ALMOST
DARK

HARCOURT BRACE JOVANOVICH, PUBLISHERS
SAN DIEGO   NEW YORK   LONDON

ALMOST DARK

Charlie McDade

Copyright © 1983 by Charlie McDade

All rights reserved. No part of this publication
may be reproduced or transmitted in any form or
by any means, electronic or mechanical, including
photocopy, recording, or any information storage
and retrieval system, without permission in
writing from the publisher.

Requests for permission to make copies of any
part of the work should be mailed to: Permissions,
Harcourt Brace Jovanovich, Publishers, 757 Third Avenue,
New York, N.Y. 10017.

Library of Congress Cataloging in Publication Data

McDade, Charlie.
   Almost dark.

   I. Title.
PS3563.C3534A79   1983   813'.54   83-6173
ISBN 0-15-105071-6

Designed by Dalia Hartman
Printed in the United States of America

First edition

A B C D E

For Rowena and Molly
with love

ALMOST DARK

PART 1

ONE:
Willie

IT's been a hell of a year. So many things have happened. I don't like to think about them, so mostly I don't. Mostly I just sit and think about where I am and where I was. That's about all I can handle, for the time being.

I am here now. Then, I was there, and I have been many places in between, but what matters now is now and, most of all, where I am: here. This room is very big, and there are beds everywhere I look. So many beds, so like one another that I don't even bother to lift my head to see how many there are. I have a table, too, alongside my bed. It is plywood, I think, but covered in veneer, which has peeled, or been peeled, in several places. Sometimes I examine a peeled place very closely and I think I can see the impression of fingers.

On the table, I have a bowl of fruit. My nephew brought it to me. I have eaten two apples, a banana, and two oranges, even though my nephew has been gone for less than an hour. Maybe longer. I have to eat what I like right away, or else stay awake all night to be sure that the others don't come and take away what *they* like. There are grapes, two kinds, sourish green ones, long ovals that have a patina like white ash, and dark round purple ones, which squirt right out of their skins if you squeeze them just right. I like grapes, too, but I can't eat all of the fruit right away. I will save the grapes until just before I go to sleep. I like them best, and they will make my dreams a little sweeter tonight.

Maybe I'll dream that I am in a room with only one bed in it. Not like the other room with one bed, a bed just like this one. I don't want to be in that room again, but it would be nice to be in a room with only one bed in it. A wooden bed. With a chenille spread, even one missing a few of its furry knobs, where I had pulled them loose in the dark. I didn't sleep alone then, but I wouldn't mind being there, either, in that room with two beds. In the other bed it would just be my brother, and I could pull some more of the furry knobs and throw them at him, just like I used to.

The people in this room are not my brothers, none of them. There are only men, except during the day, when friends and family come to see some of us, but they are not my brothers. I will not accept that. I do not *want* to discover any kind of kinship with the other men in this room. It is enough that each of us has a bed like all the others, and that we each have a peeling table beside it. But that is where the similarity ends. It isn't just that I have a bowl of fruit, because other men sometimes have bowls of fruit. Some have flowers, too, once in a while. I never have flowers, but I have had plenty of flowers in my life, and I don't want to see more flowers than I have already seen.

I had lots of flowers the last time I had an iron bed like this one. I slept in that bed for a long time, though I could not often sleep when I was there. There was too much pain for me to sleep unless I had a needle. But there were many flowers. The flowers didn't help. I remember that time whenever I see flowers in bunches, and that is probably why I don't want flowers here now, and don't envy the men who sometimes have them. I would rather have the fruit, even if I have to eat everything all at once or lose it in the dark.

It isn't only fruit that you can lose in the dark here, either. Someone here steals our sox during the night. We don't know who he is, or even whether he is one of us or one of them. Probably one of us, because there are many more of us than there are of them, and they must have better things to do than steal sox. The worst thing is that sox don't flush down the john very well, and when the thief has discovered some sox unattended, he takes them and tries to flush them down the toilet, balled up in pairs, but they don't always go down, and then we have a flood.

I don't like it here much, but I don't really mind it, either. When I try to remember what it was like someplace else, things get fuzzy on me, but sometimes I can remember a little bit of something, and it is usually enough to convince me that now there is no difference between here and there. There was once, but not now. I am better off here, I think. They don't think so, but I won't let them convince me that it is not as good here as it is someplace else. Here, at least, I get fruit once in a while, and all I really have to worry about is my sox. I just try to stay by myself. I leave them alone, and they leave me alone, too.

My mother is coming to see me tomorrow. They told me today. It's the second time, they say. I don't believe them. I don't remember my mother coming to see me here. She came when I was in the other room that had a bed like this in it. She came every day then, but I haven't seen her since I've been here. I would remember that, if it happened. I do remember little things, though, and even some big things, but they are all disconnected. I remember that Roger Maris hit sixty-one home runs in 1961. That's easy. And I remember World War II, sometimes, but I try not to. There is so little here worth remembering that something like that would have stayed with me, even if it were a long time ago.

I have been wondering how long I have been here. It doesn't seem too long, but I can't be sure. There is nothing here to help mark the passage of time. It doesn't make too much difference. It would help if I could keep track of the days, I suppose, but I don't see that it would change things any. If no one would steal my fruit, I could eat one piece a day, and mark the days by counting every piece in the bowl and subtracting the number left, but I can't be sure that no one would eat any of it when I wasn't looking. It's too bad. There are a lot of grapes, and I could count a lot of time with them. I think they would go bad before I ate them all, but it wouldn't matter. I could just take one a day and flush it down the toilet. I don't think anyone would object. There are a lot of things that go down the john here besides grapes. And sox.

If they saw me throw the grapes down the toilet, they might think it was me who was doing it to the sox. They try to find meanings in all sorts of things that don't mean anything. If they noticed that a grape has the same shape as a pair of sox rolled into a ball, they might try to draw some conclusion from that. I don't know that for certain, but it is very much like the kind of thing they do here, so it is possible. Once they make up their minds, it is very difficult to get them to revise their opinion of you. I have noticed that often, not just about myself, but about others, too. Even if I pointed out that some of my *own* sox were stolen, they would just try to explain that away by saying that I wanted to avoid being under suspicion. I don't agree with that at all, but there you go.

My father would know what to do in a situation like this, I'll bet. Boy, I never saw him stumped by anything. They named me after him, almost. He is Will and I am Willie, which is almost Will, but not quite. Smaller, I guess. The way I am almost him, but not quite. I always come up a little short, even though I am bigger than he is. Anyway, I wish he were here. Not *here*. I mean, I don't wish he were in here like me, in another one of the beds that look like mine, but I wish he were here, sitting on the wooden chair next to the night table. I could explain things to him, and he could tell them that I don't belong here. I know he could. But he's not here, and I don't know how to do it myself. I'm afraid that anything I do to get out of here will only convince them that I *belong* here. I can't win for losing. If I say I *do* belong here, like the other morning, one of them agrees with me, and nods, and writes it down on a clipboard. Some of them carry clipboards, and they are always writing things down. Some of them just stand around and talk while one with a clipboard writes. Sometimes they look at what he has written, and they look at me and talk in low voices. I think they are talking about me, but then they look at the writing on the clipboard, and I think they are talking about the writing. Maybe they can't tell the difference between me and the writing, because sometimes some of them look at me and some at the writing, but they all talk together. I think I will keep track of the conversations by putting a grape in the drawer of my night table every time they have one. I will have to make sure that I don't do it until after they go away, or else they will write that down, too.

Some of us have conversations just like theirs, but we don't have any clipboards, and we aren't allowed to have pens or pencils. They are too sharp, I think. Once I went around with another guy, and we had one of those conversations, and I pretended to write things down on a pretend clipboard. One of them saw me, though. They came right away and gave me a needle, so I don't pretend to have those conversations any more. Or a clipboard, either.

My nephew brought me a book this morning when he gave me the bowl of fruit. I wanted to read it since it was a Western. I like Westerns. I went with my nephew as far as the door with the wire on it, and when he left I was going to read my book. When I came back to my bed, one of us was there, by the table. I wasn't sure it was my bed, because they look so much alike, but he had *my* book. He was tearing the pages out of the book, one by one, pretending to read them first, then ripping them right out and flinging them in the air. I wanted to stop him, but I wasn't sure it was my bed, at first. I thought maybe *his* nephew brought *him* a copy of the same book. Then I saw my bowl of fruit, and I knew that it was either my bed or that he had stolen both my fruit *and* my book. I hit him and he fell down. His jaw went all sideways where I hit him. He was bleeding out of his mouth, kind of drooling, all over the pages of my book where they were scattered on the floor, so I kicked him. I was going to kick him again when one of them came up, and some of us, too. They all grabbed me, and I got another needle.

That was this morning, just after my nephew left. It is getting dark outside now, so I know it was a while ago. It's a good thing I woke up, because the lights will be out soon, and then somebody could steal my fruit, too. But I was lucky. The needle didn't make me sleep too long. It is not tomorrow because my fruit is still here.

If I could tell what time it is, I could tell how long I slept. I have a watch, but it doesn't work. It has one hand, the big one, but it doesn't move. It is bent, and there is no crystal on the watch. Sometimes I lie in the dark and feel the hand. I know it is the big one because that is the one closest to the numbers, otherwise it would cover the little hand sometimes. If the watch had a second hand, it would be big, too, but very thin, so you could see what was behind it. I don't know if my watch had a second hand. It doesn't have one now, though, that much I am sure of. Sometimes I lie in the dark and try to tell what time it is. I think the hand might move in the dark, so I touch it with my fingers, but nothing ever happens. Not so far. If I listen, there is no ticking sound, so I know for sure the watch is broken, even in the dark, but I will not let them take it away. I like it, even though it is broken. It makes me feel warm to have it here. I don't know why.

It was light outside when my nephew left. I could see that in the hallway through the wire door, and I could see it out the windows. When it is light outside, the shadows are different. I can see it in the hallway, and through the windows, too. The light. It is almost dark now, but it is no help to know that. My watch is broken. Sometimes I don't like the dark here, even though it is not as easy to see things when it is dark. Of course, it is never really dark, only relatively. That is the way most things are distinguished here, relatively. That is true there, too, I suppose, but here it is more so. Most things here are more so. Pain hurts more here than it does there. Happy people laugh more here, too. Until it hurts, they laugh, and when it hurts here, it hurts more than it does when it hurts there. It is better not to be happy here. Or sad, either. It is better not to be anything here, I think. In fact, it is best not to be here at all.

When I was there, I hurt. Especially when I was in the white room that had only one bed like the bed I have here. I hurt when I was in that bed. I don't think it was because of that bed that I hurt, or because of the white room. I think they were *because* I hurt. And the flowers were there because I hurt, too.

When it is dark here, relatively, and someone has flowers, especially a large bunch of flowers, I can smell them. I smell them more in the near dark than in the near light of the daytime. I am reminded that I do not like flowers, and sometimes, when someone here has some, and it is almost dark and I can smell them, I inch my arms back along the sides of the metal bed and then begin to push up on my hands until I can see all around me, except for the poles, which are painted white like the walls, and I look for the flowers. Not because I would do anything to the flowers, necessarily; it is just that I want to know who has them. And where they are. I would not do anything to the one who has them, either, necessarily. But I would make sure that I did not visit him until his flowers were gone. Not that I really visit anyone here. I don't. But sometimes I go past someone, just walking around to look at the wire on the windows, or to look at the trees out of the north window instead of the trees out of the south window. Or the east window. There are no trees on the west side that I know of. There is no window on the west. I know that for sure, and I have asked some of the others whether there are trees outside the wall on the west side of the room. Everyone says yes, there are trees outside that wall, but I don't know for sure. Why should I believe them?

If my mother comes tomorrow, like they say she will, I will ask her. She probably won't notice on the way in, so she will have to look on the way home, and tell me the next time she comes to see me. She might know already, tomorrow. I will ask her. If she doesn't know, I will have to wait. It isn't important. I have plenty of time, here. Relatively speaking. I will ask her to bring my father with her when she comes back. I would like to see him, too. I wish he were coming tomorrow, with her or instead of her. Either one. I would rather see *him* only because I have not seen him in a long time. I should ask them if *he* has come, but they always resent it when *I* ask the questions. It is almost as if they get *paid* by the question. Even if they do, they shouldn't mind if *I* ask a question. I won't ask to be paid. They can keep the money they would have to give me for that question, so it will be just like they asked it, after all. What is the harm in that?

I see someone coming toward me, in the almost dark. I think he will try to steal some of my fruit. Or my sox. I will surprise him when he gets close. I think I will wait until he reaches out to take something, then I will hit him, like I hit the one who took the pages out of the book my nephew brought to me today. The book I cannot read now. If it is the same man, I will hit him twice as hard this time. But it is probably not the same man. They took him to another place this afternoon. After I hit him. I have not seen him since, so it is probably not him, unless he is just now coming back. Here he comes, right toward my bed. He isn't slowing down, though. Now he is past. I am watching to make sure that he doesn't go around on the other side and try to sneak up on me.

He didn't, and it wasn't the man who took the pages out of my book, anyway. I am not really disappointed that he didn't try to steal something, but I would have enjoyed hitting him, whoever he was, hard.

I will put my fruit under the blanket with me, all except the tangerines. I don't like tangerines. They don't smell right, somehow, like they aren't really fruit at all. They don't smell like fruit. Maybe they aren't. I will leave the tangerines in the bowl and go to sleep. If anyone comes while it is near dark to take the fruit, he will see the tangerines and think there is nothing else left. Maybe he will even *like* tangerines. He can have them. I am going to sleep. It has been a long day. Tomorrow, my mother is coming, they told me. I must remember to ask her about the trees. I must remember to ask her about the trees. About the trees and about my father . . .

TWO

For most residents of Trenton, its history, if they were aware of it at all, had been one long, downhill slide since the night George Washington slipped across the river and caught the Hessians in their cups. It was the capital of New Jersey, and nestled in the gently rolling country at the easternmost bend of the Delaware River. It clung to life tenaciously, its energy, and that of its inhabitants, spent in light manufacturing, all that remained of the city's nineteenth-century industrial heritage. With New York City to the northeast and Philadelphia to the southwest, what growth there might have been had been blunted by the larger cities, and Trenton, like Newark and Camden, languished in their shadows, a seedling deprived of sun by much taller trees. In 1960, nothing so aptly symbolized the city's condition to its more ironically minded citizens as the neon sign on a highway bridge that spanned the Delaware. TRENTON AKES THE WORLD TAKES, it read, punning unintentionally with its missing M.

It was not unrelievedly dreary. The finer homes to the north of Trenton's only park were still grand enough to inspire the upwardly mobile. They were stately neo-colonials or sprawling brick houses, some hidden by dense shrubbery, others splendidly isolated behind sweeping lawns. They had been insulated from the more general debilitation by the park's broad meadows and scattered stands of trees, but there were not many such houses. Most Trentonians lived in more nondescript neighborhoods and unexceptional homes.

There was nothing very remarkable about the house at 224 Commonwealth Avenue. It stood in anonymous tranquillity on a tree-shaded side street that began at a college baseball field and ended at the green, gardenlike courtyard of a small Catholic hospital. The house itself was roofed in slate, which gave way to white wooden shingling over the uppermost story, then to orange brick down to the cleanly swept pavement along its free side. The front porch was of the same orange brick, its low walls capped by concrete slab, its floor a steel-gray painted wood planking. In front of the porch there was a stone-walled, shallow well full of English ivy, which crept up the front of the house as if to relax in the furniture scattered around the porch, and gave the entire front of the house the effect of a bearded smile.

The only real distinction of which 224 could boast was the spacious yard alongside, a garden, where all of the other houses along this quiet street had a neighboring home. In a row along the house stood a dozen dense hydrangeas, their summer flowers nearly the size of basketballs, now brown and brittle, with the barest hint of green leaves beginning to sprout along their stems.

Against the fence on the garden's other side was a row of nearly fifty rosebushes, and twice again as many were scattered through the remainder of the garden. They covered the spectrum of color and texture, the former running from a religious white to a violet so dark it was arguably black, the latter from a bold, fleshy petal to the most delicate of velvety silk, a single petal of which could not even be felt in the palm.

A broad swath down the middle was given over to grass, bordered by rows of roses and lilies at the front and the rear. A large, circular bed of tulips stood at the front of the lawn, and there were several other varieties of flowers, deliberately stationed to highlight their rich colors. There were three or four kinds of lily, iris, and portulaca, dahlias and asters, chrysanthemums and daffodils, their colors marching in seasonal ranks across the green open space.

On the front porch, under the shade of its broadly striped awnings, boldly colored as a medieval jousting pavilion, there was an array of brightly painted metal furniture: two chairs, one of which rocked, and a two-seater swing, its broad seats uncomfortably contoured, as if to accommodate gargantuan buttocks, the thick ridges that ran down their middles necessitating the woven straw cushions that hid them. Next to the chairs, and on either side of the swing, were chrome smoking stands, each containing a small glass ashtray, and under this metallic forest lay a fiber rug of faded earth tones, slightly frayed on the edge nearest the door, across which passed most of the traffic to and from the seats.

Will Donovan kicked open the screen door from the inside, and slipped through the narrow opening just ahead of the door's spring-propelled closure, a long, smoking cigar in one hand and a tall, bedewed glass in the other. The vigor of his movements belied his sixty-four years, an age betrayed only by the unruly shock of boldly white hair dangling over his brow to meet a pair of bushy eyebrows whiter still. He was wearing run-down canvas shoes, beltless Bermuda shorts, and a faded blue work shirt cut off just above the elbow of each sleeve, the unbasted remains of each just beginning to fringe in a fluffy billow.

He sat down cautiously, one eye on his drink, which he carefully set on the floor beside the swing, pulled the two smoking stands within easy reach, then moved his drink to sit precariously in one while depositing his barely smoldering cigar in the other. He heaved a contented sigh and began to look around, in search of something he had expected to find upon taking his seat. His bright-blue eyes glinted behind the dusty lenses of wire-framed glasses as he peered from seat to seat and corner to corner, then regained his feet in annoyance in time to greet his wife, Ella, who was just now following him onto the porch.

Under her arm she carried a crisply folded newspaper and a book. She had a tinkling, cube-filled glass of iced tea in one hand. Spotting the paper, Will returned to his seat, making room for Ella on the remaining seat of the swing, then, kicking off the battered shoes with a deft flick of each foot, he pulled one of the two chairs toward him for use as a footrest.

"I was just looking for that damned paper," Will said. "I

thought I left it on the porch when I got home, but I couldn't find it when I came out."

"You brought it in with you, like you always do," Ella responded.

"I don't always bring it in with me, especially when I know I'm going to be out here to read it in a little while."

"Will Donovan, are we going to go through this sort of thing again tonight? I declare, I don't know what's gotten into you lately. It seems like you've forgotten habits you've had for as long as I've known you."

"I tell you, Ella, that I usually leave the paper out here in warm weather. Now you *know* that, or certainly ought to."

"I know no such thing! You hardly ever leave the paper out here. As a matter of fact, you usually fall asleep under it on the couch about fifteen minutes after you get in."

"Okay, you win." Will sighed and ruffled the paper loudly to signal his concession and his intention of reading the paper rather than arguing about it any longer.

As Will gradually immersed himself in the news, Ella sat and looked out over the stone wall of the porch, the book she had brought along lying face down in her lap. She hummed lightly, in a resonant alto, pausing occasionally to watch a bird or two flitting through the leaves on the lowest branches of the two huge maples that stood in front of the house. Will seemed oblivious of her, and her humming, which she knew would sometimes irritate him. Today he was totally absorbed in the paper, not hearing her at all. It was as though she were not even there. It was so unlike her husband that she could not shake the nagging suspicion that there was something on his mind, a suspicion that only served to reinforce the impression of preoccupation he had been giving for several weeks. She resolved to take the first opportunity to ask, in a discreet and roundabout manner, what was bothering him. She had to avoid anything that remotely resembled prying, because he would only clam up. Will had an abiding distaste for interrogation of any sort, believing that he was the best judge of what Ella should and should not know. For several weeks now, he had been less than his usually talkative self, often spending entire evenings without exchanging more than the smallest of talk about the weather or the headlines.

Over the years, Ella had learned that getting Will to tell her what was on his mind required delicate navigation. Her initial tack involved a slight increase in the volume of her humming, and a selection of tunes she knew he disliked. If she were to succeed in getting him to open up, she would first have to drive him to complain about the noise, then immediately escalate the confrontation to her more serious purposes. But, a quarter hour of gradually exaggerated humming brought only a more violent ruffling of the newspaper's pages in response.

So she began, delicately at first, then more vigorously, to move the swing, knowing that the movement of the newspaper was likely to provoke some kind of response. The slow, steady motion, however, did little to disturb his concentration on the sports news, so she started a kind of zigzag movement, causing their respective seats, though welded together, to move in opposite directions. The agitation of the paper became so violent that he could not possibly have been reading it, and still he said nothing. She returned to her quiet humming, the book still lying face down in her lap. Will's absorption was unabated.

She turned her attention to a pair of robins that had been flitting into and out of the larger of the two maples. She was puzzled by their unusually animated behavior. They were flapping their wings almost spasmodically, and, even as she watched them, their chattering seemed to take on an hysterical edge. She placed her book quietly on the floor beside the swing and got slowly to her feet, hoping to satisfy her curiosity without alarming the birds further or frightening them off. She tiptoed to the edge of the porch, then slipped carefully sidewise along the low stone wall until she reached the top of the steps, where she cautiously removed her shoes and began an agonizingly slow descent.

Will, who had noticed the shift of the swing when she had

gotten to her feet, put his paper aside to watch his wife. Wishing to alarm neither Ella nor the birds on which she was so intent, he said nothing, the smile playing around the corners of his mouth the only expression of his interest. She was a large woman, but not ungraceful, and her tread was delicate as she painfully arrested the least of her motions at the first sign that the birds had noticed her; but they were intent on something more important than the large, slow-moving woman, and each time they stopped their chattering to peer in her direction, heads cocked to one side, they quickly returned to the source of their alarm.

Ella reached the bottom step and gingerly stepped onto the pavement in front of the house. She began peering up into the branches of the tree, which, because of the warm weather, had been nearly fully leaved for over a week, bright green despite the earliness of the season. Ella's own movements were becoming increasingly birdlike, as though she were trying through empathy to discover the cause of their agitation. Her head was moving from side to side, sometimes almost lying on one shoulder or the other, as she continued to approach the tree's trunk, ever more closely, ever more slowly. Suddenly she froze, then uttered a sharp cry: "Will! Will, come here, quick!"

Will, totally absorbed in her movement, was startled by the abrupt clamor, and jumped out of his seat in the swing, knocking over both cigarette stands and spilling his drink all over the porch rug.

"Look up there! Way up near the top, along the trunk," Ella directed, pointing toward the last large notch, where the uppermost large branch joined the trunk of the tall tree. "Do you see him?"

"See who? What are you babbling about, Ella?"

"It's a cat, way up there at the top of the tree, and he's after the nest."

"What nest? I don't see any cat," Will replied. "You must be imagining things."

"No. There's a cat up there, and he's after the nest! It must be full of baby robins."

"It's too early, Ella. There can't be baby birds up there yet. They haven't had time to lay any eggs, let alone hatch them."

"Are you sure?" she asked suspiciously.

"Yes, I'm sure. It's only April, for crying out loud!"

Ella seemed reluctant to believe him. She peered up anxiously through the bright new leaves for a moment longer, but the clamor had subsided as the cat lost interest in its prey, and she unwillingly conceded that there was no real cause for alarm, just as Will had said. When she turned back toward the porch, she saw that Will was watching her, smiling as though his face would split.

"I don't see what's so funny," she snapped. "It could have been something dreadful, you know."

"But it wasn't, was it?" He laughed. "It's just like you to be concerned about nothing. You always go around expecting the worst."

"Well, somebody around here has to worry about things. Since nobody else seems to care about anything until it's too late, I just have to be the one to take care of the worrying for all of us."

"What do you mean, all of us?" Will asked, smiling still more broadly. "There isn't anybody here except you and me!"

"All the same, I just thank the Lord I don't have to depend on you to worry for me."

"It's not like I don't have some worrying of me own to take care of, you know," Will said, and Ella, realizing that he was suddenly serious, saw an unexpected opportunity to find out what was on his mind.

"Other than making sure you have enough cigars in the house and some whiskey hidden in the basement, I don't think I've known you to worry about a thing on this earth, Will Donovan."

Will stared at her thoughtfully, and she was afraid she might

17

have been too obviously daring him to confess, but he nodded gently, as though confirming a long-held suspicion.

"That just goes to show how little you really know about me, after nearly forty-one years."

"Well then, if you have so much on your mind, why don't you just sit down and tell me about it? Maybe I can help."

"I was working meself up to do just that, when you started all that infernal racket, humming and pushing the damned swing out from under me."

"What do you mean?" she asked, with exaggerated innocence.

"All that peculiar carrying on you were doing! What was all that supposed to accomplish, anyway?"

"Oh, nothing! Just nerves, I guess," Ella said, then quickly pushed on before her chance could escape. "Now, what is all this worrying you claim to have been doing lately?"

Will moved toward his seat, and gasped as he stepped into the cold puddle of his forgotten drink. Ella laughed as he began to curse his own clumsiness.

"I guess you're not as tough as you pretend, are you?" She chuckled.

"What do you mean by that?" Will demanded angrily.

"You were more worried about those birds than you let on, I think. You'd never have wasted a perfectly good drink otherwise."

"It had nothing to do with those damned birds," Will snapped.

"Have it your way," she acceded. "Would you like me to get you another drink before we have our little chat?"

"Thank you, no! I'll get it meself. I've never known you to make a drink strong enough to taste, let alone enjoy. Can I get you anything while I'm inside?" he asked, softening his tone, but barely.

When she declined his offer, Will snorted and went inside, still grumbling over the accident.

"Leave the pie alone! It's for dessert tomorrow! Willie's coming for dinner with Louise and the kids," she warned, but he was already in the kitchen. She could hear him clattering around, slamming the door of the refrigerator, tinkling silverware, and rattling drawers. He came back with a new drink in one hand and a large towel crumpled in the other. He righted both stands, placed his new drink in one, then stooped to sop up the puddled mess on the floor.

"Why don't you let me do that, Will?" Ella asked. "You just sit down and relax."

"No, thank you," he said. "I made this damn mess, and I'll clean it up."

She watched him laboring over the slowly diminishing puddle, alternately stooping to soak up some of the liquid and wringing the wet towel out over the ivy bed in front of the porch. After the fourth time, he grumbled something, inaudibly but forcefully.

"What did you say?" Ella asked.

"Nothing, nothing!"

"I guess it must have been thunder then."

"I said, 'The damn stuff even ruined me cigar.' Look at this mess," Will moaned, holding up a wet stogie, which was beginning to disintegrate.

"Never mind. You have plenty of cigars. Just wring out that towel and sit down."

He sat beside her, nearly motionless for a long time, looking out into the quiet street, sighing occasionally, while Ella waited patiently. Finally he began to speak.

"I don't really know how to say this, or even if I know what I want to say." He was more subdued than Ella had seen him in a long time, his voice barely above a whisper. He was looking out over the front wall of the porch, as though unable to face her.

"Why don't you give it a try? I'll just listen."

He cleared his throat self-consciously and took a long pull

on his drink. With exaggerated care, he replaced the drink on its perch and folded his hands loosely in his lap, again clearing his throat, with more persistence than need.

"Well . . ." he began, and stopped immediately, only to plunge on. "You know, as long as I've been with the railroad, I don't think I've been away from the yards for more than a day at a time, except for vacations. Even when Emma died, I only took two days off. Now, all of a sudden, I've reached the point where pretty soon I won't ever be going back there. It seems like I have only a month to live, instead of less than a month until retirement."

"Does that bother you so much? You have always hated that job, at least as far as I knew," Ella said.

"Oh, I know I always complained about things, but it was just the way things were, the way they would be on any job, I guess. I never knew anybody, except maybe Willie, who didn't complain about his work, and, until he had that damned accident, *he* never said anything because he liked wearing a uniform and making a racket on that damned machine of his."

"Still, it's not exactly the end of the world," Ella said.

"But it *feels* like the end of the world," Will replied. "I don't know if you can imagine what it's like to work someplace for forty years. Every single night, when you go to bed, you know what time you'll be getting up, where you'll be going the next day, and exactly what you'll be doing when you get there. I'm afraid, Ella. I'm so afraid, you can't imagine. It seems like I know exactly when I'm going to die, because it's just like dying, to me. Worse, because I'll be walking around empty every day for the rest of my life. There won't even be a reason for me to get up in the morning any more."

"That doesn't speak too well for me, does it?" Ella said quietly.

"You know what I mean," Will said. "It has nothing to do with you. Work was such a big part of me life, it's like it was a separate life all its own, somehow. And that'll be gone, all gone, in less than a month."

"But there have always been so many things you wanted to do! You were always resentful of having to put things off—trips you wanted to take, things you wanted to do around here. Now you can *do* all those things, Will. *We* can do all those things."

"That sounds nice, but I don't think we'll be able to afford anything like that, Ella. I've been doing some figuring, and the money we'll have coming in won't go very far. We'll have to stretch it to make ends meet, maybe even do without some things we've gotten used to."

"That won't be so very hard. I'm sure we've gotten used to a lot of things we don't even need. I know we have. Besides, we've made do before, and we can do it again if we have to," she said, then added, with a smile, "And if you can't manage to find things to fill up your day, I imagine I can."

"But it's more than just keeping busy, Ella," Will said. "It's the purpose behind the things you do that makes them worth doing. I was always able to tell meself I was working for some reason. In the beginning it was you, then it was the kids, then the house . . . there was always something. Now the work is almost all gone, and my purpose is going with it."

"That just isn't so, Will." Ella bristled. "We still have the house, and that'll always take tending, and we'll have money, too, as far as that goes. And the kids still need us, maybe more than ever before, especially Willie. They always needed something more than money from you anyway. They needed *you*, not what you could give them in the way of money."

"But they're not kids any more, Ella. I can't treat them that way, and they don't want me to, even if I could. I think you're just trying too hard to convince me. You don't really hear what you're saying, or you'd never say it. Even Willie, who always needed somebody to tie his shoes, or help him find where he left his bicycle, doesn't really need me any more. God knows he's had his share of troubles, but he doesn't want any help from me. And you have always needed me far less than you let on."

"That's not true, Will!"

"You can't fool me, Ella. I know that I've been more trouble than you bargained for, and if I was able to help you once in a while, it can't possibly make up for all the trouble I've been." Will's voice was husky with the strain of a kind of confession he had never before permitted himself. He went on, nearly in a whisper, "As far as Emma is concerned, I've never forgiven myself for what happened to her, and I never will."

"What could you possibly have to forgive? It wasn't your fault; it wasn't anyone's fault. God wanted her, and he took her. I don't blame Him, or you, either."

"Don't start with that foolishness, Ella," he snapped, speaking in a strong voice for the first time.

"The Reverend Berland and I have discussed it many times, and he agrees that it was just one of those things that can't be helped or explained in any other way."

"That man is the biggest fool on God's green earth," Will said, "and if I had my way, he'd have nothing to do with a soul in me family, nor they with him."

"You know how I feel about that, Will, and I don't want to discuss it. We have other things to talk about," Ella said firmly.

"All right. I'd rather not waste my breath on him anyway." Will lapsed once again into a reflective silence, a silence so complete and solitary that he might have been sitting there on the porch alone, or in the middle of a desert, the bleak aridity of which was reflected in his tanned and leathery face. His hands began to move restlessly in his lap, the fingers circling one another incessantly. There was something resigned, a helplessness, in the aimless, repetitive movement, which seemed not so much something he was doing with his hands as a motion imposed on them from somewhere outside his body. Ella was watching him intently, as though she were seeing him for the first, or the last, time and wanted to etch his features clearly in her memory. He had never seemed as naked or helpless to her before, and it both appalled and fascinated her. Finally, he cleared his throat again, and resumed speaking in the same subdued, droning incantation.

"You know, I've been thinking. . . . There are quite a few things around here that I can do. On the house, I mean. And it might not be so bad as I expect. I just don't know. . . ."

"Why don't we just wait and see. There's no harm in hoping for the best, and we've gotten through some pretty rough times in the past," Ella said reassuringly. "But we've always done it together. I don't see why it has to be different just because you're going to retire."

"I suppose you're right. I hope so, anyway."

"Of course I'm right," she responded, brightening.

"I just wish I could feel as sure about it as you seem to. I mean, after all, forty years is a hell of a long time, and there will be people I'll probably never see again, once I leave the railroad."

"Why?" Ella asked.

"I don't know. It just happens, that's all. I've seen it time and time again. Somebody retires, and you make all sorts of promises: we'll have to get together; why don't we do some fishing?; we should go up to New York for a Yankee game. All that kind of stuff. None of it ever happens. One day the guy doesn't come to work any more, and that's the last you ever see or hear of him, until one day you pick up the paper and there he is, in the obituary column. His whole damn life in fifty words. If you were really close friends, you go to the funeral and you send some flowers. If you didn't know him that well, you just go to the funeral home and sign the book in the lobby. Bing! It's all over for him, and two days later it's like he never even existed. But it starts long before that. It starts the day he walks off the job for the last time."

He lapsed into silence, stared out into the quiet, shady street, and seemed to be in profound concentration, as if the leafy shade before him were the dark tunnel of his solitary future and he were searching for some light, which he did not really believe existed, at its end.

Ella watched him, and realized how deeply frightened he was, how certain he was that his life was about to end. She was at a loss as to how she could reassure him, but she knew she had to find some way before he became so accustomed to his depression that nothing could shake him out of it. She reached over to pat his arm, and shuddered in surprise as she felt the warm splash on the back of her wrist. It was the first time she had ever known him to cry, and, for the first time that afternoon, she, too, was frightened.

THREE:
Ella

I REMEMBER the night the bat got in. We had just gone to bed after a night of playing Canasta with some friends, and we were both exhausted. Will had been a bit under the weather for a week or so, and he had been up since five in the morning. I turned off the light on the night table and said good night to him, and he grunted back, as usual.

It was rather warm in the house, so I got up to open the window a little wider, and I heard a kind of flapping or scratching behind the curtains. At first, I thought it was probably just the shade, moving about a bit in the breeze, and paid no attention to it. When I got to the window, though, something went swishing past my head. I jumped back, yelled, and landed with a crash, right against the bureau. The lamp fell, knocking over some bottles of perfume, and they all spilled into my lap, some of them broken.

"What? What was that? What's going on? Ella, are you all right? What happened?" Will started spouting questions a mile a minute, and just as I'd try to answer one, he had another one on the way out of his mouth.

"It's nothing. I just tripped, Will. Go back to sleep," I told him.

But he was already getting up. I heard the springs creak a little, then a sharp click, and the room was bright as day. It seemed even brighter, the way it does when your eyes are used to the dark. At first I couldn't see anything at all, and I heard him fumbling around and cursing.

"Where the hell are me goddam slippers, for Christ's sake?"

"Will, it's all right. You don't need your slippers. I just tripped, that's all. Go back to sleep," I told him, knowing it was too late for that now. It was a funny thing about him, the way you could get him out of bed at five every morning without a bit of trouble. It was almost like it was okay, because he expected you to get him up then, but if you so much as dropped a pin when he was trying to sleep, he was like a bear.

"How the hell am I supposed to sleep when you're tearing the house down around me very ears?" he hollered.

"I'm not tearing the house down," I said, hoping just this once I could get him back to sleep.

"You sure picked a damn crazy time for demolition work, if that's what you're doing," he snarled. "And if *you're* not tearing it down, then get the hell up and help me find out who *is*."

"It was just me. I tripped and knocked something over." By then my eyes had adjusted to the light and I could see him scowling, still scrambling around on his knees looking for his slippers. Then he stopped, just sort of froze in midair, like he had been turned into a statue. He started sniffing, just a little at first, then crinkling his nose up and really snorting, fast and deep sniffs, like a hunting dog.

"What in God's name is that *smell?* Jesus Christ, it's awful. And where is it coming from?" He looked confused now.

"It's me," I said. "It's just some perfume."

"Well, why the hell do you have to try perfume on in the middle of the night? What could smell so bad you have to dump that damn toilet water all over yourself by the gallon, and in the dark yet?" He was really getting worked up now, and I knew I'd have to tell him the whole story quickly or I'd never get him back to bed.

"I'm not trying it on! I broke a couple of bottles, that's all."

"Well, why'd you break them? Why can't you just throw them out, like a civilized person?"

"You don't understand. . . ."

"Of course I don't understand. Who would? If you don't like the stuff, just don't buy it any more."

"It's not that. It's . . . I mean, I like it fine, it's what I always wear, and you like it, too. You tell me so all the time." I saw my mistake, but too late.

"So what's wrong? What did I do? Why are you so damn mad at me that you have to get up in the wee hours to throw away me favorite perfume?"

"No, Will, darn it, now let me explain!"

"Who's stopping you? Haven't I been *asking* you to explain ever since I woke up thinking the Last Judgment had come?" He gave up looking for the slippers and climbed up to sit on the edge of the bed, that patient, irritating look on his face he gets only when he thinks he's scored some great victory; but I was too anxious to settle him down to point it out, the way I usually do. I had begun to explain, when I heard it again. The swish. I looked over his shoulder and I saw it. Instead of an explanation, all I could manage was a scream. "Eeeeeeeeeeeeeeeeeeeek!"

"Now, Ella, dammit, cut that out. I . . ." He stopped suddenly, just like when he was looking for the slippers, and I knew he had seen it.

It was flapping all around the room, up by the ceiling. You could hardly hear it, except once in a while a flap, like laundry on the line. It even looked like a black rag, or a pair of sox grown wings, or something. Just flapping and wheeling around, mostly by the wall where the window was.

"Now you've done it," he said, starting to pound the bed. "If you hadn't taken so damn long getting to the point, or, better yet, if you threw your perfume out in the daytime, like a sane person, that little bugger would never have come in here. Now I'm gonna have to get the broom and chase the little fucker back out the window."

I knew there was no use trying to explain that it had come in before I got anywhere near the perfume, so I just nodded. Will was glaring alternately at me and the bat. He got up and went toward the hall, muttering something about keeping the door closed behind him until he could get the broom, but the bat must have heard him, because just as Will got to the doorway, it kind of flipped over on its side and went diving over Will's shoulder and out the door. Will didn't see it at first, but then he heard the flapping coming from in front of him, and started cursing.

"Goddam sonofabitch shit. I really don't need this aggravation. Damn it!" He muttered all the way down the hall, then he yelled, really loud, and I thought it had bitten him. I got up to see what had happened, forgetting all about the bottles of perfume in my lap, and they went crashing all over the floor.

"Ella? Are you all right? What happened?" he was yelling, at the same time I was yelling to him, afraid he might already be getting rabies. He came running back in and stepped on some of the broken glass with his bare feet. He yelled again, not words this time, though, just a kind of howl. Then he really hit the roof.

"I thought I told you to keep the door closed in here, dammit!"

"You did, but . . ."

"But nothing! But my ass! Dammit, that sonofabitch bat is out there in the hall now."

"I know it. So there's no use keeping the door closed now, is there?" I asked, all innocence in my desire to be logical. "I mean, if the bat is already in the hall, he won't come back in here and let me close the door so he can't get out into the hall, will he? Or will he?"

I was pushing it a bit too far, but didn't realize it yet. He started screaming and rubbing his foot, so I asked if he had cut himself on the glass, and he told me he had stubbed his toe on the newel post at the top of the stairs. That's when he had yelled from out in the hall.

"Well," I asked, "what are we going to do?"

"Do about what?" he wanted to know, sitting on the bed and rubbing his injured toe.

"About the bat," I said.

"Jesus Christ, I forgot all about the son of a bitch," he

shouted, jumping up and running out the hall door. He yelled "Leave the door open!" over his shoulder as he ran downstairs for the broom, still dressed only in his underwear.

I could hear him rummaging around for the broom, then a thump as he bumped into the kitchen door on the way back. He was mumbling again, louder and louder as he got closer to the top of the stairs. He came flying down the hall with the broom sticking up in front of him like a picket sign, yelling, "Where is he? Where is the little bastard? I'll kill him!"

"Not here," I told him, as casually as I could. "I haven't seen him since you chased him out into the hall."

"Dammit!" He tore out the door again, and I could hear a smacking sound, so I peeked out, and he was standing there at the top of the stairs, flailing the broom around over his head, thumping the wall on either side, and sometimes the ceiling. I couldn't see the bat, and I didn't hear it, either.

"Maybe he's gone," I suggested.

"Gone where? Where would he go? Did he go back out the window?"

"No."

"Then he's still in here. Somewhere. And I'm going to get him if it takes all night." There was a loud crash, followed by a showery tinkling sound that wasn't loud enough to drown out "Sonofabitch, didn't like it anyway." I asked what happened, yelling now, because I was reluctant to get anywhere near the door, not knowing when he, or either of them, was liable to come flying back into the bedroom.

"Broke the hall chandelier, hit the fucker with the broom."

"The bat?"

"No, dammit, I said the broom."

"I know, but I mean did you hit the bat with the broom when you broke the chandelier?"

"No, dammit, I hit the chandelier with the broom. The broom broke the chandelier. Can't you understand plain English?"

"Well what about the bat?"

"I don't know. I haven't seen him for a while. Is he in there?"

"Maybe you just better forget about it. We can look for it in the morning."

"Like hell! I'm going to kill the son of a bitch, and I'm going to do it tonight. He'll be sorry he ever flew in here!"

"Don't they bite?"

"What did you say?"

"I asked you if bats bite."

"I don't know. Do they?"

"I think they do. I think they carry rabies, too. You'd better be careful."

"Too late now!"

"Oh no! Did he bite you?"

"No. But I broke the fucking chandelier and beat the shit out of the walls in the hallway here. If I don't get the little bastard pretty soon, we won't have any place to live. Bring me raincoat. And one of your hats. One with a veil. They get in your hair, I think. Bats do, before you ask."

"Which one?"

"What one what?"

"Which hat?"

"I don't give a damn! Any one, as long as it has a veil. And be quick about it, Ella. I don't want the damn thing to get downstairs."

"I have a blue one here. Do you want this one?"

"I don't care, I told you. Any one."

"Never mind. I haven't even worn this one but once or twice. I'll give you the black one. You know, the one I bought a few years ago, for Lummie's funeral."

"If you don't get your fanny out here, and quick, and with a hat, there's gonna be another funeral. And you won't have to wear a hat for this one, either."

I tossed the hat onto the bed and went to Will's closet for his raincoat. I poked around in there, and there was this huge noise like church bells, all the hangers clanging together. Finally, I gave up looking for the raincoat, because I knew he was getting exasperated. I went to my closet and pulled out an old pink chenille bathrobe and ran over to the door. He was getting madder by the minute, and I could hear him cursing the whole time, no words that I could make out, just a rumble, like thunder off in the distance. I just stuck my arm out in the hall with the robe draped over it and the hat in my hand.

"Here they are," I said, and the words were no sooner out of my mouth than I could feel this tugging and they were gone. "Will," I said, "I couldn't . . ."

"Never mind," he said, not letting me finish. "I have to get this shit on and get the little bastard before he gets away."

"Can you see him?" I asked, afraid that the bat had already made his way downstairs.

"No, but I hear him. He's over the top of the stairs now. Flitting around by the light, where the chandelier used to be."

"Why don't you see him then?"

"Because," he began, and I could hear that he was trying to suppress the exasperation that was on the edge of his voice, "because I busted the bulb at the same time I got the chandelier. That's why I don't see him. As a matter of fact, it's the same reason I can't see a fucking thing out here. Because I broke the goddam bulb. All right?"

"Sure, all right. I was just trying to be helpful, that's all."

"The next time you feel like being helpful, leave the window shut. That will be a big help. Next time."

"Okay."

"Thank you." He was pleased with himself over that exchange. "Boy, I didn't realize my raincoat was so tight on me. I'll have to get a new one, I guess. I can't hardly move my arms in this damn thing. I guess I'll have to leave it open. Suppose he gets inside, and gets caught in the hair on me chest? What'll I do?"

"You don't have hair on your chest. And that's not your . . ."

"Sssssshhhh! I hear him again. He's coming this way, I think." There was a loud series of thumps, like wham! wham! wham!, real close together, then whamwham!, even closer together, then "Shit, I missed him. Ella, can you come out here a minute?"

I didn't want to go anywhere near the hall, not so much because of the bat, but with the way he was flinging that broom all over, and in the dark like that, I thought I'd be taking my life in my hands.

"Do I have to?" I asked.

"No, of course not," he said. "Not at all. You can stay in there. I'll stay out here. We can wait him out. He might die of hunger in a day or two, even if he can stay awake. If he can't, we'll get him. We got him either way, that's how I figure it. The only question is when. Tonight or next week? Suppose he's real strong? Then what'll we do? Maybe he can last a week. You want to miss church Sunday? If not, you better get your ass out here, and right . . ."

There was a real loud thump, a new sound, and the way he stopped right in the middle of the zinger line, I knew something was wrong. "Will? Will, are you all right?" Nothing, not a sound. I called him again, and there was still no answer, so I knew I had to go out into the hall, whether I wanted to or not. I went over to the night table and got the old flashlight we kept there, but it had been there so long, it wouldn't light. I heard a groan, now, and was really starting to worry. I forgot all about the need for a light and went running out into the hall. I couldn't see a thing, so I slowed up when I got close to the top of the stairs.

"Ouch, dammit! Get off me hand, Ella!"

"I'm sorry," I said, angry, now that I knew he was okay. "I didn't see you."

"I just got scared, that's all. I didn't hear you for a minute, after that big thump."

"Of course you didn't hear me! You weren't supposed to hear me."

"Why not?"

"Because I'm playing possum, that's why! I'm gonna ambush the little fucker when he comes over to see if he got me. Just like Hoot Gibson used to do."

"What was that thump then?"

"That was me, falling down. He has to think he got me before he'll come over to see, doesn't he?"

"Aren't you giving him just a little too much credit? Besides, you could have hurt yourself, falling like that, even on purpose."

There was another swish. It went right past my ear, where I was kneeling on the floor, and I knew the bat had gone downstairs. "Did you hear that?" I asked, knowing full well that he had.

"Yeah, I heard it. I heard it all right. He's downstairs now, and he's played right into me hands. You watch, I'll get him in a minute."

"How?"

"You just watch me!"

I could feel him stirring, getting to his knees, but I couldn't see a thing. Then I heard his steps, and a loud whisper.

"You stay here. I'll be back shortly," he said, but I knew it was far from over.

I crawled around to the top of the stairs, but I didn't want to get him madder by going down after him. At least not right away. The thumping started again. And the cursing. It went on for a while, regular as clockwork, almost. Then there was a loud crash, and glass breaking. The lights started to go on downstairs, one by one.

"Come here, you bastard," he was yelling. "You'll never get out of this alive, so come along peaceably." Will was fond of Western movies, and tended to sound like a sheriff when things were getting out of hand.

I started to work my way down the steps, cautiously, one at a time. As I got near the bottom, the last light went on, and I heard somebody pounding on the front door, yelling. The doorbell rang. Will was a sight, running all around the dining-room table, the pink chenille robe flying behind him like angel wings, the broom flailing so it looked like a broken propeller. I went to the front door, but before I could reach it, I heard a shout behind me.

"Look out, Ella! Here he comes!" The bat went right over my shoulder, and as I ducked, Will went flying past and jumped onto the sofa in the front room. The cushion slipped away from under his feet, and he pitched forward, right through the front window. There was a horrendous crash, wood splintering and glass flying every which way. The pounding on the front door had stopped, and I heard the voice of Frank Mooney, who lived across the street.

"Jaysus, Will? Is that you? What the hell's going on? Are you crazy?"

Will didn't answer right away. Then, through the hole where the window used to be, I could hear him mumble, "Did I get him? Where is he? Where is the little fucker?"

I ran to the door and yanked it open, worried that Will was hurt, and was in time to hear Frank ask, "Get who? What the hell are you talking about?" Will was getting to his feet, obviously not intending to answer, and Frank turned toward me, just as the first siren sounded, down the block. It was coming our way. Will was shaking his head, as though to clear the cobwebs. "There he is, by the streetlight," he cried, and grabbed the broom. Before I could stop him, he went bounding down the front-porch steps, howling at the top of his lungs, and started to climb the telephone pole in front of the house. Frank and I looked toward the streetlight, then at one another and back at the light, just as the police car pulled up. Lights were going on all up and down the block. People were coming out on their porches or peeking from behind the shades, and Will was still howling, cursing to beat the band. "I've got you now, you son of a bitch. I've got you now."

He was halfway up the pole, hanging on to one of the climbing spikes with one hand and whirling the broom in a big circle behind his head. Both cops jumped out of the patrol car and ran toward the porch. As they got to the top step, Will hollered again, and the cops turned right around and ran back down the steps. One of them was looking up at the telephone pole while the other went back to the car. He yelled something into the two-way radio, then came back to the foot of the pole, something white flapping behind him.

"I got the jacket, Ralph," he said, "and I called for some help. Let's see if we can get him down."

He ran back up on the porch, and I saw it was Don Reilly. I smiled at him, but wasn't sure exactly what to say, so I just looked at him. He stared at me for a minute, then asked, "Well?"

"Morning, Don. How are you?"

"Fine. How's yourself, Ella? And what the hell is Will doing up a telephone pole at three o'clock in the morning? Drinking again?"

"Well, Don," I said, "you wouldn't believe me if I told you, so I'll just wait here while you get him down, and he can tell you all about it himself. You and Ralph want some coffee?"

"That'd be nice, Ella. Thanks."

"You, Frank?"

"Yes, thank you. I'd kinda like to hang around and hear this for myself. A cup of coffee would be real nice. Light, with two sugars, if it's no trouble."

"Trouble?" I asked, glancing over his shoulder at the pole, "Trouble? I don't know the meaning of the word."

Well, I went on in and made the coffee, while Don and Ralph tried to get Will out of the tree he had jumped into from the telephone pole. A small crowd had gathered at the beginning of the uproar, but it was late, and since Will had stopped yelling, saving his wind for the chase, most of the neighbors had drifted on home. By the time they finally coaxed him out of the tree, it was just me and Frank, sitting on the porch swing, Don and Ralph, sitting on the top step, and Will in the rocker, still mumbling, still in the pink robe. Every once in a while a little shadow would flit past as we were drinking our coffee. And now and then I could hear this faint swishing sound, as the shadow got a little smaller, and a little peeping sound, almost like laughter.

FOUR:
Willie

Sometimes, in the middle of the night, I can see it coming at me again. I don't know whether I am awake when this happens, but it is real just the same. As real as it was the first time. There is nothing there at first, then the bright flash of my light on the bars of the gate. When I remember this, I don't know if I am remembering the light brighter than it was, or if they had just polished the bars of the gate, but it doesn't matter. Now, when it happens, the light is very bright, and it is shining on the surface of the gate's bars, like shiny ribbons. I can see their shadows on the stone pillar that held the gate, the dark-gray stone, narrow bands of bright-green moss hiding the concrete between the blocks of stone. I can even see, as clearly as if I have a close-up photograph, a praying mantis moving along one of the bands of moss, its head turned toward my light.

Then there is the noise. I do not remember this so clearly, but it is there, a roar, sounding like it is very far away. It sounded that way then, and it does now. Very far away, but it is there. I can hear it. When I heard it then, I didn't know what it was. I know now. I did see the car; it was long and very shiny. It was almost brand-new, and must have been waxed recently, maybe even that afternoon. I can remember seeing myself in the side of the car, and the ground and the other stone pillar, the one that held the other gate, are visible, too. I can see all of that in the door of a 1955 Buick. It is like a photograph, only it is wavy, as if the photograph had been taken of a reflection in one of those curvy fun-house mirrors that distort everything. I remember liking those mirrors as a kid, in the fun house at Seaside Heights. I would wait all summer for a chance to go to the boardwalk, just so I could walk through the fun house and see myself short and fat for a minute, in the real mirror, then make myself long and skinny in a second, without waiting a long time to grow or working very hard for a long time to lose weight. All I had to do was move my feet a little bit and I could change into any shape I wanted, like Plastic Man. It was like that in the side of that Buick, only it was real, and I did change shape afterward, for real. I can look down at this sheet now and see the bumps my toes make at the bottom of the bed. I stretch real hard, as hard as I can, toward the bottom of the bed, but no matter how hard I stretch, one bump is always closer to the bottom of the bed.

The man in the car must have been thinking of something else. I did not have anything wide and shiny on the bike for him to see himself in, so he did not see the car coming toward me the way I saw me going toward him. I had my light on, and it was so bright that I could see a praying mantis walking on some green moss behind the shiny bars, but he didn't see me. Even when I went right past him, he didn't see me. That is when the noise started, a low sound, a vibration in the ground, then a screaming. The bike began to move sideways before I heard anything, so I know that he didn't see me even then, because I would remember the sound of brakes, and of tires being ripped apart by the sharp stones in the pavement between the gates. I would have smelled the burning rubber, too, I think, but all I could smell was the metallic heat of the engine under the Buick's hood, and I could feel my leg press against the bumper. It didn't hurt, but I could feel it very clearly. I remember thinking that I was glad that the bumper was rounded and not sharp, and then I heard a tearing sound and all of the trees fell over on their sides in the dark. I wasn't even surprised as I closed my eyes. The trees seemed to be doing something perfectly ordinary, and then I couldn't see them.

Then I was there, in that whitish room, with the bed like this one in it, and the flowers were there on the table that rolled around and sometimes came over my bed, full of food. A man was sitting next to that metal bed. He was looking at me, and his lips looked funny, but they didn't have that fake smile people use when they come to see sick people. It wasn't like he was trying to cheer me up for something that happened to me. It was like he was trying to decide what he had to do with what happened to me. I was a puzzle to him, I think, just like I am a puzzle to them here. He sat for a long time, on a stool that stood between the flowers and my metal bed, and he looked at me. I know he didn't see me see him, and I didn't know who he was, but he looked like he was interested in me, or at least like I interested him. Those two things are not the same. There is a distance in the eyes of someone who looks at you the second way, and a glaze over the eyes, so that you can't even see what color they are. It is almost as if the eyes do not *have* any color. That is because of the distance. It is the way I looked at frogs when I was small, and the way I looked at Jimmy's tongue when it was swelling up in his mouth and the flies were buzzing around him. It is the way that strange man looked at me. I saw him every day for two weeks and then I didn't see him again. I didn't know who he was for the first two weeks, and then my mother told me who he was. She didn't want to—I could tell that when I asked her if she knew him—but she finally told me.

When I said hello to the strange man the next day, he got up and went away and never came back. I don't remember his name now, but it will come back to me soon, I know. Lately, many things are coming back to me, things that I haven't thought about for even a second in many years. I am not trying to remember these things, but they are coming back to me anyway. I would rather not remember many of them, but I don't know how not to remember things that come to me at night. I can't sleep very well here, and the ceiling, in the almost dark, is like a movie screen, but I am in all the pictures. It is strange to lie here, in this metal bed, and look up at the ceiling to see myself doing things I do not remember doing. I see me, and I see me do things, and when I do them, I know I did them, but if you had asked me, before I see them on the ceiling, whether they are things that I have done, I would say that I have not done them. I would not be lying, either. I am sure it is not a lie to say you didn't do something you don't remember doing. What I cannot decide is whether, if you don't remember doing something, it makes a difference whether you really did it. Yesterday, I would have said that it didn't matter, that if you didn't remember it, you didn't do it, even if you did it, but now I am not so sure.

I have a lot of time here, and I think about many things that I remember. But I am not sure whether they really happened or whether I just think they happened. I know that some of them must have happened. I know that I woke up in the white room after the trees fell over into the darkness, because I can look down at the sheet and see how one bump is farther away from me than the other one is, and there is a connection between that difference and the time when I saw the trees fall over. I saw that praying mantis walking on the green moss. I saw that gate, shining very bright, like gold. And the Buick was real. The difference is that there is something I can look at here that reminds me of those things every time. There is a connection between something I can reach out and touch with my hands and the green moss behind the bright bars. For some other things, I don't have any connections at all. When I look around here, I see all the other beds like the one I have, and I know there is a connection between something I did, or that happened to me, and my presence in this room. But I don't know what it is.

When I think of the Buick, I run my hands down along my thighs, and I can feel the ridges where my skin is all puckered there, the lines where pieces of skin were sewn together. The bump where the bone came through my leg. If I touch the skin a certain way, even through the white sheet, I can feel something tickly, like a praying mantis was walking along my skin. My fat fingers don't feel so fat on other parts of my skin. Some places I cannot even feel them at all. I can look at them, see where the sheet dents in around them, and know that I am pressing on my leg, but I don't feel anything there, in my leg. I can feel the sheet bend under my fingers, but I don't know what I am touching if I do it in the dark. If you touch *your* leg like that, you will know right away that you are touching your leg. I can't be sure. I have never told anyone this. Especially not any of them. The ones who are always asking me questions are interested in things like that, but I don't want to tell anyone. Especially not them. It is not a secret. I just don't want to tell them. I told my mother once, but I don't think she would remember it. It is hard to know what I mean if *you* can feel your own leg. My mother can feel her leg, so she wouldn't know what I meant. I told her once, but I won't ever mention it again. Even if she comes to see me, the way they said she would.

She is supposed to come today, but I don't know whether she will. They said she was here before, but I didn't see her. I think they may be testing me. I don't know why, but I'll bet that's what they're up to. They probably think they can learn something about me by telling me something like that and then watching me. They would learn more if I told them about the things I see on the ceiling, when it turns almost dark in here. But I won't tell them. I have decided that I won't tell them anything at all. Whenever I do tell them something, they make some kind of noise in their throats, like I have said something significant, but if I ask them what is so interesting, they just smile. I don't trust people who smile when there is nothing funny. There is nothing funny here at all. I haven't heard a single joke since I have been here, but I don't know how long that has been, so I don't know how long it has been since I have heard a good joke. Or even a bad one. If my father comes to see me, he will tell me a joke. I don't know where he gets them, but he always has at least one I haven't heard. I wish he were coming today. I could use a good laugh. Maybe he will come with my mother, or maybe he will at least have told her a joke to tell me. That would be like him. I will see later.

Yesterday was Sunday. I watched television in the big room where they let us go sometimes to watch it. They let us play cards, too, in the same room, and sometimes the ones who play cards make so much noise that the ones who are watching television can't hear what is being said by the ones on television. This usually doesn't bother those who are watching, because we don't really care what is being said. It is enough to watch people move around where there are real furniture and cars and bushes. We don't like doctor shows. We see enough doctors here, and we know that the ones who are doctors on television are not real doctors, and they are not at all like the ones who are doctors here. There are no mean doctors on television, and the rooms are all small, but not too small. Usually they are also neat.

If you are in a room on television, there is usually just one other person in it with you. Usually he is someone you can help or who can help you. That is the best thing about television and the people who are on it. They help one another when there are things wrong. Maybe even better is that they know *when* things are wrong, and what they are. It would be nice if things were like that here, but they are not. There are doctors here, and they wear white clothes just like the doctors on television do. That is the only similarity, though. Here, some of the doctors have bad breath, most of them in fact, and those on television do not. At least I don't think so. When one of them leans close to one of the sick ones on television, the sick one never makes a face, or turns away from the television doctor, so I think I must be right that that is one big difference. It is a small thing, I know, but when you live with fifty-three men in a big room, and each of you owns exactly the same things and has the same amount of space to move around in, little things make a big difference. Just imagine how easy it would be to spot the one bed here covered with a dark-blue spread. That is a little thing, but when there are fifty-three spreads and fifty-two of them are white, having a dark-blue one to walk toward when you want to lie down would make everything much easier.

My spread is white, and so are the other fifty-two, but I can see what a difference it would make to have one that was a different color. It would probably make you unpopular here, so maybe it is a good thing that I don't have a dark-blue one. I am not a coward, but I would not like to have to fight all the time, and to worry all day about someone stealing my spread. It is enough to have to worry about keeping all of my sox. I have six pairs, and on Sundays I only wear slippers. Sometimes I don't have six pairs though. Sometimes some of them are being washed and sometimes some of them have been stolen. You never know, when you open the drawer that is yours, how many pairs of sox you are going to find, and if you find fewer than you expected, you might have to wait all day long to see whether someone brings you those that are missing or whether they have been stolen. Sometimes you wait all day and they don't bring them back, and you realize that they have been stolen but they bring them to you the next morning and you realize that you were wrong again, and that they have not been stolen after all. They are never in a hurry to bring you your sox here, or anything else, either. They know that you are not going anywhere, I guess.

When I get out of here, I hope I am able to afford lots of sox. I will buy three-dozen pairs, so I can go a whole month without wearing the same pair. Sometimes I might wear a pair only once and then throw it away. I will do that if the yarn is rough or if I don't like the color. Here, all the sox are rough and they are all the same color, so there is no point in throwing them away, because you will not get some different ones, if you get any new ones at all.

Right now I am looking at the floor, and I notice the tiles are not all the same. They are all the same color, or were all the same color when they were first made, although they may have been made at different times, but some of them are very pale. There are small dents in some of them, deep depressions where the almost light during the daytime here makes small shadows. All of the dents are the same size but some are deeper than others. They were all made by the same thing, I think, or by several things that are all alike. That is always the problem I have here, when I try to decide what causes things. There are so many things that seem the same. I think there is a reason,

43

but it is difficult to prove something like that, and I am not free to conduct any sort of investigation. I would look around at many of the things here, if I could, and see if I could find one thing, or several things that were the same, that could possibly have made the depressions in the floor.

I don't really care, but it is a way to pass the time. It would be more interesting than just lying here and looking at the dents in the tiles and being content. I would not really be content to do that. I would not really be content to know what made the depressions in the tile, either, I guess, but at least an investigation would keep me busy. I would ask a doctor, but he wouldn't know, and he probably wouldn't care enough to find out for me or to help me in my investigation. He would probably make some notes on his clipboard, if he was carrying one, and hum to himself as though I had said something interesting. I always wonder whether they make notes later of things you say when they don't have clipboards with them. I bet they do, but I think that many of them have bad memories and put down things that you don't say, or they put things you say on someone else's record. I bet they sometimes get things mixed up and write them down anyway. They won't get into trouble, either, because there is no way we can prove that we don't say the things they say we say.

I would not even be content to lie on my bed and look at the depressions knowing what made them and knowing that my record on the clipboard was perfectly accurate. I am beginning to think that I don't belong here. I am reminded of when they kept taking skin from different parts of my body and sewing it on and making the bones grow back together, after I saw the trees fall over and woke up in the white room with only one bed in it, and the table that was on wheels. The man who used to come to see me was the driver of the Buick, they told me later. He was a doctor, and he saved my life. If I had been hit by a milk truck or a station wagon, I would have died, they told me. I was lucky it was a doctor who hit me, they told me. They used to look at me in a funny way when I'd tell them that if I were *really* lucky no one would have hit me in the first place. It is funny to be considered ungrateful for wanting to avoid pain. I can't understand it. I wish I weren't here in this room. That is what would make me really content, more content than knowing all about the depressions in the floor and knowing what caused them. What I want more than anything is not to be here. Not to be here at all is the best thing there is. Better even than knowing why things are the way they are here. Or anyplace. The best place to be is no place at all. I think I am finally beginning to understand that.

FIVE

April 28 was cool and cloudy, and the threatened rain seemed to hang suspended, just beyond the reach of the skin or the eye. Despite the unpleasant weather, Will was up earlier than usual. He had been unable to sleep, hanging in that gray space between sleep and wakefulness that allows one to hear every noise for miles around. He had tried getting up at two to make a sandwich, hoping to satisfy a hunger he did not really feel, but decided to have a cup of coffee instead, intending not to sleep at all. He puttered around the kitchen, as noiselessly as possible, then sat at the kitchen table, sipping occasionally until the coffee was cold and undrinkable.

In a sudden burst of energy, he tiptoed back upstairs, glided silently into the bedroom he shared with Ella, and gathered a motley assortment of clothing. He didn't bother with shoes. Intending only to sit in the damp chill of the front porch for a while, he contented himself with a pair of leather slippers run down at the heels. Returning to the lower level of the house, he grabbed a sweater from its hook inside the cellar door and cautiously made his way to the front door. Muffling the sound of the clicking lock in one cupped palm, he stepped out onto the porch and made his way softly to the metal swing. As he sat, he began to swing slowly back and forth in a gentle arc, and gradually became aware of the night moisture soaking through the seat of his pants.

The sounds of the night were simultaneously soothing and alarming: soothing because they were distant and unthreatening, and alarming because they were so alien to a man who had spent the better part of his life going to bed before midnight and sleeping soundly until dawn. He luxuriated in the mystery he found in the air all around him, and tried to isolate the individual sounds, to guess their cause and point of origin.

Eventually he grew bored and decided to take a walk around the block, in the hope of burning off the excess energy that was keeping him awake. He cautiously descended to the pavement, taking care that the hard leather heels of his slippers not slap the stone of the steps. He walked on tiptoe past the neighboring house before assuming his normal stride. Strolling casually along, he glanced this way and that with an idle, birdlike motion of his head, pausing frequently to linger over the shape or bulk of a tree or house whose familiarity was obscured by the night.

He couldn't count the number of times he had walked along this street, and yet there was something almost magical in its nighttime appearance. The trees, in particular, were strange and forbidding, their rough dark-gray bark darkened still further, to the color of the night itself, their branches waving mysteriously in the light of the street lamps like the arms of sirens enticing him into bizarre and fanciful excursions, lured onward by the dark and the mist.

When he reached a corner about five blocks from the house, he paused under the broad, low sweep of a fully leaved chestnut and began to fumble in the pockets of his sweater for something to smoke. He discovered a crumpled pack of Camels, and ripped its top open when his first peek failed to turn up a cigarette. Nestled in the corner, bent nearly in two but still intact, was an old, thoroughly dried cigarette, which he carefully straightened after recrumpling the package and tossing it into the gutter. The next order of business was a match, but a search of the sweater's pockets came up empty. He thrust his hands into the pockets of his work coveralls, but they, too, were empty. About to toss the cigarette away in frustration, his eye lit upon a closed matchbook lying on the curb. He rushed over to it and, on flipping it open, found two matches, which had started to crumble from the moisture on the pavement. He struck the first, which sputtered briefly before igniting with a burst of acrid smoke. As he lifted it toward the tip of the cigarette, it began to die, so he hurriedly cupped the sputtering flame in both hands, but too late. He struck the remaining match, cupping it immediately and quickly but carefully lifting the small flame toward the cigarette, which flared brightly as he forcefully inhaled. The flame got hold, and taking three quick puffs on the Camel, he inhaled deeply and slowly sighed the smoke out through flared nostrils.

He felt no more certain about his future, but the cold night air had been invigorating and he felt more refreshed, far less sleepy. He headed off down the block. After a brisk walk of some six more blocks, he came to a huge green wall, at either end of which a barred gate stood open. He crossed the street between himself and Wetzel Field, and headed for the nearer of the two gates, which led onto the broad, partially green area around the home-plate end of its baseball diamond.

Will shuffled out to the pitcher's mound and bent back at the waist so that the grandstand was barely visible at the bottom of his field of vision. He concentrated on the broad, gray sweep of the sky, kindling vivid memories of the many nights he had spent out here in the first weeks after the death of his youngest daughter, Emma. Almost nightly for the better part of a month, he had come here and lain on his back in the middle of the diamond, feeling a peculiar, unthreatened kind of vulnerability, lying there wide open to the stars, knowing he was at their mercy and knowing, too, that they would not exploit that vulnerability. It had seemed to him then, and still did, a deliberate affirmation on the part of some unknown power that his suffering was a far greater source of amusement than the abrupt and total termination of his existence would be. He had been exhausted by those endless weeks of dealing with his own anger and trying to help Ella deal with hers. They had spent long hours holding each other quietly, the consolation of one another's arms more perfect than words, and when Ella, exhausted herself, finally rose wordlessly to go to bed, Will would put on a sweater and walk to the ball field, where he had the freedom to dwell on a grief that was narrower than that he shared with Ella, but far deeper.

He had never been a religious man, and had no patience with the false assurances clerics dispensed with such seeming smugness. He wanted to understand the single most important question Emma's death had posed: Why? For that question, pious effusions about God's will and the usual affirmations that she had gone to a better world were thoroughly inadequate. If there was a greater glory elsewhere, he told anyone who would listen, there would have been time enough to take Emma there when she had had the opportunity to lead a full life. Heaven wasn't going anywhere, he declared, with an uncertainty that had more to do with his doubts about its existence than its mobility. He and Ella had quarreled over this point several times after the immediate shock of Emma's death had been blunted, Ella preferring to cling to any guarantee, no matter how feeble, rather than confront the enormity of the loss she had suffered. Will resented any attempts at consolation that required acquiescence, since he had never been a man to suffer abusive authority lightly, and would not do so then, even for the sake of Ella's peace of mind. Ultimately, of course, the pain had passed from their daily consciousness, but it lay buried deep inside each of them, and would surface at oddly unpredictable times, and each knew, without benefit of words, when the other remembered.

Despite the fact that they had three other children, Emma's death had seemed to each of them to be the cruelest possible thing they could have been asked to endure, and the surviving children had felt uneasy and a bit resentful of the intensity and the duration of their mourning. Ella had reacted as though her entire reason for being had been her youngest child, and she had never been closer to turning her back on her religious beliefs, to which she otherwise clung with a fervor all the more avid because she had been a Presbyterian by choice rather than birth. Will, on some ill-defined but passionately held principles he could not articulate, had always been antipathetic to religion of any stripe, and believed that if anything were ever to come between him and Ella, it would be religion. Lying on his back in the middle of a naked baseball diamond after midnight was as close as he had ever come to church since he had been old enough to resist being dragged into one.

Now, nearly sixty-five years old and desperately afraid for the first time in his life, he realized that the open sky *was* his church, and that it was in such a setting, and only there, that he could call on whatever forces he could not see, and in which he could not quite believe, to sustain him, his summons issued more in the form of a challenge than a supplication. No matter how willfully he had tried to extirpate the vestiges of his childhood Catholicism, he had never quite eliminated that small spark of belief that lingers in the heart of the fiercest unbeliever, masquerading as uncertainty.

Now, in a kind of reverie, he lay on his back, wide open to the stars, and waited, but found, once again, nothing in the sky but rain, a fine, mistlike drizzle swirling in small cloudy concentrations across the dark air of the vacant grandstand. He had no idea how long he had lain there, but he was soaked through and beginning to be uncomfortable. He knew it was late, but not so late that there was any discernible brightening of the sky to the east, so he climbed stiffly to his feet, intending to return home for at least a brief nap before getting ready for work. The rain had begun to pick up, and there was a flash or two of lightning and a muffled rumble off to the northeast. Quickly and carelessly brushing his clothes, he began to head back, glancing one final time at the sky overhead before passing through the gate and pulling it shut behind him with a sharp clang that seemed to re-echo again and again from the vast, vacant stands, gradually fading away to die under the hissing rain and the hum of the power lines overhead. Once across the street, he was protected somewhat from the rain, and slowed his pace to a fast shuffle.

As he reached his own block, he slowed his pace still further and regained his tiptoes as he neared the house attached to his own. He stopped at the bottom of the porch steps to remove his slippers, shuddering as he placed first one foot and then the other on the cold, wet sidewalk, then quickly ascended the steps and, quietly opening the storm door, slipped back inside the dark house. He stripped off his wet clothing, leaving on only his damp undershorts, and went to the cellar stairwell, where he dropped the sopping coveralls and sweater into the laundry chute and stuffed his damp shirt in behind them. He did it all by feel, since he wanted to avoid even the click of the light switch, which Ella might hear.

Covering his tracks as best he could in the dark, he ascended the stairs on tiptoe, avoiding the fourth and sixth steps, which creaked rather loudly, and made his way to the bathroom, closed the door, and ran a hot tub. He knew that Ella might hear the water running, but it was a risk he would have to take if he was going to avoid having a very stiff back in the morning, Doan's Pills or no. He stripped off his shorts and slipped into the steaming water while the tub was still filling, reached up to adjust the temperature once, then settled back against the cold porcelain to wait for the slowly rising water to cover his back and shoulders with its penetrating warmth.

He closed his eyes and slid down into the water as far as he could go, carefully controlling his motion to prevent any displaced water sloshing out over the rim of the tub. He could feel the gritty surface under his buttocks, and remembered that he had long intended to replace the tub but had never had the time. Now that he would have nothing *but* time, he was not sure he would have the money. Or the heart. He hunched farther down into the soothing water, leaving little but the small oval island of his features above the waterline, and his mind drifted as aimlessly as his body would have were it in open water, touching now here, now there, never pausing long enough for pleasure or pain.

He gave a sudden start when he felt a hand on his shoulder, and sat up sputtering, the surge causing a series of slowly diminishing waves to cascade onto the tile floor. He shook the water from his eyes and squinted through the too-bright glare of the overhead light into Ella's tired face. "What is it?" he asked, "What's the matter? Are you all right?"

"I was going to ask you the same thing," she said. "I noticed you weren't in bed, and when I heard the water running, I thought I'd better come to see if you were okay."

"I'm fine. Just a bit restless, I guess," he said. "I couldn't seem to get to sleep, so I thought maybe a bath would help me relax."

"Would you like me to sit up with you?"

"No, really, I'm fine. Just go on back to bed. I'll be in in a little while."

"Are you sure?"

"Of course I'm sure," he snapped.

"I don't mind staying up. I'm kind of restless myself. I think I'll go down and make some tea. Shall I make you a cup?"

"No! Yes! What the hell! I guess I'll never get any sleep tonight anyway, so I might as well let you keep me company. I'll be down in a few minutes, as soon as I get dried off."

"All right," she said, turning to leave, and Will knew that she knew he was more than restless.

She went out the door, closing it softly behind her, and Will could dimly hear her making her way down the creaking steps in the dark. He slipped out of the tub and began to rub himself briskly with a large, rough terry-cloth towel. When he was dry enough, he grabbed an old flannel robe and slipped it on, then stepped back into the still-damp, chilly slippers and clapped his way out into the hallway, reaching back through the door to darken the light as an afterthought. He clomped downstairs, humming as he went, and had begun to whistle by the time he reached the doorway of the kitchen. Ella was just sitting down at the table, having already poured boiling water over the tea bags, now floating listlessly at the bottom of twin columns of steam rising from a pair of large, chipped, and handleless cups. Next to the sugar bowl and creamer, for Ella's use, he noticed an unopened bottle of J & B, for his own. He whistled appreciatively, and nodded toward the bottle.

"Where'd that come from?"

"Danny brought it over for you, and I didn't have the heart to throw it out, since it's so seldom he thinks of either one of us."

"What's it for?"

"He said it's your retirement gift, but I think he thinks it's something for him to drink whenever he comes over. He probably won't believe that I actually gave it to you."

"Why not?"

"He knows how I feel about whiskey in the house, and he also knows I don't like to waste anything, so he thinks it'll be someplace where he can find it if he really needs it."

Will snorted, and hefted the bottle thoughtfully in both hands. "You know," he said, "I often wonder if it's my fault he drinks the way he does."

"What do you mean by that?" Ella asked.

"I always thought he might have been trying just a little too hard to take after his old man, and that was the one thing he could see me do that was easy for him. And you never liked it much, so maybe he thought I did it just to get your goat, and he wanted to let me know he was on my side, or something. I don't know—it's crazy, I guess—but I wonder sometimes, that's all."

"Lord knows," Ella said, "that it was nothing he could have done to please *me*. But I don't think you ought to blame yourself for it. I guess it's just one of those things."

"Now, Willie," Will continued, "I could understand him taking to the bottle, after the accident and everything. I guess his life has always been just a bit out of control since then. And the pain he was in must have made the booze seem pretty welcome."

"That's true enough," Ella agreed. "If you did anything wrong, with either one of them, it was taking their side whenever I said anything about it. You were always too quick to stick up for the pair of them."

"I suppose you're right," Will conceded. "But I didn't come down here to talk about me sons, *or* their drinking. I need a little shot myself, and then I'm going to try to get some sleep. The last thing I need, on me last day on the job, is to be too tired to watch what I'm doing. I don't want to retire in a pine box, at least not without a little vacation first."

"I wish you wouldn't talk that way! You're so pessimistic these days, Will."

"I can't help it, Ella. I've told you how I feel, and there's no point in my pretending otherwise, now is there?"

"No, I don't suppose so. . . . Still, I wish you'd give it a chance before you jump to conclusions. You might find you actually *like* having some time to yourself."

Will stared thoughtfully into his teacup and took a quick sip to make room for the Scotch. He tore the paper seal away from the cap, lightly unscrewed it, and set it quietly down beside his cup before carefully pouring a modest amount into the tea, which glistened as the alcohol rose to the top. He recapped the bottle, gave the cup a gentle swirl, and quickly drank off about a third. He set the mug back on the table with a sharp crack, and noisily wiped his lips with the back of his hand. "I don't know whether it's a good idea or not," he said, "but I sure like the way it tastes."

"It's *not* a good idea, if you want my opinion," Ella said.

"I didn't think you'd think so." Will laughed. "But don't you worry, Mother. I'm not about to become an alcoholic this late in the game. Just because they have me over a barrel doesn't mean I'll try to drink what's in it, you know."

Ella laughed quietly, then said, "I know you're not going to become an alcoholic, Will. But I also know you're worried about what will become of you, and I understand that. I want you to know that whatever happens you can depend on me to stand behind you. If worst comes to worst, why we can *both* get part-time jobs. I just don't want you to worry unnecessarily."

"I know, and I'm grateful," Will said huskily. "I'm not really worried as much as it must seem. I just need some time to adjust, that's all. And I *will* adjust, but you don't get used to a whole new life overnight. I can't really start until I get today over with. That's going to be the hardest part of all, saying goodbye to people I've worked with every day for thirty or forty years. I'm not saying I won't get over missing them, but with some of them, it'll take a long, long time."

"Why don't you drink your tea and try to get some sleep?"

"I think I will," he said, draining his cup of now cool tea. As Ella got up to clear the table, he patted her affectionately on the rump, saying, "I sure don't know where I'd be without you, Ella."

Rather than prolong the conversation, Ella pretended that his remark had been lost in the clatter of dishes, and shuffled off to the sink with the empty cups. Uncharacteristically, Will pushed back his chair and grabbed the cream pitcher and sugar bowl, returning the latter to its place in the cabinet and replacing the pitcher in the refrigerator, finishing as Ella came back into the kitchen. He placed an arm distractedly around her shoulder and urged her in the direction of the hallway, releasing his grip only when they reached the doorway.

Will tossed for the remainder of the night, watching the changing pattern of shadows on the ceiling.

As the sun began to peek in the window of the bedroom, Will smiled ruefully at the deft way he had allowed reminiscence to distract him from dealing with the more important matter that lay just ahead of him. He resolved to take his time this morning, as if dawdling would somehow alter the inevitable fact that as of three o'clock that afternoon he would be a *former* employee of the Pennsylvania Railroad. It was a procrastination founded more in desperation than in optimism, however, since Will had made a lifelong habit of expecting the worst, claiming that it lessened the unavoidable pain that came with disappointment. The sole exception to this rule was the most painful disappointment of his life: the single time he had refused to allow himself to believe that things would be as bad as he could imagine. When Emma had died, in spite of his unshakable belief that she would recover, that she *had* to recover, he resolved that he would never again allow himself to be deceived by false hope. And he had not faltered in that resolve in the twenty-two years between her funeral and the present. Now, more desperate than he had been at any time since Emma's illness, he had found himself with his back to the wall on a matter that meant something to him, and he had broken his own rule, hoping against hope that some way could be found to prolong his working life, even if only for a few weeks. But, struggle as he had, it was finally here, the morning of his last day of work. No matter what shape his future life was to take, there was a finality to this morning that could not be denied.

Resigned at last, Will rose slowly from the bed, trying to avoid waking Ella, who had managed to sleep only fitfully after the wee-hour cup of tea. He gathered his working attire silently and moved softly down the hall to the bathroom, where he could dress without making any noise, leaving only his heavy shoes, which he would pull on just before leaving the house. With a deliberateness that assumed the significance of ritual, he minutely examined each piece of clothing before donning it, holding each in turn for a long moment in his hands and staring at it in silence, in an attitude that resembled nothing so much as that of prayer. The nondescript striped coveralls and the faded blue work shirt were somehow transformed in his mind to garments as sacred as a priest's vestments, and the stylized movements with which he put them on suggested the carefully controlled ritual of the Mass. Ready at last, he grabbed his shoes in one hand and his peaked cap in the other and made his way to the head of the stairs, pausing to listen for Ella before descending.

At the bottom of the stairs, he again paused to see if she was stirring, but hearing nothing he walked quickly to the couch, where he sat down to pull on the shoes. He deftly knit the laces into a complex pattern through the metal eyes and pulled them taut with a tug that knotted the muscles of his thick forearms. Satisfied that they were tight, he tied a double bow on each shoe and stood stiffly to cock his head before the small mantelpiece mirror while setting his cap at the properly jaunty angle. He lingered before the glass, staring at his features as if he had never seen them before, and was startled by the bright blue of his own eyes, which peered out through his glasses and back without losing any of their icy glitter.

He made his way slowly down the steps and headed up the block toward the bus stop for the ride to the rail yards just off Monmouth Street. It was only five-thirty, and he had always enjoyed being out at an early hour, even in the worst of winter weather, savoring the quiet of his wait, with almost nothing moving until the bus finally came into view.

This morning was no different in its externals, though Will's head was full of unusual thoughts. He was turning over in his mind the pose he would assume for the day, not yet resolved whether he would pretend that nothing was happening or act as though he were glad the day of his retirement had finally arrived. He had not confided his fears to any of the men with whom he worked except for Pat Flaherty, and Pat would keep his own counsel and go along with Will's approach, whatever it might happen to be. He scuffled his feet idly in the greenish-yellow dust of the bud hulls that had fallen from the trees along Chambers Street and lay like golden snow in the cracks of the pavement and in the root crevices of the trees themselves, even dusting the rougher barks right to the limb line.

Up the block, he heard at last the subdued rumble of the approaching bus and turned to watch it lumber into view, looming suddenly over the parked cars that lined the street along its path. When it finally reached his stop, after waiting a block away for a red light, there was no one on it but the driver, who nodded only vaguely as Will dropped his fare into the fare box, and said good morning.

Taking a seat at the rear of the bus, Will turned to stare out the grimy window at the familiar houses and factories he had seen so many mornings, looking at each in turn as though it were a monument left by some vanished civilization, which, in a way, each of them was. In the first few blocks, the quality of the houses changed drastically, the deterioration that formed the topic of so much neighborhood conversation clearly in evidence. Most of the houses on the far side of the high school were old frame homes, the paint peeling away, the windows long unwashed, the porch banisters missing one or more slats where they had been kicked out by one of the dozens of working-class kids who had spent much of their youth waiting for a chance to buy houses of their own, no doubt just like these, in a section just a few years behind this one on the downward slide.

Will closed his eyes, trying to see the neighborhood the way it had been so many years ago, when he had taken this trip for the first time. He smiled as he remembered that he had gotten lost and ended up having to walk a dozen blocks to the yards. As the bus hurried into the long incline at the base of the bridge that arched for three blocks over the wide cluster of tracks at the north end of the rail yards, Will opened his eyes to take in the view for what would be his last official arrival. The sun, although still low in the east, was fully visible, its fiery red giving the impression of a size seldom seen in the noontime disc, the clouds, which were the remainder of the previous night's rain, a bright scarlet, spreading from north to south in a vast semicircle behind the glowing ball. He reached idly and automatically for the handle of his lunch pail, and when he didn't find it, looked nervously about him before realizing that he had neglected to bring it along in his distraction. He rose to make his way slowly forward, still the only passenger on the bus, which allowed him to indulge his inclination toward profanity without troubling to mumble unintelligibly.

"You say something, old-timer?" the driver yelled over his shoulder.

"Don't you 'old-timer' me, you young scalawag," Will snorted.

"What'd you say?" the driver shouted.

"I said, 'What's the matter, you gettin' deef?' That's what I said," Will yelled back.

"Jesus, what's the matter with you?" the driver asked placatingly as the bus crested the hill, its engine unwinding into a dull mumble as it began coasting down the far side.

"Nothing! Just watch out who you call 'old-timer,' that's all. I can still take you two out of three falls," Will warned.

"Sorry! Jesus, I didn't mean nothing by that," the driver whined, and Will was satisfied that he had, indeed, stricken terror into the very heart of the young man.

"Pull over at the bottom of the hill," Will directed.

"But that's not a stop," the driver protested.

"I know it's not. Do it anyway!"

"But . . ."

"No buts, son, just pull over at the bottom of the hill. If you know what's good for you," Will added as an afterthought, in the manner of Barton Maclane, who was his favorite heavy in the movies. "Son, I've been getting off at the bottom of this hill for as long as I can remember. Today is me last day on a job I've worked for forty years. Now, you don't want to inconvenience an 'old-timer' on his last day, do you? It's un-American!"

"No, sir." The driver capitulated.

"That's a nice fella. You keep on learning things like this and you might hang around a while. Do you take my meaning?" Will was alternating between the Maclane style and that of Barry Fitzgerald, slipping into and out of each nearly as fast as the young driver was swallowing.

"Yes, sir, thank you, sir." The driver quivered, staring at the powerful forearm Will had planted on the aisle gate just to the driver's right. "Here you are, sir. And have a good morning."

"Thank you, son. And remember, I got two sons at home who are twice as big and four times as mean as I am, so don't let me hear any more about you insulting old people, or you'll have a couple of unruly passengers late one night, out by Scotch Road, under the trees there, where it gets real *dark*. Mornin'," Will said, tipping his cap and stepping lightly down into the stairwell of the bus, where he hesitated just long enough to be sure he had the driver's attention before he broke out laughing and hopped off the bus without looking back.

Will stood chuckling as the bus groaned into motion, the driver staring over his shoulder at the strange old man. When the bus was out of sight, Will set his face into a grim mask and made his way across the street. The long, low sheds that formed a solid wall on the west side of the yards, and where much of the fun he would regret leaving behind had taken place, were painted blood red by the sun looming over his shoulder and casting a long, thin shadow in front of him, its legs rippling rather than bending as Will made his way toward the gate.

As he passed through the high, rusty gate, which sagged drunkenly to one side back against the fence, its bottom bar hidden in weeds that had been there as long as he could remember, Will did not see a soul. The huge, corrugated sliding door that led to the yardmaster's office was thrown wide open, as usual, but it was deathly silent, as if the railroad itself had suddenly ceased operating altogether. He climbed a rough stairway improvised from raw ties heavily soaked in creosote, and long since worn away at the center of each step, in order to reach the cement pier in front of the rollered door. Once on the pier, he turned to look around the cemeterylike expanse of rails and ties, then as he turned to cross the pier into the yawning darkness of the warehouse, a corner of which served as the yardmaster's headquarters, he heard the howl of a train off to the northeast. It came again, suddenly and higher in pitch, and he could just make out the small clouds of smoke puffing over the laboring engine, bright red like the clouds higher in the sky, and he could barely discern the chuffing of the engine and the faint rattle of its wheels on the bright rails. The blasts of the horn were becoming louder and more frequent, and squeezed toward him with a nearly tangible pressure as the powerful engine drove closer and closer and then, like an explosion, passed under the bridge with a roar.

Will entered the cavernous warehouse and looked around, but saw no sign of anyone. He walked over to his locker, one of three-dozen metal cubicles, nearly identical. None had even the presence of a number to distinguish it from any of the others. Most of the men had, more than once, inadvertently gone to the wrong locker, and not just early in their careers in the yards. Tom Rafferty was notorious for not bothering to use his own locker, preferring to take advantage of the nearest unoccupied stall when he arrived, which was usually late, and usually with a headache. Rather than passively accept the enforced anonymity the locker situation imposed, Will had made a point, as soon as he had accumulated a sufficient amount of seniority, of taking the corner locker on the left. Even Rafferty's casual approach to ownership made an exception of Will's locker. As Will slowly made his way along the row of metal doors, he idly tapped every other one in time to his advancing tread, lost in thought about the peculiar silence that seemed to hang in the cavernous warehouse like a palpable presence. As he reached the end of the long row, he paused, dumbstruck, and began looking around in bewilderment. "What the fuck is going on?" he exclaimed aloud. Then he squatted to scrutinize the small rectangular ridge of dust on the floor that was the only evidence that a locker, or anything else, had ever stood there.

"All right, you guys," Will bellowed suddenly. "What the fuck is going on here? Where's me locker? You sons of bitches, I know you're in here somewhere!" There was no response, except for a faint echo, which reverberated among the jumbled packing cases, fork-lifts, and scattered repair-shop machinery. "Anybody here?" Will yelled, now less certain that he was the victim of a prank.

He walked over to the open door of the office shared by the yard boss and the head of the maintenance staff, but there was no one inside. It was the same as it had always been—the scarred furniture looked as it always did, the sprung stuffing of Tony DeMarco's wheeled chair was as grungy as ever—but the office was uninhabited. Will shook his head in confusion and had turned to walk back out into the open warehouse area when he spotted the grimy calendar hanging beside Tony's chair. It depicted a scantily clad young blonde in a provocative pose that, apparently, was believed to be an inducement to buy a particular brand of Italian tires. Will had always kidded Tony about the calendar, and at least once a month would drop in to ask Tony if he had bought any tires lately, and when the answer was no, as it invariably was, Will would inquire if Tony had at least bought a *car,* thereby justifying the presence of the calendar on the wall. The calendar had become a shop joke, and the men would line up to take a peek at the latest version as soon as word got around that Tony's "tire ad" had arrived. He enjoyed the attention, but swore each of the men to silence outside the shop, explaining, "Rosie would kill me if she knew I had that thing down here."

Will checked the calendar to make sure that today was a Friday, and, satisfied on that score, was more bewildered than ever as he made his way back out into the locker area. Suddenly he heard a piercing hiss, and turned to see what had caused it, but still saw no one about. He sat down on the chipped bench that ran the length of the bank of lockers, though it was now inexplicably two feet longer than it had been. He was about to look for his lunchpail when he remembered that he had neglected to bring it. Again he heard the hiss, and this time traced it to somewhere out on the pier, just to the right of the door through which he had entered. He got up quickly and went to the huge, open door to step out onto the pier, but saw nothing but an empty boxcar, its rusty door yawning open as if waiting to engorge the entire contents of the warehouse. Again he heard the hiss, this time from the open door of the car, and he cautiously made his way toward it, stopping to pick up an abandoned slat from a shipping skid that had been left against the outside of the car. Brandishing the slat overhead, he leaped into the car with a yell, and was greeted by an answering roar that dwarfed his own.

"Surprise!" And suddenly he was surrounded by laughing men, all talking at once and slapping him on the back in their enjoyment of his bewildered expression.

"What the hell is all this?" Will demanded in annoyance.

"What the fuck do you think it is, you asshole?" Tony DeMarco bellowed. "It's a surprise party."

"What for?" Will demanded.

"This is your last day, isn't it?" Tony asked.

"Yeah, sure, but . . ."

"Well all right then! You didn't think we were going to let you get out of here without a little celebration, did you? Even if you aren't glad to be leaving, we sure as hell are glad you won't be around to bust our chops any more. Right, guys?"

The babbling company murmured its assent, and Tony went on. "We knew you wouldn't go for a party if we said we wanted to have one at a restaurant or something, so we figured we'd have to trick you into it. This was the best we could come up with, so don't give us any grief, you bastard. We could have had a nice dinner someplace, with a band and some dancing girls in a cake or something, but since you would have put the lid on that in a hurry, we decided that you'd have to be held captive in our secret dining room on wheels." He laughed.

Will was momentarily overwhelmed, and ashamed of the suspicions he had earlier confided to Ella. In order to gain time to compose himself, he reached into the rear pocket of his coveralls and flourished his huge red handkerchief before blowing his nose loudly into it. Then he decided to take the offensive. "Where the hell is me locker? You bastards could at least have waited until tonight to move it the hell out of there!"

"Move it out? Are you kidding? We *retired* it, man. Just like the Yankees retired Babe Ruth's number, you know? I mean, you don't have a number, so we figured we'd retire something else. As long as this railroad stays in business, which we all know may not be all that long, nobody, but nobody, will use that locker again."

They gave a loud cheer, liberally sprinkled with derisive hoots, and Tony continued. "As a matter of fact, not only are we retiring your locker, we're *giving* it to you. That way, none of us will ever have to look at the damn thing again. The last thing we want is to be reminded of the son of a bitch who used to use it. Right, guys?" Again there was a rumble of concurrence. "Right now, it's in the back of Rick Harrigan's pickup, over in the parking lot. Under a canvas, of course, since we don't know whether or not management will be as glad to see you leave as we will, and Rickie will drop it off after work tonight."

"You bastard, what do you mean you don't know whether management will be as glad to see me leave as you will?"

"Well, I gotta tell you, Will, try as I might, I just couldn't keep it under my hat that you were a real company man, you know?"

"You son of a bitch, what do you mean 'company man'? And why the hell couldn't you keep it under your hat? You got nothing *else* under there."

"See what I mean, guys? A real swell fella, that Will Donovan!" Tony laughed. "I don't guess you'll be easy to replace, Will," he said, extending his hand. "Seriously, buddy, we're all gonna miss you. We just wanted to bust your balls a little this morning, give you something to remember us by, that's all." He took Will's hand in his own and squeezed it warmly.

Whispering to keep his voice from breaking, Will asked, "Well, didn't you at least get a little booze for this party? What the hell are you, a bunch of cheapskates?"

"Booze, he says," Tony shouted. "Fellas, do you hear this? He wants to know if we got any booze. Are you kidding? Look at this!" He walked over to a heap of canvas in one corner of the boxcar and swept it aside with a theatrical flourish, accompanied by a general fanfare. Will could just barely make out, in the darkened corner, the dim bulk of three kegs of beer, bunched together in the midst of several large blocks of ice and a number of soda and liquor bottles.

"What do you say, guys? Let's have us a real party!"

As the beer was gradually reduced to urine, the men began trading stories of the past thirty years or more, many with Will as the focus, but more often as the butt. Tony, in particular, had a large repertoire of tales that revolved around Will's temper or his fondness for practical jokes, and he regaled the others with most of them before the lunch whistle blew.

To cover the shift they were supposed to be working, the men were taking turns, making the rounds of the yard and routing traffic through, shunting freight off onto sidings, and doing their best to see that nothing got too fouled up without stinting their party. There was a constant rumble of passing trains, and the thunder of the boxcar door sliding open and shut was nearly incessant. Will laughed harder than anyone, doing his best to forget the fears he had confessed to Ella earlier that morning, but he was unavoidably aware that the participants had a nearly hysterical edge to their laughter, as if they were attempting to deny the very purpose of the gathering, or to ward off some impending evil by pretending it did not exist.

By three o'clock, the normal quitting time, the party had dwindled down to a handful of men, the oldest and closest of Will's friends, men with whom he had worked for many years, and they seemed to be feeling the approach of Will's departure as keenly as if it were their own, which in a way it was. These veterans were a tightly knit group, who shared a history as well as a job, and, like old military men, they had a closeness that comes only from a commonality of interest and from danger lived through as a unit. In the early days of union activity, seeking protection from unscrupulous management and hired goons, they had all had narrow escapes of one kind or another, some to save their jobs and others to save their skins. And though the newer yardmen would confirm that the situation was far from ideal, it was the old hands, men with thirty or forty years behind them, who knew how bad it had really been.

Losing Will was like losing a brother, in the truest sense of the word, to many of them, and they were not handling it well. Beneath all the chatter and the reminiscing, there was a sense of loss slowly making its way toward the surface of the conversation. Will, who felt it more keenly than the others, decided that it could not be allowed to ruin his last hours on the job. He preferred to leave with the raucous derision and humiliating banter that would surely greet his announcement of departure rather than have to deal with the maudlin mood into which the men were slowly but surely slipping.

"Listen, guys," he said, "I promised Ella I'd be home early, so I think I'll get going."

"Aw come on, Will. It's early yet! Ella won't mind if you hang around for another hour or two. We were going to go over to Flynn's and hoist a few. What do you say?"

"No, I don't think I'd better. I got a lot of things to do around the house, and I don't want to start with me ass in a sling. You know what I mean?"

They attempted to convince him to stay a while longer, but he was adamant. "Where the hell is Harrigan, anyway? That bastard is supposed to drive me home, with my locker."

"The last I saw him, he was sleeping behind the wheel of his truck, over in the lot," Rafferty said. "Come on, I'll walk you over and we'll wake the bastard up."

"Okay, Tom, thanks. Listen, you guys, it was a lotta fun working with all of you. Keep in touch, huh?"

"Sure thing, Will. Listen, we'll have to do some fishing, huh? My brother-in-law just bought a boat, keeps it at Forked River. We'll have to go down and catch a few blues later in the year, all right?" Tony DeMarco said.

"Sure thing, Tony. Give me a call anytime," Will responded. "Ready, Tom?" he asked, turning to Rafferty.

"Yup! Let's go."

The two men rolled back the door of the boxcar and made their way out onto the pier, where the early-afternoon light made them blink after the gloom of the car's interior. They walked in silence out toward the gate, and Will did not turn back to look over his shoulder, knowing that he could take his last look from Harrigan's truck as they pulled out of the parking lot and headed over the bridge. When they got to the truck, Harrigan was sitting on the tailgate, reading an afternoon paper. He greeted Will with a chuckle, and said, "I didn't think you'd be here so soon, old buddy."

"What the hell. No use hanging around any longer than necessary, is there?" Will laughed.

"No, I guess not," Harrigan responded reluctantly. "You about ready to leave?"

"Sure am! Listen, Tom, take it easy," he said, grasping Rafferty's hand.

"Take care, Will," he responded, punching Will playfully on the shoulder. "You sure are one lucky son of a bitch. I wish it was me that was retiring."

"Yeah," Will said thoughtfully. "I just bet you do!" He hopped into the cab of Harrigan's pickup and leaned out through the open window, grinning at Rafferty, who said, "I'll call you, Will."

"Do that. Be seeing you," Will replied. "Take it easy, Tom."

Harrigan started the truck, and as he backed slowly out of his parking place, the crunching of the gravel under his tires was nearly drowned out by the blare of a speeding freight approaching the yards at full tilt. The oncoming train roared under the roadway bridge and, as Harrigan's truck passed out of the parking-lot gate, the last blast of the freight's horn faded away, and the train itself, as well as the yard, could barely be seen in the glare of the sun. When the last passing car had disappeared, Harrigan said, "Take a good look, Will. That's something you won't have to worry about again."

"Thank God for that." Will laughed. "Let's get that damn locker home, Rickie. You'll have to give me a hand getting it into the cellar."

"Sure thing!"

The truck passed out through the gate onto the street, and

67

as Harrigan crested the hill, Will looked back into the sun and saw the whole yard bathed in bright orange light, the gleaming surface of the web of rails like streams of liquid fire heading toward, or coming from, the sun. Will couldn't decide which, and was just as glad.

SIX:
Ella

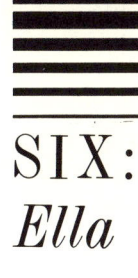

I WAS humming in the kitchen, rattling the dishes and silverware as I set the table. I was usually much quieter, but this morning I wanted to make a real racket, because Will was still in bed. It was the first time since he had retired that he wasn't up before me, and for God knows how long at that. Lately, he had been irritable and listless, managing not to accomplish any of the dozens of jobs he had been setting out for himself, in long lists. He constantly made lists and then revised them, setting priorities for weeks in advance. I was starting to think that the making of lists had somehow become a substitute for actual work, as if he were looking for the perfect arrangement. He would sit at the kitchen table, the nub of a battered, flat red carpenter's pencil clamped in his teeth, and mumble before asking me whether the basement should be cleaned before or after the roof gutters, the porch furniture painted before or after the back bedroom. When I couldn't stand it any longer, I warned him that he ought to plan less and do more, since it was starting to look like he would go to his grave with nothing cleaned and even less repainted, but my sarcasm fell on deaf ears. I was half hoping to provoke a fight, in order to drain away some of the tension, which was something I could almost reach out and touch.

Last night he went to bed at his usual time, so there was no reason to suspect he was more tired than usual, but I knew that the strain had to be taking its toll. I was hoping maybe he had made some private resolution to straighten himself out, and was starting by sleeping later.

I kept looking at the clock over the refrigerator, next to an old oilcloth sunflower whose seeds were stick matches. Finally, after staring at it off and on for half an hour, I actually took the clock down and held it to my ear. I was sure it had stopped working, but when I listened, I could hear the gears still humming. I shook it, just to be sure, then replaced it over the refrigerator, making sure to cover the lighter area on the wallpaper, because I knew that Will, if he noticed the difference in color, would probably add repapering the kitchen to one of his lists.

I slammed the refrigerator door after getting out a grapefruit, and I heard a muffled rumble upstairs. I hurried to the kitchen table, split the grapefruit in two, and began to loosen the soft pink pulp from the rind with a curved, serrated knife, the existence of which had never ceased to amaze Will. "The idea," he used to say, "to think there are people in this world who can't eat a grapefruit unless they have a special knife to cut it with!"

I began sawing at the second half of the grapefruit when a shout from the doorway nearly startled me out of my wits. "Aha! Caught in the act," Will hollered. "For years I've been trying to figure out what was wrong with me grapefruit. Now I know! You use that damn knife with the curl on the end!" He laughed and rushed over to me as if he wanted to knock me down, but he stopped suddenly and grabbed me in a bear hug, lifting me off the floor and swinging me around in a circle.

"Will, put me down! Put me down, I've still got the knife in my hand, you idiot!"

"That's all right. You can't cut anything with that damn contraption anyway."

"You never complained before."

"I never caught you in the act before! I knew something was wrong, but I never thought you'd be using that thing in secret and ruining me breakfast!"

"If I didn't know better, I'd let you cut your own, but the juice would be all over the table, and you'd probably blind yourself in the bargain."

"Well, it doesn't matter anyhow. From now on things are

going to be different around here. Ella, you are looking at a new man!"

"Lord, I hope not! I have my hands full with the old one!"

"I'm serious, now. I've turned over a new leaf. I am going to stop moping around and start doing all those things I've been talking about for so long."

"It's about time you got out of that terrible mood you've been in."

"I just realized it's time for a change. It got so I couldn't stand to look at meself in the mirror any more. Every night I'd start lecturing myself about all the things I had to do, and I'd go to bed convinced that the next morning everything would be different. Well, you know how much I got done!"

"I have to confess I was starting to get worried about you. I didn't even know if I could honestly say that I knew you, any more."

"I know, I know," he said, nodding. "Well, anyway, I finally realized that the problem was that I thought I was different, that retiring had changed me into somebody else. It's taken me all this time to understand that I'm still the same person I always was. Nothing has to be any different, as long as I don't let it. I'm not ready to pack it all in yet. Don't even know if I ever will be."

"Well, that certainly is good to hear! Now, how about some breakfast?"

"That's the best offer you ever made me. Except for one."

"Oh? And what might that have been?"

"Oh, no, you don't! I'm not a complete fool. If I answer that one, you'll accuse me of being lewd, and start preaching at me."

I could feel my face get hot, but I was pleased all the same. I was glad that his mind had started to come back to some things he had forgotten for what seemed like forever. He pulled a chair over and sat down, edging toward one end of the table to keep out of my way. He looked at the clock and, seeing that it was too soon for the paper to have been delivered, he started to drum his fingers on the table. After a moment of that, he jumped straight up out of his chair, yelling, "Damn! I forgot!"

"Forgot what?"

"I forgot that I decided you were helpless in the kitchen long enough! I made up me mind to do something about it!"

"What do you intend to do, hire a maid?" I asked, annoyed by the idea that I might be considered helpless in the kitchen. "And just what do you mean by helpless, anyway? I must be able to do *something* out here, or you'd have starved to death long ago."

"I didn't mean helpless; I meant you'd been doing it all alone for a long time. I figured that I could pitch in, now. You know, give you a hand around here."

"And just what do you think you'll be able to do?" I was trying not to smile, since he was obviously uncomfortable at his choice of words.

"What do you mean?" he asked, a little indignantly. "Of course, I don't know exactly what I can do, but I want to even things up a little, however I can. It might take me a while to get the hang of things, but I sure as hell would like to give it a try. What do you say?"

I hesitated, just long enough to make him doubt whether I would go along with his plan, then said, "All right, it's a deal! But I don't want any sass as long as you're out here. You'll do as I say, and please don't make things harder for me. If that happens just once, the deal is off! Okay?"

"Okay!"

"What do you have planned for yourself for this morning?"

"Well, I thought that it was about time I started getting this place ready for summer. It's been hot off and on for weeks, and I still haven't taken down the storm windows or painted the porch furniture. If I don't get started, it'll be winter before I know it. I can't afford to let things like that go by, or I'll just get some bad habits that'll be awful hard to break. Soooo, I thought that you and I could work on the windows this morning."

"Me? What can I do? You never want me anywhere near you when you're on something like that. You used to chase me away. And the language! It's a wonder my ears aren't blue, the way you'd start cursing!"

"Well, that was the old days. Things are different now. I've mellowed a little in me old age, I guess. Anyway, I don't expect you to hang out the attic window to put screens up, or anything like that, but you can wash the windows before I put them up, that sort of thing."

"I don't suppose there's any harm in that—at least, not as long as you promise to be patient with me. You were always yelling at the kids whenever they'd try to help you, though, so why do you think it'll be any different now?"

"It just will," he said. "You know how they were, always horsing around. Sometimes they did more damage than work, and I'd end up by having to do twice as much as I planned, just to fix what they broke."

"Now that's a fine way to talk! You used to love it when they would stand under your feet trying to decide how they could be helpful. And Daniel must have learned something from you, after all. He's been making his living as a house painter off and on for years."

"More off than on, if you ask me. That son of a gun hasn't worked two months back to back in fifteen years. If it weren't for the damned ships he runs away on, maybe he would have made something of himself by now. But every time it gets a little rough out there, off he goes! Next thing I know, you're sending him money off in Hong Kong or God knows where. I don't understand why he works on those ships if they don't pay him any money."

"They *do* pay him. He just can't hang onto it very well. You know how he is, never able to say no to a friend who wants to borrow something from him. He always *was* that way."

"Damn right he was! And it wasn't always *lend*ing he did, and it wasn't always *his* stuff he lent either." He snorted. "I never will forget the time he lent my radio to that friend of his, and right in the middle of the World Series, too. I nearly stripped the hide off him for that one. Maybe I should have."

"Well, it was a nice thought, wasn't it? His friend was in the hospital, after all."

"Sure! And wasn't it Daniel himself who put him there? Why the hell you would want to get in a fistfight that would put your best friend in the hospital is beyond me, but if you're going to do it, you shouldn't go and give him your father's radio to make up for it, for Christ's sake! I never saw the like of that one. Almost forty years old, and still floating around the world on a goddam banana barge or something, any damn time he feels like it."

"But he enjoys it so."

"Damn right he does! And why shouldn't he, on somebody else's money? I could have a good time, too, if somebody else was footing the bill. Only it's usually me that picks up the tab, and I never even know it until it's all over. You're damn near as bad as he is, only you don't have any of the fun. That's the only difference between the two of you, as far as I can see."

"You don't think it's fun being stranded halfway around the world without a dime in your pocket, do you?"

"Maybe not, but I'll bet you he had a hell of a good time getting his pockets empty in the first place!"

"Since when is it such fun to lend money to a friend?"

"What makes you think he *lent* it to anybody?" He snorted.

"He said he lent it to a friend of his, in Singapore, the last time," I said, starting to feel uneasy about the thrust of his conversation. "Don't you believe that?"

"Not on your tintype. If I know our Daniel, I can tell you exactly how he 'lent' it, and to whom, by type if not by name."

"What are you suggesting?"

"That he spent it on women, that's what I'm suggesting. Ladies of the evening, at that!"

"Oh! Oh my goodness!"

"Now, now, don't go getting all upset. He probably had a very nice time. Enjoyed every penny, I'll bet." He couldn't control his laughter, and the more upset I got, the harder he laughed.

"Do you mean he *lied* to me?"

"More like he abused your good nature, and my wallet, I think."

"Well," I persisted, "do you mean to tell me that you approve of what he's done?"

"Not exactly."

"Does that mean you don't exactly disapprove, either?"

"Not exactly. Say, look how pink this grapefruit is. I don't think I remember seeing one this pink before. And the skin is so yellow. Look at it, almost as bright as a canary, it is. Extraordinary! Say, what do you think about painting the house this color? Or the porch furniture? Maybe both?"

I listened to him trying to change the subject, and wanted to let him squirm a little. I wasn't exactly persuaded that Daniel had spent the money as Will suggested, but if he was only joking, I wanted him to pay for it a little. I could tell from the look on his face that he was just now realizing the depth of the hole he had dug for himself.

"Just what *do* you mean, then? I would dearly like to know."

"What?"

"Oh, never mind," I said, turning to my own grapefruit.

We sat in silence for a while, the only sound the occasional squish caused by our spoons. Will didn't dare look at me, fearful that the slightest glance would give me the opportunity to reopen the discussion. Then, finished at long, slow last with his fruit, he cleared his throat rather loudly and announced, "I guess I'd better go get me old coveralls on, if we're going to get anything done today."

"I guess you might as well!"

"You're going to give me a hand, aren't you?" he asked hopefully.

"Doing what?"

"The windows, of course, and the furniture, if we have time."

"Oh! Yes, I guess so, yes."

"Good. I'll go get ready then, all right?"

"Yes. You get ready."

"All right. I'll be right down, okay?" he asked, suspiciously.

"Why wouldn't it be all right?"

"I don't know. You're just acting sort of strange. Is anything the matter?"

"Do you really have to ask me that?"

"No, I suppose not," he said. "But I was only teasing you. I have no idea how he spent the money, or why he needed it. But after all, even if he did spend it on women, what's wrong with that? He's a young man, and he's not married, after all. It would be different if he had a wife, but he doesn't, so what's the harm in it?"

"The harm would be that he lied to me, Will. That's the harm there'd be in it. I don't care about the other business, not so much, anyway, but if he *lied* to me, and for such a purpose . . ."

"Don't you think you're letting this get just a little bit out of hand, Ella? Would you rather he be like Emma, now? Would you prefer that?"

"Will, I . . ."

"You think about that just a minute, Ella. Go ahead, put your hand on your God Almighty Bible and tell me that's what you'd prefer. I dare you," he shouted. His voice was knotted and nearly inarticulate with grief and rage. I couldn't quite understand how something so playful had become so deadly serious, and so quickly.

"Will, I . . . I'm sorry. I didn't mean . . . But try to understand how I feel. I never denied that boy a thing. Never! He didn't have to lie to me, for God's sake, not like that, anyway. I . . ." My own voice gave out completely, and Will took me in his arms, starting to croon as he used to to the children when they were frightened or injured, all the while smoothing my hair with his free hand, the tough skin of his palm occasionally catching in my hair, and all I could see was him at Emma's bedside, holding her to him and crooning, as if he could breathe back into her the life that had just gone out. At that point, I wasn't even sure he knew who he was trying to comfort—me, himself, or Emma. Maybe there isn't any real difference. After a minute or two, he said gently, "For Christ's sake, Ella, you're dripping all over me chest here. Let me get a towel or something, will you?"

I managed a weak laugh. "I'm all right now, I think. Why don't you go get ready, and I'll clean up here?"

"Are you sure you're all right?"

"Yes, I'm fine now. Go, get ready!"

He left reluctantly, looking back over his shoulder once or twice before finally leaving the kitchen. I sat down for a minute and leaned my chin in my hands. I could feel the wetness on my cheeks, and it reminded me of what had started it all. It wasn't so much that Daniel may have abused my trust as that he had taken advantage of my generosity, which had been all the more freely given because it had been a kind of memorial to Emma. I realized that both Will and I had separately determined that Emma's death was going to be repaired in the only way possible, by offering greater comfort to the surviving children, all three of whom had, in their own ways, recognized the change in us after their sister's death.

Katherine, to her credit, had adopted, insofar as she was able, our approach, and this had made her the most outgoing of the three children, and the most giving. Almost from the moment she learned that Emma had died, unexpectedly, of a streptococcus infection associated with an attack of tonsilitis, Katherine had changed her personality. Where before she had been fun-loving and vaguely rebellious, she then became a miniature version of me, as if she were trying to take on some of my responsibilities so that I could be free to deal with my grief. As the oldest child, it was only natural that she take the most active role in the running of the house, but I thought there was something deeper, a more mature sense of responsibility. I was aware of the change in Katie and tried to tell her in subtle ways. As time wore on, and the immediacy of the grief dulled, the new relationship that had begun to develop between us continued, although it underwent a series of changes that were marvels of wordless communication.

Willie, on the other hand, had seemed to react in a way that was diametrically opposed to Katie's. His fondness for pranks, which he got from and shared with Will, seemed exaggerated in the first weeks, and, like the change in Katie, it persisted, but was slowly muted as the tragedy dimmed. While Will had always enjoyed Willie's cutting up, he was concerned about the nearly hysterical edge he thought he detected in Willie's behavior. Rather than discuss it with Willie, he asked me if I had noticed anything, and when I told him what I had seen, he decided to wait, and to say nothing. He had not known how long he was willing to wait, but in a few weeks the edge was gone and, although Willie continued to be a handful for the two of us, he seemed to be settling down slowly but surely.

Danny, however, was a mystery to me and to Will. Outwardly, there was no sign that he had been in the least touched by Emma's death. His schoolwork continued on the same mediocre level, he got into minor scrapes at school as often as ever, and there was no sign that he had been in any way changed. Will just thanked his stars that Danny had not taken after his brother, but I was worried. I knew that Danny and Emma had been closer to one another than to either of the other two children, and I couldn't believe that the outward indifference truly reflected his feelings. Will kept telling me to leave the boy alone, insisting that I would only make him feel guilty if he were, in fact, as unaffected as he seemed to be. Try as I might, I was unable to get Will to accept the idea that Daniel had been the most affected, while least able to demonstrate his feelings. I believed that the outward calm was only a veneer, and knew I had to try to get him to open up. Despite my continuing efforts, I wasn't able to get through to him, but we did grow closer, and I guess it was around this time that I became attached to him in a way that I was not attached to the others. I guess it was the memory of that special closeness, which continued long after the immediate need, that made me feel so betrayed by what Will had told me. I couldn't believe it, but couldn't avoid considering the possibility that it might be true, and when Will came back down, I started to cry all over again. He was dressed in his old coveralls and a tattered work shirt, and he stood over me, asking, "Here now, what's all this?" He was forcing a cheerful demeanor, which didn't quite ring true. "I thought you were going to finish up here while I got ready so we could get right to work."

"I was," I said, blubbering and trying to dry my cheeks with the dishtowel I had twisted into a thick cord.

"Well, what happened?"

"I don't know. I . . ."

"Well, I know! You were still thinking about Daniel, weren't you?"

"I guess so," I lied.

"Well, there's no point in that, now, is there? What's done is done, and we don't even know what it is that might have been done. He's a grown man anyway, for good or bad, and you shouldn't blame yourself if he does something you don't feel he ought to do."

"I know that, but . . ."

"No buts, now! Listen to me. If he wants to spend his hard-earned money on floozies, you can't stop him. You don't have to *lend* him any, mind you, but you can't stop him. The best thing for you to do is chalk it up to experience and then forget about it. If it bothers you, just make sure it doesn't happen again, that's all. Am I right?"

I nodded in agreement, more for form's sake than because I actually agreed. I just wanted him to think he had understood why I was upset, rather than tell him the truth, which I knew would upset him as well.

79

"All right then," he said, "what say you get ready to give me a hand with those windows, huh?"

"All right. It'll just take me a few minutes to straighten up here, so why don't you get started? I'll be with you as soon as I can. Where will you be? In the cellar?"

He nodded, and gave me a long look, as if he were trying to look right inside my head, before leaning over to kiss me on top of it.

"By God," he said, "I don't care if you *are* old, you're still a good-looking woman, Ella. And special into the bargain."

He turned on his heel and headed toward the cellar door, whistling to create a cheer he knew I wasn't up to. Since he didn't know what else to do, as usual, he did what he could.

SEVEN:
Willie

HERE, among so many men, it is not easy to remember Louise, but there are things I can feel with the fingers, things I remember from long ago. Sometimes I look down at the sheet here, the way it lies in folds and creases. The small, round ridges cast bluish shadows in the almost light, and I remember her skin with its pale-blue veins crissing and crossing, and the small, soft part of her leg, rippled like corduroy. I could put my hand there for a long time and move my fingers back and forth over the soft skin. Sometimes I trace the patterns of bluish shadows on the sheet and I pretend that the sheet is as translucent as her skin and that the shadows are her veins. It is not the same, because the small, rounded ridges are not themselves blue. They only create the parallel blues that run and run like veins into and out of one another, but it is all I have here and, though not good enough, I make do.

It is weakness in the eyes of some of them here to trace these patterns. Some of us here do not have such things half buried that we can go back to. For those of us who don't, there is no delicate tracery to remember, and thoughts of skins under which such mysterious patterns lie are alien. They don't envy me, but they don't like it that I have such memories. To them it isn't fair that I should have such a thing to hide in, that I should be able to ride my sheet and my memories of skin like a carpet and fly high over the trees outside the windows in the three walls here and forget where I am for a while. It isn't fair to them, they must think, but it is not my fault that they don't have such an opportunity, and I refuse to forget completely what I have been sometime in the past. If I have been lucky enough to have traced such blue patterns under soft pinkish skin, or to lie with my hand in the rippled nook of corduroy, even if it has been a very long time since I have been able to, and even if I could no longer do it if I were there instead of here, it is not my fault. I won't let them make me feel guilty.

I never talk about it to any of us, but I think that some of us know what I am doing when my mind's fingers blindly retrace such patterns on the sheet. Some of the others must have done something like that in the past, I am certain. It cannot be something only I have done, a thing I have invented. I am not original, I am only a man who does things he does for whatever reason most men do ordinary things. That is why I know some of us must have done it, too. Sometimes when I do it, and half close my eyes, I can see some of the others, some of the close ones, watch me, and their hands begin to move like small butterflies, sliding along the surfaces of their own sheets, and I smile to myself.

Louise does not love me now. I know this. It is not her fault, and it did not happen because I came here. It happened before I came here. Long before. I did not know it was happening when it was, but when I look back, I can see that it was happening for a long time. I should have seen it happening, but I did not. I am not even sure that I can know when it first started to happen, but I know that when I can tell when it first started to happen was very long ago. After the war, when I could not find a job, I think it was already starting to happen, even though it was not my fault that I could not find a job. It isn't fair that I should be held responsible for something that is not my fault, but there is little that is fair in most lives. It is not fair that Louise does not love me and that all I have of the way things used to be is a pattern of rounded folds and bluish shadows on this sheet that is only one of fifty-three sheets. But it is true. It might even be why I am here, but I don't think so. Some of them, the doctors, tell me that it might be, but I don't think they are right. It is too easy. This is such a strange place that I can't believe that one would come here for such a simple reason. The strangeness is out of all proportion to the explanation.

After all, I am not the only one Louise does not love, and most of those I know she does not love are not here. And there are many here whom Louise doesn't know at all, so that is not the reason they are here. For that reason, I think it cannot be the reason I am here, either. There is no connection. I am even beginning to feel that I don't belong here, whether Louise loves me or not.

I have not told them this, but I think that it is what they would call "making progress." If that is what it is, I suppose I should be pleased, but I don't know whether I am pleased or not. If it will help me to leave here, I am pleased, and if it won't, I am not. I don't want to be here. I don't like it here. I have too much trouble here, things are not what I am used to, and I don't like being in a room with so many others. Some of us are mean, and some are almost crazy. They do strange things here, and you can tell that some of the others are crazy because the crazy ones don't even notice when someone does something strange. It is not normal. I guess I am not normal, either, but I know when I do something strange, and I can tell when it is time to stop. Some of us don't know when to stop. I think some of us don't even know what we are doing. I always know what I am doing, but sometimes they don't understand. I think that I might be looking at things a little differently from the way they are. They still talk to me in bunches, and mumble, and make notes on their clipboards, but they smile now more than they used to.

One of them is very nice. I have been thinking about telling him about Louise, but I am not sure it is a good thing to do. It is not his business. I have to decide whether it is worth it to me to tell him about Louise if that is what it takes to get out of here. They ask many questions, and they get angry when you don't answer them. Even personal questions they have no right to ask you. They never yell if you don't answer, but I can see the muscles in their faces grow stiff and their lips get thin if I don't answer some question that is none of their business. Sometimes they get stiff faces even if you do answer. That means they don't like the answer you have given them, but I don't think they should get angry if you don't answer a question the way they want you to. After all, it is not like they have explained the rules to us, and told us how we are expected to answer. There are no classes here, so we have to guess how they want us to answer, and often we are wrong. They seem to hold it against us, but I don't think it's fair to do that.

Sometimes they come and ask questions about Louise, and I don't want to talk about her, so I change the subject. They get very angry then. I think they must think there is some connection between Louise and my presence here. That would be news to me. I might have to try to make up some good answers so they can establish the connection they are looking for. It will be very hard, because I can't always figure out how they are thinking, and I have to know that to give them the right answers. They get impatient, just like Louise used to get impatient, but for different reasons.

Louise always used to get mad that I didn't make more money. She used to tell me that I was no good at anything, and I used to shout, and tell her that I was very good at many things until the man in the Buick entered my life. She used to call that "water under the bridge," but she couldn't see that it was *my* bridge and that it can change you to get run over by a Buick and have to change your whole life, the whole way you look at things, even yourself. I started drinking, sometimes because of my legs, and sometimes because my life was different. Louise didn't like that very much.

Then I started to drink because Louise didn't understand why I drank. I think I might have thought that if I gave her enough time and enough experience, she might start to understand why I drank, and then I wouldn't have to drink, and I could get down to understanding how my life was different and telling that to Louise, too. She tried, I guess, but not very hard. I couldn't help her, because one of the things about my life that had changed was that I couldn't explain things to her any more. I was learning a new way to look at things, and I had not yet learned it and could not explain it to anyone yet, not even Louise. She didn't give me enough time to learn it and explain it to her, so things started to go downhill. Once I started rolling, I kept on rolling, all the way downhill, like a fat rock, until I came to rest here, at the bottom of the hill. This is as far down the hill as you can roll and still be able to look at things and talk to people. Even if you don't want to, at least you can. I can, anyway, even if I don't always say the right things.

Right now, I am looking at the blue shadows on the sheet, and I think I can see Louise a long time ago. Back when she loved me and my life was not different. It is different now, but once it wasn't, and that is when I used to trace the veins under her skin with my fingers, which were not so fat then. My fingers got fat when I was little, then they got to be regular, except for a little while, maybe three months, and then, when things got different, they got fat again. There must be some connection between things not being right and having fat fingers, at least for me, because the worse things get, the fatter my fingers get. I don't know if any of the others here have fat fingers. It has never occurred to me to look, since I have just thought of the possibility that there might be some connection. Tomorrow I will look at their fingers, but I will have to be very careful, because they might think that I am a spy for the doctors. If one of the doctors sees me, I might get written about on his clipboard, and that wouldn't be good, either. It is hard not to have everybody mad at you at once in a place like this, but I try.

I used to sit in a bar and watch my fat fingers curl around a glass of beer, and I could hardly see the top of the glass, because my fingers were getting thicker and thicker. They were almost like sausages for a while. Then I started to get fat all over, so my fingers didn't seem so fat any more. Then I came here, and I have gotten thin again. Even my fingers are getting thinner. That is another reason I think I may not belong here. If you have to have fat fingers to get here, maybe you can leave when they get thin again. Maybe that is a good sign, and maybe that is what the doctors are always writing on their clipboards.

I hope so. Of course, if they were really scientific, I think they would want to take measurements of my fingers, and see if they were really getting thinner or if it just seemed like it. Besides, some of the doctors have fat fingers, so to them my fingers might look thinner than to some of the doctors who have thin fingers. I don't know. I don't know anything, except that I want to leave here, as soon as I can. Tomorrow, I will ask how thin my fingers have to be before I can leave. If they tell me, I can measure for myself, and I will be able to know when it is almost time. My fingers are getting very thin, now, so I think it might almost be time to leave.

I remember that time when my fingers started getting fat for a few months, and then they got thin again. I think I know why, but I have never really thought about it until now. It seems that I am learning how to think things here that I would not know about if I had never been here. I would rather not have been here, but if I have to be here, at least I can take away with me this new way to think of things. I know it would make them happy, and it might help me. At least it can't hurt, anyway. For a while my fingers were getting fat. I was almost crazy then—not enough to be here, and not even enough for anyone to notice, probably, except maybe people who knew me real well. My father noticed, and my mother noticed, too, I think, although she didn't know me as well as my father, I don't think. At least she never seemed to understand me as well as he did.

Emma was in a small room, like the one I was in after the trees fell over, and I went to see her, and her hands were stretched out alongside her, the palms facing up toward the ceiling, like she was expecting rain. I reached out to touch her hand, the one on the bed in front of me, and it was all hot, and very dry. I think her palms must have been expecting rain, even if she wasn't. They must have known how dry she was, and how hot. Her face was very white, and I would not even have seen her if her hair had not been dark and spread out around her face on the pillow. Her eyes, which were very dark, I could have seen against that white sheet, but they were closed, so I did not see them that day. They did not open the whole time I was there. She was small, because she was young, only nine, but she seemed even smaller in that room which was all white. Only her dark hair to look at in all that white, and her lashes, which were usually dark and long, seemed almost pale because she looked so small, and because her hair was so very dark against the white sheet. I kept talking to her, but she didn't answer me. I didn't want to touch her hand again, because it was so hot, and so dry. I didn't like the way it felt. It did not feel like her. It did not even feel alive, that hand, all hot and dry like that. That was the last time I saw her. I told her good-bye, but I don't think she heard me. After that she died. That same night, I think, but I'm not sure.

After that, my fingers started to get fat. They were getting to look the way they did when I was smaller, around Emma's age. It seemed like every time I looked at them, either they seemed fatter or there was something in them that would make them fatter. I was eating all the time, because I was too young to drink. Like my father. That must be the only reason, too, because now if something like that happened, the first thing I would do is reach for a drink. Then it was different. I didn't know how drinking could make things seem better, even if they weren't. I know that now, but it didn't help me then because I didn't know it yet. I learned it later on, after my legs were hurt by the Buick. Instead, I just ate food all the time. I don't know why. Maybe I thought if I ate enough to support two lives, Emma would come back. I felt as if she weren't really gone, anyway. Just away for a while, like a vacation.

Sometimes, late at night, when it is almost dark in here, I can see Emma's face on the ceiling, like a photograph, only it is real big, and I stare at it, and the lids of her eyes start to move, just the tiniest bit. I stare real hard, and I watch, and they flicker, but they never open. Even if I whisper to her, they don't open. I want them to, but they don't. They just flicker a little and then they stop. I try not to look, thinking maybe it is the pressure of my eyes on the ceiling that prevents her from opening her lids, but I can never control myself long enough to be sure that that is what it is, because I always peek, and then she is gone again, before ever opening her eyes. I think that is what I miss most about her, those eyes. Maybe I would not miss her so much now if I could have seen her eyes that day. It is nice to think so, but I can't know. Not for sure. So what is the difference? There is nothing I can do to change any of that. There is nothing I can do to change anything at all, not even myself. I try to change. I try to make myself what people want me to be, mostly Louise, but other people, too. But everybody wants me to be something different. If I make one person happy, I make someone else angry. That has always been what it is like for me. It is like that here, too. If I make a doctor happy, the others get angry at me. If I make a doctor angry, then the others like me, and they sneak me things, like in a prison movie. It is very much like that here. All of them are Barton Maclane, and we are all friends of Jimmy Cagney. All we need is for him to come and lead the rest of us against the lousy screws, and we could bust out of here. My father likes Barton Maclane, so I guess he wouldn't like it if he knew how I felt, but that is what it is like here. And that is how I feel.

I guess it is more likely that my fingers will get thin enough to leave, because I don't think Jimmy Cagney would come to a place like this, even to help us get out. Why should he? He doesn't know us. I have even been watching for him on television, in the movies, to see if his fingers are fat. If they are, then maybe he *will* come here, but I can't tell on the television. Everyone's fingers are so tiny on the screen it is hard to tell if they are fat or thin fingers. Sometimes I can't even tell if they *have* fingers. Their hands are just blobs on the ends of what look like arms. That is because the screen is fuzzy. I know how to make it not fuzzy, but I can't. There are knobs that you can turn to make things clearer, but one of us took the knobs and won't say where they are. They won't give us any more knobs, so we have to wait until somebody finds the ones that are missing. I bet they are down the john. They probably are, but I don't know for sure. I can't suggest that to them, either, because they might think it was a confession, and then they would blame me. They would probably blame me for the sox, too. That is the way they like to do things here. Just take the first explanation that comes along. It is an easy way to solve problems. It works for them, too. I wish they would let *us* use the same method, but they just get thin lips and stiff muscles in their faces whenever I try it. Some things only work one way. And some things don't work at all. Like the TV.

Sometimes I think even my idea about the fingers is wrong. I look at my fingers now, in the blue shadows on this sheet like the other sheets, and I know that it is only a sheet, and not the translucent skin of someone who used to love me, and I know that I am not ready to leave here yet. I can see that my fingers have fat shadows, even if they are thin.

EIGHT

It was the first summerlike day of the year, and even though it was only late May, Will was determined to get a head start on the heavier summer variety of gardening chores, and there was no better way to begin than to get rid of the rambling rosebush that had been driving him crazy for more than twenty years. At 6:00 A.M., when Will looked out the kitchen window, it was already bright. There was a sprinkling of high, fluffy clouds. They were bright white, edged in dark blue, and billowed as if they were living creatures, constantly changing shape and proportion, as if prodded by an impatient hand. He glanced at an old thermometer mounted outside the window, but couldn't quite read the temperature.

"It looks like it's going to be a hot one today," he said over his shoulder to Ella, who was bustling around in the small room off the kitchen. She was rattling utensils, didn't quite hear what Will had said, and came into the kitchen drying her hands on her apron.

"Did you say something, Will?" she asked. "I had the water on."

"I said it looks like it's going to be a hot one today," he repeated. "I can't quite read the thermometer, but it looks like it says seventy degrees already, and it's only a little after six."

"Well, I've never known that thing to work right," Ella said. "But it usually is a little cooler than it reads. What do you plan on doing today? Anything special?"

"I've been thinking it was about time I got rid of that damn rosebush in the back, by the cellar door. I never liked it much anyhow, and Manelli was griping all last summer about how it kept taking all the water from his tomatoes."

"Didn't you cut it back last spring?"

"Yeah, I cut it back almost to the ground, but the damn thing just took off again. I've tried to cut it right out of the ground three or four times since we've lived here, but I just can't seem to get rid of it."

"I don't know why you're going to bother with it, then. Why don't you just tell Vincent you can't do anything with it? He'll just plant his tomatoes someplace else, and you won't have to worry about it."

"I can't tell him that," Will said. "I don't want him to think I don't have any control over me own garden. He's always bragging about his, and how his tomatoes would be the best on the block if my rosebush didn't get all their water. I want to give him a fighting chance, and then rub his nose in it when my beefsteaks look like footballs and he still has those scraggly little cherries."

"But if you can't do anything about the rose, that's all there is to it," Ella said firmly. "If you like, I'll tell Millie, and you won't have to get involved at all."

"Damn it, Ella," Will snapped, "just keep out of it. I'll take care of that rose if I have to get a bulldozer in here to do it. Besides, I think at least one of Vinnie's brothers is in the mob, and I don't want to find some guy named Dominick in the back yard with a machine gun, chopping up me flowers."

"Sssssshhh. Now you just cut that out, Will. I know you don't like Vincent, but Millie is a friend of mine, and I won't have you talking like that behind her back."

"All right, I'll tell her to her face, if you want. Call her up. Just don't let Vinnie's brother know. I don't want to find my tulips in the river, wearing cement leaves."

"Now, that's enough! Drink your coffee and be on about your business."

"Okay, but remember, mum's the word! If Dominick gets wind of this conversation, I'm in big trouble, and so are you. You know, those guys don't play around. Nothing's sacred to them; they even go after the family, you know? Why, I'll bet you they'd even find a way to get to your African violets as soon as they were done with the plants out in the yard. They might even go after those cuttings you gave to Katie last year. God knows where it would all end!"

"Are you going to hush up and drink your coffee, or am I going to have to pour it down the sink to teach you a lesson?" Ella sighed.

"I'll never say another word about Vinnie being a mobster, I promise. Just let me have my coffee."

"I don't know whether I should believe you or not."

Their respective attitudes were those of wayward pupil and irate teacher. Ella's hands were anchored to her hips and Will was staring down at the cup of coffee, occasionally sneaking a look at her out of the corner of his eye. Ella often wondered what he must have been like as a boy in the classroom, but had never been able to conjure an image of the child equal to her experience of the man, and her heart would go out in sympathy to her husband's grammar-school teachers.

"Ella?" It came suddenly, interrupting her reverie, and was almost a question.

"What is it now?"

"Are you sure we ought to get rid of that rosebush?"

"Why ask me? It was your idea!"

"Not really. It was Manelli's idea, actually. I guess I might as well go and get it over with."

"I don't care where you go, as long as it's out! Now scoot! I don't want to know you're here until noontime, at least. And maybe not even then!"

"Does that mean you won't bring me some iced coffee later?"

"You've gotten all the coffee you're going to get from me. If you want some iced coffee, you can just take that cup off the table and put some cubes in it."

"Well, I'm going to go now. Out. In the yard."

"Close the door behind you. And lock it."

Will lost his composure at that point and burst out laughing. He slipped out the door and slammed it behind him, then made his way around to the back of the house. Ella peeked out the small window that looked out on the back yard, and, though she couldn't hear him, she knew Will was still chuckling by the way his shoulders shook. He got down on his knees and began digging idly at the base of the unruly rose, which was just beginning to bud, and she marveled at the way his strong, thickly veined hands tore away the soil around the thick cluster of roots. She smiled in spite of herself, saying half aloud, "Will Donovan, you are still a child, but I don't guess I'd change you if I could!"

She went back to cleaning the table, and heard the thud of the cellar door, then the heavy tread of Will's work shoes on the stone stairs down to the cellar, followed by a loud clatter of metal tools.

Will gathered some of the implements he would use for his chore—two spades, a hoe, a saw, and a rake—and took them by the handles in one hand, like a long-ball hitter coming to the plate, as he rummaged in the pocket of his gardening apron for a pair of work gloves. He bounced back up the steps, the spades clanging together, tossed the tools onto the lawn, and paused to slip on the gloves, which were still stiff around the wrists but soft and supple in the palm and fingers, a rich earthen brown, seemingly fertile enough to support a growth of vegetation.

He knelt, resting his weight on his heels, and pondered his problem, almost reluctantly, as if he was not certain that he could, or ought to, do the thing he had set himself to do. After several moments of what could have passed for prayer, perhaps of contrition for what he was about to do, he rose slowly to his feet while reaching back for the nearer of the two spades with a sigh of resignation. It went against his grain to kill anything, let alone something he had spent so many hours nurturing, even though reluctantly, but he had promised Manelli, and he could not go back on his word.

He slid the spade into the loose, sandy soil, withdrew the first spadeful, and tossed it lightly into the nearest open area. The earth was quite dry and offered little resistance. The more he pondered what he was doing, the more it outraged him, yet he continued, and the soft, dry mound of soil continued to grow in a rough cone of progressively deeper beige, shading slowly into brown toward its peak.

The work was getting more difficult as the spade had to bite through the network of rose roots. The hole around the base of the bush had reached a foot or so in depth, and Will thought he might stop at this point and merely lop the plant off level with the deepest part of his excavation. He had tried this last year, and though it didn't work then, and probably wouldn't work this time, either, it might be sufficient to buy a truce with Manelli.

The sun had risen over the nearby rooftops as Will continued his digging, and the sweat had begun to run down his neck in tickling rivulets. He worked intently and in silence, the only sound that of the sand-bright blade of the spade hissing into the soil and an occasional chunk when it came up against a particularly sturdy root or a buried stone.

From time to time, Ella would peek through the lace curtain on the back window, but she elected not to join Will in the yard. She sensed that he was less than wholeheartedly committed to his labor, and would likely be in a snippish mood and not welcome her company. As she busied herself with her daily routine, she heard the kitchen door slam and the thump of Will's heavy shoes on the linoleum. She wiped her hands dry and went into the kitchen in time to see him slump into the chair he had so hurriedly vacated an hour earlier. He pulled a large, bright-red workman's handkerchief from a pocket in his coveralls to mop the sweat from his neck and forehead, then turned to smile at Ella.

"Christ, I think I dug deep enough to strike oil," he groaned. "I don't think it will matter how deep I go, I'll never get that damn thing out of the ground."

"What are you going to do, then?"

"I think I'll just chop it off at the bottom of the hole, like I did last time."

"Won't it just come back again if you do that?"

"I don't know. Probably." He sighed. "But I won't tell anyone about Vinnie's mob connections if you don't tell him about the bush."

"I'm too tired to argue with you any more. Do what you want!"

"You won't tell Vinnie?"

"No!"

"Or Millie?"

"No, her either. Are you satisfied?"

"I suppose I'll have to be. I don't really trust you not to tell Millie, but I'm too tired to dig any more." He mopped his brow again with the huge cloth, which always reminded Ella of a movie cowboy.

"You look exhausted, Will. Are you all right?"

"Yes, I'm fine," he snapped. "It's just the heat. Don't go thinking I'm too old to do anything. I'm a long way from being over the hill yet, even if I don't go to work any more!"

"I know you're not over the hill, and I wasn't trying to suggest otherwise, but it's hot out there. Oh, never mind! Would you like some iced coffee?"

"I thought I was going to be punished," he said impishly. "How come I can have iced coffee? Wasn't I really bad?"

He reached out and grabbed her apron to tug her toward him, while she squirmed without really trying to extricate herself from his grip.

"You're feeling pretty frisky, this morning, Mister! I thought you wanted something cold to drink."

"First things first, Ella. I need a kiss to sweeten up that coffee. Seems like you put saccharine in everything these days."

"Even my kisses?" She laughed.

"Well, I don't recall getting enough lately to rightly know. I think I'll have to run a few tests. You got that little jigger you pee in anywhere handy?"

"Now stop that! You are incorrigible!"

"All right, all right. Just give me the kiss then. I can run the test some other time. Come on, lay one on me kisser, will you?"

"My goodness, you certainly are playful for an old man, aren't you? Why don't you finish your chore, if you have so much energy? I'll give you a hand. Just let me get my gloves. I'll only be a minute," she said, reaching around to untie her apron. She shucked it off and went to the cellar door, where she hung the apron and withdrew a ragged pair of cotton gardening gloves.

"Christ, I thought you got rid of those things, Ella," Will snorted.

"What's wrong with them? Why should I get rid of them? They work perfectly well."

"What's left of them, maybe. For Christ's sake, they're so old Eve probably wore them, before *she* got in trouble for gardening."

"Now, Will, I wish you wouldn't joke about something like that. You know how I feel about that sort of thing."

"You're right, you're right. I'm sorry. Let's go, shall we?"

Once outside, Ella realized just how unseasonably warm it was as they made their way toward the back of the house, where Will's pit lay like an open wound in the smooth green skin of the garden. The rose itself seemed almost humanly naked and so vulnerable with its roots exposed.

"It does seem a pity," she observed. "I don't think we got more flowers on any other bush. And we've had it for so long, too."

"I know" was all Will's response.

"You don't suppose we could move it to another part of the garden, do you?"

"No, I don't think so. Its life is all in its roots, and they go so deep we'd never be able to get them out. It's a funny thing, but I could cut the top off this thing every year and nothing would probably happen to it, but if we hurt it deep enough, it's all over. The thing is, I just don't know how deep to go to really be sure."

"Well, I suppose we may as well get it over with." Ella sighed. "What do you want me to do?"

"I'm just going to take a saw to the roots, down near the bottom of the hole, so if you could hold onto the stem I'm cutting, it'll make things a lot easier. Just grab on tight. And look out for the thorns."

He bent over to pick up a small keyhole saw and leaned into the hole to begin hacking away at the principal stems. The fibrous roots resisted the small blade, and the going was slow. Will paused frequently to catch his breath, and the sweat was again running down his neck, more freely than before, and his wind came in short, sharp gasps. As he succeeded in cutting through each of the main stems, Ella would tug it from the pit, and there was a small pyramid of tangled branches slowly growing behind them. Her exertion was strenuous enough to bring a heated glow to her cheeks and neck, not unlike that of Will's own.

"We can go in and rest as soon as you cut the last one," Ella said. "There's no hurry to fill in the hole, is there? You can do it after lunch. Or even this evening, after it cools off."

"No. I'd just as soon be done with it, for good and all, I hope. At least I'll fill the hole and tell meself it's over, anyway."

"Do you really think this will kill it?"

"No, I don't, to tell you the truth. This thing's as tough as I am. Maybe tougher. It'll be here when I'm dead and gone, you mark me words."

"Well, be that as it may," she said, laughing, "I don't think there's much hope for this plant. I'll bet you it's as dead as a doornail this time."

"I sure hope so," Will groaned. "I guess, anyway. I guess it *is* a pity to see something die before its time, and God knows we've had enough of *that* in this family."

He turned abruptly to slash viciously at the remaining stem of the bush, and tore it away from the root when it had been sawn only halfway through. With an exaggerated gesture composed of resignation and defiance in equal measure, he threw it onto the pile of severed branches and briskly clapped his gloved hands together to dislodge the small thorns that had broken off in the material. The flourish with which he removed each glove signaled to Ella the return of the good humor that had so suddenly left him. He rose to his feet and threw one muscular arm around Ella's waist, saying, "I guess I've earned me iced coffee, and some of that 'rest' you were talking about, eh, Mother?"

"If the iced coffee doesn't cool you off," Ella said, chuckling, "we'll talk about it then."

NINE:
Ella

By the middle of summer, Will was beginning to get into the swing of things. He learned to save his energy and slowly began to accept the idea that there was not so much to do that he couldn't afford to take his time. One morning, he took it into his head that it was the perfect time to repaint the front-porch furniture. Without telling me, he lugged all the heavy metal chairs down off the porch and out onto the lawn, then burst into the kitchen, where I was reading the morning paper, and announced, "Up off your duff, woman! We've got some work to do!"

"Oh, and what might that be?" I asked.

"I'm tired of that sickly green-and-white stuff we've been sitting on out front. I think it's about time it had a new coat of paint. What do you say?"

"Oh, Will, I don't know. I don't think it's such a good idea to be painting that stuff on the porch."

"Who says we have to paint it on the porch? Can't we just move it down into the yard?"

"I suppose so, but I don't think today is the best day for it. We're supposed to get some heavy rain later. We'd never get done in time."

"Oh."

"What's the matter?" I asked. "Did I say something wrong?"

"Oh, nothing! Only, I already moved the stuff out to the yard. Now you tell me it's going to rain. I guess I'll just have to move it all back up on the porch."

"Well . . . the paper isn't always right, especially when it comes to the weather. Maybe we can get it done anyway. Shall we give it a try?"

"I don't know. Let's go take a look. It's clear right now, and we might have enough time to get it all painted. By the way, what's that smell? You baking something again?"

"Yes I am. It's a pie. But don't go getting your heart set on having a piece. It's for the bake sale."

"What bake sale? You haven't mentioned it before. Where is it?"

"At the church."

"Jesus Christ!"

"What's the matter?"

"That damned Berland is going to drive me nuts! Him and his damn schemes to make money. He's as bad as the damn Catholics. Next thing you know, he'll be having Bingo!"

"I just don't understand why you resent the Reverend so much," I complained.

"It's not that I resent him so much," he explained. "It's that I don't *like* the son of a bitch."

"Will, stop that! Don't talk like that about a minister; it isn't right."

"Well, anyway, I *don't* like him. And I don't trust him, either. I'll bet you every damn penny he raises goes right into helium for that damn blimp of his."

"I thought we were going to check out the weather," I reminded him.

"All right! All right, let's go!" he grumbled. "You put on an old dress or something, and then we'll go check the weather."

I went upstairs to get ready, still not quite sure I knew what I was letting myself in for, but unwilling to argue any more. Will had always been a stickler for precision, and more than once I had seen him come in from the yard or up from the cellar fuming at the damage Willie or Daniel had done by trying to help him. I recalled the time Daniel had come running in, Will right on his heels cursing like a prophet. Daniel's face was blue from ear to ear, and Will had a smear of the same color on one cheek, running down his chin to drip on the front of his shirt.

In one hand, he was carrying a small paint can and a brush, dripping the same bright blue.

I stared in astonishment at the two of them as they raced past me, Daniel yelling at the top of his lungs. They made two or three trips around the dining-room table, Will hollering, "I'll teach you to paint me face, you rapscallion!"

"I didn't mean it, Pop, honest. I didn't mean it!" Daniel cried.

Before I could interfere, Daniel shot off toward the kitchen, Will right behind him. Daniel managed to get the cellar door open just as Will got close enough to grab him, and plunged down the stairs into the dark just ahead of Will's outstretched fingers. There was a growl, like a wild animal, and then Will was gone into the darkness after him. I could hear him bounding down the steps, then a tremendous clatter of cans and jars. I knew Daniel couldn't see anything in the dark, and he must have been desperate to find a place to hide.

"Gotcha, you rascal!" Will hollered.

"Like hell you do, too! Ma, Ma, he's gonna kill me! Help!"

There was another roar and a tremendous crash. I was certain that one or the other of them would break a leg in the dark, so I clicked the light on and hurried down the steps.

"Will? Daniel? Somebody answer me!" I was whispering, for some peculiar reason. "Where are you? Answer me! Daniel?" No one answered, so I went into the back room, thinking that Daniel had managed to get to the steps and Will had followed him into the yard. But the back door was still locked from the inside. I started toward the front of the cellar, and heard a groan coming from somewhere up front. The voice was deep, so I knew it was Will. "Will, where are you? Will, is that you?" Another groan, and suddenly I saw a hand, still waving a paintbrush, emerge from behind a pile of cardboard cartons. "Will, are you okay?" He groaned again. Then silence, complete and utter silence. I tiptoed over to the cartons just in time to see Will, his entire face now the same bright blue as Daniel's, climbing slowly to a sitting position. The front of his shirt, too, was now almost entirely blue.

"Oh my God! Will, what happened?"

"I almost had the little bastard, and then I tripped. The damn paint can was in me hand, and it went splashing all over the place. I went right through it, face first. Thank God it's only that! At first, I felt all sticky and I thought it was blood. Wait'll I get my hands on that boy. Where is he?"

"I don't know. Isn't he here?"

"Now, don't you go hiding him, Ella!"

"I don't know where he is. What happened, to start all this in the first place?"

"I'll break his neck for him, that's what I'll do!"

"Calm down, will you! You've nearly broken your own neck, and that should be enough for one day. What started all this?" I asked again.

"We were painting his soapbox-derby racer, and all of a sudden he ups and smacks me right in the kisser. With his paintbrush, yet."

"Why did he do that?"

"Why don't you ask *him*? That's what I'll do, after I break his neck. Are you sure you don't know where he is?"

"I told you, I don't know. What happened next?"

"Well, I asked him what he thought he was doing, and he says there was a bee on my cheek. 'He was gonna sting you, Pop!' he says. So instead of letting the damn thing go away on its own, he smacks me with the brush."

"Go on," I urged, trying to hide a giggle.

"That's about it," he said. "Are you sure he's not here?"

"How did *his* face get covered with paint?"

"Oh, that! Well, I was mad at him, of course. He damn near put me eye out, and covered me with paint, to boot!" Will explained.

"That doesn't explain how *he* got paint on *his* face," I said again, suspecting there was more to the story than he was willing to tell.

"*I* did it! I painted the little rascal," he confessed. "I grabbed him by the scruff of the neck and I told him that since he was my son he ought to *look* like me, which meant he ought to be blue, too! So, I painted him. Now he *is* blue! Or almost. I'm not through with him yet, either. Not by a long shot!"

"You painted him blue? So he'd *look* like you?" I could hardly believe what I was hearing.

"Damn right! Well, don't look at me that way! I'm blue, ain't I? Well, so is he!"

"Why don't you just go upstairs and get cleaned off? I'll see if I can coax him out of wherever he's hiding," I said.

"All right, but if you *do* find him, he's *mine,*" he said ominously.

A half hour later, Will was clean again, although smelling strongly of turpentine, but there was still no sign of Daniel. Not even an hour later. By dinnertime, Will had finally cooled off, and he and I were both starting to worry. We went to the cellar hoping that Will could entice Daniel out of hiding with a promise that there would be no further reprisal. Still no sign, and I was about to go upstairs to call the police to report him missing when I heard a muffled voice from somewhere in the cellar.

"Daniel?" I called, but there was no answer. I heard another sound and went to the foot of the stairs and called again. When I heard a creak behind me, I turned to find myself staring into a bright-blue face, peering out from the open door to the laundry chute. One blue hand was on the sill of the chute, and a pair of sox, rolled into a ball, was stuck to a bright-blue cheek.

"Pssst!" Daniel hissed. "Is Pop still mad?"

I chuckled now at the memory, still so vivid, of my younger son peering out from the laundry bin, and hoped that I would not meet a similar fate that morning. I put on an old dress and hurried back down to Will, who was sitting impatiently at the kitchen table.

"I'm about ready, I guess," I said. "You know, I was thinking . . ."

"I know what you're thinking, but don't worry. I'm too old to paint anybody any more. Even somebody who can't run any faster than I can." He laughed.

"How did you know?"

"I can't pick up a paintbrush without thinking of that. I have never been as mad in my life as I was that afternoon. He still kids me about it whenever he sees me with a paintbrush. It's like it happened just yesterday." He sighed. "I wish it *had* been only yesterday."

"Let's go see if it's going to rain," I said. "With any luck, it will, and I'll be off the hook for a while."

We went outside, and the sky was pale gray, the sun just a yellow blur behind the clouds, but Will wasn't one to give up too easily.

"It looks fine to me," he said. "I think we'll have plenty of time to finish up, even if it does rain."

"What about the peach tree? You haven't finished that yet, and if we get any wind, it could do some damage. Maybe you ought to do that instead."

"You may be right. Why don't we pass for today, then? And I'll lug all that damn stuff back on the porch."

"I think that might be the best thing to do. Why don't we have a cold drink first, though? It's hot out here."

"Okay. What do you feel like drinking?"

"Iced tea?"

"Are you asking me or telling me? If you're afraid I can't make it, don't be. Just let me know how much sweetener you want in it."

"I always put sugar in it," I said, a bit timidly, knowing what was coming.

"I know you do, and I also know you're not supposed to. Why the hell do you go to that doctor if you're not going to listen to him?"

"But it tastes bitter without sugar in it," I said.

"I know it does, but I want you around for a while yet, and so long as I have anything to say about it, you'll do what the doctor tells you to do."

"Three tablets," I said, reluctantly. "And one sugar!"

"No sugar, dammit! Do you want three tablets or four?" Will insisted.

"Two, I guess. Scrooge!"

He just grunted and headed across the lawn toward the house. I sat back in the grass, enjoying the feel of it on the backs of my legs, then, beginning to feel uncomfortable, I got up to sit on a chair, and leaned back with my eyes closed. I knew that Will was right about my unwillingness to follow doctor's orders, but I hadn't gotten used to the idea that I was diabetic yet, and for one so used to cooking elaborate meals, and eating my share of them, it wasn't easy to accept. The only evidence that I was ill was my daily test, which I resented, but which Will absolutely would not let me ignore. After every meal, I had to urinate into a small vial, then drop a tablet in and compare the color of the fluid to that on a chart, so I could check the level of blood sugar.

When we had company for dinner, I was usually able to get around the rules, mostly because Will wouldn't argue with me in front of guests. I always took advantage of visitors and asked Will to pass dessert. He would ignore me. So I would start to talk to myself, ask if I wanted some pie, or whatever we might be having that night. I would take a generous slice, then ask if I wanted seconds. The first time I had tried it, everyone at the table had laughed, including Will. But afterward, when the guests had left, he let me know that it wasn't a habit I ought to plan on cultivating, because he wasn't going to stand for it. I wasn't easily intimidated though, and the next time we had company, I tried it again. Will didn't laugh, and he didn't make an issue of it, either. But I heard about it later. He was really angry.

"You know, you may think that's real funny, that talking to yourself. But I'm not going to be around here forever, and if you can't control yourself, what will happen when I'm not here to argue with you? Did you ever think about that?"

I had been good for the first couple of weeks after that, but it wasn't long before I started slipping back into the old routine. I couldn't bear to look at Will when I did it, however, because the pain I knew I would see on his face would have spoiled everything for me.

When Will and I ate alone, it was a different story, and he wouldn't allow me to use any sugar at all, not even in my iced tea. He had even gone so far as to gather up all the sugar in the house and toss it into the trash, saying that, by God, if I couldn't resist the urge to eat sugar, there wouldn't be any around for me *to* eat. For a few weeks after that, he took to sweetening his coffee with saccharine, and although I knew he couldn't stand the taste of it, he kept it up until I finally promised him I'd cooperate, as long as I could keep some sugar in the house for cooking. He relented then, but only after warning me that a single relapse would put an end to sugar altogether.

Now, sitting on the lawn, I remembered his warning that he wasn't always going to be around to look after me, and I couldn't help but feel that there was no way I could stand to lose him. It was so comfortable, being with him. Each of us seemed to know what the other was thinking, even when there was no logical clue in the conversation. But it was more than that. It was something I knew but could never explain to someone who had never felt like that about someone else, and anyone who had wouldn't need an explanation. Besides, we had already lost Emma, and it was only having each other that got us through that. Who would help me if I lost him?

I opened my eyes when I heard his elbow thump the screen door, and looked up in time to see him edging sidewise across the back porch, a glass of iced tea in each hand. He made his way down the steps, trying not to slosh the tea out of the glasses, and came across the lawn to sit in the grass beside my chair. He gave me one of the glasses and set his own down on the grass, then reached into his coveralls for napkins.

"Here, take one of these."

We sipped our tea in silence, and I was still thinking about what it might be like to live without him when there was a sudden burst of rain, which we heard rather than felt, the fat, heavy drops drumming on the seat of the other metal chair, and splattering in every direction. There was a momentary silence, then the rain began again, more gently this time, but more steadily. It was like a drifting mist, swirling in the breeze, and Will shuttled rapidly back and forth with the porch furniture, finishing just as the sky opened up and it began to pour in earnest. We heard an ominous rumble off in the distance, and there was a bright flash of lightning. Will took a look at the maples out front. They were bending and swaying, their leaves rippling wildly and glistening with rain. The limbs of the peach tree, which were already full of large green peaches, were swaying under the pressure of the wind. Will hurried inside, saying he had to get the cellar door open.

"Will, you're not going to try to do anything in this storm, are you?" I hollered after him.

"I have to do something to that tree or we'll lose it," he yelled back.

I followed him into the house and down into the cellar. I could hear the wind flapping the awnings of the front porch and the hiss of rain against the side of the house. Through the cellar windows, I could see the rain running in torrents over the glass, and the great muddy splashes made by the larger drops as they landed in the soil along the hydrangea clumps at the side of the house. Peal after peal of thunder boomed and echoed in the basement as Will gathered some pipe and a coil of heavy wire. He worked quickly, as if he had been planning to shore up the tree under exactly these circumstances.

"Get me my raincoat, will you, Ella," he asked over his shoulder.

"I don't think you ought to go out in this," I said. "Besides, there's a lot of lightning." As if to justify my warning, a bright flash seemed to explode in the interior of the cellar, momentarily throwing everything into bold relief. Almost immediately, there was a tremendous clap of thunder, which started with a sound like tearing cloth and ended in a tremendous, echoing boom.

"If I don't get out there right now, we're liable to lose that tree altogether," he said.

"Maybe not. Anyway, we raised it from a pit, and we can just as easily plant another one. It won't matter that much."

"Like hell," he snapped. "I've been looking after that tree for nearly twenty years. I don't have enough time to raise another one. I'm going to do me damnedest to save this one, and that's all there is to it."

"If you insist on making a fool of yourself, I suppose I have no choice but to help you," I said sarcastically. "Let me get my own coat and I'll be out in a minute. What shall I bring?"

"I'll take all the pipes; you just bring whatever is left here. But be careful, will you?" Will warned.

"*You* be careful," I responded. "I don't like the looks of that lightning. It's too close for comfort."

"Never mind the lightning," he snapped. "You just bring the wire, then get back inside."

He threw open the cellar door and grabbed a handful of pipe before plunging out into the downpour. Elbowing half of the longer pieces, he grabbed a shorter piece, and began to screw it into one of the elbows. After threading a crosspiece into another elbow, he slipped a second long pipe into the elbow and threaded it home. When he had finished, he had a long inverted U shape.

Then he measured the nearest heavy lower limb of the peach. Leaning the U against the trunk of the tree, he ran back to the cellar for a small sledgehammer, splattering water all over me when he dashed past. As he was about to remount the stairs and head back into the rain, there was a bright flash and a roar of thunder. He shook his head once or twice, and I knew his ears must be ringing from the explosion, which seemed to have been right over our heads. He took the stairs two at a time back into the storm.

I went to the top step, just out of the rain, and saw him grab the U and position it quickly under the limb before driving it several inches into the ground. He leaned into it with his shoulder to force it toward the trunk of the tree, where the crossbar met one of the heavily laden limbs. He seemed satisfied that the pipe would take a good deal of the strain from the area where the limb met the trunk. Turning to begin fashioning the next support, he noticed me, a bandana over my head, running toward him with the coiled wire trailing behind me.

"Throw it down there," he said, "and go to my workbench and get the wire cutters, the small blue ones." He seemed satisfied that his scheme would work, and when I got back with the wire cutters, he had already made three more of the U shapes. The wind was roaring around him, and the leaves of the peach tree were hissing like angry snakes. He drove the second support into the ground, and leaned it in place. When he had finished, I tapped him on the shoulder and offered the cutters to him. He cut a length of wire, which he wound repeatedly around the supported limb and the support itself, binding the limb to the pipe to ensure that any sidewise gust of wind would not force it away from the prop.

He did the same with the second supported limb, managing to stick himself several times with the now slippery, stiff wire, drawing blood from one thumb and the back of his left hand. As he was forcing the third support into the ground and in toward the tree, a violent gust of wind whipped through the tree, driving the streaming leaves into his face and causing him to lose his grip on the support momentarily. He shook the water out of his eyes and ears in time to hear a horrible rending sound, and as he watched helplessly, the tree split wide open right at the fourth of the limbs he had planned to shore up. The heavy limb sagged in slow-motion toward the ground, and the squalling sound increased in pitch, sounding now like tearing metal.

"Shit! I thought I was going to make it after all," he yelled. "But I guess not!" He threw himself back into the work as if to spite the storm and quickly bound the third limb in place. Turning his attention to the last, now nearly severed, limb, he scrutinized the damage carefully, surveyed the area beneath it, and, having decided on the proper position for its support, drove it into the wet earth with several heavy blows. Pinning the skirts of his raincoat between his knees, he bent to grab the damaged branch with both hands.

It was heavy, and the bark was slippery, but he managed to get a fairly secure grip and tugged upward. At first, it refused to yield, its torn fibers resisting his effort to force it back into position. Slowly, agonizingly, the rent wood began to give, and to mesh as he strained steadily upward. He paused, out of breath, to rest the heavy limb on his knees, then bent his back into the job again, refusing to admit that he would be unable to save this one last limb.

The remaining branches, higher up the tree, were lighter and more resilient. They lashed wildly about in the downpour, but were unlikely to sustain any serious damage. I wanted to help, but there was nothing I could do but stand and pull with my heart, amazed at his determination to assert himself against nature in order to preserve something he had tended with such care for so long.

Finally, Will managed to get the torn branch to shoulder height, where he again rested it, struggling to get his wind. His breath was coming in short, jagged gasps. The rain ran down over his chin in a steady stream, and his hair was plastered to his brow like white leaves. At last rested, he wrenched the heavy limb sidewise and brought its weight down on the crossbar of its support. Waiting for a break in the wind, he maneuvered the coiled wire close to his feet, where he could bend to pick it up, fearful that the wind would blow the branch off its prop before he could do so. I wanted to remind him that I was there, and could help, but he seemed hypnotized by his struggle and there seemed to be no place for me in the contest. Twice he bent to grab the wire, and twice the limb started to slip, pressured by the wind. On his third attempt, his luck held, and he retrieved one end of the stiff wire without losing control of the branch.

He pulled a length of the wire loose from the springy coil, reached into his pocket for the cutters, and snipped several feet loose with one hand while holding the limb in place with the other.

Letting go of the branch, he held his breath and began winding the heavy wire around the limb and the support in loose coils. He gave the wire a few twists with his bare hands, then cut another, longer, piece free from the coil and began threading it under the first winding. Swiftly, he finished the threading, twisted it taut, and cut a third piece of wire, which he wrapped as tightly as possible about the tree itself, at the base of the torn branch. "I'll probably have to do that again, and tar the damn thing up," he yelled over his shoulder. I jumped, even though I could barely hear him, because I had been so absorbed in watching him and thought that he had forgotten I was right behind him.

Satisfied that he had done all he could for now, he grabbed the remaining wire and, shaking the streaming water from his head and face, made his way back to the cellar door. I followed, and made it down the steps just ahead of another flash of lightning, which threw my shadow roughly to the floor of the cellar. He pulled the door shut behind us, the rain beating on the broad planks as if it would come right in after us. Will slumped heavily to the steps, heaving his breath in great whistling gasps. He seemed to be only dimly aware of my presence.

"Will, Will, are you all right?" I was frightened by the deathly pallor of his face. He didn't answer, and slumped back against the dusty wall of the stairwell. "Will! Oh my God! What's the matter?"

"Nothing, nothing. I'm just out of wind, is all," he mumbled.

"Are you sure? Shall I call a doctor?"

"Nah. Not unless you know a good tree surgeon. I think I may have been too late!"

"Don't make jokes, now! You gave me a fright. Are you sure you're okay?"

"Fine, fine. Just leave me be a minute, will you? How the hell can I catch me breath if I have to answer all your fool questions?"

"Let me help you upstairs, at least."

"I'm okay, I tell you! I only hope I can say the same for that tree."

"It doesn't matter."

"Like hell it doesn't!"

TEN

THE trip to the Jersey shore was not one Will anticipated with enthusiasm. He had made this kind of trip before, and it usually ended badly. The ride itself was pleasant enough, but he had made too many trips to too many new ventures of Willie's for him to expect this one to be any more fruitful.

The drive went smoothly, rolling through the flat, almost featureless countryside, so broadly anonymous that something as simple as a horse farm outside New Egypt would explode on the horizon, its lush grass and split-rail fences running for hundreds of yards where before, and after, there was nothing but weeded sand, fields of yellow corn, or acres of beans. Will used to look forward to visiting the shore because the trip took them past Lakehurst, where they would pull the car over to the side of the road to watch the big U.S. Navy dirigibles maneuvering in to the tall, wheeled mooring masts, drifting so slowly in the light winds that they seemed not to be moving at all. They could just as well have been underwater, if the sun had not had that hard, flat edge it seemed to get away from the smoke and dust of the city. Lately, though, since Ella had become involved with her pipe-dreaming pastor, even the modest joy of the dirigible base had been less welcome.

God only knows, Will thought, what this new idea of Willie's will turn out to be. He had been excited on the phone, but then, he always was, and he had refused to give any details. He insisted they come down to see for themselves, promising only that they would be "amazed."

"I don't doubt that at all," Will had told Ella when he first learned of the new business. "I hope I never live to see the day

I'm not amazed by one of Willie's adventures. I'd begin to doubt me own sanity, for sure."

"Now, Will," Ella had cautioned, "you know Willie really wants us to be proud of him, and he tries these things as much because he wants to please you as because he thinks he'll become a millionaire."

"Hah!" Will snorted. "Millionaire, that's a laugh. I've worked all me life and never expected to be a rich man. Why the hell should me son be any different?"

They were carrying on in this same vein in the car on the trip down to the shore, and as they drew inexorably closer, Will seemed to grow more sensitive. Ella finally said, "Will, we've been through all this before. I know how you feel, but he's our son. I worry about him, and I want him to succeed because I know it means so much to him. If it hadn't been for that horrible accident, he'd still be a policeman, and he wouldn't be so lost now."

"Ella, for Christ's sake," Will exploded, "Willie hasn't been a cop for five years. He can't spend the rest of his life wishing he could still ride around on a motorcycle. Sometimes I think you're as bad as he is. You try so hard to understand him, you've started to think and sound like him."

"Just because I try to have a little sympathy for him doesn't mean I don't realize the mistakes he's made, but I think we owe him all the support we can give him."

"All right, all right," Will said, trying to placate her. "Don't lose sight of the real world, that's all I'm asking."

"You're a fine one to talk," Ella retorted. "After all, it wasn't me who thought his insurance business was a great idea. Who was it who insisted on trotting right down to his office the first day and buying a life insurance policy he didn't need? And then there was the Cheese-of-the-Month-Club. . . . You thought *that* was wonderful, too!"

"I know, I know, dammit. You don't have to rub it in, Ella. But I've learned my lesson. That's all I'm trying to say. It'll be a damn cold day in hell before I get excited about another one of his hare-brained schemes."

Katherine, who was driving, had thus far kept silent. Now she glanced at her father in the rear-view mirror. "Daddy, how can you say that?" she asked, tapping her hands on the steering wheel to give her words added emphasis.

"Damn it, Katherine," he sought to explain himself, "I'm not saying that we shouldn't try to help him, just that we oughtn't to go overboard. He gets himself all worked up every time he has one of these crazy ideas, and we're all there on the sidelines cheering him on. Did it ever occur to you that maybe the best thing we could do for him would be to be more honest with him? Never once has one of us said, 'Now hold on there, Willie! What happens if this doesn't work out the way you expect?' Would it be so horrible of us to say something like that to him, if that's what we really believed?"

"No, I suppose not, Pop," Katherine agreed, uncertainly. "But you make it sound so . . . heartless, so cold, when you talk about it this way."

"Ah, Katie," Will responded, "I never once wanted anything but the best for any of you kids; you know that. But lately . . . I don't know. I just look at the way things have turned out for all of you and I think maybe I wanted too much for you, more than anyone has a right to expect for his children. Sometimes I think that by encouraging you, I was setting you up to be hurt, to be let down too hard. That's sure as hell not what I wanted, not for any of you."

"Pop, we don't any of us want so much, but even if we want more than we should, we have to expect to be disappointed once in a while," Katherine said. "If things haven't worked out for us the way you wanted, you can't blame yourself."

"Maybe not," Will replied, "but I keep thinking that if I hadn't pushed your brother so hard to get that job on the police force, he'd still be walking around on two good legs. I guess maybe I'm bending over backward now just so I don't push him into another disaster we'll all be sorry for. I don't know. Maybe I'm just getting old."

"You're not old, Daddy," Katherine said kindly. "Tired, maybe, but not old."

"This is one time I'm happy to agree with the old goat, Katherine." Ella chuckled. "If you could hear the noises he makes getting out of bed in the morning, you'd *know* he was old. I never heard such creaking and groaning in all my life."

"I don't notice you doing much dancing in the morning these days," Will retorted.

"Did you use to dance in the morning, Grandma?" Patrick piped up from the front seat, where little but the top of his Yankee cap could be seen by either of his grandparents.

"She did," Will snapped, "but your Grandma thinks dancing is sinful now."

"It is!" Ella interrupted. "Well, shameful, at least."

"Well, I think it's *neat,* Gram, but I won't tell anybody you used to do it if you don't want me to."

"Thank you, Patrick. I'd rather you didn't. It might get back to the Reverend Berland, and I don't know if he'd be too pleased if he were to find out about it."

"Ah, for Christ's sake, Ella," Will exploded. "He's as full of hot air as those damn blimps he's always talking about! Don't worry what he thinks. I'm sure the good Reverend has done more than a little dancing in his time. And worse than that, unless I miss my guess."

"Now don't start up on that subject again, you two," Katherine pleaded. "If I have heard that argument once, I've heard it a hundred times. Neither one of you has anything new to say on the subject, I'm sure, so there's no point in going over it all again, is there?"

"But the man's a fool, Katherine."

"Daddy, I know *you* think he's a fool, but Mother doesn't," Katherine said in exasperation. "Mother won't change any more than you will, so why don't the two of you just forget about it, at least for the rest of the afternoon?"

"All right, Katie, you win. I won't say another word. Besides, maybe he really *wasn't* drunk," Will mumbled.

"Drunk? When? Where?" Katherine asked.

"Never you mind, Katie, just never you mind. You'll not find *me* spreading vicious rumors about a man of the cloth. No, sirree, not on your life! Even if he *does* hoist one on occasion, he's still a man of the gospel, after all."

"Ooooohh, you . . . !" Katherine groaned. "You're impossible."

"And what have I been telling you for thirty years?" Ella asked, the assumed edge in her voice barely concealing her amusement at Will's ingenious baiting of their daughter.

"Can we stop for a hot dog?" Patrick asked hopefully.

"Not now. We're going to have lunch in a little while," Katherine said. "Why don't you just look at the dirigibles, Patrick?"

"Because Grandpop says dirigibles are only interesting to sailors and Presbyterian ministers," Patrick informed her.

"Will," Ella exploded, "have you been filling the boy's mind with some of your nonsense about the Reverend Berland?"

"Not at all, not at all," Will said dryly. "The boy is just a natural judge of human character, and a damn good one, too, if you ask me."

"I know better than to ask you," Ella said. "And I'll thank you not to mention Mr. Berland behind my back. Especially to the grandchildren!"

"Whatever you say, dear." Will smiled as he turned his attention to the passing scenery, satisfied that he had worked enough mischief for a while.

They rode on in silence for fifteen minutes or so, except for Patrick's occasional observations of horses and cows. Will was absorbed in reassessing what he thought about Willie's frequent business failures. He and Ella had never really discussed their respective attitudes toward their son's futile efforts to overcome the disappointment he had suffered when he had had to leave the police force, each believing that whatever was done independently would somehow reinforce the other's efforts. Now Will wasn't so sure, and he was even less certain that either of them, especially he, had taken the proper approach. Neither of them had sat down with Willie to talk the matter through from *his* point of view, and although Will had always believed he knew how Willie felt about things, and what it was Willie wanted to do with his life, he was no longer satisfied that he knew his son at all.

Still, he didn't feel very comfortable with the prospect of having to make too obvious an adjustment, especially not at the moment, when Willie had just undertaken a new business proposition. To present too new a façade to Willie at this time might very well cause more problems than it would solve. On the other hand, to sit back and wait was a curious kind of betrayal, assuming as it did that this business, too, would be a failure. It would be as if he were saying to himself, "Wait until he messes *this* up; then you can sit down and hash things over with him."

Ella devoted her share of the silence to considering the delicate balance that persisted between her and Will on the matter of religion, a balance that often, as this morning, came perilously close to tipping into open conflict. Ella was not preachy by any means, but she did take her religion seriously, the more so perhaps because Will was so antagonistic toward her pastor, but it caused her considerable alarm that Will seemed to be growing even more scornful in recent months. She kept asking herself whether there could be any truth to Will's frequent assertion that there was less to the Reverend Berland than met the eye, or whether the bombast was simply designed to tease her, and to be Will's safety valve for the scorn he readily summoned when confronted by odd human behavior.

She considered the possibility that Will was uncomfortable with the proximity of his own death, which had come increasingly to concern him in the months since his retirement, and to which he more and more frequently alluded in his sarcastic asides. It might be his own uncertainty about the future, particularly the effect of the irreligious, though not immoral, life he had chosen to live. Although he had never spoken to her at any length about his religious background, she knew that he had been raised a Catholic, in a small Midwestern town of few Catholics, and it now seemed likely that his vigorous rejection of religion was nothing more than protective coloration he had adopted early on.

As the car sped on through the Pine Barrens, they looked out their respective windows in motionless concentration, totally absorbed in their personal ruminations, and reflected in the window glass so they seemed to be in the process of splitting into identical halves that were mirror images of one another, or fusing into a denser, more concentrated humanity, as though their meditations were lending them a gravity and substance they had not previously possessed.

Abruptly, the pines gave way to flat, rush-filled lowlands, and the car's tires began hissing on the sandy highway, scattering the smooth oval yellow stones that filled the shoulders of the road. As they approached a major intersection and stopped at a light, Will picked up the tang of the salt in the air and called it to Patrick's attention.

"Do you smell that, Paddy? That's the bay, and we're getting pretty close now."

"How far, Grandpop?" Patrick asked eagerly.

"Oh, not far, ten miles or so, maybe less. We should be there in fifteen minutes, I guess."

"Where are we going?"

"To your uncle Willie's new house. He has just bought something on the bay that he wants us to see."

"What is it, Grandpop?"

"It's a business."

"What *kind* of business?"

"I'm not exactly sure, Paddy. It has something to do with boats and such. Maybe your Grandma knows more about it," Will said.

"I think he rents boats to people who want to go crabbing, Patrick," Ella explained, uncertainly. "I don't know much more

119

than that. We'll see when we get there, and maybe you can even go crabbing."

"What's crabbing?"

"Catching crabs," Will said.

"What do I want to catch crabs for?"

"To eat. They're real tasty, and it's fun to catch them, too."

"Don't they bite?" Patrick asked nervously.

"No, they don't bite. They *do* pinch you with their claws, but you don't have to worry about that. You just keep them in a basket so they can't crawl around the bottom of the boat."

"Wow, it sounds neat! Are we going to go crabbing today?"

"If you want. And if your uncle Willie has any boats that he hasn't rented." Will laughed.

"Boy, I sure hope he's got one left," Patrick said excitedly.

"I hope that's *all* he's got left, Paddy," Will said, and he noticed Katherine glance at him in the rear-view mirror.

"If you manage to catch any crabs," Ella observed dryly, "I just might manage to make a big bowl of crab-meat salad. I haven't made it in years, but I think I still remember how."

"What do you mean if 'you' manage to catch any? You'll be out in the boat with us; so if we don't, it most likely will be your fault."

"Not on your life! I will not go out into any boat with Will Donovan *and* a basket full of live crabs."

"We're here!" Katherine announced.

"Thank God!" Ella sighed.

"Here" was a huge, rustic, and ramshackle building that looked like a barn, its faded cedar shaking looking forlorn and misplaced in the bright sunshine streaming from overhead and glinting in ripples off the bay. To one side and to the rear was a wide parking lot of the same pebbled, sandy soil they had first encountered ten miles back, and beyond it stretched waving reeds and rushes for as far as the eye could see. The building fronted on the bay, and a freshly cut boardwalk ran from the broad front porch down to a rather rickety-looking pier that extended along the bay shore and out into the oily water for nearly fifty feet. Bobbing silently, amid softly lapping waves, lay more than a dozen old row boats, two or three of which had been freshly painted a dull-gray color, except for the slat seats, which were bright red. On the bow of each, a bright-red number had been hand-painted in uneven strokes, and many of them tailed off in trickled strands. The boats all bobbed up and down at the end of their mooring lines, nuzzling up to the dock like a crowd of sluggish puppies ready to nurse.

As they all got out of the car, Patrick ran down onto the pier, but his excited yells were lost on the stiff breeze, which whipped his hair into a small cloud and brought the others only the squeals of the dozens of gulls which circled lazily out over the bay.

"Ahoy there, ye swabs" came booming from the interior of the building, and was soon followed by the slamming of the screen door as Willie stepped out to greet his visitors. He was wearing a spanking brand-new yachting cap, decorated on its peak with crossed anchors, each trailing a length of line up and over the crown of the cap. One length of the white braid had started to come loose and was flapping in the breeze as if to gain someone's attention. The rest of Willie's attire consisted of a soiled tee-shirt, drawn tautly over his generous stomach, a pair of baggy dark-blue Bermuda shorts, and tattered sneakers, laceless and worn through at each big toe.

His skin was bright red, and his cheeks, under a huge pair of aviator-style mirrored sunglasses, were puffy from the sunburn. He limped noticeably as he rushed over to the car. "Can I give you a hand with anything?" he asked. They shook their heads no, but he snatched the bulging woven bag Katherine was holding and with a cheerful "Follow me!" led the way toward the boardwalk porch, where he set the bag carelessly against the wall beside the rusted screen door.

"Well, what do you think?" he asked proudly, clearly expecting unqualified praise from the new arrivals. "I have a lot of work to do on this place, but it should really be something when I get it fixed up, don't you think?"

"Absolutely," Will said. "It's shaping up already, as far as I can tell. It won't be long before you'll have to beat people off with an old oar, I'll bet. Or at least to buy more boats."

"Oh, I already have to do that, Pop," Willie said. "Yesterday, I could have used twice as many boats as I have, maybe more. I never saw anything like it. I think I finally struck oil in this place."

"I sure hope so, Willie," Ella said, with a glance toward Will. "God knows you deserve it!"

"Thanks, Mom. I don't know if I deserve it, but I sure as hell am going to try to earn it. Come on inside and let me show you around. Then we'll have some lunch."

"Are we going to go crabbing, Uncle Willie?" Patrick asked eagerly.

"Why sure, if you want to, Paddy. After lunch, you can go out with Danny and me and Pop, okay?"

"What about David? Can he go?"

"He's away at camp this month, Paddy. But the rest of us will have fun anyway."

"Okay, great! Boy, I can't wait!" Patrick responded, jumping up and down. "I'm gonna catch a million crabs!"

"Let's go on in, everybody," Willie said. "Louise is at the store. She should be back in a few minutes. Come on in," he said again, holding the battered screen door wide open.

Will looked around curiously, even before his eyes had adjusted to the comparative gloom. He was in the middle of a large room, which obviously served as both kitchen and dining room, and heard the others filing in behind him. Spotting a large, draped sofa, he sat down stiffly and slowly, with a suppressed yawn, and watched the others looking around the room. There was a huge, circular table, where Willie, Ella, and Katherine deposited the various bags and bundles they had carried in from the car.

"Okay! Everybody ready for the grand tour?" Willie asked cheerfully.

But before anyone could answer, a car could be heard pulling up onto the gravelly sand alongside the building, followed by the squeak of brakes and a beeping horn.

"That's probably Louise," Willie said. "I'll have to give her a hand with the groceries. Danny is with her. Have a seat, everybody."

"I'll go with you," Katherine offered.

"No, you sit down and relax, Katie; I'll go," Will said. "I could use a little stretching after that long ride."

"Well, what do you think?" Ella asked, when they were alone.

"About what?" Katherine responded.

"Of this place? What do you think?"

"Mom, we've only been here five minutes. How can I possibly have any idea of what to think in so short a time?"

"I'll bet your father has already made up his mind," Ella whispered.

Before Katherine could reply, the men came back inside, their arms full of groceries, followed by Louise and the younger of their two sons, Danny. They deposited their packages on the table, and Louise greeted each of the women with a wet kiss and an abundance of vaguely avian cooing. Danny and Patrick stared at their elders in some bewilderment, then looked at one another in embarrassment. With a shrug, Danny went back outside, waving to Patrick to follow him, which Patrick gladly did.

"So, Pop, what do you think of your son's latest loony idea?" Louise asked.

"I don't know. I haven't really had much of a chance to look it over, but I think it has possibilities," Will replied.

"Ah, yes! Possibilities! There's that word again. Lovely word, 'possibilities.' It comes with a capital P I think, doesn't it, Pop?"

"All right, Louise, we went all over this stuff this morning. Why don't you just get off it, huh? Let Mom and Pop relax a little, will you?" Willie snapped.

"What about me?" Katherine piped up. "Don't I get to relax, too?"

"Not if I can help it." Willie laughed.

123

"And why not?"

"Willie likes to see all the women in his family break their asses, Katie. You should know that," Louise said sarcastically.

"How about lunch, everybody?" Willie asked loudly, trying to defuse a situation that was threatening to get out of hand.

"That sounds like a good idea to me," Will said, anxious to join in the diversionary maneuver. "Why don't I just give Louise a hand putting these groceries away while Katie and Ella make some sandwiches or something?"

"No, no! You just sit down, Pop. I'll help Louise," Willie said, plunging a hand into the nearest bag.

"Why don't you all sit down and get out of my way?" Louise asked. "I'm used to taking care of everything around here anyway."

As she began shuttling back and forth among cabinets, refrigerator, pantry, and table, leaving only those items to be used at lunch, Will raised a questioning eyebrow at Willie, who responded by rolling his eyes heavenward. When Louise had finished, she summoned everyone to the table, advising them to round up something to sit on.

Conversation was initially delayed by the scraping of chair legs on the rough planking of the floor, but when everyone had been seated, except the two boys, who had taken sandwiches outdoors, the only sound was the tinkle of silverware on the rims of the open jars. Sensing that any further hesitation in opening conversation would be likely to prevent it altogether, Will cleared his throat to announce, "Well, Willie, I think this looks like a hell of a good idea you have here." Ella almost choked on her pickle, and kicked Will under the table, but it was too late. "I mean," he went on, "there must be a lot of people here on weekends renting boats, buying bait, and stuff like that, no?"

Before Willie could answer, Ella broke in to ask Louise whether she and the children were going to live in the new place all year round, but Willie answered for her.

"Louise doesn't know where she wants to live. One day she

wants to move in here permanently and give up the house in Trenton, and the next she wants me to move in here alone and she'll keep the house. Does that about sum it up, Louise?"

"Just about, I think," Louise said, pushing back her chair. "If you all will excuse me, I have a headache."

"You married a headache is what you mean, isn't it?" Willie shouted. "Well, I've had to take a few aspirin in my time, too. Don't forget that."

"I can't remember the last time you were feeling any pain at all," Louise rejoined.

"Sorry I asked," Will mumbled under his breath.

"Why do you think I kicked you, you fool," Ella whispered. "Anyone could see it would cause trouble."

She turned to Katherine, asking her to follow Louise and Willie to try to coax them back to the dining room, but just then they heard a door slam that rattled the jars on the table. This was followed by a second, louder, slam, and then by muffled shouting, alternately shrill complaining and baritone admonishment. "I think I better leave them alone," Katherine said. "I don't know about you two, but I don't feel much like eating. I think I'll just go outside and get some sun."

"Oh, I wouldn't worry about them too much, Katie," Will said soothingly. "Your mother and I used to argue all the time. Like cats and dogs, we were, but we're still together, aren't we?"

"It's not the same thing," Katherine replied, opening the screendoor.

"Now you've done it," Ella said. "Now everyone's upset except you."

"What did I do? I was just trying to be positive, that's all," Will said, defending himself.

"That's what you call it? Positive?" Ella said scornfully.

"Well, what would you call it?" Will demanded.

"Never mind what I'd call it. I'm going out to get some sun myself. Why don't you just stay here and try to keep your nose out of other people's business for a while?" Without waiting for a reply, Ella pushed her chair back and stomped out to the porch, forcefully closing the screen door behind her to emphasize its function as a temporary barrier.

"That's a fine how-do-you-do!" Will observed aloud to no one in particular. "A man tries to make his son feel good, and everybody jumps down his throat. The hell with it all, anyway. I'm hungry and I'm going to finish me sandwich!"

He chewed disinterestedly on his lunch without really tasting it, then went over to sit on the long, low day bed under a large window, where he found a two-day-old newspaper.

Willie soon appeared and walked slowly over to the day bed, trying to minimize the effect of his limp, and sat heavily on a vacant corner.

"Sorry about that, Pop," he said with some embarrassment. "Lou hasn't been feeling well lately, and she just took it out on you, I guess."

"I'd say she took it out on you," Will observed.

"Well, what's the difference. She didn't mean anything by it, is all I'm trying to say."

"I don't know, Willie. I think she must have meant it. You don't say something like that unless you do mean it."

"I'm afraid to find out, Pop. I swear to God, I can't take much more. It seems like everything I try is either too little or too late. And I'm not just talking about me and Louise. I mean everything. I keep looking for that golden goose, but I keep looking in the dark, and the only way I know it's there is when I step on it, you know?"

"If you're running around in the dark, and you know it, that's half the battle."

"What if the battle's all over, only I don't know it? What then?"

"Well, the way I see it, the sooner you find out for sure, the sooner you can go on about your business. If things are bad, they sure as hell aren't going to get any better on their own."

"What can I do?"

"For starters, you can talk to Louise. Talk to her about what's bothering her, the way I do with your mother. It doesn't always work, because there's always lots of stuff neither of you knows is there, but you have to give it a try."

"What about the kids?"

"What about them?"

"Well, it won't be easy for them if Louise and I decide to split up."

"Do you think it's easy for them now, the way you two are at one another all the time?"

"No, I guess not."

"Well, I *know* not. I can tell just by looking at them that they're unhappy. You two are so wrapped up in your own troubles, the only time you think about the kids at all is when you try to get them to take sides."

They lapsed into silence, and Willie stared out the window, which overlooked the bay. In the quiet, he could hear the gulls crying shrilly, cresting air drafts, circling lazily, effortlessly, over the water of the bay, and he wished his own life could be that easy, or his flight, if it should come to that. Will watched his son without speaking, and the pale blue of Willie's eyes seemed to ebb and flow, as though the color was a barometer of his moods, brightening when he was thinking positively, and fading to a nearly flat gray when things seemed hopeless.

He wondered whether he had been blunt enough, or too blunt. All the best advice in the world was no substitute for the determination to act, and Willie's problem, Will understood, was largely one of paralysis. He knew that there was no possibility that Willie would be able to work through problems the way he and Ella had, because his son was so very different, and had never been able to confront emotions as directly as Will himself. They were elusive, mysterious things to Willie, and slipped through his fingers like smoke when he tried to gather them closer for analysis.

Now, with the gulls wailing overhead like lost souls, Will stared at his older son, someone for whose very existence he was responsible, and he was at an absolute loss as to how to give effective counsel. He wasn't even sure there was such a thing for someone like Willie, who could not rely on a sensitive radar like Will's own, since he did not have it, and it could not be cultivated. It was a natural instinct, and Willie had been born without it. For Will, it was almost as if all of his real communication with Ella was not speech at all, but a nerve-to-nerve transmission. Maybe that's all love was, the ability to read signs you carried around in your body, and the ability to present these signs to the one you loved in an intelligible way, who in turn had the instinctive ability to read and present other signs, congruent at best and, at worst, not contradictory. Maybe it was why so few people ever really were in love at all, preferring to settle for approximations, accepting limits that had been too early imposed and become chains, too painful to break and impossible to do without. If so, that was surely Willie's problem. The chains were too strong for him, and he wasn't clever enough to slip out of them, or brave enough to try. Either way, Will could understand, knowing that the most difficult thing one can do is admit to having made a mistake when that admission will hurt someone you care for, but he also knew that living a lie was more hurtful, and Willie would have to come to terms with that painful truth as best he could, and in due course, for there was nothing Will could do to help him.

ELEVEN

WILL had gone to bed early, tired from a long day on the ladder, painting the shingles on the upper stories of the house. Restless and unable to sleep, he was thumbing carelessly through a magazine when he heard a thump from the living room below. He could not identify the sound, but knew it was something out of the ordinary.

"Ella, what was that noise?" he called. "Ella, are you all right?" Receiving no answer, he hopped out of bed and went to the head of the stairs, where he again called to Ella, who still made no answer. Worried now, he bounded down the steps two at a time and stood on the landing below, peering around the dining room and into the living room beyond. "Ella? Where are you? Are you all right?" he called. He heard a groan in the darkness beyond the dining-room table and ran to the source of the sound, knocking over a chair in his haste.

Ella was sprawled on the floor, moaning softly, one arm folded beneath her and the other sprawled out beside her motionless figure. Hurriedly, he knelt beside her, taking her free arm to feel for a pulse. There was a faint throbbing in the veins at her wrist, but it was intermittent and feeble. "Ella, Ella, what is it? What's the matter with you?" he asked. In fright, his voice took on an edge of annoyance. "Can you hear me? Why don't you answer me, dammit?"

She groaned again, louder than before, then stirred. "Stay there, I'll get you some water," he said, running to the kitchen. He grabbed a bottle of ice water and ran back into the dining room to find Ella struggling to get to her knees. "Just lie there for a minute, will you! Don't try to get up!" he said sharply, kneeling again to hold the jar to her lips. In the struggle to swallow, some of the cold water spilled down the front of her dress and seeped into the open bosom. She gave a start at the cold shock and pushed the jar away distractedly, shaking her head as if to clear it. Reaching again for the water she took a long swallow, holding the jar in both hands.

"What happened? Are you all right?" Will demanded.

"Oooohhh, I don't know," she answered dazedly. "I was going out to the kitchen, and I felt light-headed all of a sudden. I just couldn't stand up any more, I guess."

"Why didn't you call me?" Will asked in irritation.

"It all happened so quickly. At first, I thought it was going to pass, but it came on me so quickly I didn't even have time to sit down. I just fell right over, I guess, right where I stood."

She reached up to rub her upper arm and left shoulder. "I must have landed on my arm, I guess."

"Let me see," Will said, rolling the loose sleeve of the dress up toward her shoulder. A broad, faint smear of a bruise was already beginning to appear, and Will went back to the kitchen to get some ice. "Don't get up," he called back over his shoulder. "You stay right there. I'll be back in a minute."

She heard the crack of cubes being pried loose from their tray, and the running of tap water as Will tossed the cubes into a bowl. Soon he was back, a large basin of water, full of rattling cubes, sloshing over his bare knees as he rushed back into the dining room, a pair of dish towels over his shoulder. He knelt beside her again, sloshed one of the towels around in the cold water, and wrung it out before wrapping her upper arm in the now freezing cloth.

"Lie back down," he commanded. "I don't want you to move for a while."

"But I'm all right," she argued. "It was just a fainting spell, that's all! There's nothing to get so upset about."

"I don't care. I don't want you to move for a bit," he said, soaking the second towel in the water and wringing it out more thoroughly than the previous one. He twisted the towel into a thick rope before placing it across her forehead, then jumped up to run into the living room, where he grabbed a pillow from the sofa. Rushing back to Ella, he placed the pillow under her head and pushed her firmly down on it, saying, "Stay there! I'll be right back. Don't move!"

"Where are you going?" Ella asked weakly.

"Upstairs to put some clothes on. It's chilly down here, you know!"

His heavy steps thudded on the floor of the hallway above as he ran toward their bedroom, where he quickly put on an old flannel bathrobe and a pair of battered leather slippers, then clattered back down the stairs. As he reached the landing, he noticed that the room was considerably brighter, and when he rounded the dining-room table, he knew why. Ella was gone, and so was the pillow he had placed under her head. He heard rattling in the kitchen, and exploded. "Ella, dammit, I told you not to move! What the hell do you think you're doing? What's the matter with you, anyway? Can't you ever listen?"

Ella was in the pantry, making tea and whistling softly to herself. "What did you say, Will?"

"I asked you what the hell is the matter with you. What do you think you're doing, fooling around out here? You should be resting. For God's sake, you don't even know what happened to you, and here you are running around in the kitchen."

"I'm all right now. It was nothing, just a fainting spell, that's all," Ella responded brightly. "Don't get all upset. I'm fine."

"Maybe so, but I'm going to call the doctor anyway."

"Whatever for?"

"Because I want to know why you suddenly have a fainting spell in the middle of the night, that's what for. You never had one before, and I don't think you ought to be so damn sure there's nothing to it. Now sit down in the living room while I call the doctor," Will ordered.

"Oh, Will, don't be silly. I don't need a doctor. I'm fine."

"I'd rather have him tell me that, if you don't mind."

"If it'll make you feel any better, I'll call him tomorrow, but I don't think I need him, honestly."

"Are you sure?" Will asked suspiciously.

"Of course I'm sure!"

"You'll call him tomorrow, regardless of how you feel?"

"Yes!"

"Promise?"

"Oh, Will, please stop!"

"Not until you promise."

"Oh, all right, I promise!" Ella said, as if placating an importunate child.

"All right, you go sit down," Will said. "I'll bring you your tea in a minute."

Ella shuffled off to the living room, and Will heard the click of the television, followed by the whoosh of sofa cushions as Ella settled down to watch a movie. He busied himself making tea. He watched the water intently, amazed at the subtle gradations of color as they spread uncertainly from the bag in small amber clouds, extending slowly toward the walls of the cup like the fingers of a groping hand, the curls twisting this way and that as if responding to unseen currents in a small, warm ocean. Satisfied with the color of the tea, he hoisted the bag out by its stringed tab and crushed it gently between tab and spoon, generating a small, dark stream which cascaded into the center of the cup and gradually lost itself in the swirling contents. "That'll probably be just enough to make it too strong." He smiled ruefully, placing the bag and spoon on the stove top with a soft clink.

"Ella," he called, walking to the kitchen doorway, "Ella, do you want milk or lemon in your tea?" There was no answer, so he walked into the dining room to call again, but changed his mind when he noticed her leaning back on the sofa with her eyes closed, as though against a bright light he could not see. He tiptoed over to her and stood staring down at the deep, regular rise and fall of her breathing. It was chilly, and he dragged a knitted afghan from the back of the sofa, where it lay folded in neat rectangles, and quietly flapped it open to spread over her sleeping form. He clicked off the TV set and tiptoed back to the kitchen, where he dumped the tea down the sink and went to the refrigerator for a beer, which he set down on the Formica table top, taking care not to make a sound loud enough to wake Ella. He popped the lid carelessly and drank slowly, savoring the first few sips until his mind began to wander, and he lost interest in the beer.

He didn't think he could stand another shock. When Emma had died, he threw himself into his family with demonic intensity, as if he could force them to live for her, and her to live in them. Then when Willie had his accident, he realized the fragility of life, understanding for the first time that he could no more control its end than he could its direction. To lose Ella now, after all they had been through, would be too much, more than anyone ought to have to endure, and he wasn't sure that he could endure it. He was losing his grip, not only on his own life, but also on that greater, more elusive life that embraced his own. He took another pull on the beer, but it was bitter and flat, tasting more of metal, or ashes.

Hearing, or thinking he heard, a noise from the living room, he got up to check on Ella. She was sitting up, shaking her head groggily when he entered the room.

"How are you feeling? Better?" he asked.

"Much, I think." She smiled sleepily. "I'm not really awake yet, but I think I'm all right. How long did I sleep?"

"Not long. About a half hour, I guess," he responded. "Do you want to go to bed now?"

"Yes, I guess maybe I should."

"Are you sure you don't need the doctor?"

"Yes, I'm okay. I just need a little rest, I guess."

"You gave me quite a scare, there. Especially when I first came down. You weren't moving, and you were hardly breathing at all."

"I'm glad to see that I'm not so old that you don't care," Ella said mockingly, "but there really is no reason for you to worry. I may be getting old, but I'm not senile, and I know when something's wrong with me. Believe me, I'll holler loud enough if I have to."

"That's true enough." Will smiled. "Still, you've been pretty feisty these past few months. I just don't want you to get the idea you can handle anything that comes along. I want to feel like I'm still useful around here, and for something more than pushing a goddam paintbrush around all day long."

"Is there something the matter?"

"What?"

"Is there something the matter?"

"No. Why?"

"I don't know, I just have the feeling that there's something on your mind, that's all."

"Of course there's something on my mind. It's not every day that you fall on your face, you know."

"I don't mean that. I mean something else. You seem . . . I don't know, distracted, I guess."

"It's nothing," Will said evasively.

"Then there is something. What is it?"

"Forget it. It's just silly. An old man's foolishness, that's all."

"Well, an old woman can probably understand, maybe even help. Why don't you tell me about it?"

"Before, when I went upstairs to get dressed, you know, while you were lying on the floor, all of a sudden, I felt like there was somebody else there. I got chills."

"That's nothing. It happens to me all the time. It has nothing to do with age or anything else. It happens to everybody."

"No, this was different. I know what you're talking about, but this wasn't like that. It was real."

"You mean there was somebody there?"

"Yeah, there was somebody there."

"Upstairs, in our house?"

"Yeah . . ."

"Well, who was it? Don't just stop in the middle like that. Who was it?"

"It was me."

"Is this another one of your jokes? If so, I don't want to hear it."

"I told you you wouldn't understand."

"Are you serious?"

"I've never been more serious in my life. Never! I felt like there was somebody there, and I looked up, and I was in front of the mirror, and there was somebody staring back at me, only it wasn't me, so I got scared. Then I realized it *was* me, and that was worse. I didn't recognize meself. I looked so different. I might as well have been a total stranger looking through a window as somebody staring into a mirror. Then it dawned on me that I was not seeing meself the way I thought I looked, but the way I really looked. I've gotten old, but I didn't know *how* old until that moment. It was like I had been remembering the me that used to be. Every morning, staring into the mirror to shave, I might as well have been looking at an old snapshot. The face that looked out at me from that mirror tonight was as different from what I thought I looked like as it could possibly be. First, I thought it was just because I was scared by what happened to you, you know? But it's not that. I'm just now coming to see how much has changed and how little there is left for me."

He stopped talking, and Ella cast about for something to say, but found nothing appropriate. "Is that all?" she asked softly.

"Pretty much. I guess, finding you like that, it hit me. I don't have much more time. You, either. One of us is going to be alone pretty soon, and I guess it sank in for the first time tonight. What I hate is knowing that there's nothing I can do about it. And what's worse than that is thinking of what it'll be like for me if it's you who goes first. I thought that was happening tonight. I know it can happen any time, and there's not a damn thing I can do to stop it. I hate that."

"It doesn't have to be for a long time yet, Will," Ella whispered.

"Ella, when you've been together for as long as we have, any time at all is too soon. Much too soon . . ."

TWELVE

CHRISTMAS in the Donovan house was something of a ritual, and the entire family participated, with Will as the presiding genius of the always elaborate affair. It was as if the family had come to view itself as the conservator of a valuable tradition that had elsewhere been eroded or, worse, perverted. Even the departure of the Donovan children to homes of their own had little impact on the tradition. For weeks before the holiday, Will would be dropping hints about the gifts he expected to receive, leaving notes on particular items that had caught his fancy. He would deliberately forego acquiring a new tool or bottle of shaving lotion for months, simply so that he could experience the thrill of unwrapping it on Christmas Day, the grandchildren scattered around him like admiring disciples.

This year, the tradition was to have added significance, symbolizing the maintenance of a way of life that had recently seemed to Will to have been dangerously imperiled. He looked forward to the arrival of Christmas from the opening day of the football season. Where, in the past, he had waited until the last possible moment to do his shopping, this year he had begun during September, and hardly a week went by when he did not mysteriously disappear for a few hours one afternoon, to return, furtive and grinning, with a glistening package peeking from a brown paper bag. He would skulk past Ella, taking great pains to hide his purchase behind his back, and flit up the stairs to bury the gift in a corner of his closet, which had been declared off limits to Ella on September 1. On pain of dismemberment, she was not, except in case of fire, to venture anywhere near his closet, whether or not its door was closed, and more than once he had bounded up the steps intent on apprehending her in the act of rifling his cache, only to discover that she was merely emptying a wastebasket or sorting magazines and newspapers in the bedroom rack.

Once, Ella had tried to tease him by implying in a roundabout manner that she had actually been cleaning his closet and only run to the magazines when she heard him coming, but his reaction was nearly apoplectic, and Ella, deciding that the fun was not worth the effort of having to soothe his suspicions afterward, had foregone the pleasure of teasing from that point on. She did not touch the closet, she did not go near it, she even felt guilty looking at it, as though Will would find her trying to peer through its very walls in an attempt to divine its contents.

One afternoon in mid-November, Ella was sitting in front of the television, absorbed in the teeming complexity of her favorite soap-opera lives, when she heard a strange rustling beneath her feet. At first, she thought she had been mistaken and went back to her viewing, forgetting the noise until it happened again, this time more clearly audible above a lull in the televised conversation. Baffled, she got down on her knees and put her ear to the floor. It came again, still indecipherable. Afraid it might be intruders, she went softly upstairs to get her husband, who was working in the front bedroom, but when she got there, the room was empty.

It must be Will, she thought. He probably finished and went down to the basement to find something else to do.

She went back to the living room and sat down for the next soap. For a long while, the basement was silent, but then, during a commercial, the noise started again, this time more insistent and clearly audible.

"Whatever is he doing down there!" she mumbled aloud. Getting up, she went to the basement door, which was open a crack, and pulled it wider to call down, "Will, is that you? What are you doing that's making all that racket?"

"Nothing! Go watch your shows," came the guilty reply.

"Is everything all right?" she asked.

"Yes, I'm fine. Go watch television, will you?"

Something in the tone of his voice urged her to go down, but she was unwilling to spy on him.

"I'm coming down," she called.

"What for?" he asked, the sound of his voice growing louder as he walked to the bottom of the stairs. "There's nothing going on down here that concerns you. Leave me alone! Go watch your shows. You'd have a fit if I asked you to give me a hand with something while they were on!"

"It's a commercial," she said.

"So what! The show isn't over yet. It can't be. They seem to be on forever, so there must be more yet. Go look!"

"I'm coming down," she repeated.

"So, come down then," he snapped.

She took one tentative step, then, steeling her nerve, quickly descended the rest of the way. Will was standing in the middle of the floor, surrounded by wires and glowing lights.

"What are you doing?" Ella demanded.

"If you must know, I'm testing the Christmas tree lights!" Will said truculently.

"Whatever for?"

"Well, we want to have lights on the tree, don't we?" he asked.

"Yes, but . . ."

"Well, how will we know whether we need any new bulbs if I don't test the ones we've got? For Christ's sake, if I left it to you, there'd *be* no Christmas around here. Now, you found out what you wanted to know, so go back upstairs," Will said, trying to conceal his embarrassment.

"Will, it's only the middle of November. Why do you have to test the bulbs now, and down here?" Ella asked, barely able to control her laughter.

"Well, why wait? I mean, I have plenty of time, and this way, if we do need any bulbs, I can pick them up without having to fight with those crazy crowds at the last minute."

Ella, hands on hips, was no longer able to suppress her laughter.

"I don't see what's so funny," Will said, pouting.

"Why did you decide to do all this today? It's not like you to prepare so far in advance for something. You'll end up spoiling your Christmas if you're not careful."

"What do you mean? How could I spoil it, just by trying to be prepared?"

"You seem to be making such a big thing out of it all, bigger than usual, I mean. It's almost like you can't wait for it to come. Why?"

"I don't know. You tell me! It seems to me that if anyone is blowing things all out of proportion around here, it's not me. You seem to be playing amateur psychiatrist or something."

"But I'm not the one who sneaked down here six weeks early, am I? It wasn't me who decided to haul all of this stuff out and sit here with it, trying to make things into something they aren't. *You* did that, and what I'd like to know is why you did. Why today? Why not last week . . . or next week? There must be something on your mind you're not telling me. I just know there is. I can feel it."

Will sighed, and was silent for a moment before responding. "Maybe you're right. Maybe I am making this into a big deal. It's just that I feel like I need Christmas more than usual this year. I feel like I need the lift I usually get from the holidays. There's something missing, is what it is, I guess. I'm not even sure I know what. I just know there's something I used to feel that I don't feel right now. Maybe Christmas will bring it back, whatever it is."

"Will, I'm not trying to say that it can't be done, or even that it won't work. All I'm trying to do is make you see that it *might* not, and I don't want you to get hurt, that's all. All I'm asking is that you not build it up to such a point that you can't be satisfied with what it really is. Please?"

"I know what you're saying, Ella. I do, but I want to try this, that's all. What's the harm in that? The worst that can happen is that I'll have a lousy Christmas. You'll see, this one's going to be something special. Now let's quit all this jabbering. I have a lot more to do."

Will turned to the tree stand, and began to sand its pocked surface. He had made it himself in the machine shop at the yards, a fairly simple construction of heavy steel pipe and wing bolts. As Ella watched him now, bent over the laborious job of sanding smooth the lower extremity of the stand, pitted by years of week-long immersion in water, she realized that, for the first time since Emma had died, he was going to put his heart and soul into the season with the kind of single-minded passion only he was capable of. He was screwing up his face as he sanded, periodically holding the stand up to the overhead light, and long after she could no longer see any evidence of corrosion, he continued to rub away at the metal, until she feared he might sand it away to nothing. His attention to the surface was so intense that she doubted he would hear her should she venture to say anything. After another ten minutes, he held the stand to the light yet again and, satisfied at last, placed it on the concrete floor with a thud.

"There," he grunted, "that ought to do it. Look at that, Ella. That thing hasn't looked that good ever, not even the day I finished making it."

"Why were you rubbing so hard on it, anyway?" Ella asked.

"I don't know. I guess maybe I was thinking I could rub away all the years since I made it. Stupid, I guess, but you know how it is. You start doing something, and pretty soon it's the way you feel instead of what you're doing that's important. I was thinking about all the time that has gone by since I brought this thing home, and some of the things that have happened that I wish hadn't."

"Are you sure you wouldn't rather get all new things, sort of start over again, fresh?" Ella asked.

"No. I want things to be just like they used to be. That's what this is all about. I told you. Restoration. Preservation. And that's exactly what it's going to be. Sort of a monument to the old days," he said, clicking off the dim light overhead.

"All right, as long as you're sure. What do you want to do now?"

"I guess we should put these lights back, so we can argue about them on Christmas Eve, the way we always do. That's part of it, too, you know." He smiled.

"All right, let's get to work then," Ella said cheerfully.

They began unscrewing the bulbs, some of which were so hot that Ella had to wrap them in her skirt before she could grasp them in her fingers. They worked quickly, and the gradual encroachment of darkness, as each small colored bulb was extinguished, seemed to Ella like the gathering darkness before a winter storm. She shivered at the thought.

"If there's anything else you want me to do," she said, "just tell me. I know how much this whole thing means to you, and I want to do whatever I can to help. *Somebody* has to look after you."

Will merely nodded that he had heard and unscrewed the last bulb, plunging the basement into its usual pervasive gloom.

By Thanksgiving, Will's Christmas fascination had reached fever pitch. He spent hours reading advertisements in both daily papers, and when he wasn't scanning them, looking longingly at things he couldn't buy, he was in the basement, clearing space for his "project," about which he would tell Ella nothing. At all hours of the day and night, Ella could find him down there, shifting cartons about, freeing the floor space he claimed he needed for his secret conception. After three solid days of maneuvering, which even saw him begin to sort things he felt were expendable, Will had freed enough space to work in, and set about improving the lighting in the chosen area. He constructed partitions of thin plywood, behind which the clutter could be concealed, and repainted the floor a bright, slippery steel gray. He whitewashed the cinder-block walls, and the basement began to look as though he had stolen it from beneath someone else's house. He then declared it off limits to Ella, who was enjoined from entering the front room of the basement until further notice.

One afternoon, when he had been at his renovation for nearly two weeks, he called Ella down to see his handiwork, and she couldn't believe her eyes. The basement glowed like a department store, and there, spread out beneath glaring new fluorescent lamps, was a vast expanse of freshly painted plywood, six full sheets that lay in an unbroken plane, twelve feet by sixteen feet.

"What do you think of it?" he asked proudly.

"It's very nice, I guess," Ella hazarded, "but it seems like an awful lot of work just to make a big table. What's it for?"

"Trains," Will said. "Toy trains, the biggest damn set you ever laid your eyes on. There's going to be a whole damn city sitting right there, and woods and farms, too. All of it right there."

"Will," Ella said with alarm, "where are we going to get all that stuff?"

"Don't worry about it," Will said hastily, "I got that all figured out."

"But . . ."

"No buts, now. I said I'll take care of it and I will. I've even got it all planned out. See here," he said enthusiastically, grabbing a huge folded sheet of paper from one end of the table. "I drew everything to scale, and I know just what's going to go where. Look at this," he said, thrusting the plans before her.

She spread them out on the table, smoothing them down to keep them flat at the creases. There was, as Will proceeded to explain in elaborate detail, a complete layout of a railroad system, including rural and urban stations, farmland, forest, mountains, and running streams. There were tunnels in the mountains, a sawmill in the forest, a dairy in the country, and a warehouse in the city, each accorded its own quadrant of the available space, and each designed to accommodate a special car and special accessories, which were available to model-train enthusiasts. The place where each would stand was clearly marked on the plan, and he had gone so far as to color in the rivers and lakes with blue crayon and the vegetation with green.

"I've got it all figured out," he said. "I'm going to paint the whole thing up, just like you see it here. There will be cows out here, where the dairy farm will be, piles of logs over here, and boxes over here. You should see the stuff they make for these things nowadays. It's incredible! They have a dairy car, and you stop the train at the right spot and a little man comes out of the dairy and loads milk cans—you know the kind I mean, the big metal ones—right into the dairy car. They have the same thing for the sawmill, only they're logs that get loaded instead of milk. They have a car that carries real coal, they have coal loaders, and they have a water tower that actually fills a little tank in the engine with water. Why, they even have tablets of some chemical that you put in the engine and it makes little puffs of smoke while it goes around the tracks. Can you believe that?"

"I don't know what to believe, looking at all this. Are you sure we can afford it?"

"Don't worry about it. It won't cost very much. I'm going to do the work myself, and all the equipment is already available. We don't have to buy anything at all, or almost nothing, anyway."

"Where are we going to get it, then?" Ella asked skeptically.

"The kids. They already have all of this stuff. So I had this great idea. I said to myself, Why not combine all the train sets, make one great big layout that all the kids could play with? Well, here it is. All I have to do is paint this thing up and put it together. What do you think?"

"I don't know," she said uncertainly. "How do you know they'll all fit together? They're not all the same kind, are they?"

"No, but they're all the same gauge, and that's the only thing that counts. They're all HO—that's the real small stuff—and the cars on any one of them will fit the tracks of the others. If you look real close at this plan here, you'll see that there are two separate loops of track. I laid it out so that at this point here

I can either break it into two completely separate layouts on the same board, or have one big, double line. If the couplings are different, I just run two separate railroads at the same time, that's all."

"What do you mean, you?" she demanded. "I thought you were doing this for the kids? After all, you are planning to use their trains."

"Well, yes, of course it's for the kids. But they can't be here all the time, can they? I mean, they won't object to their grandpa playing with their trains, do you think?"

"No, I suppose not," Ella said slowly. "But I know how you are, and I'll bet you that after about six weeks, during which time I won't see you except at meals, if then, you won't feel like playing with this stuff any more, and then I'll have to argue with you about taking the whole thing apart."

"Well, so what?"

"Nothing, I guess, as long as you don't get carried away."

"What do you mean?"

"Just try to keep it in mind that these trains are toys, and they're not yours, at that. All right?"

Over the next several days, Will worked straight through lunch, and often had Ella bring him a tray down to the basement at dinnertime rather than stop work to join her at the table. He had finished painting the table layout, and had been accumulating the various accessories and lengths of track from the grandchildren. He had planned very carefully and found there was little that had to be redone.

His deadline for the completion of the project was rapidly drawing nearer, and as it did, his pace increased. The track was all in place, but he had been careful not to nail any of it down until it had been tested. On the evening he slipped the last piece of track into place, he took a small engine from a box of cars and placed it gently on the tracks in front of the larger passenger station that marked the focal point of his plan. Everything was in place, even the small automobiles he had placed between the narrow white lines painstakingly drawn around the sides of a rectangle of flat black paint to one side of the station, representing a parking lot. He checked the lines from the transformer and, satisfied that everything was properly connected, he plugged it in and turned the handle slightly. There was a quiet hum in the basement, and the small engine began, almost imperceptibly, to move away from the station. He increased the power, and the engine began to move a bit faster.

He folded his arms across his chest to watch the engine, now beginning to smoke from its stack in small, perfect donuts of pure white, make a complete circuit of the outside line of the pattern. Since he had learned that the couplings on both sets of cars were identical, he had constructed one complete, interconnected rail line, replete with a figure eight at the center of the smaller, inside oval track. He had also built switching track into each oval, so that either circuit could be used separately, and he had a second transformer so he could run the individual trains at separate speeds, and so that both Patrick and Danny, the owners of the components of the merged railroad line, could play individually when they were both visiting.

Now, after nearly a month of work, he sighed contentedly as the train slowly completed its baptismal run around the outside track. As the small black engine returned to the station in front of him, he turned the transformer off and added a pair of boxcars. He sent the engine around again, this time at a higher rate of speed and, as it drew near the three-quarter mark, he worked the switch that would allow the train to pass to the inner route. He slowed the speed a bit, until the engine had safely passed over the switch, then increased it until the engine, with its boxcars in tow, was traveling past the scattered rural buildings and small plastic animal figures which marked the dairy farm at a fairly good clip. He pressed the small button marked "whistle" and a low, eerie moan emanated from the small train's innards. Will smiled in amazement as the ghostly sound seemed to trail back behind the train, echoing through the trees and across the broad, blue-painted river, almost as if it were a real train, barreling through the countryside on a cold winter afternoon.

"Damn," he hollered. "Hot damn! Ella, Ella, come look at this, will you?"

"Did you call me, Will?" Ella yelled down from the kitchen.

"Yeah! Come here. Hurry up!" he called excitedly.

"Land sakes, what is it now?" she grumbled, clattering down the cellar stairs.

"It's all finished, just like I planned it, and it works beautifully. Wait till you see it. It's fantastic."

"I don't know what's so important that it couldn't wait till after dinner," she mumbled.

"Never mind dinner. You have to see this! Get the switch over there, will you?"

She clicked the lights off, and the only illumination in the basement was that cast by the small bulbs mounted inside the passenger station, the sawmill, and the larger buildings of the dairy farm. Each of them took on a stunning reality in the dark basement. Will pushed a small button mounted alongside the transformer, and two dozen small streetlights and two blinking traffic signals went on, throwing the pavement of the tiny city into bold relief.

Ella, despite her annoyance at being called away from her cooking, caught her breath. "Glory be! It *is* amazing, Will! I've never seen the like of it in my life. It's beautiful, simply beautiful!"

"Isn't she something?" Will said proudly. "I knew it would look nice, but I never expected it to look like this! Wait until you see the train moving around out there, toward the other end of the table. You won't believe it."

He cranked up the transformer, and the train began to chug along, quickly leaving the station behind. As it approached the papier-mâché mountain range and was about to enter the tunnel through it, he leaned on the whistle button, without giving Ella any warning.

"Whooooooooooooooooo. Whooooooooooooooooo." The eerie and evocatively rich sound of the whistle floated back out of the tunnel.

"Cripes," Ella said, startled. "What was that?"

"It's the whistle." Will laughed. "Isn't that something? You'd swear a real train was coming in through the front wall any minute. I can't believe how real it sounds, being so small and all."

"Whoooooooooooo. Whoooooooooooooooo," the train called, as if warning Will that it would be back again when he wasn't expecting it.

"It gives me the chills." Ella shuddered. "Can we put the lights back on now?"

"Sure." Will laughed again. "Maybe you won't be so superstitious, once you see the thing in the light."

"I don't know. I don't like that sound at all," she said nervously. "I'm going to put the lights back on."

She stepped over to the bottom of the stairs and clicked the lights on. The entire panorama lost its supernatural presence as the buildings shrank once again to toys in the bright overhead glare.

"What does this thing do?" she asked, pointing toward a small platform at one end of the table.

"That's a mail drop," Will said. "Want to see how it works?"

"Sure."

"Okay, watch!"

He rummaged around in the carton of cars and accessories until he found a silver boxcar that bore the legend "U.S. MAIL" in bold letters along both sides and in smaller letters along the roof. He fitted the car to the rear of the second boxcar already coupled to the train and started the engine off at a fairly good clip, heading in the direction of the platform that had aroused Ella's curiosity. As the train drew near, he slowed it down a bit and, when the engine was passing in front of the platform, he pressed another button in the array beside the transformer. Suddenly, one end of the platform moved toward the tracks, while an arm affixed to a pole swung out toward the train at the same time as a door in the mail car swung open. There was a sharp click, and Will tooted the whistle as the train roared off and the platform returned to its former configuration. Now, however, a small canvas pouch dangled from the end of the arm atop the pole.

"That's the mail," Will explained. He pressed another button and the pouch fell to the platform with a small clink. "Now, I can also pick it up, the same way, but I have to hang it on the pole myself. It won't do that, but I guess you can't have everything, can you?"

"The kids are really going to get a kick out of this, I'll bet," Ella exclaimed.

"I sure hope so," Will said. "The way I see it, they will each be able to use some of this special stuff that they don't have in their own sets. I was thinking that we might leave it up all year round, down here, and they could come over anytime, even after school, if they wanted to. What do you think about that?"

"Well, I don't know. I'm not sure it's a good idea to have something like this available when they have schoolwork to do at night. But I guess if the kids are interested, we can leave it this way. At least until they get tired of it."

"What if they don't get tired of it?"

"Then I guess I'll have to live with it." She laughed. "Has Willie seen this yet? You know how he used to love to play with trains when he was a boy."

"No, but I'll bet you the whole reason Danny and David have these things in the first place is so Willie can use them. He sets them out under the tree every year, and Louise says she doesn't even see him at all for most of the holidays because he's always playing with the trains."

"That's just what I need, my husband *and* my son locked away in the basement like two lunatics, playing with toy trains. I declare, for grown men, the two of you don't seem to be much more than children yourselves. I wonder why?" she mused slyly.

"Well, the only thing we have in common is you," Will observed dryly. "But I don't know whether that has anything to do with it or not. What do you think?"

"I think you better watch your step. If you want any dinner tonight, you'd better not try to blame any of this foolishness on me, that's what I think!"

"I swear, I can't wait till the kids see this thing," Will said, trying to change the subject. "I'll bet Patrick will be down here for hours at a time. He seems to love the railroad even more than I do."

"As if that were possible." Ella laughed. "I wouldn't be surprised if you were down here all day long, pretending you were still at work, only here you can be the boss of the whole thing."

"I guess I might do that once in a while. You know me pretty well, don't you?"

"I'm not sure," Ella said thoughtfully. "But there's one thing I know, and that's if you want to have dinner, you'll have to come up and help me. I'm way behind schedule as it is."

"All right, I'll be up in a minute. You go ahead, and I'll be there as soon as I finish tacking this track down," he said.

"Okay, but don't be too long." She smiled. "Or we'll both be eating burned food tonight." She went back to the stairs, pausing at the bottom to ask whether he wanted the lights on or off.

"Leave them on, I guess," he said. Then, changing his mind, said, "Wait, why don't you turn them off again? I want to watch this little thing a while."

She went on up the steps, and he pulled over an old wooden stool, so he could sit comfortably at the transformer. The table was low enough so that he could see its entire surface, except for the area directly behind the mountain range, while sitting on the stool. For a minute, he just stared off at the far side of the board, checking to make sure that everything conformed to the mental image he had carried for so long in his head. Satisfied that everything was in order, he started the small engine and watched it move slowly along the rails. It seemed to be straining slightly, as if it trailed a long train of heavily laden boxcars behind it. He thought about adding another specialty car or two, but decided that he would rather just watch the train make its endless circuit without any distraction. He didn't even bother to use the mail car, and arranged the switches so the train would circle the outer line, enter the nearer side of the inner circuit, and make its way slowly through the figure eight and back to the outer line, where it would go through the same route again, without anything required of him.

He moved his stool slightly to the left, leaned his arms forward to the edge of the table, and placed his chin gently on his folded arms, so he could see the train at eye level. As it continued through its limited, repetitive journey, he began to imagine that it was real, and that his whole life had been reduced to watching the small engine, trailing the same three cars, again and again, around and around. The mail car left no mail, and it was because there was no one in this strange, diminutive world to write to and no one to write to him. There was no need for milk, or logs or coal, and the train itself continued to clack and clack, around and around. The broad surface of the table began to assume a flat, colorless reality for him, and each time, as he watched the train approach him, it was with some expectation that this time it would be different, this time there would be mail, even if it wasn't for him. He could read it anyway, and no one would know, because he was the only one there. But each time, as the train neared the mail platform, he couldn't bring himself to interrupt the hypnotic clatter and clack of the rails or to interfere with the smooth, liquidly curving rhythm of the train's endless route, the small rods on the drive wheels of the tiny engine rising, falling, rising and falling. Their motion seemed to be the center of the universe, the focus of all existence.

On and on plunged the Lilliputian freight, on and on into the darkness of the tunnel that bored its way through the very heart of the green-and-brown mountains of papier-mâché that now, from his diminished perspective, seemed to tower over the flat world into which he had been thrust. Each time the train pulled out of its interior circuit and rounded the curve toward his cradled head, it was all he could do to keep from crying out as the small headlight bored into his eyes out of the darkness around the bend. The terror he felt each time was more real than anything he had ever experienced, and it began to feel as though he had somehow been reduced to a stature commensurate with that of the train. The trees no bigger than his fingers, light as feathers, which he had clustered in his hands like a fistful of darts, now towered over the landscape before him unlike anything he had ever seen. Once, when the train had careened around the curve toward him with what seemed to be a greater than normal velocity, he had moved away, unable to control the instinct to hurl himself out of the path of the onrushing locomotive, and his elbow had depressed the button nearest it. "Whoooo . . ." the whistle had moaned, fading away into Dopplerian oblivion as the speeding train roared past, and he could not suppress an involuntary shudder. "Whooooooooo," it seemed to wail, over and over, though his elbow was no longer on the button. "Whooooooooooo . . . ," it echoed, and he knew it was in his head that that sound lingered on, no more real now than the world he could not escape yet had built with his own hands. "Whoooooo . . ." and then, suddenly, silence. The train had stopped without warning. It had plunged at what seemed breakneck speed into the tunnel and had not come out the other side. There was not a sound to be heard. He pressed the whistle button, and the moan in response came from far away. "Wuuuuuuuu . . . ," like a lost soul in the darkest night, it wailed and then it, too, was still, and the silence came flooding back, bringing a chill, all the more powerful because of its utter lack of meaning. The whole wide, flat world was gone, and before him lay nothing but a sheet of plywood and plastic, its water reduced to blue paint, its ponds to shattered mirrors once again. The train had been the source of the planet's hold on him, its motion the magnetic fist that held him captive, and when it ceased to move, the world created by its motion had ceased to be. He was back in his own basement again, free again, and did not wish to move. He lay staring toward the tunnel, as if the pressure of his straining eyes could force the train again to move, could restore that delicate balance its sudden failure had destroyed, but nothing happened. The spell was broken, and the train did not move, though he knew that, even if it should, it was too late. There was no way he could recapture the icy chill of the careening locomotive threatening to run him down, its tiny moan ballooning out into the heavens like the voice of doom.

He stared a moment longer, feeling the beginnings of hunger stirring, turned off the transformer, and climbed slowly toward the light above.

THIRTEEN:
Willie

SOMETIMES some of us have company. They take precautions with us, because there is no telling what some of us might do. Some of those who come to see us are people we don't want to see. These people can just walk in, and one of them is with them, in a white suit that sometimes shows what they had for dinner in the commissary last night. Sometimes you can even tell what they had in the commissary for a few days. There is one of them who is not very careful. I call him Menu, partly because I don't know what his real name is, and partly for obvious reasons. If he were my son, I would probably go down to City Hall and make it official. But maybe if he were my son, it wouldn't be necessary. I don't know.

Sometimes I wonder what you can do as a father that hasn't already been tried. I am a father. I have two sons, both with Louise, but I don't think I have done a good job with them. I know Louise doesn't think so. What she thinks doesn't really matter, I guess, except that she has my sons, and if they want to see me, she can stop them. I haven't seen either of my sons since I have been here. I think it might be Louise's doing, but I can't ask anyone, because if I ask one of them, they will think I am demonstrating an unjustified hostility toward Louise, and that will make it harder to leave here.

I stay awake at night, when it is almost dark, and I think about Louise. And about my sons. I know Louise doesn't love me. I don't know if my sons do. It doesn't matter if Louise doesn't, because she did once, and I wrecked it, so it is my fault, although it is not a thing I wanted to do. With my sons, it is different. I never knew, and now I don't know if I will ever have the chance to know. I don't mean that I will never get to leave here, because I know I will. I will manage to get out of here if I have to kill somebody. I might even get out without doing that, and then come back later and do it anyway, when they wouldn't suspect me. Some of them ought to be killed, I think. If I tell anyone that, they will think I am being hostile again, so I never say it to anyone. I go in the john and write it on the metal mirror with soap, sometimes, but they don't know who does it. I disguise my handwriting so they won't suspect me.

Some of them have control over us and they don't know what to do with it, so they make us miserable, mostly just so they will know they are doing something with this power. I don't really blame them, I guess. It is not very often that you get a chance to have that kind of power over someone, especially someone who doesn't want you to have it. I know that some of them wouldn't bother to do anything mean to us if we all got together and asked them to. It is because we don't want them to be mean that they are. People are predictable that way. Louise was predictable that way, too. Just like some of them. There is even a woman here who looks like Louise, except that she smiles once in a while. She has big hands, bigger than Louise's hands, and she smiles sometimes. Otherwise there is no difference that I can see. I don't know what her skin is like, where you can't see it with clothes on, but I don't think there is that much difference in skin.

I think it must be how you feel about someone that makes them different from everybody else. Otherwise how would you know you loved somebody, especially in the dark? There must be some kind of language that we can speak with only a very few others, and when you find someone who speaks it, you grab on and squeeze, so they can't pull their hand away and leave. Louise used to speak to me that way, but not any more. Now, she doesn't even have to try to pull her hand away. I let go of it. My father told me once about that language, and how it was special and very important. He could speak that way to me, and to my mother, too. It is a special language that is used only for special things. When my father told me a joke, he always used

English, because that special language is not made for funny things. It is for very serious things. Things like knowing how Louise feels about me. I know, now, because she doesn't talk it any more.

I look at the ceiling, when I think about that language, and I try to remember if I ever used it with my sons, the way my father did with me when I was little. I don't remember. I think that might mean I didn't, and I am worried. It may be why my sons haven't come to see me here. If Louise isn't stopping them, it must be because I never used it to tell them how I felt about them. I guess I fucked up again, not telling them, but that would not surprise me. Or Louise, either. Nothing I do surprises her. Whenever I lose a business, or get a speeding ticket, or can't find my shoes, she always says she's not surprised.

There are a lot of new things I have learned about myself in the time I have been here, mostly things I already suspected, but now I am sure about some of them. A lot of them, even. It feels good to have one's beliefs confirmed, even if they are your worst fears. That's what's happened to me here, more than once. I thought that Louise didn't want to be with me any more, and since I have been here I have learned that for certain. She has never come to see me, and there is no reason unless it is because she doesn't want to. She is certainly old enough to come in if she wants to. At first I wasn't sure that she hadn't been here, but I asked one of them, and he told me. I asked about my sons, too, and they said they hadn't been here, either.

This morning one of them came to see me. They are very good at coming to see people here. Some of them don't do anything else. They just go around and visit us, and nod sagely, sometimes taking notes if something very important has been revealed. They never take notes when they talk to me any more. I have decided not to reveal anything to them that is still secret. It is not always easy to have secrets, but especially here, because nothing ever happens here, at least nothing much. That means that there are no secrets that you can have about anything that happens here, partly because nothing much ever happens, and partly because whenever something does happen, which isn't very often, somebody is so excited they tell everybody else as soon as they can. That is their big mistake.

I would just wait for something to happen, and then not tell anybody. That would be one good way to leave here, but I might have to wait a very long time. That's why I don't tell them everything about me before I got here, so that I can have some secrets and act like people with secrets act. That is supposed to be a good sign, I think. I would even make up a secret about something that happened here, but in order for them to know I was keeping it a secret, I would have to tell them that something happened and then not tell them what it was when they asked me. They would think that was antisocial behavior and would make me stay here even longer. That's not a good idea, so I just won't tell them everything about me before I was here. They will talk to my father and my mother, who will tell them things about me that I never told them, and they will know that I have secrets and belong someplace else instead of here. Then they will send me there.

There are quite a few rules here, and I don't know them all yet, but I am trying to learn them all as quick as I can. I have to leave here soon, so I can go ask my sons if I ever spoke to them in that language. If I don't do that soon, Louise may take them away, or they may not know what I am talking about because it will have been a long time since I used that language with them, if I ever did in the first place. I think I must have, because I love my sons, just like my father loves me. He doesn't always say it that way, but I know he does. I mean, he doesn't come up to me and say, "Willie, I love you, son." But he tells me other things that mean the same thing. I can always tell when he is telling me that, even if we are talking about politics or business, or about the time my sister died, the young one. It was bad then, and my father was very sad, but I knew he loved me then because he looked at me a special way when he talked about my sister. He looked at me the same way I used to look at my sons when Louise and I had a fight.

I know I used to look into Louise's eyes and I could see everything. I could see the way I felt about her, and the way she felt about me, and the way she felt about the way I felt about her. All of it was right there. Not any more, though. Lately, when I saw her at all, I tried to look inside and see if I could see anything, but I couldn't see inside at all. All I saw was me looking at her, trying to look inside. Once I looked real hard, and when I didn't see anything inside, I looked at me looking, and I got real close to her face, and I could see two of me staring back at me, there in her eyes, and where my eyes were supposed to be, there were question marks, and I looked even closer, and I could see that my cheeks were wet. I think it was because I couldn't see anything inside her, and was straining my eyes very hard to see something that wasn't there, and my eyes started to water. Maybe not, maybe I was crying, but I don't think so. I don't think I cry any more. Not since the accident.

Once, when I was renting boats at the shore, I talked to my father about this kind of thing. I think we might even have used that special language that people who love one another use at special times, but I don't remember. I know we talked about it. He was feeling bad about me and Louise, and our not getting along well together. He was feeling bad about some other things, too, that day, but we didn't have a chance to talk about them at all. I will ask him what they were the next time he comes here. Maybe it will be tomorrow, or even later today. I know my mother is supposed to come soon, and he will probably come with her, so I will ask him then. It is the least I can do, I think. Sometimes even a fuck-up like me can help somebody else. You can almost always help somebody if you really care about them, even if you can't do anything about the problem they are having.

It is always nice to know that somebody cares, and if you care, you can help someone just by telling them that. That's why I want to see my father, to tell him that I care, and maybe that will help him with the thing he was feeling bad about that time at the shore. I know he cares, and I care, too. I know he will tell me he cares, even if I don't ask him. I probably won't even have to ask him, or even hint around about it, because he knows how to do things like that without anyone asking him. He is a good man. I love him. He will tell me he cares because it is true, and because he will know that I have to be able to believe something like that before I can leave here.

He might even know that it was not believing it that got me here in the first place. I think that is the truth, too, even if it does sound like something one of them would say. Sometimes they are right by accident. I know it is what helped me to get here, anyway, especially when I knew that Louise didn't care any more and I couldn't find anybody else who did, except my mother and father. Especially my father. But that didn't mean anything then, because they are supposed to do that for you, your mother and father. It comes with the territory, and most of them do it without trying, or even thinking about it. They don't always do it too well, but they do it. Sometimes they even do it when they shouldn't. It is sometimes not good to care for someone, especially if it is someone who will hurt you if they know you care. Louise isn't like that. She hurt me because I hurt her, not because she knew I cared and she didn't.

The thing to do is try to leave here and see my sons before they think they have to hurt me, too. If I had it to do over again, I don't think I would hurt Louise, but I can't say for sure, because I didn't do it on purpose. It was an accident, but it never helps very much to tell someone that. I told that to Louise, but it didn't make any difference. She just thought I was careless. With my sons, it's different.

I can't wait to be someplace else, and lately I have been pretending that I am just here waiting for my papers, like Ellis Island. I am here to have someone give me my papers and to make sure that I don't have smallpox, and then they will take me on a boat to New York, and I can go on my way. They might even change my name, if I don't say it right, but I don't care about that too much. Sometimes I don't even try to say my name right, and they don't even notice. If they change my name to be what I make it sound like, I can pretend that none of this ever happened. No one else will know, because they will know me as Willie Donovan, and if I tell them that my name is Helmut Albricht, or something like that, they won't know it's me, and everything will be all right. If I can only find a name that I like, I will be okay. I want to sound like I am successful, and then I probably will be. At least that is how people will treat me. It is very important to sound all right to other people, because most of them don't know how to look inside you and see things. Those who can are the ones who really care about you, and they don't mind if you're not successful. All except Louise. She cared, but she still minded. It was probably my fault, though. I'll have to think about that a while, I guess.

FOURTEEN:
Ella

WATCHING Will and his obsession with the holiday season, I began to get a strange foreboding, as if something were out of control. I don't think it was Will, and I don't think it was things so much as it was the way they were affecting him. As long as I have known that man, I don't think I have ever seen him so much at the mercy of the things around him. Things that were perfectly innocent, and didn't seem to have the slightest effect on me, or on anyone else I knew, were getting him down. If I had to say how he seemed to me, to find one word that would describe him, it would be victim.

Something had its teeth in him, and it wasn't trying to bite him but it wasn't going to let him go, either. I could see the look in his eyes when we were in the basement, cleaning the tree ornaments, and especially when he was polishing the tree stand. He didn't have to tell me what he meant when he said he wanted to sand away some things that had happened that he wished hadn't happened. And he didn't have to tell me that the plural wasn't necessary. I know him pretty well, and there is only one thing that has happened that he would try to change if he could change only one thing. And if I didn't know just by knowing him, the way his eyes kept sneaking over to the angel that was Emma's favorite thing would have told me. I don't mean that he wouldn't want to have spared Willie the troubles he had, and all the misery of the accident, but that was something that was manageable. I know he thinks that Willie shouldn't have had to suffer, what with all of the skin grafts, and the broken bones, and everything the accident did to his mind, changing his whole life around the way it did. All that is something that Will would prefer hadn't happened. I know that. But at least we still have Willie, with all his troubles, and we don't have Emma. That's what Will would change if he could change only one thing. There isn't a doubt in my mind.

This morning, I realized that it was his unwillingness, after all these years, to let go of that pain that has gotten him in such a state. I wish to God I could talk to him about it, but I know I can't. He has buried it so deep inside him that he doesn't really know it's there. And even if I tried to make him talk, to let it out, and hope that he could feel better just by talking to me in a way he never has been able to, I know he wouldn't be able to. I think it might even be my fault, because he tried so hard to help me get over it that he never had the time to feel it himself, let it burn itself out the way hurtful things do if you face them honestly. Painful things have a way of cauterizing the very wounds they cause, and they heal, but you have to admit that they hurt you, almost fall in love with the pain, just so you can really feel it, and measure it. That's the only way you can overcome it. I have seen too many people walk around denying to themselves that something hurt them, and all they manage to do is hide from themselves something that anybody else in the world can see just by looking.

Now, I don't know whether I ought to try to do anything or just hope that whatever it is that's got hold of him will let him go. I love that man, and if I didn't think about it, I'd be tempted to say that whatever it was, he could beat it. With one hand tied behind his back. But I can't say that, because I know what it is, and I know he can't beat this one. He would have been able to if I had let him, but I never did, and now it's too late. Sometimes I think pain is like the roots of a tree that go down into the ground as far as the tree is tall, so that it takes as long to get over something as you have suffered from it. I know Will won't live forever, and it has been buried in him a long time now, longer than the time either of us has left. I would share it with him, but I don't think that can be done, and even if it could, I don't think the two of us together have enough time left. Maybe that scares me. It probably does, and I guess I just can't make up to him for what he has done, as much as I want to. Sometimes the only thing I can think of doing is praying, and, as mad as I know that makes him, it's for him that I do it. He knows that, too, I think, so that he teases me, just to make me more determined to go ahead with it. He doesn't know whether there's a God in heaven, but I think he has a sneaking suspicion, and he's not going to stop me from putting in a good word for him, no matter what he tells other people.

This morning I am going to church, as I do every Sunday, and I'll sit in the front pew and pray until my eyes are red from squeezing them shut. I'll come home, and he'll ask me if I have been up all night drinking, or some such thing. That's just like him. It's his way of saying he knows what I've been doing. I know he appreciates it, and it's the only thing I know how to do to make it up to him for leaning on him so hard for so long. It's always a little harder this time of year, because it brings back so many things, but that's exactly why it's most important now. That, and the way Will has been feeling lately.

I get ready, the way I always do, and Will is lying in bed, the way he does every Sunday, one eye open so he can reach out and touch me with the back of his hand when I'm ready. He always pretends that he just rolled over in his sleep, and if I say something to him, he doesn't answer, but I don't think I could leave for church without it. It's almost as if he's saying, "I know where you're going, old girl, and I'm glad." I know that, deep down, he *is* glad, much as he will grumble at me when I get home.

This morning, even before I get downstairs, I know that it's cold, much colder than it has been, and the sky is grayer than it usually is at eight o'clock. I never have breakfast before I leave, and I like the few moments alone at the bus stop. They are probably more important than the time I spend in church. I can think about the things I want to pray for, and it gives me a chance to sort through the week. I always pick out something special, something that has come to mean something or to require particular attention during the past week. I always pray for Will, of course, and for Emma, but it is usually not necessary to ask anything special for him. Today, though, I'm not so sure, and I start thinking about it even before I put my coat on. By the time I reach the sidewalk, I know that there is nothing more important this week, and maybe nothing has ever been this important. It's almost too important to pray for, and I think I know why Will gets so angry about religion. It's as if he's saying that anything that's so important that you have to go to church to pray for ought to be important enough that you shouldn't have to pray for it. God ought to know about it and take care of it without being asked. Will's stubborn that way, but sometimes I'm not sure that he isn't right. There are some things God ought to take care of on his own. He owes us that much, I think. It scares me to think that way, mostly because I'm not as certain of things as I let on to Will. In a way, I have to be certain for both of us, and it's not easy sometimes. Will knows that, but he'd never admit it. Too much energy has gone into that gruff exterior he has been cultivating for so long. He spends more time on it then he does the garden, and it has grown very well over the years, maybe too well. I'm not always sure he knows how much is show and how much is what he really believes, but I guess it doesn't really matter. Not this late in the game.

I wish he would soften just a little, just once. Maybe he could come with me once. It would make me happy, but I don't dare ask him, because he would do it for that reason, and that's not why I want him to come with me. I want him to do it because it will make *him* happy. I can't ask him, but I hope someday he will ask if he can come along. He always says he doesn't need church, but I can tell that he's not happy, not at peace with himself, and I know he needs something, just like I have always needed something, and church is as good a thing as I know, and probably as good as any. When I sit there, and hear the choir up in the loft, the church might as well be empty. It's like I'm there alone anyway, and I don't think about anything except whatever the special thing I have picked out for that week might be. I don't really talk to God, the way some people say you should when you're in church, but I think a lot about whatever the thing is, and I know that it makes me feel better just to do that. I don't know whether God actually knows what I'm thinking about, but if I feel more hopeful, I don't think it makes any real difference. There are a lot of ways to communicate, and mine is as good as any, I guess.

Just being inside those thick stone walls is a comfort, and I feel more peaceful there, as if the walls are between me and whatever it is that threatens me or Will. It's almost like I bring him with me, just by thinking about him while I'm there. He's as safe as I am just because I bring him with me the only way I know how.

This morning, the Reverend Berland gives a good sermon. It is about the only time I am aware that someone else is in church with me, and he is a good preacher, although he has a tendency to talk over our heads sometimes, mostly because I think he tries too hard. He's a good man, but I don't think he's altogether comfortable with us, as if he weren't sure he ought to be preaching to us at all. I don't know why he should feel that way, because he always manages to touch on something that means something to most of us. He has common sense, and I think that is one of the things that I like about him. He seems always to know the right thing to do or say, even if he sometimes has trouble saying it. Will always says that his intentions don't make any difference, since the road to hell is paved with them. He thinks the Reverend Berland's problem is that he thinks he's too good for us. Will says he's always talking down to everybody, but I don't think that's true. I just think he has some difficulty relaxing with his parishioners, possibly because he takes his work too seriously. He can't seem to realize that we're all just people, and that what we need most when we're having a rough time is another ordinary person who has some insight into the problem. I think he has insight, but he's not comfortable with it, almost like it *would* be talking down to us if he were just to say what he thinks and say it as plainly as he could. Still, I don't blame him, because it can't be any easy thing to do, dealing with so many people, some of whom only seem to be around when they need something from you. It must be difficult to give all day long, seven days a week. I think it might make me uncomfortable, too.

   I know he was a great help to me when Emma died, more help than anybody except Will. He might have been more help than he was, I guess, but only because I think Will scared him. They had such a fight, I thought Will was going to punch him. I think of that every Sunday, and I think the Reverend Berland thinks of it every time he sees me. He doesn't come over to the house much, even though I know he wants to. I think he's afraid of Will, and he doesn't understand why Will acted the way he did. How could he when he doesn't really know how Will felt about Emma? And how cruel it seemed to him that Emma should be taken so young. He just said the wrong thing to Will, and he didn't stop to think about it or I'm sure he wouldn't have said it. This morning, the Reverend Berland is standing in the vestibule after the service, as he always does, and he nods to me as I leave.

   I stop to chat with him, and he suggests that he'd like to pay a visit during the holidays. I don't want to discourage him and I think to myself that I have nearly three weeks to prepare Will for the visit, so I agree. I always dread it when Mr. Berland pays a call, but I have to stand up to Will, just so he can't think he has me completely buffaloed. He'd never respect that, and I think I'd be letting him down if I didn't fight back once in a while. At least, that's what I tell myself. It's the only way I can go through with it, I guess. To tell the truth, I was more afraid for the Reverend Berland than he was for himself that morning. Will would never have hit him on purpose, but if he had by pure accident, we would have needed an ambulance. Will was fit to be tied, and beside himself. Well, now I have to plan how to break the news to him. At least it won't be for dinner! I'd never get him to sit down for two hours without trying to provoke a fight, just on general principles. Sometimes he just carries things too far, and doesn't know when to stop. He won't listen to reason when he gets like that, and there's no holding him, either. He just goes on and on until he runs down, like a wind-up toy. I don't suppose this time will be any different, but I can always hope.

FIFTEEN

By the beginning of the last week before Christmas, Will's anxiety had reached a pitch that made Ella wince just to look at him. His conversation was limited to the subject of Christmas. He devoted the better part of his waking hours to preparations, and was on pins and needles lest Ella's reluctance to accompany him on a search for the perfect tree result in their getting no tree at all. Unable to stand the tension any longer, Ella called Katherine to complain.

"I don't know what to do with your father any more. All he talks about is Christmas," she wailed.

"Oh, Mother, don't be so hard on him," Katherine told her. "You know it means a lot to Daddy. Even if you can't get as excited as he does, try to understand and go along with him. It'll all be over soon anyway."

"I suppose you're right," Ella agreed reluctantly. "But I can't help worrying about it, all the same. I don't want him to be disappointed."

"I don't think you have to worry, Mother. He'll get it out of his system, and that will be that. You'll see."

"I hope you're right," Ella said.

"I know I'm right! Do you have your tree yet?"

"No, and your father is driving me crazy. Every day for nearly two weeks he's asked me whether it's time to get the tree. I try to tell him it's still too early, but he just gets sulky and stomps off to sit by himself, or goes down to the basement to play with the train set."

"Then why don't we get the tree this afternoon?" Katherine asked. "I'd be happy to drive you. I've heard about a place outside Princeton where you cut down your own tree. I can find out where it is, and we can go this afternoon, if you like."

"I don't know what your father has planned for this afternoon, but it sounds like a good idea to me. Why don't you get the directions and call me back?"

"All right. I'll call you back in about an hour, okay?"

Ella hung up the phone, paused to assess the probability of Will agreeing to go along, and resolved that she would press the issue, if necessary, so they could get the nagging problem out of the way. She went down to the basement, where he seemed to live when he was not dogging her footsteps and talking about the tree.

The basement was dark except for the lights from the train set, and she found herself more than a little intimidated by the other-worldly atmosphere, particularly the eerie beam of the engine's headlight as it rattled around and around the rails, the clatter interrupted occasionally by the demonic wail of the engine's whistle, which had so disconcerted her the day Will first demonstrated the layout. It still chilled her to the bone whenever she heard it drift mournfully up through the floor. To Will, it seemed to have become some kind of oracular utterance which baffled and intrigued him. He would depress the button over and over, as if he were trying to squeeze a meaning out of the noise, or trying to reconstruct an entire language from a one-word vocabulary.

As she drew up behind him, the whistle moaned and the train roared into the tunnel at the far end of the table. She grasped his shoulder gently, but at first he seemed not to be aware of her presence. As she increased the pressure and shook him a bit, he muttered, "What is it?"

"I just spoke to Katherine," Ella replied.

"What did she have to say?" Will asked, uninterestedly.

"She's heard about a nice place, outside Princeton, where we can cut down our own tree. She offered to drive us this afternoon. Is that all right with you?"

"I suppose so," he responded dully.

"What time shall I tell her?"

"I don't care. Any time is all right with me."

"One o'clock?"

"Yes, one o'clock is fine."

"All right, I'll . . . Will?"

"What is it now?" he asked impatiently.

"Nothing. I . . . I just want you to know that I'm not trying to interfere with your plans, or anything like that. I just . . ."

"I don't think that," he said gently. "Though I can't say I blame you for thinking I might. I know I haven't been the most pleasant person to be around lately. I'll be better soon, I promise. Just bear with me. And don't hesitate to let me know if I get too irritable." He smiled.

Will stayed with the trains until nearly noon, then bounced up the basement stairs to make himself a cup of coffee and a sandwich. Ella heard the commotion in the kitchen and found Will rubbing his hands together vigorously, pausing now and again to rub his shoulders.

"Boy, I must really be going downhill fast," he observed. "Either that or that basement is a lot colder than I thought. I feel like I slept out in the snow or something. You wouldn't believe how stiff I am."

"Maybe it's just your circulation," Ella volunteered.

"Well, even so, it must be because I'm getting old. Why else would my circulation be so sluggish?"

"Maybe it's not. Maybe it's just the way you hunch over those trains for hours at a time. That would make anybody stiff. Just make sure you dress warmly this afternoon. It's cold out!"

"Don't worry about that," Will said. "I might even wear me longjohns, just to make sure."

At one o'clock, Will was on the front porch, wrapped in heavy woolen coat and muffler, his hands in heavy woolen gloves, rocking on his heels and impatient to be going. Ella, who had always been the first one ready for any excursion, and more than willing to tease Will about his reluctance to undertake the simplest trip, was still inside, determined that she would not put on her coat until Katherine arrived, partly because it was Will's show and partly because she saw no point in waiting out in the cold.

Will watched his breath cloud and drift slowly upward into the vacant, brittle gray of the maples in front of the house, slowly dissipating as it climbed until, reaching the lowest of the trees' limbs, it was barely visible. It required an act of the will to trace the wispy ascent. He toyed with the idea of blowing smoke rings, but after a few desultory attempts, gave it up, deciding that the breath was too elusive a medium for such precise artistic endeavors.

From time to time, he would sit down on the cold concrete slab atop one of the porch walls, but the chill seemed to seep through as soon as he made contact, and the nervous excitement he felt only added to his general discomfort. Since he had insisted on waiting out front, however, to return indoors would be an admission of defeat, so he endured the cold and tried as best he could to keep warm. There was no one on the street in the noon cold, and his attention kept wandering from house to house along the block as he tried to occupy himself and to ignore the chill.

He began minutely examining the bark of the taller of the two maples in front of the porch, and fancied that he could read history and the future in the chilly gray parchment. The curious curlicues and interlacing ridges and grooves seemed to contain a metaverbal chronicle of the entire family. He saw some of the distortions of the bark as representations, even embodiments, of the various traumas and catastrophes that had befallen the Donovans, as if the tree itself had been a participant in those events, or so empathetic an observer that it bore the scars of their pain. He fastened his attention on one particularly gnarled segment of the bark and wracked his memory for some evidence that it had been so tortured before Emma's death. He believed, though he could not be sure, that the area in question had been relatively unmarked until that time. Intrigued by the idea, he attempted to correlate other features of the bark with other events, but gave it up for the foolish fantasy it was when he could not decide what aspect of the tree's surface would signify some happy circumstance, although he was satisfied with the equation of the normal flow of uneventful time with the smooth, almost tediously regular flow of ridge and rook in the bark's broad, simple expanses.

While he recognized that he was making a great deal of pointless effort, he couldn't dismiss from his mind the correspondence between Emma's death and the heavily scarred knot of bark there in front of him. "Of course," he told himself, "it's just nonsense." But he stared nonetheless at the darkly convoluted clot that could speak only of something horribly painful. Absorbed in his meditations, he did not notice the arrival of Katherine, who parked her Chevrolet at the curb in front of the house. Even when she popped the horn button, his attention was unwavering.

Katherine got out of the car, leaving the engine running, its gray exhaust rising quickly from the tailpipe, as if hot on the trail of Will's escaping breath. At last feeling her presence, rather than seeing her, Will turned as she mounted the steps, saying, "Hi ya, kitten, when did you get here? I didn't see you pull up."

"So I noticed," Katherine teased. "You look like you were engaged in some pretty serious thought there. I beeped the horn, but I guess you didn't hear me."

"I guess not." Will laughed. "But it's probably just me ears. They say the hearing is one of the first things to go when you're over the hill."

"Try again."

"Nothing, really, just some foolishness. Old men are entitled to some of that, you know."

"Come on, Daddy, I know you well enough to know that there's more to it than that. Fess up."

"Christ, next thing I know, you'll be breaking out the rubber hose to use on the old man."

"If I have to beat you black and blue to make you talk, I'll do it."

"You know, Katie, sometimes I think you have more than a little of me in you, even if you're not my daughter. It scares me, sometimes."

"I know what you mean, but you won't get off that easily!"

"Mostly I was just looking at that tree there and thinking about things in general," Will said evasively.

"What kind of things?" Katherine persisted.

"Lots of things, most of which don't mean anything to you, and aren't very important anyway."

"Does that mean that some of them *do* mean something to me and are important?" she asked with a laugh.

"I guess so." Will smiled. "But they aren't particularly pleasant, or else they're pretty silly, so . . ."

"Come on, Pop. Quit beating around the bush. Something's on your mind and it's too cold for me to stand here and play guessing games. Now what is it?"

"Your sister . . ."

"Oh!" Taken aback by the brutal abruptness of Will's answer, Katherine could not immediately respond. While she searched for some way to continue the conversation, her mother opened the front door and pushed open the storm door just wide enough to say, "Oh, you're here." She ducked back inside and almost immediately reappeared, buttoning her heavy winter coat.

"How come you didn't let me know you were here?" Ella asked as she locked the inside door behind her. "Have you been here long?"

"No," Katherine responded. "I just got here, and Daddy and I were just chatting."

"What, do you mean to tell me the great ogre has decided to be sociable again? Land sakes, let me go back inside and call the papers. It'll be front-page news." Ella laughed.

"Oh, he's not an ogre. Are you, Daddy?"

"No indeed." Will smiled, relieved to have the subject changed. "I am a troll, though," he added.

"At least you can make a good living at that," Katherine

said. "It's almost a respectable profession."

"You'd be surprised how few dumb goats there are around nowadays," Will replied.

"I can think of at least one," Ella put in.

"I didn't say old goats, I said *dumb* goats," Will shot back.

"It's cold out here," Katherine said. "Why don't we get going?"

For a few moments no one spoke, and the overcast seemed to dampen whatever interest there was in conversation, so they rode in silence. There was something slightly discordant in the presence of so many festive lights and decorations dangling dully against the gray sky, and Will stared at them as if they were messengers of bad news. As the car drew out of the city and began to hum steadily along the highway between Trenton and Princeton, the quality of the houses improved enormously, and the wide lawns, many still a lush green, seemed barriers deliberately erected between travelers and residents. Many of the homes could not be seen at all, and others barely peeked from behind tall hedges or between trees.

The greenness of the countryside was less deep but more pervasive than that of the lawns, and at odds with the season. Despite the coldness of recent weeks, the weather had been warmer than usual for most of the fall, and the fields did not have the pinched barrenness Will associated with winter, when the dull grayish soil lay frozen in hard clumps where it had been turned after the harvest.

Ella and Katherine exchanged cursory conversation about Patrick's performance in school, Andy's job, and the usual trivia people resort to when a pregnant silence weighs too heavily on them, but Will remained quiet in the back seat. Somewhere ahead of him, he knew, lay a small green cone that had come to dominate his attention like a grail that of an errant knight, and he was burrowing straight down into the core of himself, trying to understand the true nature of his mania for Christmas, about which he had come to feel increasingly nervous. He had long since decided there was nothing he could do about it, but he frequently felt a tension, a disquiet, he could not articulate. If the truth were known, he thought, I would just as soon Christmas were over.

"Here we are," Katherine announced cheerily as the car's tires suddenly crunched into a gravelly parking lot.

Will looked up from his ruminations to see a long, low shedlike structure of peeling clapboard in front of the car and several signs hand-lettered in what appeared to be a childish scrawl of crayon, each of which read "Office" and pointed in the same general direction as the others. Will asked Katherine if she wanted the car locked.

She shook her head, saying, "There's nothing worth stealing in here anyway."

Will led the way toward the office, where they found a gruff, heavyset man with chill-reddened cheeks and a ready smile sitting behind a battered desk.

"Howdy, folks," he boomed as they entered. "Looks like snow, don't it?"

Will nodded. "Yup, looks like we got here just in time."

"Sure does," the man agreed. "What kind of tree you lookin' for? Got anything special in mind? We got all kinds, you know, all kinds."

"I don't know about you, Daddy," Katherine said, "but I was thinking of a Scotch pine for a change. What do you think?"

"Oh, yeah, we got a bunch of them out back," the man said before Will could answer. "Cute little buggers, they are, too. Good shape on them, and pretty tall, too, as those things go."

"Scotch pine is all right with me, too," Ella chimed in.

"I don't know," Will said hesitantly. "I was thinking of a more traditional tree, a spruce, probably. Somehow a Scotch pine doesn't seem like a Christmas tree to me."

"I know what you mean," the salesman grunted. "I like a spruce myself, but some folks don't want a great big thing like that in their living rooms. I do, but not everybody does. No matter. I got all kinds. Just let me know."

"Can we look around a bit?" Will asked.

"Sure thing," the man said heartily, "sure thing. Look around all you want. I'll just come outside to point you in the right direction is all. I'll be here if you have any questions."

"I have a couple right now," Will replied.

"Shoot! No sense in goin' out in the cold yet is there?"

"Okay. First off, how much are they?" Will asked. "Do they go by the foot, or what?"

"Nope, by type," he said. "The Scotties are three bucks apiece, and the firs and spruces are five bucks, and I don't mind telling you you'll have to go a pretty far piece to beat those prices. Fact is, the bigger the tree you get, the bigger the bargain you get, too."

"They seem reasonable to me," Will agreed.

"Reasonable? Whew, I'll say they're reasonable. They're cheap, even." He laughed. "Yessirree, cheap, that's what I call 'em. I mean you can buy a fifteen-footer for five bucks. Try and beat that price anywheres around here. Now, what was your other question?"

"What about a saw? Do you have one I can use to cut the trees down?"

"Sure, sure I do. I got saws, axes, anything you want, long's you bring 'em back. What do you want, a saw or an ax?"

"A saw, I think," Will said.

"Good idea." The man nodded. "Damn good idea. You get down under one of them suckers with an ax, the next thing you know you got a neck full of needles. Take my word for it, a saw is better than an ax any day of the week."

"Okay, I guess I'll take a saw, then. I get enough needling around home as it is." Will laughed.

"Know what you mean," the man whispered conspiratorially. "The wife does the same thing to me. Here, take this here saw. It's real sharp though, so be careful. I don't mess with no insurance."

"Thanks. Now, which way do we go?" Will asked.

"Here, follow me," he said stepping through the door, which closed behind them with a rattle of loose panes. "Now, your

Scotties is over there, behind that barn. The whole field's full of them. Just take your pick and cut her down. All I ask is that you make up your mind for certain before you do any cutting. You'd be surprised how many people start hacking away before they have any idea what they want. They make up their minds after the damn tree is cut down that it's too big, or too small, or too something. Jesus, I had one guy here a couple of years ago, I caught him tying a tree up with string. Said he cut the thing down, then his wife changed her mind. Jesus!"

"Well, you don't have to worry about me," Will assured him. "I'll make sure I've made up my mind first."

"I know you will, I know that. Anyways, the spruces are over here, behind the shed here. There's three fields full of 'em, all sizes and shapes, but they're all beauties. Almost all of 'em, anyways. You won't have any trouble finding a real nice tree out there, I'll guarantee you. I even got a few that run over twenty feet, or even taller if you want."

"Thanks again," Will said. "Shall we bring the trees over here, or can we leave them at the car when we're done?"

"Oh, hell, leave 'em at the car, I guess. No sense luggin' 'em all the way over here if you don't have to. Just let me know when you're finished, and I'll come out and give you a hand tying 'em on."

He waved cheerfully, stepping back into the office, rubbing his hands together to restore some circulation. As he followed after Ella and Katherine, Will could hear the man stamping his feet. The women had already moved into the lot of pines, where Will could just make out the bright-red tail of Ella's scarf as she moved among the lanes of trees. He was content to trail along behind as they scrutinized prospective trees, idly fluffing the branches of likely choices and exchanging comments on the flaws of various candidates.

Finally, Katherine said, "I guess I don't want a pine, after all. We might as well go look at the others. These are nice, but they look like they'd be too hard to decorate. How do you get the tinsel on them, anyway?"

"I think you're right," Ella concurred. "What do you think, Will?"

"Personally, I don't think a Scotch pine *is* a Christmas tree, but don't let that influence you. If you want a pine, take your time and pick one out. It won't be any harder to cut down."

"No," Katherine decided. "Let's go look at the spruces."

They headed back through the narrow lanes between the rows of pines, Will drinking in the strong scent, sharpened by the occasional raw stump where one had been cut down by an earlier customer. They headed into the long aisles of tall, deep-green spruce trees, many of which were, as the salesman had indicated, upward of twenty-five feet in height. It seemed cooler among the taller trees, even though they more effectively blocked the wind. Will took a more active interest in the selection process now that the trees were more to his liking. He would find a possible candidate, walk around it with intense concentration, stroking his chin occasionally and often stepping back to see how it looked from a distance.

"Here's the one I want, Daddy," Katherine called from a few aisles over. "Did you find yours yet?"

"Not yet," he called back. "Let me cut yours down while you and Mother see if you can find another one." He went over to Katherine and Ella, who were still scrutinizing the tree Katherine had chosen. "What do you think? Does it look all right to you?"

"It looks fine," Will said. "It might be a bit too tall, but I think we can fix that without too much trouble. I can just whack a foot or so off the bottom if I have to."

"Wouldn't that be too much trouble?"

"Nah," Will replied. "No trouble at all. I'll just wait until we get it home, though. No sense taking if off now, because if I take too much, I can't put it back, you know."

"Oh, Daddy, I thought you could do anything," Katherine teased.

"Now, Katie, I asked you not to let your mother know that. She hardly gives me any peace as it is."

"Peace, is it?" Ella laughed. "I'll give you peace, all right. Katherine, I have to wake this galoot up just to tell him it's time to go to bed. I can hardly watch my shows for the snoring, these days."

"Come on, come on," Will said. "Let's get down to business here. We can talk about my snoring later. Go pick out a tree, for Christ's sake, will you, Ella? Let me get this one cut."

"Don't you want to pick it out, Daddy?" Katherine asked.

"Your mother knows what I want," Will said. "I'll trust her. Besides, I'm the one with the saw."

"All right," Katherine said. "We'll be over there. Mother saw one she liked a bit earlier. Call if you need a hand."

"You go on." Will smiled. "I'll be right here."

He watched the women move off among the trees, then dropped to his knees on the heavily needled earth, bending over to peer in under the lowest branches of the tree Katherine had chosen. It was full and well shaped, and the lowest branches were barely above ground level. He lay on the ground on his back, and squeezed his right side in toward the base of the tree, tugging the saw in alongside him, wriggling until he found a comfortable position. He enjoyed the acrid bite of the needles and lay still for a moment, feeling the tingle of the breeze down his open collar.

It was so comfortable, with the thick layer of needles between him and the cold earth, that he felt almost as if he were settling down to sleep. He stifled a yawn and began to saw away at the pithy trunk, the fragrance of the tree's sap welling up around him as the blade bit into the bark. He worked slowly but steadily, beginning to raise a sweat under his heavy coat and sweater. The coat was hampering him with its cumbersome bulk, and he paused in his work long enough to climb out and remove it, then spread it beneath him like a ground cloth. He resumed his sawing, pausing now and then to examine his progress. The wood wasn't hard, but he could not bring too much pressure to bear on the blade because of his awkward position, and the work went slowly.

Thank God I didn't decide to be a lumberjack, he thought, or I'd probably have starved to death. So intent was he on the job at hand that he completely forgot the others until Katherine's sudden shadow startled him.

"Christ's sake, Katie, why didn't you holler or something? You scared me half to death," he spluttered.

"I did holler, Daddy." Katherine laughed. "Twice! When you didn't answer, Mother figured you had fallen asleep. She found a beautiful tree, a few rows over. How are you doing on this one? Can I help?"

"Almost finished. Maybe you can just hang on to this thing, and push it away from me a little, so the blade won't stick so. I was trying to do it meself, but I was getting pretty tuckered out."

Katherine leaned into the tree, pushing the trunk at shoulder height, and Will had soon sawed completely through. They left the tree where it fell, and Katherine led the way to where Ella waited beside the second tree.

"I didn't see anybody else here," she said, "but this is so pretty I didn't want to take a chance of losing it. What do you think, Will?"

"It's perfect." He nodded, a smile of satisfaction creasing his work-ruddy cheeks. "I think I have the hang of it, so I'll have the little bugger down in no time at all."

He fell to his knees and had the women each grab an armful of branches. "Whatever you do," he advised them, "don't let go of those damn branches, or I'll end up with a mouth full of pine needles."

"Finally, I have a way to shut you up." Ella chuckled mischievously.

The threat seemed to galvanize him, and he began to saw with desperate fury, the entire tree shaking as though it were being uprooted. The cascading needles bothered him not at all, a minor annoyance in comparison to Ella's threatened attack. The tree gave way suddenly, and Ella, who had been leaning in toward the trunk, collapsed in a heap, much to Will's delight.

"There," he chortled, "that'll teach you to threaten an unarmed man."

"Don't just lie there, cackling like an idiot," Ella exploded. "Help me up."

"I think you better help Mother up, Daddy. It's starting to snow, and we have to get a move on."

No sooner had she finished speaking than Will felt the first cold flakes land on his flushed cheeks. He quickly shrugged into his coat, leaving the scarf dangling freely, and hauled Ella to her feet.

"You better button that coat, Will," Ella warned. "You're overheated, and it's pretty cold."

"It'll keep until we get to the car. Here, Katie," he said, "you take the saw, and I'll get the trees."

The manager saw them returning and met them at the car, where they gave him the money for the two trees. They chatted and exchanged holiday greetings while the men tied the trees onto the roof of Katherine's Chevrolet.

"Pleasure seeing you folks," the man said cheerfully. "Enjoy your trees, and hope we see you again next year." As the car, now nearly buried under the trees tied to its roof, backed into the road, Will saw him pause to look at the sky, one hand extended to gather a few of the large, fluffy flakes, which were falling with greater intensity, seeming to cluster like angry bees in small clouds that momentarily obscured the man and even the buildings.

"It sure looks like we're going to have a white Christmas," Katherine observed. "I hope it doesn't get too bad until we get home, though. I hate driving in the snow."

"Boy, oh, boy." Will chuckled. "Just what the doctor ordered. Even the weatherman is pitching in. This is going to be one bang-up, perfect Christmas, I can tell. I can hardly wait."

SIXTEEN

By Christmas Eve, the snow was deep, and had been falling, off and on, the better part of the week. Will was in his glory, his spirits mounting as rapidly as the snow, and every morning he would stand gleefully in front of the dining-room window chuckling as the rosebushes sank slowly out of sight until only their tips could be seen, bony brown fingers desperately clutching the air to avoid disappearing altogether.

The whiteness seemed like a promise to Will, a clean slate. It was as if God had thrown a vast, amnesiac blanket over history, totally erasing everything that had gone before. After checking with Ella to see whether she would need him for anything, he set about erecting the tree, although it was only ten o'clock in the morning. Ella suggested he might want to wait a while, but he told her he was going to work slowly, savoring every last strip of tinsel. He was like a man obsessed as he mounted the tree securely in its stand, checking to see that it was straight, that the branches fell properly, that the thinnest area of the tree would be hidden from view. Three times he had to pull the tree from its stand to adjust the lower branches, but he seemed to relish each and every annoying detail. When he was finally satisfied that everything humanly possible had been done to ensure perfect alignment, the tree's branches fanning out in perfect circles, he went to the kitchen to have a cup of coffee with Ella.

"Are you finally satisfied, Mr. Perfection?" Ella teased.

"Just about." He laughed. "That was some job, getting that thing lined up like that."

"You'd think the world would come to an end if it weren't just so, the way you were carrying on!"

"Well, no need to worry about that now, even if it's true. It's up! I'm going to take a little walk before I start trimming. Why don't you come with me?"

"A walk? In this weather? Are you crazy?"

"Sure, why not? It's beautiful out there. We can even fall down in the snow and make angels. Remember how we used to do that with the kids, and even before that? Willie made the fattest angels I ever saw. Huh, they'd be really something now, I bet."

"Of course I remember. But I'm too old for that sort of nonsense now. . . . And so are you! And you shouldn't talk that way about Willie," she scolded. "He can't help his weight."

"Suit yourself! Maybe I can find someone else to make angels with. You never know."

"Not likely. You're probably the only one in town fool enough to go out in this weather. Even the kids are indoors today, and happy to be there."

"Maybe so, but that doesn't mean I have to be. That's the nice thing about being grown up. You can do all the things you always wanted to do when you were a kid but weren't allowed to do. Now, there's no one to stop me, whatever I feel like doing."

Will chuckled as he donned his heavy overshoes and coat. He opened the door with a surge of expectation, and was not disappointed. The cold air was swirling around the porch, and two huge snowdrifts had come to rest against the stone walls of the porch, swooping gracefully up and over the walls to plunge into the more monstrous drifts collected against the front of the house.

He pushed the storm door closed and grabbed an old, worn-down broom leaning against the wall to sweep the snow from the rubber mat that ran from the porch steps to the front door.

Quickly, he scraped away at the snow until only a few small clumps, which had been crushed under his feet, remained. These he kicked loose and swept off the porch. He stood on the pavement for a moment to watch the snow rise in whirls from the sloping roof of St. Andrew's Hospital at the end of the block.

Looking in the opposite direction, he could see nothing but swirling snow and muted, shadowy fragments of trees, which seemed to float above the ground.

He felt the urge to get away from the house, to plunge into the white heart of the storm and merge with it. He strode, stiff-legged, down the block toward Wetzel Field, lifting his legs sluggishly over the deeper drifts, kicking playfully through the smaller ones, and soon the house was invisible in the snow swirling behind him. The wind was howling through the trees, whose brittle branches slapped against the icy wires threaded through them. Reaching the corner, he decided it would be easier to walk in the deserted street. Not a single car had passed him since he left the house, and the only noise was the scraping of a heavy plow a few blocks away, its huge blade grating on the paving with a constant grinding rumble, sprinkled with the clink of heavy chains. The going was easier in the street, and he had nearly reached the fence around the ball field before he realized it. He hoped that the gate had been left open.

He worked his way along the fence and smiled when he saw that the second gate had indeed been left ajar. Going through, he plunged on toward the center of the diamond. When he stopped to catch his breath, he could no longer see the fence behind him, and the grandstand was only a gray shadow behind the screen of whirling flakes, now as dense as smoke. He fell slowly over backward in the deep snow and began to beat his arms back and forth as rapidly as the heavy snow, which clung to his sleeves, would permit, as if he sought to take wing, and opened and closed his legs several times. Satisfied, he lay still, smiling up into the storm with an expression of beatific serenity, licking the flakes that landed like feathers on his lips, almost numbing in their cold, pure clarity.

His breath was rising in small clouds of dense gray, sometimes in nearly vertical columns, which were suddenly ripped aside like filmy silk and seemingly knotted in midair by the violence of the wind. He watched the slender gray filament which seemed to connect him to the heart of something above him he could not see. The solitude was total, tranquil and elusive, yet he felt more a part of life than ever before, more connected to things and people, and all of the unbearable tension that had weighed so heavily on him for so long seemed to drain away as if it were no more than electricity ascending the wire of his breath into a vast reservoir of neutrality. He was calm, his breathing slow and deep, and his knotted shoulders relaxed. He saw, with a clarity he never had before, that the meaning for which he had strained was not only illusory, but unnecessary. It was enough, he now knew, simply to be.

Feeling as if he had been purged, he rose, as if the weight pressing on him had been all that held him to the earth and now, with it gone, he would fly through the air like a balloon, following the trail blazed by his breath into the swirling gray, which crystallized and showered down around him unremittingly. It seemed that he was rising through the snow rather than it falling around him. His cheeks were nearly numb, and he realized that he had not stopped smiling since he had completed the angel in the snow. He had the urge to cover the entire diamond with hundreds of interlacing angels, their wings linked together in a continuous heavenly scrawl across the snow. But "No!" he shouted. "Noooooo! One is perfect! That's all I need—one!" and he danced in his joy, laughing into the teeth of the wind, which grew suddenly still, his laughter booming from the depths of the unseen grandstand as if the hundreds of angels he had envisioned were there, cheering him on.

He couldn't wait to share his joy with Ella and began loping across the snow, following the rift his passage had created. Short of wind, he beat his clothing free of snow and bounded back toward the house, still laughing, catching wayward flakes of snow on his tongue, swallowing the wind hungrily.

As he drew near home, he realized that there was no way he could share his new serenity with Ella, just as he had been unable to share his agony. Even had she come with him, to dance in the snow and shape her own vacant angel, it could not have been shared. Her joy would have been hers, as surely as his was his, and his alone. He climbed hesitantly up the porch steps, kicking off his boots at the door and padding through the living room in his stocking feet.

"I'm home," he called to Ella, who was still in the kitchen. "I'm going to change and take a hot bath. I'll be down in a bit."

When he came down after his bath, Will set about the decoration of the tree, after checking its alignment one final time. He smiled as he gathered the numerous strands of lights, remembering the afternoon he had spent with Ella in the cellar a few weeks earlier.

"Hey, old woman," he called, "do you want to come argue with me about the lights? I'm ready to start putting them on now."

Ella came into the living room, drying her hands on her apron. There was flour from her wrists to her elbows, yellowish in spots where it had gotten wet. "I don't think I'm going to have the time," she said. "I've got to make three pies, and I'm not as good at rolling the dough as I used to be. Do you really need help, or were you just being contrary?"

"I can handle it. I just thought it might not seem like a holiday if we didn't argue about the lights, that's all."

"Well, you go ahead then. I'll pick a fight later, if I have the time." She smiled as she turned to go back to the kitchen and warned him over her shoulder, "Just make sure you don't have any yellow lights. I hate yellow lights on a Christmas tree."

Will chuckled and turned back to wrestling with the strands of wire. Once he had the sockets securely in place, it was relatively easy to screw the bulbs in, taking care to equalize the color distribution.

He then turned to the placement of the glass ornaments, locating each with an eye to its eventual framing of tinsel, so it would seem to hang suspended in a silver cloud, a thousand miniature replicas of itself swarming in glittering miniballs of color, like electrons orbiting their nucleus.

When all the balls were in place, it was time to drape the glittery tinsel, which Will always insisted should be done strand by strand. He and Ella constantly disagreed on this point, and she would attempt to catch him placing a fistful at a time, which he often did, but with such circumspection that she never managed to catch him in the act. When she peeked in to see how he was doing, she saw two miniature trees reflected in his glasses and two more, smaller still, in his eyes. He seemed to be emitting the tree by some mysterious astral projection, as if the power of his commitment to the holiday were creating an image of the season more powerful than substantial.

"Almost finished?" she asked.

"Not for quite a while yet. I just started the tinsel, and it has to go on piece by piece, you know."

"Do you want me to give you a hand?" she asked, ignoring the provocation. "The pies are in, and I don't have anything to do for an hour or so."

"All right. But only if you promise to do it a strand at a time."

"I promise," Ella said, laughing, "if you will."

"What do you mean by that?" Will asked, assuming an expression of great injury. "I always do it that way."

"If you say so," Ella grunted, taking a stiff cardboard card full of foil strands. She began to place them with scrupulous care, string by string, taking great pains to see that each hung free, ending in space rather than bunched against a lower branch. Will insisted that the point of tinsel was to simulate icicles and never tired of reminding her that icicles hung straight down and did not meander around corners in defiance of gravity.

They trimmed in silence, Ella continuing surreptitiously to monitor Will's technique, but she was unable to catch him breaking his own rules, and was determined that she would not be the first one to place more than a single strand at any one time. Will stopped from time to time to stand back and scrutinize the tree from a distance, once or twice climbing halfway up the stairs to check the view from above. The progress was apparently to his satisfaction, because he said nothing, and other than sticking a strand or two into a bare spot, he made no adjustments to those areas already trimmed.

A short while later, Ella announced that she had to return to her baking, and left Will to complete the trimming. He worked steadily, maintaining a deliberate pace, savoring the placement of each metallic strip. There seemed to be one for each needle on the tree, so shimmering and silvery was the mass of light that hovered in the corner. When he was satisfied, he pulled a dining-room chair over to the tree and kicked off his shoes to mount it, angel in hand. He had to lean precariously in order to reach the tip of the tree and slip the tubular base of the supreme ornament in place, but when he had finished, he hopped down like a man half his age and danced back toward the dining room, where he stood as if mesmerized, basking in the cascading glow as the tinsel undulated slowly in the rising currents of air. The angel's wings had been polished until they shone like mirrors, and the entire swirling blaze sparkled like lightning on their surfaces.

The spectacle exceeded his expectations, and he sank down onto the sofa with a sigh, pulling a Cuban cigar from the box on the coffee table. He struck a match and, with audible pops, puffed the stogie into a glow, his smile of satisfaction wreathed in heavy, fragrant smoke that drifted toward the kitchen to do battle with the cooking aromas. He propped his feet on a battered hassock and lay back to lose himself in the play of illumination and swarming color.

Ella was up at six o'clock the next morning, and Will was already gone. She dressed hurriedly to go down and get the turkey into the oven. When she got to the foot of the stairs, she saw Will sprawled out on the sofa, a bright-red smear of stocking across his stomach and a small heap of coal in his lap. For many years, she had been filling his stocking with coal, knowing that he would be unable to resist the impulse to open his packages long before the grandchildren arrived. There was no harm in his finding the coal ahead of time, but the small stocking gifts were another matter. One time, she had chanced to put them out the night before, and he had mangled each of them in a desperate attempt to determine its contents without actually opening it. She had had to rewrap each and every one of them, and just managed to get them finished before Willie and Louise arrived, their two sons in tow. She was amazed that he still refused to accept the fact that she was no longer foolish enough to put the gifts out until the last minute, and invariably rooted around among the lumps of coal in search of the gifts, which were safely hidden in the attic.

Later in the day, when the kids arrived, he would again delve into the bright-red, fur-trimmed stocking, and this time the gifts would be there, neatly wrapped and ribboned, along with a generous helping of coal, walnuts, tangerines, and filberts. Each of the small gifts would be ceremoniously unwrapped, accompanied by histrionic oohs and aahs from Will and enthusiastic applause from the grandchildren. There was, of course, an exchange of more substantial gifts, but the highlight of the day was always the stocking, and Will took great delight in playing to the hilt his role of astonished recipient, often feigning heart attack or coma, falling silent and unconscious on the sofa.

She tiptoed over to Will and, as she stood over him, smiling at the contented look on his face and the heap of shiny coal in his lap, he opened one eye and said, "Well, you got me again, didn't you?"

"Why don't you go on back to bed?" she asked. "You must be exhausted."

"Nah! I'm fine. Do you want some help with the bird?"

"No. All I have to do is get it in the oven. It's already stuffed and ready to go."

"What time does the company get here?"

"Andy and Katherine will be here around ten-thirty, but the rest of them aren't due until noon."

"Why is Katie coming so early?"

"She's going to give me a hand with the coleslaw, and the other cold food."

"I could have done that."

"I know, but I want you to relax and enjoy yourself."

"I'm a little anxious for things to be over with, I guess, but that'll come soon enough."

"Not soon enough to suit me." Ella laughed. "I think I'm getting too old for all this work. It wears me out."

"Well, we don't have to do it any more after this year," Will said. "It's working out so nice that I don't think we could match it anyway. Look at that tree, would you? It's perfect! Here, let me plug in the lights."

He got heavily to his feet and walked over to the far corner of the room. There was a soft click, and the room was bathed in a rainbow of colors, a thousand tiny points of a dozen shades of red, blue, and green dancing from every shiny surface on the tree. "Look at her," he said proudly. "Did you ever see such a pretty tree?"

"I have to admit it's beautiful," Ella said. "Are you happy?"

He put an arm around her waist, tugging her toward him and slightly off balance, so they swayed a bit, almost in time to the sparkling sway of the tinsel. "Yeah! Yeah, I really am." Will sighed. "I never thought I'd manage to pull it off, but there it is. The perfect Christmas tree, all ready for the perfect Christmas dinner, with the perfect family."

Ella extricated herself from his grasp, saying, "I think I better go put the oven on, or we won't have that Christmas dinner." She gave him a peck on the cheek and went out to the kitchen. Will sat down in the chair nearest the tree, staring into the lights, and beyond, into the bright, shiny caverns behind the bulbs, and lost himself in the hypnotic spectacle before him. He fell sound asleep, his head cradled on the arm of the easy chair.

When Ella returned from the kitchen, she quietly covered him with a knitted red-and-green afghan before going softly upstairs to lie down, setting an alarm for nine-thirty. She wanted to be up and dressed by the time Katherine arrived. As she lay staring at the ceiling, her mind began to wander back through previous Christmases, and she had to admit that, despite her initial resistance, Will had been right in trying to make this one special. Their lives had been made over that year, and in a way it was as if they had never had a holiday together. This was the first one of their new lives, and it *ought* to be special, because they had reached that point when any moment might very well be the last. The past few years had seen many of their friends die, and hardly a month went by that didn't bring some depressing news of old friends, or friends of old friends—a broken hip here, a stroke there, a heart attack, a death. She realized that this was implicitly what Will had been afraid of facing when he retired. It had not been the retirement itself that so scared him, but the unwelcome luxury of time to dwell on the misfortunes and afflictions that lay in store for each of them, things that could be ignored only so long as there was no time to dwell on them.

She snuggled down under the feathered comforter she had drawn across her shoulders and closed her eyes, deciding that it was better not to think so much about so depressing a subject on a day like this.

The alarm startled her back to wakefulness, and she rubbed her eyes to see the blurred hands of the clock. She lay still for a moment, savoring the remnants of sleep and the special warmth that always seems to exist only under the covers on a cold day. Finally stirring herself, she went into the bathroom and turned on the water. She hummed tunelessly as she pinned her long gray hair back in a secure bun, taking extra care with the loose ends at her nape so they wouldn't trail in the bath water.

Her face loomed before her in the mirror, and she stared at her features, which seemed lighter today than they had in a long time, almost as if they were floating on the surface of the glass, deriving an uncharacteristic buoyancy from the rising steam. Her eyes, like Will's, were blue, though inclined to be slightly gray except in the bright light of summer. This morning, they were their brightest blue, despite the gray weather, as if they had somehow partaken of the glow from the lights on the tree below. By the time she had finished with the stray ends, her image had all but disappeared, drifting back out of reach of those bright-blue eyes as if into a heavy fog. She amused herself by partially clearing the glass, and her face bobbed to the surface, now streaked and running in rivulets, the face of a young child, the marks of age still hidden by the smoky veneer of the glass. She was struck by the similarity between her face and the photograph of Emma that sat on her nightstand in a small, ornate oval frame. She had never realized the likeness before, despite years of comments from friends and family, especially when Emma was very young and Ella younger. It frightened her to see herself transformed and staring back out of a smoky other world like an apparition. It seemed almost as if it *were* Emma, looking through a window from another place and time. With an involuntary shudder, she breathed heavily on the glass to cloud it over again, rather than wipe it clear, afraid that even a pristine glass would bear the hovering shade.

Without stopping to make sure that her hair was securely pinned, she backed away from the mirror and turned, almost in a daze, to the tub, dropping her nightgown to the floor with a shrug. She stepped over the edge of the cold enamel into the tub and was shocked back to reality by the steaming water. She slipped down into the bubbling bath with elaborate care, giving herself up to the water's heat, closing her eyes against the swirling steam. It had been a long while since she had allowed herself to think of Emma, and the strength of her impressions was so overwhelming that she could not shake the feeling that she was not alone in the bath. Her spine, even buried under the billowing suds and swirling mist, was chilled, yet her skin told her the water was far hotter than she was used to. She laughed aloud at her cowardly conduct, saying, "I'll be pink as a lobster when I get out of here if I'm not careful."

"I like you pink" came a response from somewhere in the fog, and she gave a shriek.

"It's only me." Will chuckled. "Take it easy, will you? What's the matter? Did I scare you?"

"You most certainly did! What are you doing in here, anyway?"

"I was just going by when I heard you talking. I decided to pop in so you wouldn't feel silly talking to yourself."

"Well, you surely gave me a start. I'd appreciate it if you'd knock from now on," Ella said acidly.

"All right! All right! I was only joking. Jaysus, you'd think I threw cold water on you or something, the way you're carrying on. Are you sure you're okay?"

"Yes! Fine. Now leave me be. I want to relax before Katherine gets here."

Will didn't answer, and Ella heard the door close with a muted thud on Will's grumbling. She hadn't meant to snap at him, but her fear, and the embarrassment at being discovered talking to herself, made her respond more fiercely than she intended. She'd make it up to him later, when an apology would satisfy him without an explanation, since she knew she would feel foolish explaining what she had experienced.

She hurried through her bath, now unwilling to spend any more time alone in the fog-shrouded bathroom. She patted herself cursorily dry, then slipped into her robe, the sleeves of which clung clammily to her arms and back as she hurried down the hall. When she got to the bedroom, Will was sitting on the side of the bed, tying his shoelaces. He looked at her quizzically as she entered, but said nothing. When she took off her robe, he noticed that she was, indeed, quite pink, and couldn't resist the urge to tease her about it.

"Boy, you are pink!" He laughed. "But I was right, I kind of like you that way."

"Oh, mind your own business!"

"Why so touchy? Is something wrong?"

"Nothing that a little peace and quiet won't cure," she said conciliatorily. "I'm just a bit on edge, I guess. I have so much to do this morning, and Katherine will be here any minute. I wanted to have everything ready, so we could get right to work, but I can't manage it now. What time is it, anyway?"

"It's only ten-fifteen," Will said. "I'm ready to go down, so if you tell me what has to be done, I can start on it."

"That's all right. Thanks, anyway, but it would take me longer to tell you than it will to get ready and do it myself."

Will sat and watched her as she pulled her slip on. When she saw him smiling foolishly at her, she said, "What's so amusing?"

"Oh, nothing, I guess."

"What do you mean, nothing? You don't get a silly expression like that on your face for no reason."

"I was just thinking that I did all right for myself, that's all."

"What are you talking about? Did all right for yourself how?"

"Marrying you," Will said, sheepishly. "I did all right. You're still a good-looking woman."

"Oh, stop talking nonsense!" Ella said in irritation. "I don't know if I *ever* was a 'good-looking woman,' as you put it, but I certainly am nothing much to look at now."

"I wouldn't say that," Will said firmly. "And after all, it's what I think that matters, isn't it?"

"If you say so," Ella said, thankful that she was still pink from the hot bath. She knew she would have been reddening slowly under the compliment and, especially, his fondly appraising gaze. "Why don't you go on downstairs and let me finish up here?"

"Whatever you say." Will grinned. "I might lose control of myself if I stay here any longer."

"We'll just see about that, Mister," Ella snapped, laughing in spite of herself.

Will whistled cheerfully as he stomped down the stairs. The heavy tread of his Sunday shoes on the steps faded gradually, then disappeared altogether into the dining room carpet. A moment later, she could hear muffled voices, followed by the slamming of the front door. The voices grew louder, and Katherine called up, "Mother, we're here! Do you want me to start?"

She finished tugging her dress into place and, taking the small poinsettia corsage Will had left for her on the night table, she made her way to the top of the stairs, calling, "I'll be right there. Just make yourself comfortable."

As she was about to descend, she got the urge to peek into the bathroom. She clicked the light on and tiptoed cautiously to the mirror over the sink, as if she expected the image that had so disconcerted her still to be floating there, but the room was cool and the cloudy glass long since clear. When she peeked into its corner, only her own features peered back. She smiled suddenly, relaxing. When she reached the first floor, Katherine was hanging coats in the closet, and Andy and Will had already begun arguing good-naturedly about the outcome of a football game.

Patrick amused himself with crayons and coloring book while Katherine and Ella finished preparing the food.

When Willie and Louise arrived, with their kids, both women came out to say hello, then returned to the kitchen.

"How's Daddy doing?" Katherine asked Ella when the two of them were again in the kitchen.

"Oh, he's all right I guess," Ella said uncertainly. "You know your father!"

Katherine nodded and gathered place settings for the dining-room table. As she headed out of the kitchen with her arms full of dishes, Will bustled in, heading straight for the table, where he proceeded to pull a small, crisp strip of skin from the steaming turkey and pop it into his mouth.

"I wanted you to help me get that thing out of the pan," Ella said, "but I had hoped to do it in one piece, not bit by bit."

"Don't worry," Will said, chuckling, "I'll be good. You know I can't resist the skin when it's done like that, but I won't take any more of it, I promise."

"You'd better not," Ella warned. "I've had more than enough to do this morning. Don't you add to my problems."

They lapsed into silence, and Will devoted his attention to the risky job of extracting the enormous fowl from its pan, trying not to do any unnecessary damage to the taut, brown, parchmentlike skin, while Ella gathered the ingredients for her gravy. When the bird had finally been transferred to a carving platter, Ella took the pan to the pantry, along with its payload of giblets. Will, with all the ceremony of a musketeer tending his sword, stroked the carving knife briskly along the sharpening stone. She paused long enough to peer around the corner, just in time to see him try the blade's edge on his thumb. He gave it a few more honing strokes and, after careful examination, picked a paper napkin from the table. Unfolding it to dangle carelessly in one hand, he drew the carving knife across the waving paper, which parted without a whisper, the severed half fluttering away to one side like a drunken butterfly.

Feeling Ella's eyes on him, he turned to smile at her, nodded, and said, "Thanks for everything, Ella. You've been wonderful."

Then, without a backward glance, he hefted the platter to his shoulder and headed into the dining room, where she heard him unceremoniously announce dinner with "Let's eat!"

SEVENTEEN:
Willie

LATELY I am trying to remember things, mostly about my life before I was here, and I try to think of reasons why I might have had to come here in the first place. They are always asking me about things like that, when they come to see me, so it must have something to do with the way you get out of here. I am not sure exactly what the connection is, but I have my suspicions. I am starting to think that it is important to have secrets, but not too many. If you have too many, then they think that you are afraid of people, and don't want them to know anything about you. On the other hand, if you don't have any secrets at all, then they think you are weird and like to impose yourself on people in order to gain their attention. Most of my time here now is spent trying to draw the line between being too secretive and too open. I don't know how much time, though, because my watch has only one hand. I try to remember if it was always like that, but I am not sure. I don't think so, though. I think the difference is a line, a very narrow line, and one must walk it very carefully and surely, like a Flying Wallenda. We all work without a net, and if we fall off the line, we end up here.

I say that I spend most of my time here trying to draw that line, and that is true, but it is only lately that I became aware of that. This morning, in fact, I realized that it was nearly two weeks since I discovered the calendar in the television room, where they let us go to watch some shows. If we are good. Don't ask me to define good. That is their job. The calendar was a nice one, with some lady in underwear selling Italian tires. I don't know what the connection is, but I guess it works. I have seen a lot of those tires around town over the years. I don't know whether the calendar is a new one or not, but it probably isn't.

It said November 12, 1961, on it, and when I looked outside, through one of the windows where there were trees, there were only a few leaves left on them, and they were all brown. Underneath the calendar was a light rectangle on the paint.

Maybe there was something else there, like a picture I didn't notice, but I don't think so. The calendar was probably there, but I didn't pay any attention to it. It is even possible that they made it look like it was always there, but that is a lot of trouble to go to to fool me. They are not the type to waste much time on people like me, so I think they didn't do that. Besides, they couldn't fake the trees, and there is no reason to all of a sudden place a calendar on the wall unless you want to fool someone, and the leaves that were left on the trees outside one of the windows looked like fall, and the calendar said fall, so I think it probably is fall. Besides, there is no way, from looking at the calendar, that I can tell how long I have been here. I can tell how long I will have been here from now on, but that doesn't really help much unless I knew when I came here.

There is one good thing about the calendar, though, besides the lady in the underwear, and that is that I can tell how long it has been since someone has taken my sox. It is twelve days now, exactly the number of days since I discovered the calendar. Not once since I have been able to keep track of the time has anyone taken my sox. I almost hope they will, since I could then see if there is a pattern to the thefts, like I could do when I was still on the police force. I was a motorcycle patrolman, but I always used to hang out with the detectives, and sometimes they would ask me what I thought about some case or other. Once or twice I had a good idea, and they always used to kid me about it, when I went into the squad room. They even, one or two of them, started calling me Sherlock. Once there was even a deerstalker in my locker one morning. I don't know who put it there, to this day, but I have a good idea. I think it was Fred Doerhmann. He used to tease me more than the others, and we started out together on motorcycle patrol, so he knew me better than most of the other detectives. It was probably

Fred, but I'm not sure. I was never able to crack that case. I'll look into it when I get out, though, unless the trail is cold. It probably will be. And there weren't any witnesses.

Anyway, I am trying to remember some things that happened to me before I came here, mostly because I think I have to have some secret things to tell them about if I am ever going to get out. I am tempted to make some things up, but I don't think that would work, because they probably check with other people to see if you are telling the truth. I notice that I have two kinds of remembering, one of which is very clear, and comes on like a television picture, almost like I pushed a button in my head and POP, there it is, the memory of the thing I am remembering that happened to me a long time ago. I can sit in bed and watch it happen, just like it was not really me, in the picture of the thing I am remembering. Sometimes there is another kind of remembering, though, and I am not so sure about this one. It takes a long time, and it is not very clear. It comes only very slowly, and it is like I am washing a photo in a developing pan. The details are very fuzzy, and they get clearer and clearer, and I am not always sure that that thing happened, because I don't always remember all the details. There are some blank spaces, sometimes, and I try to fill them in, but I don't even know some of the people, sometimes. It is like somebody gave me a page with a lot of dots, like the kids' game, and I connect them up. Only there are no numbers, and I can make the picture almost anything I want, depending on how I choose to connect the dots and draw the lines. I have told them about both kinds. When I have one of those television sort of rememberings, they nod and they shake their heads and they make notes on their clipboards, if they have one of them along. The other kind they don't seem to pay any attention to at all. They just go "Ummm, yes, yes, I see." Then they ask me something that doesn't have anything to do with what I was just telling them. I think they must be talking to somebody about who I was before I came here, and they only care about memories that somebody else has told them about.

Once in a while I think about telling them something that happened here. That would be a good way to tell them something without giving away a secret from before, one of those I would need to make sure I am still walking the line properly. That might help me get out of here, but I might have to wait a very long time. Sometimes there is nothing at all that happens here, for weeks, I think, though I can't be sure since I have only known about the calendar for twelve days. That would not be a good way to get out, since everybody talks about something that happens here, if it does, and it would not be a secret. I could make something happen, in secret, I guess, but then they would know it was me that made it happen, if I tell them about it. There are some people who do things like that here, and they usually never tell anyone about them. Sometimes they write about them on the wall, in the men's room. Late at night. I do that, too, but they never catch me. I disguise my handwriting.

I wish I knew the exact kinds of things that have happened to me that they are interested in, because then I could tell them about some of them, and they would let me out of here. I have been thinking and thinking, but there aren't too many things that seem to make much difference, no matter how much I tell them about those things. I will have to ask my mother or my father about some things that happened to me a long time ago, things that only they know about me. I could tell them some of those things, and that would satisfy their curiosity. Maybe even enough to let me out. I will have to think about that a little, and maybe I can ask my father about some things when he comes to see me here the next time. Mostly, when I sit down and try to think of the kind of thing they want to know, I end up thinking about Louise. I don't like that too much, because it hurts to think about her. I don't like to hurt. Sometimes I know that she hurt me only because I hurt her and she didn't know any other way to get back at me. That is usually the way we get even with people who hurt us, by hurting them back. I am sure that is why Louise hurt me. To get even. I guess I don't blame her. I will decide when I get out of here.

I have been trying to think about my brother while I am here, too. Mostly because it doesn't hurt as much to think about him. He didn't hurt me, and he didn't put me here, either. I have a hard time thinking about him, though. I don't know his name. I mean, I am not sure that I know his name. If it is a name like George or Henry, or even Ralph, then I know it, but I don't know that it is his. If it is some name I have never heard, then I don't know it at all. There are some names I have heard that I don't like, but I don't think his name is one of those. I don't think his name is Schuyler. Or Austin. Or Mario. I don't care for those names, but I don't think they are his. They don't sound like the kind of names my father would inflict on anyone. Especially not someone in his family. On the other hand, George is not such a great name, but it would be all right if it were my brother's name. I will ask my father, the next time I see him, what my brother's name is, and he will tell me. I hope it isn't Austin. If it is, I would rather not know. Ralph would be okay, though. But not Mario.

Sometimes, when I think about how much I want to be able to leave here, I wonder whether I am doing the right thing. It is hard to admit, but maybe there is some reason why I ought to be here. I don't know what that might be, but it might be connected to the kind of thing I am supposed to remember. It is hard to know, but there could be something that I should remember that would make me feel better. Things are awful here, though, and I don't see any reason why I couldn't stay home and try to remember things there. It might even help, seeing familiar things when I look around. The things here are starting to get familiar, but it is not the same. They don't have any connections to the way things used to be in my life, and they can't help me remember something that happened. I know when I used to look at the wooden boat that my brother, Daniel, gave me, I used to think about him all the time. I would sit and look at the boat and try to imagine what it was like where he made it, out on the ocean. He used to write to me what it was like, long letters about how dark the sky is and how bright the stars get when you are in the middle of the ocean and all the lights on the shore are gone. I sort of knew what he meant, because it was like that on the troop carrier I was on in World War II. But that wasn't the same. I wasn't there by choice, so it was hard to know how I would feel about it if I was there because I wanted to be. He was, or at least he thought he was. I don't know if anyone can run away as much as Daniel has and be able to say they are anyplace at all just because they want to be. It has been a long time since I thought that way about him. At least I remember his name now, so it was worth it, I guess.

I shouldn't blame him for running away, even though I never did it. I always tried to stand up to things, even when they weren't the kind of thing I knew how to stand up to. Even now, here in this place against my will, I am able to do things that tell me that I have not surrendered completely. I don't mean that I am a troublemaker, because I am not. There is no way I would ever get away from here if I were a troublemaker, unless I ran away. Only Jimmy Cagney can make trouble in a place like this and still manage to get out, and that is only because he has friends on the outside who will put him up. If I make a break, I don't have anyplace to go, except home, and that is the first place they would look. That is always what happens to those who manage to run away from here. Of course, most of them are not in very good shape. They get confused, and they head for home, like lost dogs you read about in the papers, and there is always one of them waiting there on the front porch. I would hate for it to be like that when I get out, so I will wait, and try to walk that line and make them let me go their way.

There is another way, too, but I don't like that way at all. It is the reason we are not allowed to have radios, or electric razors here. One of us got tired of all the nonsense, and took his radio apart, to get even. Some of us were watching him, and we were all laughing and joking with him, while he took the back off and took all the tubes out, one at a time. He made a neat little pile of the tubes, then he started to take out the resistors, then the condensers, and pretty soon he had all these little piles of electronic parts. They were very pretty, especially the resistors, since they had all different-color stripes on them, red, green, blue, brown. The tubes were ugly, or at least not so pretty, because they had dark spots on their sides where they had been burned. He had listened to the radio a lot, and even though it was pretty new when he got it, the tubes were burned black on their sides, I'll bet.

After he had the parts arranged in little piles, he took the knobs from the front, and stuck the skinny parts in his nose. He said he was a radio, and everybody laughed, because he looked funny with the knobs in his nose. He took the wire, too, and he disconnected it from the inside of the radio, and he took the insulation and pulled it apart down the middle, tearing it along the little indentation between the wires. He took some insulation off each piece, about an inch or so, and was fooling around with the knobs, trying to improve his reception. He was clowning around so much that the wire knocked over my pitcher of water, where he had put it on the floor. We were all drinking from it, because it was hot in there, even though it was November. I remember how his face lit up when he felt the water soaking through his pants. He just smiled, almost like a clown on television, or a saint in a religious movie. Then he stuck one wire in each ear and plugged himself in. There was a pop, and the place got dark for a minute. When it got light again, some of them were standing around, and there was one fewer of us. That is the other way to get out of here. Officially, it was an accident, but we all know better. I wouldn't want to leave that way.

Not unless I have to.

EIGHTEEN:
Ella

THERE are some days when I just don't know what to make of Will. Even after more than forty years, I still find things about him that I don't understand, and I don't imagine that will ever change. It's almost as if he were always trying to catch me off guard, by finding the least likely thing to do, and doing that one thing precisely because he knows I'd never expect it of him. Sometimes he will do something that makes no sense at all, and the only reason he could possibly have is because he knows it will surprise me. I guess that makes him hard to live with, but it always seems worth it, no matter how much of a nuisance he manages to make of himself.

He can be as ornery a man as you'd ever want to meet, especially when he's dealing with someone he doesn't particularly like. I guess you'd have to say that includes most people, but if there's one thing I can say for him, it's that if he's your friend, it's for life. I know it wasn't easy for him to put up with John in the beginning, when John started to get peculiar notions, and a lot of men would have run off rather than deal with John's temper, but Will never batted an eye. Sometimes, when I think about them, and sort of put them up side by side in my mind, I can't imagine how I could have loved the two of them, they were so different from one another. I don't mean at the end, either, when John wasn't particularly likable. I mean at all times, from the first day I laid eyes on John Flynn until this morning, when I woke up next to Will Donovan. In all that time, I don't think I ever saw Will do something that reminded me of what John would have done in the same situation. It's almost like Will knows what John would have done and deliberately tries to do something he knows would have been out of character for John, just so he doesn't put me to mind of him. I know that's not what he does, but it's so peculiar how different they are, that it seems that way.

I never talked much to anybody about John, not even to Will. I guess especially to Will. Katherine knows about him, but she never knew him, and I never tried too hard to tell her about her father, since there was nothing I could change by talking about it. Will was sort of curious, but he never pressed me, and I have always been thankful for that. Will pretends that he's hard-hearted, but he knows how difficult it was for me to lose my husband, being pregnant at the time, so he just left it up to me to talk about it or not. So far it's always been not, and it's getting kind of late to change that now. Not that I've forgotten; not at all. Neither the good times, and there were a few, nor the bad times, of which there were more and more toward the end. I think I would have lost John even if the flu epidemic had never happened. There was something happening to him; he was changing so fast that the man who left for work in the morning never came home that night. There was always somebody new, wearing the same clothes, and looking pretty much the same, but I could tell it wasn't the same man just by looking at his eyes. Something was going out of them, and something else was taking its place. All the goodness was going out of him, and the meanness that was taking its place was like a shadow that was hanging in the back of his mind, even when he smiled. There was something hard about his eyes then, and they never smiled, no matter what the rest of his face did. I guess that's the main reason I never talked to Will about it. I can't explain it any better than that, and it's always better to be careful when you are talking about somebody you used to love, especially when you are talking to somebody you still love. It's so easy to hurt him, not meaning to at all, and you say something that doesn't mean what he takes it to mean, and he never knows to ask you, partly because he's afraid and partly because it never occurs to him to ask what you mean in the first place. People can be so sure they understand you that it never crosses their minds that they might not.

Will is like that, and he's so quick to jump to conclusions that I would die before I would mention John's name in front of him, even though they used to be the best of friends. John knew Will before I did, in fact; I never knew him until John brought him home to dinner one night, just after they started working the same shift on the railroad. I can still remember how John was teasing Will about this tattoo he has on his left arm. Most of the time you couldn't even see it, because it ended just about the spot where his sleeve would start if he had it rolled up. But this particular night, it was very warm, and they had put in a long day, so Will had rolled his sleeves up higher than normal. It wasn't much of a tattoo, just a heart with the name Sara in it, but John grabbed hold of it and wouldn't let go. Poor Will was so desperate; he kept looking at me, a total stranger, and begging with his eyes for me to change the subject or ask him to help with the dishes. I could see he was getting uncomfortable, so I tried to change the subject a little, but John either couldn't or wouldn't take the hint. It was before he started to change, so I think he just didn't realize that Will was uncomfortable. Later on, after he started to change, he would hang on to something like that with all his might, and the more he knew something irritated you, the more he would push it. But not then; unless it was just starting.

I remember when it first started to get bad between us. He came home from work, and he wasn't sick, not really, but I knew something was wrong. I thought he might be upset about the baby on the way, and I guess it wasn't the best approach to have served up the news over coffee and the morning paper, especially on a workday, but I had to do it that way even though I was so excited and didn't want to wait to tell him. That night, I could tell by the set of his jaw that it was risky to ask him anything at all, let alone what might be on his mind, but I had to know. He hadn't been thrilled by the first baby, and I always suspected that he had been uncertain about the circumstances surrounding my first pregnancy. I think he might even have suspected that he wasn't the father, though he never said that. It wasn't his way. He always liked to brood on things until he couldn't stand it any longer, then explode.

This time, I was afraid to ask him, because I knew that the question might plant a seed of doubt in his mind where there wasn't one; but I had to know what he was thinking. Besides, I suspected that he already had his doubts—he was so suspicious—so asking him wouldn't really be any worse than watering a seed already growing deep inside him. I didn't want him to think I had tried to trick him into the marriage by so desperate a lie, but I guess he might have believed that anyway, the way he was so jealous and seemed not to trust me at all. Mary had been his; there was no doubt of that in my mind, and I was the one to know it. The one in my belly was his, too. I knew it was a girl, and I had already settled on the name Katherine. I hadn't told him that in the morning, but I might as well have gone all the way, I realized now that it was too late. Not that John had been my first, but there had been only one other man, and there was so much time between Michael and John that Mary had to have been his. Any other possibility was unthinkable, at least to me. I think he was secretly glad when we lost Mary after two months, just because he couldn't stand to have raised another man's child. And there was no way on earth I could convince him she was his if he didn't want to believe it.

When he came in that night, he threw himself down on the old red sofa, and I steeled myself for the argument I knew was coming. We had been fighting every night for several weeks, and I guess I have to take my share of the blame for that. I had gotten so used to it that I had developed my own style, sort of wry and hesitant, where his was brutal and direct. Almost like I was trying to generate light where he was interested in heat. We never seemed to get anywhere, mostly because I would have had to fight like him to hurt him, and his anger just rolled off me because it was too heavy for me to take seriously. All that seemed to happen is that we would tire one another out and go to bed tense, exhausted, and no closer to a solution than when we started. I finally concluded that afternoon that things could not be allowed to continue the way they were going. I had to know what lay behind his hostility. I had made up my mind that, pregnant or not, if he didn't tell me what was bothering him, I would leave. And I'd have to do it, because he wouldn't believe I'd actually go until he heard the door close behind me.

"God, what a day, Ella."

"What happened? Nothing bad, I hope."

"God Almighty, what didn't happen? It's not bad enough down in the yards, but today we got two new men. Together, they don't have sense enough to come in out of the rain."

"Oh, now, it can't be that bad. You always say that whenever you get a new man. He's always the dumbest thing on two feet, according to you. For about two weeks, that is. Pretty soon he catches on, and six months after he starts, you're all sitting around in a bar complaining about the latest new man. And so it goes."

"Maybe so. Maybe that's been true, but not this time, I swear. These guys probably have to pay somebody to tie their shoes, for Christ's sake."

"Now, don't be so hard on them," I said. I was trying to keep him from getting too surly before I got to the things I wanted to discuss. "Maybe it just seems bad because you got two rookies at once. Do you think?"

"I don't know. Maybe. It's never happened before. Getting two new guys at once, I mean. Maybe you're right. I wish to God we didn't have to deal with it now, either, but we don't have any choice. Even with the new guys, we're undermanned. Since that damn Spanish flu started going around, we've lost seven men, and that's only been . . . what . . . four months, now?"

"Speaking of the flu, how is Will Donovan?"

"Getting better. He's supposed to be back next week, if he's up to it, and if I know Will, he'll be back whether he's up to it or not. He's lucky to be alive, I guess, but he shouldn't push it."

"Does he have a choice? He's not getting paid as it is, and they won't keep his job open too long, I don't suppose. Will they?"

"You're right about that. They sure as hell won't. He's lucky he still has a job to come back to. He's been out three weeks already, and if we hadn't lost so many men in the past few weeks, he'd be out of work for sure. But they can't afford to have too many green hands in the yards at one time or there'd be a fine mess. As it is, we had two near wrecks already this week, and it's only Wednesday. God knows how long we can continue getting by like this."

"Well, I'm sure things will get better when Will comes back to work."

"Yeah, I guess so. He's a good man, all right. But what's made you so damn high on him all of a sudden? Used to be you would hardly speak to me at all if I so much as stopped off for a beer with him. It's sure not like you to worry about him."

I could tell he was starting to let his suspicious nature get the better of him, and there was an edge creeping into his voice. I didn't want to fight about the wrong thing, but it was hard to keep myself from answering back when he got started like that.

"You know how you used to come in after drinking with him. And you also know you never saw the day it was one beer. No one I ever saw could put it away like Will Donovan, and I hope to God he's unique. In your acquaintance, at least. He must be, for all of that. We have been paying the rent every month."

"Are you sure?"

"What? That we've been paying the rent? Of course I'm sure. You don't think they'd carry us here too long if we hadn't, do you?"

"That's not what I mean, and you damn well know it." His teeth were starting to grind a little now, and the bright-blue vein in his left temple was beginning to throb. As much as I usually dreaded what I knew was coming, tonight I welcomed it. I was ready for him. He had given me the opening I was looking for and, by God, I was going to go right through it, without stopping to peek ahead at what might be on the other side, the way I usually did.

"Well, what *do* you mean, then?"

"You're quite the cute one, aren't you, pretending you don't know what everybody else in town knows."

"Oh, and what might that be? You're not the brightest man of my acquaintance, John Flynn, and I'm sure there's not a little knowledge around that has somehow escaped your notice."

His thick fingers were starting to dance on the arm of the sofa, and his neck was turning a red almost as dark as the upholstery. I was always afraid of his temper, but I had to get this over with, and if it meant taking the risk of making him uncontrollably angry, then I would have to do it. His voice was getting thick with anger, and it seemed to strangle in his throat as it descended to a whisper.

"I've no patience, tonight, Ella. Don't shilly-shally. You think I haven't heard the rumors around town?"

"What rumors, John? And have you heard, perhaps, that Will Donovan and I are the only two living fools willing to put up with your nonsense? For if you have, you can bet a few dollars on it; it's no rumor at all. It's the truth!"

"Don't provoke me, Ella! You know . . . ."

"I know I'm sick and tired of your coming home and arguing with me about gossip and idle speculation. I know that! And I know I'm not going to put up with it any more, John. You have been nearly eaten alive by God only knows what lately, maybe jealousy, though God knows you've no earthly reason for it."

"Damn it, woman, don't lie to me. I'm not stupid, you know."

"Now that's something I *didn't* know. Are people going around town spreading the rumor that you're not stupid? How silly! They should know better than that!"

I regretted that almost as soon as I said it, and I knew that I was letting my frustration get the better of me. If I was going to achieve anything, I would have to keep my wits about me.

But it was too late. Before I could say another word, he was up and headed for the door. I yelled to stop him, to say I was sorry, but he never heard me between the slamming of the door and the curses he was yelling as he went up the street. It was three hours before he came home, drunk as a skunk, and if it hadn't been for Will Donovan, he would never have gotten home at all. Will brought him in, and his face was all red from the cold, with angry welts on his cheeks. Will told me John had been crying, and the tears got frozen, but he never told me anything more about it, not even later. Two weeks afterward John was dead. The flu killed him, and to this day I'm not sure if he would have been spared if he hadn't gone out into the cold without his coat. I don't know whether it would have made a difference, but the funny thing about guilt is that if there's the slightest chance you were responsible for something, you decide you were. I don't know why it is; maybe just because we all feel so helpless that we take any opportunity we can find to feel that we control things, even just a little. It's a terrible thing to feel so helpless.

When John died, Will was a great help, and it wasn't easy for him to come around, because he knew, somehow, what John had been thinking. Even though he knew it wasn't true, there is something about an idea like that that has power over us. If someone suspects you of something, you do everything you can to prove the opposite, even though you know it isn't true in the first place. It was like Will thought John was looking over his shoulder, just waiting for the chance to say "I told you so!" Will never spoke about it to me, but there was something in the careful way he looked at me, like he thought someone was watching him, and waiting. In the end, his concern for me got the better of his fear of John's memory, and he asked me to marry him, mostly out of concern for Katherine, although she wasn't born yet.

He always used to refer to her as "the one on the way." It was like he loved Katherine sight unseen because he wouldn't let himself love me. And it was a long time before he got over that. Some things you never do get over, I guess. Just like I still think about John, and feel a little guilty about his death, I think Will still feels there might have been a grain of truth in John's suspicions, even if neither of us knew it.

NINETEEN

"Now remember, Will, I want you to be on your best behavior when the Reverend Berland gets here," Ella said sternly.

"I don't see why I have to be here at all," Will responded surlily. "I'd rather take a walk instead of sitting around with that blowhard. He's only going to try to get you to do something for nothing. Worse yet, he might try to sell you something."

"Are you going to start already? Why can't you give the man a chance? He means well, and he tries to do good for those who need it most."

"If he wants to do good for me, he can move to California."

"Now stop it," Ella snapped. "I don't want to hear another word out of you. You'll just get yourself all worked up and you'll have to start something just to prove how clever you think you are."

"You don't have to be clever to know a fool when you see one."

"Shush! Why don't you find something to occupy yourself until Dr. Berland gets here?" Ella asked. "Go clean the basement or something, will you?"

"What? And have to shake hands with your almighty minister with dirt all over me? Do you want me to make a good impression on him or don't you?"

"I don't think that's possible. All I want is for you to avoid making a scene when he's here. That's good enough, thank you!"

"All right, all right!" Will laughed. "I'll be in the basement. Call me when he gets here. Or, better yet, after he leaves."

He went down to the basement with a thoughtful expression, as if the very act of navigating the cellar stairs was a problem requiring close concentration. In the basement, the gloom

213

seemed heavy, the glow cast by the lighting seemed to be swallowed up within inches by some unseen presence. Beyond the partition that separated the train room from the storage room of the basement, the contents were as they had been for many years, a fabric of shadow and memory, indiscriminately jumbled together, and they seemed less distinct than usual today. He had no intention of doing any work, since he believed that greeting the minister with work-blackened hands would be a mistake, not so much because it would make a bad impression as because it would, in some ill-defined fashion, give Berland the upper hand in what Will, despite Ella's plea, viewed as the impending confrontation.

Will had been leary of Edward Berland ever since he had arrived to minister to the parishioners of the Third Street Presbyterian Church. There was something in the man's manner that didn't quite set well with him. He had to admit that the man had an extraordinary amount of energy, but, insofar as he could tell, very little of it was channeled into the more traditional concerns of the ministry.

For several years, Berland had been drumming up support for a small aviation company of which he was president and prime mover. For some reason Will had been unable to fathom, the minister was obsessed by lighter-than-air craft, and the principal purpose of his company was the development of an improved form of dirigible. It seemed to skeptical observers, among whom Will could be counted, that most of the cleric's free time, and a good deal of time that should not otherwise have been free, was invested in flitting about from place to place and potential investor to potential investor in attempts to raise cash for the company's experiments. When times were flush for the small firm, he even went so far as to engage the services of armed guards, culled from parish volunteers and captained by two retired army men, who were posted outside the hangar where his prototype was stored whenever the heavy canvas wrappings were to be removed for some additional modifications to the constantly evolving, though seldom-tested, design. This uncommon devotion to his project troubled Ella not at all, but Will was considerably more suspicious of the man in general, and of his pursuit of financial support in particular. Will couldn't care less about the effect of any impropriety on the other parishioners, but his concern for Ella was unbounded, and he knew that she would be crushed if the minister was abusing the trust of his flock.

Like Will, Ella had not been much of a church-goer until Emma's death, but where Will had merely been confirmed in his skeptical attitude toward the Almighty, Ella had turned to religion to relieve the burden of her daughter's death. Never one to go halfway, she had first felt as if she had been abandoned; then, when the shock had worn off, she plunged headlong into the church and its activities, both charitable and social, and a good deal of her time seemed to be spent preparing for some sale or other, or cleaning up after one. Originally, Will had not been concerned about the intense way in which Ella had gotten involved in church affairs, but the arrival of Berland, who seemed to be a very different sort of man from his predecessor, had changed all that.

Sitting on a stack of cartons in the basement, Will felt a little like a banished child, consigned to the basement for behavioral reasons, and he couldn't shake the feeling that something unfortunate was going to happen when Berland arrived. Not that he was intending to be contrary, but somewhere in the back of his mind was the nagging suspicion that Berland was going to get on his nerves in a way that he would be unable to ignore.

He walked past the toy trains and into the storage room, straining his eyes against the gloom, but he was unable to derive any comfort or distraction from his surroundings. On the contrary, nearly everything his eye lit upon was symptomatic of what he perceived to be his own failure. The room was cluttered with things broken or past use, things not quite whole and never to be mended, things that had no use at all. There were jars full of bolts without nuts, and nuts without bolts, coffee cans of the old flat nails no longer used by any self-respecting carpenter, rusty-lidded paint cans, their sides covered with faded drippings of no longer fashionable colors and bastard tones he had mixed himself.

Peeking out from the litter could be seen the frame of an old painting, the picture itself long gone, that he had been saving against the time he would discover the perfect illustration to hang in the kitchen. Now chipped and split along one corner, it stared vacantly into a pile of yellowing newspapers. Will walked over to the dust-covered frame and pushed it idly aside to get at the papers, the topmost of which he picked up carelessly, only to have it fall apart in his hands. He picked up the next, more carefully, and made his way back to the light and began to turn the pages. The headline of the paper, from 1940, blared about a long-since-forgotten fire in the heart of the city, a department store burning nearly to the ground. He did not remember the blaze, and the store itself was gone, so he turned to the inside pages, scanning casually for something of interest. He saw names of politicians remembered dimly, if at all, incidents that had no doubt formed the basis for several days' worth of small talk, tragedy and meaningless violence, all now reduced to yellow paper so brittle that it could barely support its own weight in his hands.

He turned, on sudden inspiration, to the obituary page, and quickly scanned the column and a half for familiar names, but saw none. *So that's what it all comes down to. You do what you can for as long as you can, get yourself condensed into fifty or sixty words, and twenty years later nobody even knows who the hell you were. Me, too,* he thought. *That's what I'm heading for, and all of the sweat, bruised thumbs, and blisters on my feet, the headaches and colds, all of it, the pain, and the joy, too, all gone. What's the use of any of it?* And he had no answer. He returned the old paper to its stack and stared into the distant dust and gloom of the basement, which seemed to recede as if he were traveling at incredible speed. Everything around him seemed to swirl and grow tiny, then tinier still. He shook his head to clear it and looked up at the bulb overhead. It, too, seemed to be receding, and he grew dizzy with the sensation of overwhelming motion. He grabbed hold of a pile of cartons in order to maintain his balance, and as suddenly as it had come, the giddy nausea was gone. He took a deep breath and put one unsteady leg out, still clinging to the cartons for support. His head was now clear, and he breathed deeply again, then expelled it in a long sigh. I *must* be getting old, he thought. I never felt anything like *that* before.

He walked back toward the cellar stairs, extending his hand toward the nearest support, and gave a sigh of relief as he reached the bottom step, where he could grab the banister securely. He climbed the stairs carefully lest his dizziness return and catch him in mid-ascent. He did not care for the prospect of falling and breaking a bone on the hard wooden steps.

He got to the top landing just in time to hear the front doorbell. He was undecided whether to leave the basement or go back down. He preferred not to confront the minister while feeling so vulnerable. The bell rang again, and he heard Ella running from the kitchen. "Coming, coming!" she sang, and her heavy tread thudded past him on the other side of the cellar door. The bell rang again, and he could hear Ella muttering to herself, "Land sakes! I said I was coming, didn't I? Hold onto your hat."

Will chose to sit on the top step, where he hoped to regain his composure before venturing out to meet the unwelcome guest. He heard the mumbled pleasantries exchanged by Ella and the minister, gradually growing in volume as she led him back toward the kitchen. There was a burst of illumination as Ella yanked open the cellar door and called to Will to come up. She stopped in amazement as she saw Will sitting on the step, and asked, "What in the world are you doing there?"

"Just sat down to get me breath is all," Will lied.

"Well, I hope you didn't work too hard down there," Ella said.

"Don't worry about that. Just a little winded is all."

"Come out here and say hello to Dr. Berland."

Will got reluctantly to his feet and turned into the glare, where he could see the minister's supercilious smile hovering over Ella's shoulder like a pink balloon, and pushed Ella gently aside to grasp the minister's outstretched palm.

"How do, Reverend," he mumbled. "Nice to see you again."

"My pleasure, Will," Berland boomed heartily, "my pleasure, indeed."

"Why don't we all sit in the kitchen and have something hot to drink," Ella said. "It must be cold out there. The weather report said we might even get some more snow tonight. I think some tea or coffee would be just the thing."

She went on into the kitchen, followed by the two men. Without ceremony, Will pulled a chair out from the table and nodded to the minister to do the same while Ella went on to the pantry. As he sat down, Berland unbuttoned his fashionable suit jacket and revealed a gaudy silk vest and an elaborate gold buckle on his belt. His chubby, well-formed hands were of the same pinkish hue as his cheeks, and Will observed that they were rather soft-looking and well manicured.

"Well, Will, how's retirement agreeing with you? You look well," Berland said cheerfully.

"I'm getting used to it all right, I guess," Will answered.

"I'd say. Ella told me you were not adjusting too well at the beginning, but it looks like you've gotten over that pretty well."

"Yes, I guess so," Will said distractedly, glaring toward the pantry where Ella was busy with the coffee.

"I had hoped we'd start to see you at church on Sundays, now that you have more time," Berland continued.

"I'm not much of a churchgoer, Mr. Berland," Will observed with restraint. "Never have been and never will be, I guess."

"You know, we have a number of interesting programs for older people at the church. They're nondenominational, and we just might have something that would interest you."

"I don't think so," Will said firmly. "I don't really have much free time, Mr. Berland. I have all I can handle right here. I'm always just one step ahead of Ella and her ideas, anyway."

"Now, Will! You'll give the Reverend Berland the wrong impression of me. Don't pay any attention to him, Dr. Berland. The truth is, he spends most of his time trying to get *out* of work that needs doing."

The minister laughed heartily, but Will just glowered. He wasn't happy to be made sport of for the benefit of the minister, but he bit his tongue. Ella had finished preparing the coffee and brought in two cups, which she set in front of her husband and the minister. She bustled back out to the pantry and returned with milk and sugar.

"Now, I'll just get my tea and I'll be right back," she announced.

She returned with the tea and pulled aside the curtain to examine the sky before taking her seat. "It certainly does look like snow," she observed. "I hope it isn't too bad, if we do get any. People do so much traveling during the holidays, it would be a shame if the weather interfered."

She took a long, careful sip of the hot tea, then asked, "Would you like some sugar, Ella?" "I think so, two teaspoons, please!" she answered, and reached for the sugar bowl, but Will covered her hand, saying, "Now don't think just because we have company you can get away with that! I've told you that more than once."

The minister, who had been smiling at Ella's dialogue with herself, was surprised by Will's vehemence. He looked quizzically at the older man, who wrested the sugar bowl from Ella's grasp and placed it out of reach. "If you want something to sweeten your tea, use saccharine."

"Oh, Will, a little sugar won't hurt me!" Ella said imploringly.

"No, a little sugar won't hurt. But I don't like the idea of your using the Reverend here as an excuse to indulge yourself."

"Will, I don't think she's using me as an excuse," Berland said.

"Maybe not," Will responded, "but she shouldn't have the sugar, just the same."

He got up to retrieve the small bottle of saccharine tablets from atop the refrigerator and set it down with a crack, just beside Ella's tea. She jumped as the bottle struck the table, and the minister also flinched at the report. Unscrewing the top of the bottle, Ella whistled to cover her embarrassment. "Well, I didn't really want the sugar anyway. I guess it's just as well I have a doctor in residence here. I'd be breaking the rules pretty often, I guess."

Taking her hint, Berland said, "You're a pretty lucky woman, Ella, to have Will to look out for you. A lot of husbands wouldn't take the trouble to keep an eye on something like that."

"I know and, believe me, I'm grateful," Ella said, glaring at Will over the steaming teacup. Will remained silent, unwilling to make things any easier for his wife. He knew that she had been trying to make an ally of the minister, but Berland had declined the offer to join forces. Will sensed it was because the minister had a larger purpose in mind, and he determined to watch and see what it might be.

"What did you have to talk to me about, Dr. Berland?" Ella asked.

"Oh, yes! I knew there was something I wanted to ask you," he replied, clearing his throat and imbuing his voice with additional resonance. "I need your help for an affair we're planning at the church next month."

"What kind of affair?" Ella asked.

"We're planning a bazaar, for charity of course, and I was wondering if you'd be willing to lend a hand, since I have several other things to attend to in the next few weeks."

"I'd be happy to," Ella said. "What can I do?"

"Well, I'm not sure exactly. I know that we expect several hundred people each day, and we'll have to have plenty of food on hand, ice cream, cake, you know, the kind of thing people can eat while they roam around. We plan to have several games of chance, wheels, ring toss, that sort of thing, and sales of some secondhand items, some raffles. The usual."

"Bingo?" Will chimed in.

"Oh, no," the minister said, "not Bingo. That's too . . ."

"Catholic?" Will ventured.

"Well, not exactly," the cleric stammered.

"But sort of?" Will persisted.

"Well, yes! I mean no offense to our Catholic brethren, of course," he added hurriedly. "But they do have a lock on that sort of thing, and I don't think we'd get too many people. After all, they can play Bingo three nights a week as it is. We need something different, which will attract people, something they can't get all the time."

"I think it's a good idea, Dr. Berland," Ella said, attempting to pave the way for his escape. "I always enjoy the rummage sales, and games are a nice idea, too."

"Yes, we're quite enthusiastic about the idea," Berland said. "Do you think you'll be able to help?"

"Of course!" Ella replied.

"Of course!" Will mimicked.

"Will!" Ella reproved. "You'll have to excuse him . . . He's not himself today."

"Well, I don't want to impose on you, Ella. If it's too much of a burden, by all means say so."

"No, no, not at all. I'd be delighted to help."

"Wonderful! I'll tell Mrs. Berland that she'll be able to count on your help. She specifically asked that I try to get you on the committee. She thinks very highly of you."

"Why, that's nice," Ella chirped. "Do thank her for me."

"Is that about it?" Will asked.

Ella shot him a warning look, but Will ignored her. He looked inquiringly at the minister, who looked back in bewilderment. He sensed that Will was unhappy with the discussion, but wasn't quite sure why.

"Well, actually, there is something else I wanted to discuss. With both of you," he emphasized.

"What's the matter," Will demanded, "you short of volunteers down at the church?"

"Well, it's got nothing to do with the church, actually. It's more of a . . . ah . . . business matter, I guess you might say."

"Aha, now we're getting down to the heart of the matter, eh, Reverend," Will said, nodding.

"Why, what do you mean?"

"Well, I was just telling Ella before you got here how you were probably just using this church thing as an excuse to come see us. I said, 'He probably really wants to cut us in on a big deal of some kind; you'll see.' Didn't I say that, Ella?" Will grinned.

"You most certainly did *not*, Will Donovan. Don't pay any attention to him, Reverend Berland. He's just teasing you," Ella said nervously.

"Actually, Ella, he's not far wrong."

"There, aha, there, what'd I'd tell you, Ella. We're gonna be rich. The Reverend here will see to that. God's no slouch as a businessman, and Mr. Berland here is his right-hand man. Isn't that right, Reverend?" Will asked smugly.

"Well, I don't know if I'd say that," Berland stammered.

"No, of course you wouldn't," Will blurted out. "Of course you wouldn't! But you don't mind if *I* say it, do you? You're a humble man, Reverend, but you have no objection to the truth being spoken, do you?"

"Will, why don't you keep still and let Dr. Berland tell us whatever it is he has to tell us," Ella snapped.

"Of course, you're right, Ella," Will apologized. "I just lost my head there for a minute. I've always wanted to be rich, and this is my chance. I can *smell* it. Go ahead, Reverend, tell us *all* about it," Will said, making a great show of rubbing his hands gleefully.

"Well, it's nothing really," the minister began tentatively.

"You're too modest," Will interjected. "Of course it's something. Of course it is. What is it? Come on, tell us now! Don't keep us guessing like this; it's not polite."

"Will, will you *please* shut up?" Ella said angrily.

Will mumbled another apology for the cleric's benefit and winked at Ella, as if to say "Didn't I tell you so?"

"Go ahead, Dr. Berland," Ella said. "Will will behave himself, I'll see to that."

"Well, as you know," the minister began again, then paused to clear his throat self-consciously. He knew that Will was egging him on for some reason. "As you know, I have for some time been involved with a small firm doing aeronautical research. We have, ah, been exploring the feasibility of using lighter-than-air ships as a means of expanding the possibilities of the ministry, and . . ."

"I knew it, Ella," Will shouted, "I knew it. *Blimps!* He wants to cut us in on the blimps action."

"Will, hush! I'm sorry, Reverend Berland. I don't know what's the matter with him today. He's been carrying on like this all morning. Please go on." She shot Will a deadly look over the rims of her glasses, and he returned her venomous glance with a beatific smile.

"Will is very close, actually, Ella. We—that is Aeroministry Research Corporation—have been underfunded, and we have nearly exhausted the available capital. We have decided—the members of the board and myself, that is, have decided—that the best method of raising additional cash would be to sell stock to interested investors. These would be private shares, of course, since our program of research and development is largely secret, and we'd like it to stay that way."

"Of course you would." Will nodded. "No sense in letting anyone know what you're up to if you can help it, is there? Especially the SEC, eh?" Will grinned, shooting a vicious poke of the elbow into the minister's ribs just as he was about to sip his coffee. The coffee sloshed over the rim of the cup and splattered all over the saucer on the table beneath it. "Sorry, Reverend. Or should I say Captain?" Will chortled. "I hope I didn't get any coffee on that fancy vest of yours." Then he added hopefully, "I didn't, did I?"

"No, no, I'm fine, Will. And may I say that I appreciate your enthusiasm. This is an extraordinary opportunity."

"I'll bet, I'll bet. Say, I guess there's no truth to the rumor that there's one born every minute, is there? I mean, they must be hard to come by these days, eh?"

"Pardon?" the minister said, puzzled.

"Suckers, Reverend, suckers. What did you think I meant? After all, that's what you take us for, isn't it? Well, I have a better idea. Why don't you just pass the basket? Call yourselves Blimps for Jesus, or something like that. Boy, I bet the money would come rolling in then."

"Mr. Donovan, I don't know what you're trying to insinuate, but . . ."

"Like *hell* you don't, buddy. Like hell you don't," Will cut in. "I've had your number for a long time."

"Now see here . . ."

"No, sir, *you* see here! I resent you abusing the trust and the faith of my wife, buster. But I'm not going to sit still and watch you take advantage of her any longer."

"But . . ."

"Hang on, I'm almost finished!" Will had been steadily raising his voice and was now nearly shouting. "It's one thing for you to talk her into giving up her time and working herself half to death for all those church schemes of yours. At least some people get something out of it, even if it *is* something the damn church ought to be paying for with all that money you raise. She feels good about helping folks, and I appreciate that. But it's a horse of another color when you start coming around here asking us to take money we don't have and stuff it into one of those holy balloons of yours."

"Mr. Donovan," the minister said icily, "are you suggesting that I have been behaving improperly?"

"I'm not suggesting anything but what I've heard around. I don't know whether it's true or not, and I don't give a good God damn, but you'll get none of *my* money, for all of that. No more, do you hear me. I have sat back long enough and watched you pull the wool over her eyes. But you never fooled me, not for a minute. And I'll tell you another thing: I've had it up to here with your holier-than-thou attitude. You walk around like you're the greatest thing on God's earth. You think you're so much better than the people you're supposed to be helping. I don't know much about churchgoing, but I know enough about the Bible to tell you Jesus never had men like you in mind for his work. Not by a damn sight!"

"Mr. Donovan, I resent what you're trying to imply!"

"Resent it all you damn please, but I'll thank you to go outside and do your resenting. I won't have you in my house a minute longer."

"Will," Ella managed to whisper. "Please, don't say any more!"

"Don't worry, Ella, I've said all I'm going to say to this bag of hot air."

The minister rose stiffly, his back rigid, and turned to Ella.

"I know Mr. Donovan isn't speaking for you, Ella. I understand men like him. I've met them before."

"Reverend Berland," Ella stammered, "I'm dreadfully sorry, I . . ."

"Never mind, Ella. Never you mind. This needn't interfere with our relationship at all. I can make allowances for fools as well as the next man."

"Fool is it?" Will snarled, rising to his feet. "I'll show you who's a fool. Just step outside, and you'll see who's a fool." He clenched a fist and shook it in front of the blushing cleric's face. Will was trembling with rage, and the minister was clearly frightened. His doughy cheeks were quivering as though they would fall off the bone. He backed away from Will, half raising one arm as if to ward off an impending blow. He nodded curtly to Will, then said, "I'll find my own way out, Ella. My wife will call you. Good afternoon to you both." He strode stiffly toward the front of the house, after pausing in the kitchen doorway, turning to Will, and saying, "By the way, Mr. Donovan, if I should hear any of your accusations repeated, my lawyer will be in touch with you."

"Lawyer is it?" Will shot back. "I'm glad to see you're interested in more than one kind of windbag. Lawyer, eh. Well, let him come see me. I can give him a hundred people to talk to about what I've said. Who knows? He might even find out whether any of it's true, don't you think?" He winked at the minister, who reddened still further and turned on his heel, striking his elbow on the door frame.

"Now don't go telling other people I broke your arm. I never touched you," Will called after his retreating figure. "Though God knows I would have liked to," he mumbled.

He turned his attention to Ella, who had slumped forward, resting her face in her hands, which were supported by elbows propped rigidly on the table. He walked over to her and put a hand gently on her shoulder.

"How could you *do* that to me?" she sobbed. "How could you embarrass me like that?"

"I can't say I'm sorry for what I said to *him,* but I didn't mean to hurt you," Will said softly. "I just can't stand to see him make a fool of you like that. And God knows how many others he takes advantage of the same way."

"Oh, Will, you're terrible. You're a cruel and thoughtless man sometimes. Even if you *did* hear those things you said, you didn't have to repeat them, and to his face!"

Will pulled a chair over to the corner of the table and sat down, pushing Ella's hand away from her face as he did so. "Look at me," he said. "Look at me, I say!"

Reluctantly, she turned her face toward him, and he reached out to wipe away the tears that were running down her cheeks.

"Ella, as God is my witness, I never meant to hurt you. But that man is no good. He takes advantage of his position, and abuses those who can't believe that a minister could possibly be no good. I've never seen it to fail! If you give somebody too much trust, they cheat you. One way or another, they cheat you. And people like you make it easy for people like him. It's like taking candy from a baby. For Pete's sake, Ella, didn't you hear the man? He was asking us to give him *money,* and for *what.* A bunch of *blimps,* for crying out loud! That's not what ministers are for! If he's so god-almighty fascinated by the damn things, fine, but he shouldn't go around as a minister asking people to pay for them."

"I know how you feel, Will," she sobbed. "I do. But did you ever stop, even for a minute, and think that maybe what *I* feel is important, too?"

"You know I have! I've never once said anything against your going to church, even *his* church. I know it's important to you, and I respect that. But the whole point is that what he was talking about had nothing to *do* with church. He knows you can't make the distinction, and he counts on that. I won't let that happen, that's all there is to it. Did *you* ever stop and consider the possibility that I might be *right*? What then? What then? What if I'm *right,* Ella? How would you feel then? Wouldn't it be *worse* for you then? Look at me, now! Well, wouldn't it?"

"I don't know," she whispered, "I don't know. But you *can't* be right, don't you see, you *can't* be right. He's a good man."

"We'll talk about it some more later," Will said gently. "Why don't you drink your tea before it gets cold?" He stroked her hair absently as he stared out the window, and noticed that it had begun to snow.

TWENTY

The new year began with a burst of bright sunshine, whose fire danced and glittered on the mounds of snow in the yard. It was cold, and Will's breath began to cloud the window as he stood, his eyes hooded against the glare, watching a few stray birds bouncing aimlessly on the hard, white crust, nearly two feet above the seeds they knew he had scattered over the lawn in late autumn. The dizziness he had experienced in the cellar the morning of his argument with Berland was back, and he rubbed carelessly but insistently at the base of his neck where he had felt an uncomfortable throbbing ever since he got up to look out at the snow.

He wondered whether the snow would thaw in time for the spring flowers to be out by Easter, and the probability seemed to diminish even as the clarity of his vision receded behind the thickening haze on the inside of the glass. He rubbed idly at the fog, and pulled his hand away in amazement at the fine ridge of frost that grew like a tiny glacier and steadily advanced ahead of his fingers. I guess it doesn't much matter, he thought; I've got time, if I've got anything at all. He laughed in soft irony, and Ella, who was comfortably ensconced in the depths of an old easy chair, looked at his broad back.

"Did you say something?" she asked.

"No," he answered unconvincingly.

"Anything wrong?"

"Not really."

"Want to talk about it?"

"Nope!"

"Okay, but you know where to find me if you should change your mind," Ella said.

Will let the lace curtain fall from his hand and stood looking through it for a moment, blinking away the ghostly image of the winter that hung before his vision. He turned and walked over to the sofa, grunting as he eased himself down.

"I was just thinking, that's all," he explained.

"About what?" Ella asked, folding her newspaper into her lap and peering at him expectantly over the top of her reading glasses.

"The flowers. Nothing much."

"What about the flowers?" Ella persisted.

"I was just thinking how it seemed like the snow might not thaw in time for the spring flowers, that's all. It seems like that snow has frozen so hard that it's turned to stone. It just sits there, getting gray, getting covered, then getting gray all over again. It doesn't get much deeper, but it seems to get more permanent by the day."

"You always get that way this time of year. I guess most people do. All summer long, they complain about the heat, and keep saying how they can't wait for winter to come, and as soon as it really gets here good and proper, they can't wait for it to leave. Never satisfied, any of them!"

"And I suppose you are?" Will asked.

"You suppose I am what?"

"Satisfied?"

"Reasonably so, I expect, yes," Ella said.

"Now, don't go getting your back up. I told you I wasn't thinking about much, but you kept at me, and now you want to start a fight."

"I don't either. I was just wondering what was on your mind. You've seemed so . . . preoccupied."

"Not really. Just getting old is all," Will said softly.

"Are you sure there's nothing more to it than that? Something you're not telling me that I ought to know about?"

"Not a thing! You know I've never been one to keep secrets. No way I could ever hide anything from you even if I wanted to. Not for long, anyway!"

"That's news to me." Ella laughed.

"Well, it's true." Will smiled. "God knows I've tried, but somehow, sooner or later, whether I want to or not, I tell you every damn thing that runs through my head."

"That's just a convenient fiction we've lived by all these years," Ella said. "It's true you've told me things when I've insisted on knowing, but that's only because I knew when not to ask you anything."

"Well, it hasn't hurt us any, has it? I mean, we've been together for a long time now."

"Maybe so, but you've changed a lot over the past year. I look at you sometimes and I don't even recognize you. You've changed, and you've shut me out. Shut me out of things that I ought to be a part of. You look the same, but you're not yourself. I don't think I know you at all, somehow. It scares me—I don't mind telling you—but I don't know what to do about it."

"You've never mentioned it before," Will protested. "Why all of a sudden now? I haven't changed overnight, and I'm not convinced I've changed at all."

"You don't have to be convinced. I *live* with you, and I can see it with my own eyes."

"Well, I wouldn't worry about it. It'll go away when the weather warms up a bit, whatever it is."

"I certainly hope so," Ella said uncertainly.

"Take my word for it, it will. Or I will, anyway. The new me, that is."

"We'll see," Ella said, shaking her head.

"Now, how about you and me play a game of canasta? What do you say?"

"But it's so early, Will!" Ella protested. "I have a lot of things to do. Can we do it later, after lunch?"

"If you say so," Will grunted. "I just thought it would take your mind off things, that's all. Help you get introduced to the new me, or whatever. We can play later, any time you like, or not at all if you don't really want to."

Ella got up from her seat and headed slowly toward the kitchen, saying, "I'll be done soon, about half an hour. All right?"

"I'm not going anywhere." Will's noncommittal grunt drifted in her wake, barely audible over the swish of her housedress. When she was gone, he sat staring at the glare outside, barely able to fight its way through the thick lace of the curtains over the dining-room windows. He got up and walked toward the glowing rectangle, pulled the shades down one by one, tugging each one firmly down to the windowsill with an air of theatrical finality, then walked indifferently back to the living room, where he sank into the soft cushions of the sofa, snuggling himself precisely into the still-visible depressions his body had left.

He stared uncertainly around him, and the shadowy objects that loomed dimly in the obscurity assumed a menacing unfamiliarity, as alien as a lunar landscape. The dull throbbing he had first felt while staring out at the snow was still with him and seemed, if anything, to be more insistent. He pressed one hand absently to the base of his neck, and that seemed to relieve the pain somewhat, but it was still noticeable, dull but continuous. He found it distracted him, and he tried to make his mind a total blank. He knew that reading would only make the pain worse. So quiet and motionless was he, there in the darkness, that he seemed to be of it more than hidden by it, while the distant pounding in his ears grew to a steady thunder.

Ella, wiping her hands on her apron and untying it as she came through the door, did not notice him at first. She jumped in fright at a groan, reaching for the light switch as she warned him, "Now don't you go trying to scare me, Will Donovan. I'm not one of your gullible grandchildren. I know you too well to fall for any of your nonsense." She turned toward him, smiling, and blinking away the bright blindness caused by the sudden flash of illumination. Will groaned again, as if reluctant to give up his joke, and pitched forward to the floor in front of her.

"Now, you be careful." She laughed. "You're not as young as you used to be, you know!"

He didn't answer her, and she reached down to shake his shoulder in exasperation. Then, seeing the bilious green foam around his lips, she cried out, "Oh my God, Will, no, Will," and she knew, even as she ran screaming for the phone, that it was too late. Will Donovan was dead.

PART 2

TWENTY-ONE

WILLIE was slumped in his favorite chair, *Sports Illustrated* face down in his lap, his head nodding in ever-deepening plunges toward the splayed magazine, when the phone rang. He looked at the clock, and couldn't believe that the caller could be trying to reach *him*, not so early on New Year's Day. He reached idly for the insistent instrument and smiled at the recollection of his father's wild denunciations of the telephone, triggered by a simple wrong number or a persistent salesman who refused to let go long after Will had resorted to profanity in an effort to make it clear that he was just not interested in storm windows. Before he even had the receiver to his ear, he knew it had to be bad news, and the tone of Katherine's voice confirmed it.

"Willie, it's Dad," she said huskily.

"What is it? What's the matter?" he demanded.

"He's had a stroke," she said, struggling to maintain her composure.

"Well, where is he? What hospital? Is he all right?"

"He's dead, Willie. He's dead," she sobbed.

"No, he can't be! Where's Mom? Are you sure?"

"It's true, Willie. Mom's sleeping. The doctor was here, and he gave her a sedative. Andy and I are with her."

"I'll be right over," Willie shouted, his voice breaking with the desperation of one who wants to believe the impossible, that he can prevent something already done. "I'll be right over," he repeated, this time barely whispering.

"No," Katherine said. "Don't come now; there's nothing you can do. I'll call you when Mother wakes up. She'll need you then."

"I'm coming anyway," he said, as if to defy her was to deny

the substance of her news. Numbly, he replaced the receiver in its cradle and stared toward the window, the glare from the bright morning stinging his eyes. He started to rise, and the magazine slipped to the floor with a soft hiss of its slick pages. Sinking back with a groan, he stared dumbly at the watch Will had given him for Christmas, the week before. Its hands seemed motionless and suddenly its ticking was the only sound in the room besides his labored breathing. The two sounds seemed to swell and subside, swell and subside, like waves slapping the side of a derelict ship.

His mind began to race over the past, images of his father flickering and flitting at blinding speed, like an old newsreel run amok. He was searching for that one moment when he could have or should have done something differently, some small thing that would have changed the course of time, shifted the present moment into some other dimension and allowed things to continue as they had been before the telephone irreparably altered his personal history. The images themselves were black and white, as if the life and color had been drained from them, bleached out by the same insidious force that had deprived his father of breath and beating heart.

He turned his thoughts to his mother, and he saw her as she must be now, lying drugged and nearly lifeless herself, sleeping, though not quietly, her mind as blank as his father's own, wiped clean for the moment of the terrible pain of her loss, perhaps dreaming in desperate hope that what had happened that morning was also a dream, something horrible that would be obliterated by the first flutter of her eyelids, lingering only as a nightmare lingers.

He turned back to his father and sifted through the jumbled, senseless memories for the essence of the man, some single event that embodied the best and worst of him, some time and place where he was most alive, and would stay so, forever insulated from the horrible reality in which he no longer moved. Willie was unable to choose such a time, such an event, as if his father's maverick personality refused to allow itself to be fixed in a single facet. He remembered instead the time he and Daniel had stumbled upon their father's best-kept secret, buried in the darkest part of the cellar. It was strange that an incident in which Will participated only through representation by a thing he had made should produce the strongest impression on his son at this moment, and yet it was peculiarly typical of the range and kind of influence Will had wielded over his family that he could control them as well in his absence as in his presence.

Willie, in his recollection, was so distant, so removed, that he seemed a stranger to his own memory. He remembered the small room at the front of the cellar where it all happened. It was an area that he and Daniel seldom visited, and the room huddled in its shadows and cobwebs until one rainy afternoon when they were trapped indoors and restless for something to do.

They had been getting on Ella's nerves with their repeated giggling fits and roughhousing forays which threatened to destroy most of the furniture. Her patience finally frayed, and she banished them to the cellar with a pair of brooms and strict instructions not to return until they had thoroughly cleaned it. Grateful for something to do that would get them out from under their mother's eye and allow them to burn off the excess energy bred of their confinement, they threw themselves into the work.

During the first half hour, dust rose in palpable clouds, and rattles followed clunks up through the floorboards. The clouds quickly dimmed the stark illumination from the bare bulbs overhead, but the strenuousness of their labor soon began to dampen the enthusiasm that had marked the opening of their assault. It was only the certainty that they would not be allowed out of the underworld until their mother was satisfied that enabled them to push on.

Winded, they decided to stop for a breather, and Willie bounded up the steps, to return shortly with a pitcher of lemonade and the news that their mother had gone out to do some shopping and would not return until three o'clock. She had left a note under the lemonade in the refrigerator, warning them to be finished with their chore by that time. With the peculiar confidence of children working at an unpleasant task, they decided that far less time was needed than they had been allowed, and they began to horse around, tossing the less lethal objects that came to hand at one another with sufficient force to break a bone or two. While hiding behind a tall stack of cartons, Danny noticed the old wooden door in the wall behind him.

"Hey, Willie, look at this," he called.

"What is it?" Willie asked suspiciously, certain that Danny was laying some sort of trap for him.

"I don't know. It's a door, in the wall back here."

"What kind of door? Where's it go?"

"I don't know. I never saw it before. It looks like it goes under the front porch."

"If this is a trick, Danny, I swear I'll break your neck. There better be a door there, boy!"

"There is! Come here! I swear it's not a trick!"

Willie wormed his way between two stacks of stained cardboard boxes, one hand poised to ward off the surprise attack he was certain would be coming. His younger brother was standing, hands on hips, before the faded wooden door. The rusty trip latch bore a deep, shiny scratch where it made contact with the latch seat, testimony to its recent, and probably frequent, use.

"What do you think's in there?" Willie wondered aloud.

"I don't know. Maybe something Pop wants to keep a secret."

"Like what?"

"Well, if I knew, it wouldn't be a secret, would it, dummy?"

"What's he got to keep stuff secret from us for?"

"Yeah, I guess you're right. But what *does* he have in there?"

"Why don't we find out? Mom's out until three, and Pop won't be home until nearly four. We could take a look, as long as we don't touch anything, and he'll never know we were in there."

"I don't know. He'd be awful mad if he found out. He must

have it hidden, whatever it is, for some reason," Danny said uncertainly.

"It's no big deal. Come on! It's probably where he hides Christmas presents, and stuff like that," Willie suggested, feeling the need to convince Danny quickly, before his own nerve could slip away. He began to slide his hands along the edge of the door and bent forward, peering through the murky air like a nearsighted old man.

"What're you doing, Willie?" Danny asked, his voice just above a whisper.

"Looking for something. Sssssssssshhh!"

"What are you looking for?"

"I don't know."

"Well, how will you know when you find it, then?"

"Don't worry about it. I'll know, that's all."

"Want me to look, too? It'll save time," Danny volunteered.

"Nah. You don't know what to look for. Leave me be."

"If it's here, I have to find it, or Pop'll know we've been in the room."

"How will he know if you don't even know what it is? He won't know what it is, either, or even if he does, he won't know you found it, will he?"

"No, but he'll know if I *don't* find it, though. Now shut up and let me look! You keep distracting me."

"Sometimes I think you're crazy. You're standing here telling me that you're looking for something, but you don't know what it is, but you have to find it because Pop will know if you don't. That doesn't make any sense at all, Willie."

Willie heaved a sigh, steeling himself for one last stab at explaining the nature of the elusive concept baffling his younger brother.

"Look, if Pop wants this place to be a secret, it means he doesn't want anyone, including us, to go in there. That means he probably wants to know if we, or anyone, have been in there. The only way he can do that is if we leave a sign, something that tells him we have found this room and gone inside, see?

He probably has something on the edge of the door, like a thread, or a hair, or something like that, you know? Something we wouldn't see unless we were looking for it. If we open the door without finding it, he'll know somebody was here, because the hair will be gone. That'll tell him somebody found this place."

"Okay, okay. So we just play dumb. If he asks us anything, we just say we never saw the door. Why don't we just open the damn thing now and see if there's even anything in there, huh?"

Willie surrendered. "Okay, Dan. But if he finds out, we'll both be sorry. Remember I told you so."

He pulled up on the latch, and the horrendous screech made them jump. They peered cautiously into the shadowy room, their eyes registering little more than silhouettes in the gloom. There were two tall, shadowy outlines against the dim light sifting through the high narrow windows in the front wall, where the leaves of the ivy outside moved waywardly.

"Wow, neat!" Danny exclaimed. "Look at that! What is it?"

"Jeez, I don't know," Willie answered, equally impressed, "but there's two of them!"

The boys tiptoed forward, very cautiously. Willie reached the substance of the nearer outline first, and his eyes widened. Jumping back, he exclaimed, "Holy Cow! Would you just look at that thing? I never saw anything like *that* before! Godalmighty!"

"Me, neither," Daniel whispered.

Willie reached his hand out but hesitated a moment before making a final commitment to tactile exploration. Finally, his reluctant fingers came into contact with a cool, metallic surface, and he stroked it gingerly. "I think it's metal, Dan," he whispered. "But what is it? What's it doing down here? What the hell is Pop up to, I wonder."

Danny remained silent, but reached out to join his brother in the Braillelike examination Willie was engaged in. "I wonder if the other thing's the same," he said.

"Wait here, Dan," Willie whispered, "I'll be right back."

"Where're you going, Willie?" Danny asked, his voice trembling.

"To get a light. Pop has one of his lanterns down here somewhere, and I'm just going to get it. I'll only be a minute."

He backed quietly out of the murky room, and Danny could hear his quick step as he ran to where their father usually kept one of his yard lanterns hung on a large hook. Danny closed his eyes while he waited for his brother's return, as though his inability to see the looming device would protect him from whatever malevolence it might be capable of. A sudden loud thump caused him to jump, but the muffled curse that followed reassured him that it was only Willie, who had stumbled over some obstacle or other in the cluttered darkness behind him.

"I'm back," Willie whispered, "and I got a big light. Now we'll be able to see what the hell these things are." His voice rose nearly an octave. There was a sharp click, and the small room was suddenly alive with dancing light.

"Wow," Danny yelled, "look at that thing!"

"Christ!" Willie exploded. "It's a still! No wonder Pop has it hidden down here. I'll bet Mom doesn't know it's here."

"What's it for, Willie?"

"To make whiskey."

"Pop's really something, huh? I bet Mom would go through the roof if she knew this thing was here."

"That's for sure! We gotta be real careful, because if she ever does find out, Pop'll be sure it was us who told her about it."

Willie stepped back a bit from the gleaming coils and began to play the light around. He noticed that the other outline was another still, but it seemed incomplete alongside the obviously working model directly in front of him.

"Willie?"

"Not now. Let's look around and see what else is here. We have to get out and finish cleaning before Mom comes home, remember?"

The light flicked this way and that, its hard round focus picking out likely shadows here and there, reducing their mysteries to piles of cartons. Willie went toward the nearest carton, then stopped suddenly.

"What was that?"

"I didn't hear anything," Danny responded.

"Sssssssshhhhh! Listen!"

Both boys leaned back toward the doorway, straining their ears. After a minute, Willie shrugged, saying, "I guess it wasn't anything." He turned back to the top carton of the nearest stack, reached in and tugged, removing a gleaming bottle.

"Christ, Pop doesn't mess around, does he? That's a pretty classy bottle," he said in admiration.

"Willie, do you think we could do it?"

"Do what?"

"Make some whiskey?"

"I don't know how you do it. Anyway, Pop would be sure to find out we've been in here if we start messing around with this stuff. And suppose we wrecked it. He'd kill us."

"Yeah, I suppose you're right," Danny said wistfully. "Still, I'd really like to try it. Maybe there's some whiskey here already."

"Maybe, but Pop probably knows just what's here, and he'd be sure to notice it if we took a bottle."

"Yeah, I guess so. . . ."

"Although . . ." and Willie hesitated the way he did when he was up to some mischief, usually at Danny's expense.

"What are you thinking?"

"If there *is* some here, and if we took some, and if Pop noticed, he probably wouldn't say anything."

"Why not?"

"Because he'd have to tell us what he was talking about to ask us anything, and he couldn't do that because if we weren't the ones who took it, we'd know about it when he asked us, and he wouldn't want to take that chance."

Then Danny noticed a small petcock on a large container

at the end of a tightly wound coil of copper tubing coming out of the working still's top.

"Look at this, Willie! There's something in here!" He brought his cupped hand over to the lantern, and they stared at the damp gleam.

"Taste it," Willie said eagerly. Danny lifted the wet hand to his lips and licked the moisture, then nearly gagged. "Ugh, it's awful!" he said, screwing up his face. "You try it, Willie."

Willie went over to the still and opened the petcock to let a bit of the whiskey dribble into his own hand. He lifted the liquid to his mouth and sucked it up in a single gulp. "Wheeew! That sure is strong stuff, pardner!" he drawled. "It stinks, but I think I like it. Wait here a minute. I'll be right back." He handed the lantern to Danny and started toward the stairway.

While he waited for Willie to return, Danny amused himself by trying the bitter stuff again, and found that it did not taste nearly as bad as it had initially. He wet his palm a third and a fourth time, each time licking it dry and smacking his lips as thirsty cowboys did in the movies.

"Here I come," Willie shouted from the head of the stairs, and clattered clumsily down, accompanied by a slight tinkle. "Ta daaa!" he trumpeted. "Look at what I have here."

He held two small tumblers in one hand and a bottle of Coca-Cola in the other. There were two cubes of ice in each glass.

"What's that for?" Danny demanded.

"We're gonna give this stuff a real test, Daniel me boy. Yessirree, a real test." He stepped toward the still and dropped to one knee. "Bring the lamp over here and shine it on this valve thing."

Willie opened the petcock and decanted an inch of the homemade brew into each glass. "Now shine the light down here so I can see what I'm doin'." He filled each tumbler to its brim with Coke, set the bottle next to the full glasses, and handed one to his brother. "There you are, sir. One Scotch-and-soda. Drink up!"

"How do you know it's Scotch?" Danny asked.

"What difference does it make what we call it? Drink up!" Willie instructed his brother jovially.

The boys sipped their drinks slowly at first, then more rapidly as they realized the sweet soda had hidden the bitter taste of the whiskey. "Barkeep, set 'em up again!" Danny said, plunking his empty glass down beside the Coke bottle.

"Yessir, comin' right up, my good man!" Willie replied, in the best Dodge City fashion. He refilled both glasses, this time adding a bit more whiskey before topping off with soda. "Just a little extra, to cut the taste of this sodie pop," he said, licking his lips. "Here's mud in yer eye, *hombre*!"

Danny nodded, a little sluggishly, and returned the salute through thickening lips. "In yer eye, too!"

"How about another?" Willie asked when he had drained his glass. "You know, a man gets mighty thirsty out on the prairie all day long, not to mention down in the basement. You ever spend any time in the basement, Nevada?"

"Sure have, Montana," Danny retorted. "I been in the basement mor'n once in my life, I'll tell *you*. And it weren't no picnic, neither."

"Know whatcha mean, Nevada, know whatcha mean. Sholy do!"

"How about a little somethin' to wet my whistle, barkeep?" Danny asked, holding his empty glass toward his brother. "There ain't nothin' for a man who's got a lotta straightenin' to do like a little Sotch 'n' scoda, know what I mean, pardner?" He sat down heavily, with an exaggerated groan, and looked up at his brother. "Yuh know, I reckon I'm gonna need some shuteye afore I ride my broom out yonder any more. Wake me up in a while and we'll break camp. What say?"

"I'll do that, Nevada. Fact, think I'll join yuh," Willie said, slipping down to the floor by Danny's side. He looked dopily around the small room and noticed that the shadows were moving a bit. He was about to call this strange phenomenon to his brother's attention, when Danny started humming, then broke into full-fledged song, " 'Ome, 'ome on the range-uh, ahwhere the beer and the cantaloupe pulay-uh . . ." Danny bellowed.

"Sssssssshhh! Shut up, Dan. Somebody'll hear you."

"Whassamatter? There ain't no Injuns in these parts no more."

Willie giggled in spite of himself, and was about to respond in kind when the front door slammed. "Sssshhhh! Dan, somebody's here, upstairs. It must be Mom. What are we gonna do?"

"I reckon we'll have to saddle up and ride outta here, Montana, ole buddy. That's all there is to it. Saddle up and ride out . . ."

Willie had been startled into abrupt sobriety by his mother's return and frantically tried to get Danny to his feet. But the younger boy was too far gone to be aware of the imminent danger. Willie heard his mother's footsteps moving toward the top of the basement stairs. "William? Daniel?" she called, and Willie knew it was all but hopeless. He dragged Danny out of the distillery and called up toward Ella's feet, hoping to distract her, or at least retard her descent. "We're almost finished, Mom. Be right up!" Then, as an afterthought, he added, "No need for you to come down."

He turned and began tugging Danny by both arms. Remembering the back door of the basement, which led out into the yard, he headed toward it, literally dragging the younger boy behind him. But Danny had begun to find everything amusing, started laughing, and took his brother's urgency for some kind of game. He was determined to play along, and dug in his heels, yelling, "Whoa, pardner, hold on just a minute, now!"

"Damn it, Danny," Willie hissed through gritted teeth, "will you cut it out! If Mom sees you like this, the shit will hit the fan."

"Fan? Fan, you say? Why, pardner, I don't reckon I've seed a fan in nigh on to a year, now. You got one? About yer person, I mean?"

"You'll need a fan, all right, to cool your ass after Mom gets done warming it for you."

Danny finally reached out to grab a pillar supporting the floor above. Willie tugged and twisted, but Danny held fast. Willie tried tickling his brother, and Danny collapsed in a heap, a giggling shambles. Even as Willie bent down to muffle the laughter, he knew it was too late, for he could hear their mother's footsteps drawing near the head of the stairs. She was humming in the animated manner she reserved for moments of total exasperation. All they needed to precipitate war was for her to get a peek at Danny, who was now crooning and laughing by turns, a bit of mindless drool creeping over his chin.

Willie looked around in desperation, and his eye lit upon a large steel-lipped cardboard drum. He raced toward it, hoping it was empty. It was, and he grabbed it by the lip and raced back to his brother, inverting the drum on the way. He slipped it over Danny's head, then jumped up to sit on the metal bottom, gaining his balance just as Ella rounded the corner at the bottom of the staircase.

"Oh, there you are," she said ominously. "Didn't you hear me calling you? And where is your brother?"

"Oh, he, ah, that is . . ."

"Come on now, where is he?" she demanded, and her eyes quickly scanned the cellar. She noticed the disarray at the other end almost immediately, and her jaw seemed to harden even as Willie cringed from her gaze, which returned to him with a new fire prominently in evidence. "Why is there such a mess over there? Can't the two of you ever do what I tell you to do?"

"Oh, well, we, ah . . . I mean, Dan had to go out for a minute, and we were . . ."

"Oh, he had to go out, did he? And where might he have had to be going in the rain? And why?"

"He, ah . . . forgot his glove, over at Bill Deagan's house, and he, ah . . . he wanted to get it before he forgot it again."

"I see, his baseball glove, was it. And I suppose that filthy leather lump I sat on at breakfast this morning was my imagination, eh?"

"Yes, ma'am."

"What did you say?"

"I said, 'Yes, ma'am,' but I meant to say 'No, ma'am.' "

"No, no, I mean after you said 'Yes,' which was meant to be 'No.' You said something else. What was it?"

"I didn't . . ."

"I said, 'It's not a filthy leather lump, either.' " Eerily muffled by the drum, Danny's voice could just barely be heard. Willie kicked the drum in frustration, but he knew the game was up and jumped down before his mother could reach out to pull him down. She stood, hands on hips, as the large drum wobbled, then began to rise slowly, lifted by the barely visible fingertips of the sequestered inebriate. Finally, the drum fell to one side, and Danny rose slowly to his feet, extending his hand toward his brother at the same time. He blinked once, then said, "Howdy. You must be the new school marm." He blinked again, sat down rather heavily, and began giggling.

Ella glared long and hard at each of the boys in turn, then, slowly, like cobras in slow motion, her hands extended, capturing an ear of each. "Upstairs, march!" she commanded, and Danny, who could sense trouble through the alcoholic fog, which thinned somewhat under the influence of the viselike grip, led the way toward the stairs. Willie looked woefully over his shoulder, but could not make out the door that had opened on such a Pandora's box.

As the trio arrived in the kitchen, their mother stepped briskly to one side of the table and indicated the two chairs on the opposite side. "Sit down," she barked. The brothers sat in unison, stiffly.

"Now," she began, "does either of you care to tell me just exactly what was going on down there?" She gimlet-eyed each of them in turn. She had remained standing, knowing the advantage this gave her would be a valuable concession to make if she had to soften her approach.

Willie cleared his throat a bit, lamely flapped his jaw a couple of times, and blew out his cheeks in resignation. Before he could begin, his mother recognized the opening he had unconsciously given her, and bore in for the kill. "Well? I haven't got all day," she snapped. "Your father will be home soon, and I haven't even started dinner, so I'll thank you to be quick and to the point."

"Well, see, we were taking a break. And we, uh, we . . . I mean Danny found this door, and, you know . . ."

"No, I don't know, but I would like to learn. Educate me!"

"Well, we were curious and, ah, we, ah . . ."

"Don't 'ah' me, boy. Out with it before I lose my patience altogether!"

"We opened it."

"And?"

"That's all. We opened it, and, ah, well, we lost track of what time it was I guess," Willie stammered, his cheeks slowly reddening as he approached the unavoidable end of his narrative.

"That's all? You just opened the door and lost track of the time?"

"Yeah, I guess so."

"And your brother? Was he stricken with an attack of cerebral palsy?"

"Ma'am?"

Willie screwed his eyes into their corners to look at his brother, trying to buy some time. He knew there was no way out, but hoped Danny would speak up in order to spare him the ignominy of complete confession and finking both. Danny was slowly splitting into two parts, the upper half of his head rising inexorably, by minute degrees, gradually pulling away from the rest of his body. Then Willie realized it was merely a lunatic smile.

"Well, ma'am, it's like this," Danny said. "We was mighty thirsty, yes indeed, powerful thirsty, punchin' all that junk down there, and we seed the barroom and decided to have us a little drink."

"Young man, let me smell your breath."

"Yes, ma'am," Danny mumbled, casting a glance at Willie before leaning forward.

"Exhale!"

Danny complied, and their mother screwed up her nose, then turned her attention to Willie.

"Have you two hooligans been fooling around with your father's still?"

"You mean you *know* about it?" Willie said in astonishment.

"Of course I know about it! You don't think he could keep something like that a secret, do you?"

"Well, no, I guess not, but I . . . I mean we thought . . ."

"I know what you thought. But I know a few things you don't give me credit for. Of course, your father doesn't know I know, and that's the way I would like to keep it. He likes to think he's put one over on me with that little contraption, and if that's what he wants, I guess he's entitled. I don't like it, but I guess it's harmless enough."

"But . . . but it's illegal."

"I know that, and so does your father. That's why you can't let him know that we know, especially not me. If he thought I knew about it, he'd get rid of it just so I wouldn't be upset. If you let on that any of us knows about that still, you'll both answer to me. Do you understand?"

"Stills."

"Pardon me?"

"Stills. There's two of 'em."

"Two?"

"Yeah! Didn't you know?" Willie asked.

"Well, yes . . . of course I did."

Now, Willie smiled as he remembered the look on Ella's face. It was the first time he had been able to appreciate the delicate balance that obtained in his parents' marriage, Ella maintaining more influence on family affairs than he had ever suspected, and displaying strength of character she seldom betrayed in public. And Will's managing to have secrets within secrets, things Ella thought she knew, but not quite, was no more and no less than he would have suspected. He knew, looking back on that incident, that Ella understood Will far better than anyone else in the family did, and knew, with unerring accuracy, when to bend to accommodate him and when to put her foot down—no easy matter with a man as fiercely independent as Will Donovan. She also knew when she had been bested, and there was no doubt in Willie's mind that his father was probably the only man who could pull that off.

He knew too, staring again at the glare outside, that Ella would be all right, if her children helped her over the next few months. But he also knew that each of them would be required to give rather than take, perhaps for the first time, and he had doubts about their ability to meet that obligation. Except for Katherine. She would be there for Ella, as she had always been there for any of them, no matter what the circumstances. She had kept things together when Emma died, and it would probably fall on her shoulders to shepherd their mother through the rough weeks ahead. He felt guilty about that, but he knew that his best, which he was determined to give, would probably not be good enough.

With a sigh, he rose from the chair and headed into the kitchen, where he took a beer from the refrigerator, popped the cap on the edge of the sink, and drained it halfway down in a single pull. He went to the back door and flung it open, to lean against the doorframe and drink in the cold, bright air, twirling the bottle carelessly in his hands, wondering how long it would be before he would know whether he had the courage to be his father's son. And his mother's.

TWENTY-TWO

ELLA looked at the five faces ranged before her like a hand of poker, stared at each in turn, then silently shook her head. These people all seemed like total strangers, though three of them were of her own flesh and blood, and all were family. She wasn't sure whether she had changed or if they had, or if it was simply a matter of circumstances, which had bound them so closely together for so long, having been so radically altered.

As the silence grew heavier, it began to seem a thing Ella could touch, like a heavy curtain hanging between her and her family, their restless movements no more than sluggish responses to passing currents of air. She reached out with her hands and clenched them into tight, veined fists, as if she had taken hold of the impenetrable veil and would rip it aside by force of a rage unbetrayed by the dull serenity of her expression. One by one, the hands fell back into her lap, two dying birds, quivering slightly, then lying still.

She suddenly saw that they were looking to her for guidance, as they had once looked to Will. Now, when she needed them most, they were going to lean on her for support. Painful as it would be, she saw that she would have to take the lead. She stared hard at Willie, and his eyes began to wander around the room, finally coming to rest on the mantelpiece behind her and to her left.

"Does anyone want to say anything," she asked, "or do you want me to tell you what has to be done?"

No one answered. Each studied the pattern in the carpet or the faded wallpaper, and she waited before continuing, hoping one of them would save her from the need to do so.

"Well then, here's what I intend to do," she said, with a

confidence she did not feel. "I mean to have a church funeral, and I would appreciate it if you would all pitch in."

Willie cleared his throat, as if finally summoning the courage to speak, then looked helplessly at Katherine, who could sense that he wanted her to object. She glanced at his face, which looked puffy and redder than usual, before saying, "I don't know if that's what Daddy would have wanted, Mother."

"I don't suppose he would," Ella said calmly, "but I don't know what else to do. And it would be a comfort to me."

"Are you sure?" Katherine asked. "I mean, would you really be comfortable with a ceremony Daddy wouldn't have wanted?"

"I don't know," Ella admitted, "but I don't know what else to do."

"Maybe we could just have a small ceremony at the funeral parlor," Willie suggested. "We could limit it to a few close friends, and Pat Flaherty could say a few words, nothing elaborate, and let it go at that."

"Is that the way you want to send your father off to the next life?" Ella demanded. "Nothing elaborate? Doesn't he deserve more than that?"

"I didn't mean it that way," Willie said, beginning to falter.

"Daddy didn't believe in that sort of business, Mother," Katherine cut in, coming to Willie's defense. "I mean, he couldn't stand that sort of hypocrisy, and I don't think it's right to inflict it on him when he isn't here to speak for himself. It's not . . . I don't think it's fair, that's all."

"What does fairness have to do with any of this? It's not fair that he's dead, either, is it?"

"You know that's not what I mean," Katherine persisted. "It's just that Daddy hated that kind of thing, and it doesn't seem appropriate to make him a part of something he didn't believe in. Besides, where would you have the ceremony?"

"At the church, of course," Ella said, barely whispering.

"What church?" Willie asked softly. "Not Third Street Presbyterian!"

"Of course, Third Street Presbyterian," Ella snapped. "Where else?"

"I may not know much," Daniel said, speaking for the first time, "but I know Pop wouldn't want that. He hated Berland. I agree with Katie. I don't think it's right, at least not there, anyway."

"I don't understand you, any of you," Ella exploded. "Not five minutes ago, there wasn't a soul among you who had anything to say, and suddenly you all seem to know what your father would have wanted. Well, if you can't come up with a better idea, I'll thank you all to keep your opinions to yourselves."

"Take it easy, Mom," Willie said. "Nobody wants things to be any more difficult for you than they already are. It's just that we think, or at least I do, that if we're going to do something for Pop, it ought to be respectful of his memory. Making him the center attraction in one of Berland's circuses doesn't strike me as particularly respectful."

"And since when has respect for your father been so important to you? It's a fine thing, to be sure, but you should have shown a little more of it when he was here to appreciate it."

"Mother, that's not fair," Katherine put in sharply. "Willie's right. It wouldn't be respectful. I think we ought to do something else. Nothing at all would be better than that."

"So, even you turn on me, do you? I never would have expected that of you."

"But I'm *not* turning on you, Mother. None of us is," Katherine protested. "We just want to do what's right."

"Then mind your own business, the lot of you. I have to do this for me. Your father is gone. He'll know that I had to do things as I saw fit. He'd respect that. A lot more than you all seem to."

"Maybe you're right, Mom," Daniel said. "Funerals are for the living anyway, aren't they? I mean, they're supposed to help *us*. What other purpose do they have?"

"I'm not sure that's precisely the attitude we ought to be taking," Ella said, "but I'll take it as supporting my position, anyway."

"I suppose that settles it then," Katherine said. "Just tell us what you want us to do, Mother."

Andy and Louise, less involved with their own feelings than the others, nodded in agreement, and Ella smiled warmly at them, in appreciation of their tactful silence during the discussion.

"I'll call the Reverend Berland in the morning, if you like," Willie volunteered.

"No," Ella said. "You're too much like your father. You'll end up insulting him. I'll take care of that myself. Why don't you and Daniel take care of making arrangements for the wake—get whatever we'll need, make arrangements for the food, the chairs, that sort of thing. Katherine and I will handle the more delicate affairs, if you don't mind."

Willie looked hurt, but recognizing the justice of Ella's charge, he acquiesced gracefully. And, for a moment, he seemed to Ella to be ten years old again, an apologetic child who meant well but just couldn't keep out of trouble.

"I think I'd rather be alone for a while, if you don't mind," Ella announced. "You're all welcome to stay, of course, and you know where everything is. I'll be down after a little bit," she concluded, rising stiffly from her chair. She walked slowly to the foot of the stairs, where she turned to look at each of them in turn, then, wordlessly, ascended the stairs.

They listened to her footsteps along the softly creaking hallway above their heads, sitting motionless, their breathing nearly synchronous. The collective hissing and sighing seemed to grow louder and louder in Katherine's ears, and her own breath began to accelerate, in raspy, ragged rhythms. She felt such a great weight, such responsibility, it was as if the five of them were charged with breathing for the entire human race.

"I don't know about you," Daniel said softly, "but I feel like a drink. Anyone else?"

"Yeah, me, too! Yeah, a beer, if there is one," Willie responded.

Daniel rose to his feet, staggering as if already drunk and went to the kitchen. The others just sat, listening to him rattle around, and they sighed in unison with the air escaping the beer cans as he tapped them. He was soon back, handed Willie a beer, then plopped back onto his chair, straddling the back and propping his arms on its top. He took a long pull at the beer, then stared thoughtfully into the triangular openings he had gouged in the can's lid, as if he expected something other than foam to emanate from the apertures.

Willie sipped his beer silently, as Katherine and Louise murmured softly to one another, not so much to avoid being overheard as to avoid disturbing the others. Andy just sat on the sofa, his thick arms folded across his chest, while his eyes drooped and his head wobbled.

"What are you girls whispering about?" Willie demanded. "This isn't the time to be making secret plans."

"We're not making secret plans," Louise snapped. "We're just talking about something that doesn't concern you."

Taken aback, Willie looked quizzically at his wife, then turned to his beer with the same intense scrutiny Daniel continued to lavish on his own drink.

"I still don't think Mom's doing the right thing," Daniel said suddenly.

"I don't think it really matters," Katherine replied. "Why don't we just help her do what she wants to do, instead of telling her what she ought to be doing? That really won't hurt us any, will it?"

"That's not the point," Willie put in.

"Well, what *is* the point?" Katherine demanded. "Is there a point to any of this?"

"Hell yes, there's a point. It's got to do with who Pop was, and what he was. And he wasn't exactly a fan of Berland's, as you damn well know. And for good reason, if you ask me. *That's* the point."

"I'm not so sure it is," Katherine replied. "I'm not so sure we have any right to interfere in this at all, no matter what we think. It's got to be up to Mom."

"You've changed your tune pretty quick, haven't you, Katie?" Willie asked. "It was you, after all, who first said it wasn't fair to subject Pop to this kind of thing. What made you change your mind?"

"I don't know! Yes, I do know. It was what Dan said, about funerals being for the living. He's right, and this has to be for Mother, not for Daddy."

Daniel got to his feet, asking, "Anybody want another beer besides me?"

Willie nodded and turned to his sister as Daniel headed back to the kitchen. He stared at Katherine through pinched eyes and seemed to be mulling over a new tack, but she beat him to the punch.

"Willie, will you just stop and think for a minute? Does it matter how we feel if it goes against what Mother wants?"

"Damn right it matters," Willie barked. "Will Donovan was my father, and everything I am that man is responsible for. And that's a damn sight more than you can claim, if you don't mind my saying so."

"If you're an example of his best work, maybe we ought to bury him in an unmarked grave." She burst out sobbing, shaking her head slowly from side to side. She looked at Andy but he was oblivious to everything going on around him, including his wife's distress. "I don't believe this," she continued. "The man has been dead for less than twenty-four hours, and you'd think he had never been alive at all, the way we're carrying on. Didn't we learn anything from him? Any of us?"

"You're right, Katie. I shouldn't have made that crack. I'm sorry," Willie apologized. "I guess we're all just a little on edge. But I still say we have a right to make our opinions known. If there's one thing I did learn from Pop, it's that you have to take the first opportunity to speak your mind, because you may never have another chance. And that was never truer than now. I just don't want us to do anything that we'll regret, that's all."

"But you seem to forget Mother's opinion," Katherine insisted. "Hers has to count for more than ours, more than all of our opinions put together. Daddy was hers before he was ours. They lived together for over forty years, Willie. Surely that gives her the right to decide."

Daniel was back, with a pair of beers in one hand and a highball in the other. "Now, where were we?" he asked.

Katherine opened her mouth to make the same argument to Daniel, but Willie interrupted her. "Katie was just saying that Mom has the right to decide because she lived with Pop longer than we did."

"What the hell's that got to do with anything?" Daniel exploded. "For Christ's sake, we're not talking about staking a claim here. We're talking about burying the head of this family. It's a family matter, and, as part of the family, I think my feelings ought to be taken into consideration. That's all I've got to say on the subject."

"I suppose you're too drunk to say anything else, anyway, so it's just as well," Katherine jabbed.

"Who's drunk?" Daniel demanded. "I know how to handle my booze; just don't you worry about that, Katie. And I'm entitled to my opinion, too."

"No, you're not," Katherine insisted. "None of us is except Mother."

"What do you mean? She didn't own Pop, did she? I mean, he's related to us, too, isn't he? Wasn't he?" He looked embarrassed at his use of the wrong tense and stared moodily into his glass, swirling the ice around with a gentle tinkling sound.

"Yes," Katherine said softly. "Yes, he was related to all of us, but, of all of us, it was Mother who loved him best and who loved him longest."

"Don't try to tell me I didn't love my father," Willie said heatedly.

"I'm not telling you any such thing, only that there are different kinds of love. Mother loved Daddy in a way I doubt any of us can understand. Look at us, will you? We're squabbling like a pack of thieves or spoiled children. For God's sake, Willie, Danny, if we loved her just half as much as you claim to have loved him, we'd be up there with her now instead of arguing in circles like this."

Katherine stared around the room, desperately looking for support, but Andy had long since fallen asleep, despite the heated exchange, and Louise was only willing to support her sister-in-law with a nod or two of encouragement, preferring to avoid becoming entangled in a separate, far more bitter argument than the one taking place in front of her, something sure to happen if she should cross Willie in his current state.

Daniel glared at his sister, drained his glass, ice and all, and began to crunch remnants of the cubes loudly and contemptuously. "I don't give a shit what we do, I guess," he said. "I just want to get the damn thing over with and get back to my own life."

Katherine stared at him unbelievingly. She knew that Daniel could be callous, especially when he had been drinking, but she simply could not believe he had said what she just heard. She closed her eyes and lay back against the sofa, biting her tongue in rage and frustration.

The sounds in the dark were painfully familiar to Ella as she lay and strained against the night and the dark, her ears waiting for the first gruff word that would follow the loud creak of the door, when Will, tired of his newspaper and the television news, finally came to bed. She opened her eyes as wide as she could at every squeak and thump, waiting to see what she had seen for the last time only three nights before. He used to amble in, his heavy coveralls dangling over his hips, the heavy woolen underwear damp under his arms, the wet circles just barely visible in the dim light from the hallway framing him like some nineteenth-century Romantic portrait of a laborer.

She knew she would never see that again, and that the noises she was hearing in the dark were never again to be followed by the creaking of the door and the dim portrait framed there. Only three days, and already it seemed like an eternity. She felt as if he were even slipping away from her memory; the details of his face, the contours of his body, things she had known better than she had known her own skin, were flickering in and out of focus. The more she tried to fix them, the more elusive they became, as if they belonged more to him than to her, as if they, too, were dying, and were to be buried the following morning as surely as he was.

Once, she heard so loud a thump that she sat bolt upright in bed, pulling the covers around her chin against the chill. She sat that way for nearly an hour, hoping against hope that she had only been dreaming a long dream, but she knew it was real, and that only the noise had been illusory, some casual night sound transformed by the fervency of her desire into something which no longer existed. From time to time, sitting there immobile, she would catch the play of headlights from a passing car on the ceiling, the pale illumination broken here and there by the dark-gray shade of a tree limb, winter-gnarled, arthritic fingers twisting in the stiff winter breeze outside as if beckoning to her. It might have been some suitor, precariously perched on a ladder lodged against her window ledge, urging her to come out into the cold darkness against her will. Once, the light was so bright, and the shadow so black, she was sure there was someone there. She half rose from the bed, and was brought back to her senses only by the shock of the cold linoleum under her naked foot.

It shot a chill through her unlike any she had ever known, as if all the painful truth of the past three days were compressed into a single sensation, and she moaned against the frigid aftershock, drew her foot back under the heavy comforter, and rubbed away the cold with both hands, a grotesque parody of Lady Macbeth, trying to expunge a crime she had no part in. She reached over to click on the lamp, and the shadows fled, taking with them the frail promise of company they had so cruelly extended to her.

She had been having second thoughts about her decision to have the Reverend Berland officiate at the funeral, swayed by her own sense of what Will was, had been, rather than Katherine's reasoned arguments or the boys' passionate invective against the minister. It had seemed right, the thing to do, at first, but now she recognized it for what it truly was, a feeble attempt to assert some influence over something she could not hope to control. It was almost as if to tailor the interment to her wishes were to obviate the necessity for it. How frail and foolish that hope was had been brought home to her in gradual increments, and each of the last three nights had brought her closer to the certainty that she had been wrong, and to the knowledge that it was too late to do anything about it. She could not bear to call the minister and tell him that she had changed her mind, and even if she could bring herself to do it, she knew she could not face the children. Not that she was afraid of admitting that she had been wrong, but she could not bear to confess how little she understood what had happened to her, and to Will, and how much she had used her will as an instrument against the inevitable, to deny what she could not stop, to overlook for the moment what she could not ultimately forget.

Perhaps worst of all, she knew that Berland would ramble on and on, alienating the children all the more with what would have to be a eulogy composed entirely of hypocrisy and generalizations, since Berland had had no more use for Will than Will had had for him. Even this sudden reconsideration was little more than a mask, a temporary skin drawn tautly over the open wound of her solitary future, which stretched before her in the night like an endless red desert of bright, sticky sand. Day upon day of climbing and descending stairs, night after night of televised company and solitary card games. No one to talk to, no one to argue with, no one to . . . love, no one to be loved by, teased by, touched by. She clicked off the light again and lay back heavily on the pillow, imagining the feel of Will's callused fingers on the soft fold of skin under her chin. He had teased her so mercilessly about the slackening of her skin that she had once challenged him to pay for a face-lift, but he had begged off by explaining that anyone who loved sweets as she did would surely split right through an artificially tautened skin. He had laughed until tears rolled down his cheeks as he described how the old Ella would come bursting through the new one, like a large balloon being inflated inside a smaller one until the full, fleshy woman he knew and loved would appear once again to capture more than her fair share of the mattress. At the time, she had laughed with him, but it had hurt her to hear him describe her this way. If only he were still there to tease her, she would gladly bear it again, even beg him to do it, and worse, if that were the price she would have to pay to have him with her. She could bear almost anything except his loss, and there was nothing she would not do to retrieve him, if only for one more day.

Her hearing seemed to be growing more acute, and she could hear footsteps blocks away, even tell when someone turned a corner or mounted the steps to a porch. She was attempting to give Will life through audibility, as if she could drag him back to life simply by hearing him. It was almost as if she were merely waiting for him to return from a trip to the store. He had not been gone so long. Surely he had only stepped out for a pack of cigarettes or a bottle of beer. Surely he would be right back, and she lay there in the dark, listening, waiting.

She had not slept, but it didn't matter, since she felt nothing—not tired, not sad, nothing. She wanted only to get through the day as best she could and as quickly as possible, with as little as possible to remind her why it was not like any other day, even if it meant turning a deaf ear to condolences and well-meaning expressions of sympathy. The warmth of the bath, which she normally found so restful, was barely noticeable, so dulled had her senses become. She went about the business of dressing in a perfunctory manner, paying little attention to her hair, which she planned to hide under a hat, and not bothering with make-up at all, less out of propriety than indifference. At seven-thirty, she was downstairs, seated stiffly on the sofa, even though Andy and Katherine were not supposed to arrive until eight-fifteen. She stared at the clock, trying to freeze the motion of its hands, and so nearly did she succeed that she thought for one fleeting instant that there was yet hope, for if she could stop time itself with so little effort, might she not succeed in reversing it, if only she tried hard enough? And yet, the hands moved, inexorably, and eight-fifteen arrived, as she knew it must, and with it came her daughter and son-in-law, the former puffy-eyed and tear-stained, the latter stiffly uncomfortable, yet determined to be as supportive as he knew how.

Katherine let herself in with her own key, and as she and Andy stepped into the living room, she thought that her mother must not have come downstairs yet. Ella, wrapped in shadows on the couch, said not a word, and Katherine called upstairs, urging her to hurry.

"There's no real reason to hurry," Ella whispered, "is there?"

Katherine turned with a start, then laughed nervously. "Oh, there you are. I didn't think you were ready yet."

"I'm not ready. I don't think I'll ever be ready, not for this. But I guess that won't change things any, will it? Not being ready never really changes things. I used to tell you that every morning when you dragged your feet getting ready for school."

"Please, Mother, don't. Not now. Not yet."

"All right, I'm ready, just let me get my coat. I don't really want to go, but I don't really want not to go, either. I don't really want to do or not do anything, so I don't suppose it matters whether I go or stay." Ella sighed.

"I'll get your coat for you, Mom," Andy said. "Where is it?"

"It's in the hall closet, Andrew, thank you." Ella rose and

went to the mirror over the mantelpiece, where she straightened and repinned her hat, brushing back a few stray strands of hair and tucking them up under her hat. "Thank you," she said as Andy helped her into the heavy black coat. She stepped closer to the mirror and peered minutely at her face, then lowered the dark veil over her red-rimmed eyes.

As Andy and Katherine made their way quickly toward the door, Ella followed them more slowly. Reaching the doorway, she turned to scrutinize the living room as if searching for something she had forgotten. Andy was about to ask her what she was looking for when Katherine nudged him and put a finger to her lips when he turned to see why she had struck him. It was clear to her that Ella was trying to fix every last detail of the room in her mind, almost taking a mental photograph, in sad, silent recognition of the fact that, henceforth, the room would no longer be what it had been. It had become, by virtue of Will's death, a kind of time capsule, which would be entombed, even as Will's body was about to be, with a lifetime of petty details and innumerable conversations lingering in the still, almost musty air of the room.

Ella turned at last and, silently, nodded toward the door, signifying that she had fixed what was fixable and relinquished forever what could not be retained.

TWENTY-THREE:
Willie

My father is dead. He won't come to see me now, and I can't ask him about the trees or tell him about the ones who steal things here. Everybody leaves me, but I never thought he would do that. It didn't surprise me when Louise said she had had enough, although she could have been more understanding, but a father is supposed to be different. Fathers aren't supposed to leave anybody they are in charge of. I don't think my father left me on purpose; I mean I don't think he wanted to die just so he wouldn't have to have anything to do with me, but you can never be sure about something like that. I know that people sometimes do things for reasons they don't understand, and my father was no different from anyone else in that regard, I don't think. I know it was nothing personal, but it felt like it all the same.

When I was little I used to think he wouldn't ever leave me, and then when I got a little older, I would get scared every time he went to work. The days were so long, and he was away for so long, that I started to think he wouldn't come back. Especially when I had done something wrong. I thought maybe he had left just to punish me. It never occurred to me that my mother was more important to him than I was, and that he would never leave her, even to get even with me. He would never leave my mother unless he had to. I guess he had to.

Some days when he went to work and was away for a long time, I used to promise myself that I would get even. I used to think that I would refuse to go to his funeral when he died. I thought that would pay him back. It's funny how you can think something that seems perfectly logical to you only because you don't know anything. Later, when you learn things, and you understand that the whole world doesn't exist just to make you happy or miserable, you're embarrassed about those kinds of things, and you never tell them to anybody, because you think they'll laugh at you. Sometimes, you realize that everybody else was just as silly, and you manage to do okay, and to forget about that kind of thing altogether, except when something particular happens that reminds you of one of them. Some people never learn that, though. They just carry all those silly ideas around, and pretend to themselves that things are exactly the way they used to think they were, and they act just like they had never learned differently. If you're really good at that sort of thing, this is where you end up. There are some people here who have some really strange things in their heads. I guess that's why they spend so much time asking us all those questions. I guess it helps you to get better if you tell the truth. It's hard, though, because you never know who to trust.

    I have a new doctor, now, and he asks me a lot of the same questions that the other ones asked me, but he doesn't ask them the same way. He also asks some other questions, which I was never asked before. I try to answer them all honestly, because I realize that I have to trust someone here who can get me out. That is the only way. I even told that to the new doctor, and I was afraid that he would think I was only telling him things so I could get out. I asked him about it, and he said it didn't matter why I told him anything as long as I told the truth. He said I would help him help me as long as I kept talking, because there was no way I could completely hide things that were important for him to know if I kept talking. I feel better, so maybe he is right.

    This morning we talked a lot about my father, and I learned that I didn't understand him at all, and that I tried to live my life for the longest time for reasons that were completely off base. I told him about the funeral, and about how I didn't want to go, and what it felt like when I did go. He asked me what it felt like at least four times, and every time I tried to tell him, I started to cry, but I didn't care, because he was the only one there, and no one would know about it except him, because I trust him. He wanted to know what I thought about when I learned that my father had died, and at first I couldn't tell him. I thought it was because I was numb, but he made me keep trying, and I started to feel things that I probably felt then, or that I should have felt but didn't.

I told him how I sat in my chair and thought about almost everything that I ever saw my father do. And about how I would sit now and look at the watch he gave me. I remembered it was the watch my father gave me when I moved the big hand on it to 4:00, because that's what time my father used to come home from work. I thought about all those times he would come home and how I would be on the front porch, not believing that he was going to come home at all, and how I would run down the block, all the way to the corner, when I heard the bus coming up Chambers Street. Sometimes he wouldn't be on it, and I used to get mad at him, thinking that he was playing a trick on me or that he really was gone for good. When he finally did come, it would be all better, but I guess I never really got over that feeling of being left behind. It's dumb, but I can't help feeling that, so I guess it's important to know about it, and maybe try to get over it. He never came to see me in the hospital much, when I had the accident, and I never knew until years later that it was because he couldn't stand to see me all broken up, in the casts and everything. I thought it was because he didn't care what happened to me. Later, I tried too hard to make him care, and everytime I saw a chance to make things better, I took it. All I could see was that if things worked out the way I wanted, he would love me, and I would be all right. My mother told me why he hardly ever came to see me, but I didn't believe her. It wasn't until we went fishing one time, and we were out on a boat where nobody could hear us, that he told me how he really felt.

I believed him, but it's hard to get over having misunderstood someone for so long. Things get all twisted up, and some of them you don't even know about, so when you think you finally got things all sorted out and squared away, there are these little secret things inside you that still hurt. You feel them, and they remind you of the other, bigger, pains, and it's hard to forgive somebody for something like that. Sometimes I think it's even harder to forgive somebody for the pains they didn't mean to cause you than for the ones they did. It's like it's a bigger injury just because they knew so little about you, or cared so little, that they didn't even know what they were doing was going to hurt you. They *should* know, but they don't, and that makes it worse. Of course, it's usually your own fault, because you never bother to tell them, and it's arrogant to think that someone should take the time to try and understand you completely before they do anything. Nobody has that much time.

I told all that to the doctor, and he thought it was a good sign that I was able to look at things that way. It's too late, though, for me to make any real use of it. My father is dead. There is a whole lifetime of confusion that I should have had the chance to clear up before one of us died, but it's too late. I can make things better for my mother when I get out, though, so I guess it's not totally wasted effort.

That morning at the funeral home I learned something about myself, and something about everybody in my family, a lot of which I didn't want to know. I learned some good things, too, about my mother, especially. She was stronger than I thought she could be. She was stronger than any of us. She was almost as strong as my father, I think, and maybe stronger, but none of us ever knew it, mostly because she just sat back all her life and did the hard things she had to do without making any fuss about them. She never complained about anything, and when things were really tough, she was as important as my father in getting the family through. We never knew that, any of us, I don't think, because we were so used to thinking of making money as the really important thing, and she was always home while my father went to work to make what money there was. Sometimes there wasn't much, but it was always just enough to get us through, and that was her doing.

The best thing about her, I think, is that she knew when to be stubborn and when not to be. Like a lot of people would not do what she did at the funeral, even after they realized that they had made a mistake. They would rather pretend that things were going just like they wanted, instead of getting up in front of everybody and taking the chance of being laughed at behind their backs. Not Mom. When Berland started making the kind of speech we all hoped he wouldn't and all knew he would, Mom just went up to him and asked him to stop. He didn't like it, but it mattered to her, because my father mattered to her, and she made that fat clown shut up. That couldn't have been easy for her, especially since he was her own minister, and she had been the one to insist that he be in charge of things in the first place. That's a hard thing to do. I could never do it. If I could have, I think I would still be with Louise. I was never able to face up to my mistakes, any more than I was able to face up to the possibility that I might make them in the first place, and that's how I managed to fuck everything up for sure.

The bad things I learned were more important, though, and they were about everybody except my mother and my sister. That means me and my brother. I want to say mostly my brother, but that isn't fair, because there are a lot of bad things about me that I already knew, so I think he is no worse than me, only it's news about him and not about me. For one thing, he is a bastard. I don't mean literally, but he is a selfish son of a bitch, and I don't think I would trust him as far as I could throw him. That's a terrible thing to have to feel about your own brother, but I don't see how I can feel any other way. It was like he was looking out for himself, trying to get whatever mileage he could out of the funeral. I think he thought my mother was probably vulnerable, or maybe he thought she couldn't have been very smart anyway, but whatever his reasons, he started in trying to get something for himself before we even went to the cemetery. He was talking all sorts of schemes about how my mother should sell the house and go to live with him. How he had the nerve to do something like that I don't know, but then he has done so many things just like that that it shouldn't have surprised me. I kept wanting to pretend he wasn't doing what he was doing, but it was so obvious that there was no way for me to ignore it. At least twice I was ready to take him aside and talk sense to him, or beat the shit out of him if that was necessary. I didn't have to though, because my mother was up to it. She just told him to shut his mouth and have some respect for his father. He shut up, but I knew he was only pretending to have respect. If he really had it, he never would have started trying to get my mother to sell the house. You could tell that he wasn't at all interested in what the best thing for her would be. He only wanted the money. I think I may have to watch out for her against my own brother when I get out of here. I know a little about business, even though I couldn't prove it by my own history, so I think I can make sure that he doesn't take advantage of her.

I don't understand why he should feel that way, that he had to try to con his own mother out of her house, but I guess there is something wrong with him. What worries me is that maybe I'm just like him. I don't know why he's like that, and I wonder whether it can have anything to do with the way he was raised, because I don't know any other explanation for it. If that's true, then maybe I have some of the same thing in me. I hope not, but there's no way to be sure. Maybe the only difference between us is that I try to screw myself out of things while he is smart enough to concentrate on other people. Neither one of us is very successful, though. I mean, I succeed in screwing myself out of things, but that's exactly what makes me a failure. He's just a plain failure, because he never manages to pull off any of his fly-by-night schemes. He probably only tries to stiff his own family because he doesn't have a chance unless somebody is at least half willing to let him get away with something. Still, I think I may have to make sure that he doesn't take advantage of Mom, because she may have her mind on other things now, and not be sharp enough to see what he's really up to. Or maybe she just won't care any more, now that Pop is gone. You never know. When you lose somebody close to you after so long, it can do funny things to the way you look at things.

I guess Daniel doesn't mean any harm to anyone; he just doesn't give a damn about anyone but himself. I remember, when we were making plans for the funeral, he actually said he couldn't wait until it was over so he could get back to his own life. Hah, that's real ambition. His life is no prize, that's a sure bet. He's even worse than I am, if you look at it honestly. Every time he screws something up, he runs away on a boat, and we don't hear from him for months, until he's in some kind of jam and needs money to get out of it. Pop used to get mad at Mom because she was always helping Daniel out. I think she must have had some special reason for it, but I don't know what it was. I used to be jealous of him, how she was always looking out for him and I had to take care of myself. I used to think that if she helped me as much as she helped him, I wouldn't be as big a mess as I was. Maybe I was wrong. Maybe she helped him because he was a bigger mess than I was, and needed more help than I did.

When I get out, I'm not going to make the same mistakes twice, that's for sure. I know more about myself, and more about how to know things about other people. If I had known those things all along, I never would have come to be here in the first place, because they are the kinds of things you have to know to stay out of places like this one. In fact, you could even say that places like this are designed especially for people who don't know anything about other people, or at least people who don't know how to act with other people. It's not that everybody here is violent, because most of us aren't. Most of us are better at hurting ourselves than we are at hurting anybody else. I guess that's true of everybody, but we seem to be better at it than those people who never have to come here. I think some of us who hurt other people only do it because we don't know how to hurt ourselves enough, and want someone to help. They don't belong in here, not with the harmless nuts like me. They belong someplace else, because they hurt those people here who are as bad off as they are, only smaller. It's not right, somehow, to hurt somebody who is already hurt. It doesn't make sense, either, because if you really want to enjoy hurting somebody, why hurt somebody who wants to be hurt. You're actually doing them a favor, after all, and that's not what you want to do if you are interested in causing somebody else to suffer. Fortunately, there aren't too many of us who are like that in here. They have a special building for them, the Vroom Building, I think it's called, and I don't know if it is named after somebody or if it got that name because of the noise all the machines they have inside there make. They have electric machines there that some of us get taken to sometimes. They never took me, and I am glad, because I have seen those who have been taken, and they look like zombies for a week when they come back. If they come back. Sometimes they don't. I don't know if it's because they die or because there is something in the machine that makes them have to be kept there. Maybe it is both. I hope I never find out. I'll never get out of here if they ever have to take me to that building and use the machine on me.

Tomorrow, the doctor is going to let me go for a walk outside with him, if the weather is all right. He said it is supposed to be very cool, but clear. We can't leave the grounds around here, but it will be nice to get out in the fresh air and to see if there are trees on all four sides. I am looking forward to that very much. I won't have to wait until my mother comes to find out, now. I can see for myself, if the weather is okay and the doctor remembers to come to take me for a walk. I don't think he will forget. He seems very interested in helping me, and I know I am getting better, just by the way I am able to remember things. I can almost remember whole things at one time, now, instead of bits and pieces, like I used to. Sometimes, before, what I would do is remember parts of different things and make them all part of one thing. That used to confuse me, and it used to confuse them, too, because I could tell that they weren't able to make any sense of what I was trying to tell them. I think they thought I was crazy, just because I was only remembering bits and pieces. It wasn't like I was trying to say things happened the way I remembered them. I was just trying to tell them what I remembered, and if it didn't always make sense, that wasn't my fault. It was better than making things up, I think. Now, I don't have to try so hard to do that anyway, because whole things come back to me all at once, and I can see things in my mind just the way they happened, how one thing led to another, how I felt when something happened, why I did some of the things I did, and even why I shouldn't have done some of those things at all. Some of them I am still glad I did, but there are some that I wouldn't do now if I were in the same situation. Not just because I ended up here, either. There are some things that just don't make sense doing, because they don't help things get better, and sometimes they only make things worse. I did a lot of those, but no more. I have to get out of here, and soon. I have to take care of my mother now. My father is dead.

TWENTY-FOUR

"Mom, I told you we shouldn't come here, not now. It's too soon. You're not ready for this yet."

"And I told you I'll never be ready, but I have to be here, now, today! I owe it to your father, and I need it for myself. I have to show him that it mattered, all of it, and I have to prove to myself that I can do it, that I can go on by myself. I have to."

"I know, I know. You know I understand, but why now? Why so soon? He wouldn't have expected it of you, wouldn't have made you come until you were ready."

"That's the problem with you, Katherine. You don't seem to understand that all my life it was your father who shielded me from things he thought I wasn't able to handle, who made all the hard decisions for me, decided when I was ready when I wasn't, what I could handle and what I couldn't. You really don't see that, do you? You really don't."

"Of course I do, Mom. I see it. I always saw it. But I also saw that you were much stronger than either one of you gave you credit for being. I know it was one of the reasons why you loved him, because he cared enough to protect you whenever and wherever he could. But there was a reason for it. He wanted to spare you from whatever suffering he could."

"Yes, yes! You see that, but that's all you see. You don't see how it crippled me. You don't realize what it's like for me now. Don't you understand? Your father is dead. Nothing can change that and nothing can change me, nothing and no one but me. I came here precisely because he wouldn't have let me, because I have to start making my own decisions and paying whatever price my mistakes require. I've got to start relying on my own judgment, and making decisions in the knowledge that if I'm wrong, there is no one there to bail me out. I don't say I blame him. He meant well; I know that, just as surely as you do. But, right or wrong, it's over now; there's no one to make decisions for me any more. I am sure of that, just as sure as I am that the house is empty at night, and empty in the morning. There's nobody there but me, now. I am alone, for the first time in over forty years. I'm alone and I've got to start living like I'm alone."

"Oh, Mom, I know what you're trying to say. I know. . . ."

"Do you? Do you really? Do you know what it's like to get up at six o'clock in the morning every morning for forty years, make coffee and eggs, with a raspy voice singing any one of three songs in the background, the sun, red in the winter, a dull blur against the frost on the window, or bright, so bright it hurts your eyes, even that early, in the summer? Think about that for a minute, Katherine. What could you possibly know about that? Do you know, could you possibly know, how much I hated that sometimes? And, God, how much I wish I could do that just one more time. It was so much more than a habit, Katherine. It was my life. And now it's over, finished."

"No it isn't; it's . . . Patrick, Patrick, put that down, whatever it is, and come over here, now."

"Oh, Mom! It's nothing. Just a piece of wood. It was lying here and I . . ."

"Put it down, I said. This minute. And get over here."

"Leave him be, Katherine; he's not doing any harm. God knows, he'll have his own troubles soon enough. Just let him be."

"Mother, I just . . ."

"You know what I've noticed about you, Katherine? You always give it away when you know I'm right. You don't even realize it, I guess, but you do. It's like you're confessing, even while you're arguing with me. It's the only time you call me Mother. Usually it's Ma or Mom. But when we have a spat, and I'm right, you call me Mother. I wonder why?"

"Oh, Mother, don't be foolish. I . . ."

"You see? You see, you did it again. It makes it very easy

to fight with you, because I can always be sure when I'm right. It's very convenient. And I think I know where you got it, now that I think about it. You got it from your father. That's the kind of thing I mean, Katherine, the things that you pick up from people that you don't ever think about, the little things you know without even knowing that you know. No one could ever fool you, when you're that close to someone, because you know more about them than they know about themselves. I'll bet if you ask Andrew, there are things he knows about you just like that. You have to be with someone night and day to learn them, the way I was with your father. That's the only way."

"You can't inherit something like that, though."

"I wouldn't be so sure about that, if I were you. Maybe you can't inherit something like that, not exactly, but you got that habit from Will, all the same. He did the same thing. Except when I was right, he called me Ella, and the rest of the time it was anything but Ella. Not unless we were fighting, and I was right. Funny, I . . ."

"Mom, we've got to go. It's getting late, and it's cold out here. Patrick! Patrick, come here. We're leaving in a minute."

Ella shuddered against the late winter wind, pulled her thin no-longer-stylish coat a little tighter against the chill, and began searching in her purse until she found a rumpled tissue. She bent stiffly, her bulk shortening her breath, frosting in small clouds, and wiped some mud off the newly laid stone, a plain reddish granite that said simply

DONOVAN

WILLIAM   ELEANOR

1895–1961   1900–

She fumbled a moment with the stiff bunch of carnations, getting brittler by the moment, now a little discolored, turned the bronze vase a little tighter into the lip that served to hold it in place. Straightening, she let her eye roam out over the small pond, which glistened from a thick layer of ice around its edge that grew thinner and lacier out toward the center, where it looked more like rock candy crystals coating the inside of a jar. She did not want to look again at the new stone, or at its companion, under which her daughter Emma lay.

She chose instead to let her eye wander over the snow-patched brown grass of the cemetery, almost pastoral in its expansive serenity. She was remotely aware of, and grateful for, the cemetery rule that disallowed stones above ground level. There were no garish monuments towering over the lawns here, the wealthy lording it over their less fortunate but equally deceased neighbors, as in so many cemeteries. It seemed almost possible that she stood in an open field, looking at the last vestiges of winter, fading away of their own accord rather than waiting to wilt under the rising heat of spring. Would that the endless winter of her own life, which lay before her now as bleak as these quiet meadows, held the same promise of coming green.

"You know," she whispered, "Emma would be thirty-three now."

Katherine said nothing. They turned toward the hedgerow behind which the car stood, its motor idling, a small cloud curling around the exhaust pipe. Even Patrick, somehow aware that it was appropriate, was silent. Ella turned and said, "If you don't mind, Katie, I think I'd like to go back. Just for a minute."

"Sure, Mom, go ahead. I'll wait here."

Ella, head down, slowly retraced her steps, seemingly intent on placing her feet in the bright islands their previous passage had made in the frost, small snatches of dull green leaping out as if to deny that this was a cemetery. Here and there, gray patches of snow lay in clumps, like old papers full of older news. The wilting carnations looked all the more desperate against the bright stone, even in the graying light. At the foot of the stone, Ella bowed her head even farther.

She knelt on the cold earth and turned her eyes from the raw wound beneath her to the gathering darkness above, as if searching the bottom of the sky for some explanation of her predicament. It had been only six weeks, just forty-two days, and yet she was unable to determine in her own mind whether she had been bereft for only a day or if she had never known the man who lay in the ground beneath her.

"Will," she whispered, "Will, it looks like snow again. I love you. God, I love you still. Pray for me. Please."

She reached out to touch the stone again, her fingers ungloved in the cold, and traced the new engraving, lingering on each letter for a moment before pushing on to the next, her tracing as inexorable as the press of time that would, one day, bring her here one final time. She rose, her eyes still fastened on the stone, then turned to look out over the pond at the foot of the hill, its naked willow branches frail and fragile in the gray light, whipping lifelessly as the breeze picked up, rippling the darkening jewel of clear water at the center of the lacy ice. Resolved at last, she turned toward the car and got in without a backward glance.

On the way back from the cemetery, neither woman said a word, and Ella stared dumbly at her hands, examining each of her fingers in turn as if it were some peculiar biological specimen to be tagged and catalogued. It seemed to Katherine as if her mother were reading something in the elusive highlights of her skin, a language she had shared with Will perhaps, and for which Ella was now the sole curator, a language that, with her passing, would fade from human memory as surely as that of Tasmania or Easter Island, leaving behind only the stiff, wrinkled fingers of this woman who had been her mother, monuments to a way of life no longer real.

As she drove mindlessly home, Katherine remembered the haunted look her mother had worn as they had made their way down the front steps to the waiting car, newly washed for the funeral procession as if for some festive occasion. The gleaming paint had offended her, and she remembered thinking that the car would more appropriately have been draped in purple cloth, like the Stations of the Cross during Advent, when suffering was something to be hidden rather than an object of contemplation. Not that any mere drapery could deny the horrible reality they were to witness, even usher to its conclusion, that morning, but bright metal seemed an unspeakable effrontery. She could still clearly see her mother, pausing, as if frozen, punished for daring to peer at the unspeakable, her eyes dull sparks visible behind the veil as she glanced around the neighborhood, fixing forever in her memory each little gesture, each sound, each bright burst of light.

It seemed so long ago, but it had been a mere few weeks, and the process of realigning lives had all but been completed for most of the family. All of them, in fact, except Ella. Willie had gone back to his pipe dreams and illusions of financial security that loitered, for him, just around the next corner. Daniel had gone again, sending cards home from Singapore and Saigon, when he could remember how to write and was sober enough to recall someone's address. Even she and Andy, who had been closest to Will, had managed to pick up pieces of a life less shattered than it had seemed, the pieces themselves larger than expected, their relationship more clearly discernible than she had at first thought possible. Freest of all, of course, were the grandchildren, who could not quite understand the crowded room, stinking of gladiolus and lilies, where their grandfather lay in a long metal box, sleeping more quietly than they had ever seen him. If they thought about it at all, it was only to wonder when he would sit up to wave his gleaming false teeth at them and snarl as he brushed his thick eyebrows down over the bridge of his nose, seeking to seem, for one last time, the monster he could never be.

It had all been so simple, so quick, almost as if it had never happened, or as if Will had never existed. Katherine resisted the resilience she found buried deep within herself, and resented it in others, but there was nothing she could do about the fact that life went on, for everyone. She could go for days on end now without feeling the persistent emptiness that had grown in her like a cancer in the first few days after Will's death. True, it still would come back, now and then, its pain all the sharper because of the suddenness with which it reasserted itself, and she hated the growing immunity to her loss she found in herself, as if it were a betrayal of her father rather than life itself demanding that she be about its business once again.

As the car turned into Commonwealth Avenue, she smiled unconsciously, as she always had when she went to visit her father. It was only when she looked to her right, and saw Ella quietly weeping, that she realized how irretrievably things were not as they had always been on this quiet street.

TWENTY-FIVE:
Ella

WHEN John died, I don't think I allowed myself the luxury of grieving for him. I guess I was so concerned with taking care of myself and the baby I was expecting, I couldn't really afford to stop and think about what he had meant to me. Later, I didn't want to give Will any reason to be jealous of John's memory, so I tried not to think about John at all. Will never seemed to be curious, and I was not really anxious to confront the pain, so I just let John lie there, someplace in the back of my mind. He was never really with me, but never very far away, either.

I guess I was afraid that it would be disloyal to spend any time thinking about John, even though he had been Will's friend. In some ways they were closer than John and I were, and I guess maybe that's one reason Will was so precious to me. Will and I were more than husband and wife, we were the best friends each of us had. That's why I miss him so. The strange thing is that now that Will is gone, too, I can't seem to think about him without thinking about John. Not that I miss John in the same way I miss Will. It's just that I had to bury two men in my life, and whatever their differences, there must have been something about the two of them that made them alike. Most of the time that I think about John it's to compare him with Will, usually to John's disadvantage, but not always. Not that I would have preferred John to have been more like Will, but Will wasn't perfect. I don't think I do any disrespect to his memory by saying that, because he would have been the first one to admit it. But he believed in himself, and he never once had any doubt that he was as good as the next man. That was probably the biggest difference between the two of them. If John had only believed in himself a little more, he might not have been so confused, or so mean, toward the end. There was something he was afraid of, that he would never talk about, and all of his anger was some kind of protection from that fear.

I don't think John really believed I wasn't faithful to him, because I never did a thing to make him think I wasn't. But, whatever that fear was, it came from inside him, somewhere down so deep that even he didn't recognize it as part of himself. I remember reading about a fish they caught someplace off the coast of Africa. It was a fish they thought had been extinct for fifty million years, and yet there it was one afternoon, on the end of somebody's fishing line, looking exactly like it did fifty million years ago. I think that for John looking at that fear deep inside must have been something like looking at that fish was for other people. It's something that looks so alien you just can't imagine where it could have come from. Will would understand that kind of thing, but John never could. He was so frightened of anything new, or anything he didn't understand, that he would just freeze up, or explode, when he had to deal with it.

Maybe the best thing about Will was how much common sense he had. Not that he couldn't do something silly. He was better at that than many men half his age, but it was mostly just his high spirits that made him that way. He was a little bit like a child, I guess, and spontaneous, like children are. But he had a good head on his shoulders, and you could tell him something about himself that he had never thought of, and he would listen to you. He wouldn't always agree with you, but at least he'd consider what you had to say. He had enough confidence in himself, and knew himself well enough, that there wasn't anything he could learn about himself that would make him feel he was worthless. He knew better than that. John didn't, and that was the reason he was so suspicious. It was as though he secretly believed he wasn't worth my time, and that as soon as I caught on to that I would find an excuse to leave him. That wasn't how it was, though. It was just the opposite. He kept making it harder and harder for me to feel secure with him, and it was like he was trying to drive me away, just so he would be able to say that it was he who made me go. I have to admit that I was starting to think about it a bit, toward the end, but I don't know if I ever would have had the courage. That might have been the only way to prove to him that things were out of control. It's curious how little we understand ourselves sometimes, and how we go around pretending that we're something we're not, and acting as if we were what we thought we were. Then we resent it when people start to treat us the way we're asking to be treated.

One morning, when Will had been dead for about three months, I got curious about how I would feel visiting John's grave, something I had not done since the day he was buried. I wasn't even sure I knew where it was, except I had some papers somewhere that had the name of the cemetery on them. I decided that I would go and pay a visit. It couldn't really be wrong, what with Will gone, too, and I don't think Will would have objected even if he were still alive. I thought I might learn something about myself, something I needed to know. There's something about standing face to face with cold stone that makes you think about things and talk to yourself a little more honestly than you otherwise might. Visiting John's grave just might do that for me.

I wasn't used to traveling on my own, but I didn't think I ought to impose this on Katie. I'm not sure she would be able to understand what I was doing, or why, so I knew I would have to take a bus to Philadelphia, where the cemetery was. It was spring, and the trip was likely to be relaxing, as long as I didn't let myself think about it too much on the way. I didn't know exactly what I would do, or how I would feel when I got there, but that was part of the reason I wanted to go in the first place. I didn't even want Katie to know I was going, so I just went ahead and made my plans like it was an ordinary outing or shopping trip.

It was a nice day, and the bus ride was smooth. We went down Route 1 most of the way into Philadelphia, but we weren't as close to the Delaware as I hoped, so the scenery wasn't all that nice. There were a lot of dull, flat spaces between Trenton and Philadelphia, and I swear that, if you fell asleep for a bit, when you woke up you wouldn't be able to tell if it had been for five minutes or five hours, even though the bus trip is only about two hours. Everything looks the same along the highway. Then, I guess I really wasn't as interested in looking at things outside as I was things inside.

When I got there, I had to find a taxi that would take me to the cemetery, on the outskirts of the city, more in Germantown than not. I think the driver must have been a little surprised when I got in and asked for the cemetery, because he had seen me get off the bus, and folks don't usually come such a long way to do something like that, but he was very pleasant, and even knew the place I wanted. It wasn't exactly the best-kept place I had ever seen, but I didn't expect it to look like I remembered it, since it had been so long. It was kind of cluttered up with headstones and such things. I had a map with the plot marked on it, and when the driver found the intersection of two roads that looked like they were pretty close to the plot I wanted, I asked him to stop and wait for me, because I didn't know how I was going to feel, and wasn't really prepared to have a total stranger with me.

My hands were shaking, and I could hardly walk, but I made myself push on. Most of the names were Irish and a few German and Polish ones were sprinkled in. I saw a few Flynns, but I wasn't sure whether I was in the right section, because I couldn't find any John Flynn. I kept looking, and finally found it, but the dates were wrong. They said 1856–1895. I looked at the map again, and then I realized that it was a family plot, and that the John Flynn buried there must have been a relative, maybe even John's grandfather, or an uncle. The time was about right for that, although I had no recollection of his ever having mentioned another relative with the same name. After two more Flynns, I finally found it.

I knelt there, and the first thing I could think of to do was to try and remember what John's face looked like. I could almost catch it, but it kept slipping in and out, like it was on water, and the wind would keep blowing it away, or making it too ripply to focus my eyes on. When it got close, I would try very hard to fix it in my mind, but I just couldn't. Four decades is a long time, I know, but we had been married for two years, and I had carried two of his children. It upset me that I couldn't really remember what he looked like. All the while, I kept thinking of Will, and wondering what he would think if he knew I was here, and then it dawned on me that if I was right, he *did* know, and I got a chill. I started to shake, worse than before, but I wasn't going to leave until I got what I had come for, whatever that might be.

I guess I expected some kind of explanation, or maybe a cleansing, as if coming here would chase away the devils that had followed me for over forty years, devils that just might have had more influence on me than I knew. I started to realize that I had allowed the way things were with John to influence the way I did things later, not just in my relationship with Will, but in the way I looked at everything. I don't think, from the time I first became aware that John was suspicious of me, that I ever was quite as free in being myself as I ought to have been. That wasn't fair to Will, or to the kids, and most of all it wasn't fair to me. I had never really been free from the suspicions that John had hung around my neck, and I guess I used to stop before I did anything to ask myself how John would have reacted, what he would have thought. You can't really be free if you have to worry about what somebody else thinks. I guess I was lying to myself all those years, depriving myself of part of what I was, and part of what I had to offer. That cheated Will and it cheated me.

I think Will must have known that, but I don't think he blamed me, knowing what he did, and guessing what he was able, about what my life with John must have been like.

Knowing that, or learning it for the first time there in the cemetery, I realized that the understanding of myself I had come for was not some secret knowledge, but an understanding that would allow me to be something I had never permitted before—myself. In a strange way, I think I owe that to Will. He cared how I lived, and he wanted me to be secure. That's why he protected me the way he did, but he might have protected me too well, maybe not understanding that the best thing he could have done for me would have been to allow me to make my mistakes, to suffer for them, and, ultimately, to learn from them.

There were times, especially after Emma died, when I know I could not have gone on if it hadn't been for him. In those first weeks, just seeing the sun come up in the morning was unspeakably cruel. It meant another day I would have to face, knowing that my daughter was gone, that I could never send her out to play in that sunshine, the way she used to, the way other children her age would be playing. It didn't seem fair that the sun should come up for them and not for Emma. It was Will who made me see how wrong I was to feel that way. He listened when I talked that way, and he didn't argue with me, not at first, not until he thought I had had a decent time to get it out of my system, but one day I said that if I had my way, the sun would never come up again, and he asked me if I would want to be the one to deprive all those other children of the things I wanted, but couldn't have, for my own daughter, and he kept at me until I saw how selfish and wrong-headed I had been. It made me see that what had happened wasn't directed at me alone, and I didn't feel as bitter about it after that. He never said another word, and he never did lecture me. That wasn't his way. But I knew he was keeping a watch on me, determined that I would not slip into that bitterness again without an argument from him. Just knowing that let me know that someone else cared, and it made me see that he felt the injustice of it every bit as keenly as I did. He just knew that there was no point to carrying a grudge against the irreversible nature of the thing that had happened, and that the only way to deal with it was to get on with living the rest of my life. I guess I came here for some sort of reaffirmation of that, something I had delayed for over forty years, in the case of John, and that I could apply to losing Will in exactly the same way. The funny thing is, Will was never able to practice that kind of forgiveness himself. He never got over losing Emma, even though he helped me forget as best I could. Even now, when he had been gone for three months, I was still learning from him, but this time I was learning that I had to stop trying to learn from him, and start learning things on my own, the way he had.

I looked around at all the stones and thought of all the people who must have come here over the years, some every day or every week. Others, like me, took forty years to get here, but the lesson was the same for all of us. The only difference was that some never paid enough attention to learn it. I knew that what I had to do was to go on with my life, not as if Will had never been, but as if the fact of his having been was something precious to me, precious enough that I would not allow self-pity to tarnish what we had had. I suddenly understood that he loved me for what I was, and what I was able to be, as much as for the more ordinary reasons that we always think of when we try to explain what it is that so draws us to someone.

There wasn't a sound in the cemetery except my beating heart, the soft chuffing of the taxi engine, and the wind. The wind seemed to have a voice of its own, almost as if it were trying to speak to me, as if it were speaking for Will, saying what he would have said if he were standing beside me. "Mother, there is no reason for you to stand there and wonder about what you are going to do with the rest of your life," it said. "There is a lot you can do for yourself, and for the children and the grandchildren. I don't want to see you waste yourself on the last two. Do for yourself, do as I would do for you if I could." I know that sounds silly, but it really seemed like I could hear those words in the air, and there was almost no breeze to speak of, just enough to move the young leaves a little. I looked up, and the sky was bright blue, with huge, white, fluffy clouds that seemed to float along like ships. The sun was coming out from behind a great big cloud, the edges of it a dark blue, and bright yellow rays spread out in every direction. It was so beautiful, I knew that the voice I was hearing wasn't Will's and it wasn't even my own; it was just an expression of nature, the will to go on in the face of pain and the kind of loss that everyone experiences, but which seems so personal and brutal when it happens to you.

I looked at the headstone in front of me, and the sun was flashing so on the bright edges of the stone that I could no longer read the inscription, or even the name, and I began to see that it really didn't matter who was buried there. It could have been Will or Emma or John, and it wouldn't have made any difference. The important thing was that I had loved each of them as best I could, but they were dead and I was still alive. I had to carry on, no matter how difficult it might be, and no matter how much it might hurt to think about the people I had had taken from me. My turn would come soon enough, but until it did, I had no real choice but to live as though it would never happen to me. There was no point in living at all if you had to spend most of your time thinking about the end that was going to come, sooner or later, to you. Daniel had said that funerals were for the living, and he was right. What he didn't say, because he probably hasn't learned it yet, is that there is nothing more important for the living than the ability to live in the face of death. To live as though death didn't exist at all. That's what I was going to do. It was the only way to live. It's what Will did, and he'd expect no less of me.

TWENTY-SIX

In the weeks immediately following the funeral, Ella had lain awake nights, haunted by a thousand fears, some economic and some far more personal. She had never really had to fend for herself, and although she was determined to be self-sufficient, it did not come easily to her. When it came to money, Will had always insisted that she leave it to him to worry about. But when she paid her visit to John's grave, she realized that this might be more of a liability than she had thought. Although she didn't blame Will for his overly protective attitude, she now frequently found herself resenting her lack of preparation for living by herself.

With the kids no doubt having money problems of their own, she couldn't very well expect them to carry her burdens. Willie had become increasingly distant as his problems with Louise escalated, and Daniel . . . well, he was just Daniel, for better or worse. She had quickly gotten used to the idea that emotional solace could not readily be had, and when Willie called, which he seldom did any more, it was more likely to be to ask her for comfort than to offer her something in the way of consolation, or companionship. When he did ask her about her situation, she could tell by the tone of his voice that he wanted it kept short and would prefer that she simply assure him that things were fine. She usually complied with this unspoken wish so he could feel he had performed his filial obligations without actually having to deal with anything. She hadn't heard from him in nearly two weeks, and the last time had not been pleasant. She knew there wouldn't be a permanent break, at least not in the sense that she would never see him again. But it would not be the same. Neither of them could ever see the other in quite the same way again.

Ella's relationships with nearly everyone in the family seemed to be changing, often dramatically. She seemed to be asserting that the direction of her life was going to be governed by new considerations. It was almost as if she were deliberately, provocatively, demanding that others sit up and look at her, perhaps thinking that it would register on them, if only subconsciously, that she was alone now, that she had to be perceived as something other than a simple appendage of her husband. She seemed to be seeking new perspectives, new directions. Her children had only slowly become aware of this new resolve, despite her insistence on having Will's funeral the way she wanted it.

It struck her as rather curious that Andy, of all the family, was the only one who tried to help her define herself, to find herself, instead of trying to force her to be what she had been or to reshape her to suit a personal need. As a result, she had come to value his opinion more and more, even going so far as to call him at work on occasion, to be certain that she could solicit his opinion without any interference from Katherine, who would otherwise have hovered in the background, distracting both Andy and herself. She usually reserved her requests for his advice for particularly sticky matters, such as the one she was now facing, the most difficult decision she had yet to make since Will's death.

Willie, Katherine, and especially Daniel had been pressing Ella to sell the house, and the question had been hotly debated off and on ever since it had first arisen in the week after Will's funeral. Katherine, with Andy's blessing, had suggested that Ella move in with her, while the boys were more interested in the sale of the house than in the question of where Ella would live once it had been sold.

Ella had been mulling the question over in her mind, and had finally come to a tentative decision. But she was anxious to try it out on Andy before doing anything irrevocable. She decided to call him at the plant.

"Andrew, I'm sorry to bother you at work, but I wanted to talk to you about something I don't want Katherine to know," she began.

"That's all right, Mom. What can I do for you?"

"You can start by telling me, honestly, whether or not you object to my moving in with you and Katherine," she said.

"Of course I don't object, Mom. The only thing I want is to be sure you feel comfortable doing it."

"In that case, do you think I should really sell the house?"

"No, I don't, Mom. It's a good house, it's paid off, and the maintenance won't be that much. Katie and I can always give you a hand with it if it's necessary. If you want to move in with us, you're more than welcome, but you don't have to sell the house to do that. You can rent the house out. That way you'll have a little more money coming in, because I know Pop's pension isn't that large. I'm sure the rent you could get would more than cover the taxes and maintenance, so you could supplement your income a little. Not much, maybe, but you'd still have the house to sell later, if you had to. On the other hand, you'd always have it to go back to if you found you didn't like living with us. Sometimes it makes it easier just knowing that you have someplace to go."

"That's pretty much what I think, Andy," she said. "But Katherine insists that I sell. Why do you think she feels that way? Does she think I can't take care of myself, is that it?"

"I honestly don't know, Mom. I know she wants you to move in with us, and I guess she figures that if you hang on to the house, you'll be less likely to do that. And I know she worries about you being alone there."

"Well, I'm not all that helpless, not yet, anyway. I've decided not to sell, and I'm going to live here as long as I can afford it. Will would have wanted it that way, I know, but even that isn't the reason. I just don't think I can afford to give up my independence, not if I want to keep my self-respect."

"I understand how you feel, Mom," Andy said. "I think you have to do what you want to do, no more and no less. The worst possible thing you can start doing at this point is allowing somebody to tell you how to run your life. Katie will just have to understand that, and I'll do whatever I can to make her see things your way. But remember, anytime you change your mind, all you have to do is say the word, and there will be no questions asked. Will you promise me that?"

"Yes, of course. And thanks, Andy, I appreciate that. But let me tell Katherine before you say anything to her. I know she can get her hackles up when she thinks she's been crossed, and I don't want her to think you had a hand in persuading me to go against her."

Andy knew that Ella was right. She had slowly but surely regained her equilibrium, and to knuckle under to outside opinion now, no matter how well meaning, would surely upset it once again. He felt it was essential that Ella be in charge of her own life, and make her own decisions. Had she moved in with them, she wouldn't have been as likely to do so, or even to think through many questions on her own, with Katherine there to intrude at every turn.

It soon occurred to Ella that she had more room than she needed in the house, and since she was a good cook and didn't have more money than she could use, she began toying with the idea of taking in a boarder, someone who could help defray the expenses of the house and who would not intrude on her own life, but who would provide her with some much needed company. She didn't want an old woman, or an old man, for that matter, who would have the better part of life to look back on and not much to live for or talk about. She didn't feel anything incongruous in this attitude, since she was not in the habit of thinking of herself as old, despite her frequent references to her "advancing senility." She felt that she could derive a certain vicarious vitality from a younger person, someone whose presence in the house would provide resonant echoes of her own children.

The loneliness that seemed to gather in the attic and the cellar, seeping like cold dark air through the cracks in the floorboards and down the attic stairs, could only be kept at bay by someone young enough to radiate youth, someone with enough energy to permeate the house and ward off the more onerous emotional aspects of her widowhood. She knew that to raise the question with Katherine would only provoke a new storm of opposition, so she took an advertisement in the *Trenton Times* without consulting her. She did let Andy know, and he suggested that she be careful in screening any applicants. He told her there were plenty of people who would be glad to rent a room, with board, when it was her cooking, so she needn't feel that she had to take in the first person who came to the door.

The first three or four responses were enough to make her reconsider the idea, but on the third day after the ad had appeared, she answered the bell to find a tall, young, well-dressed man shuffling nervously on the front porch.

"Yes, can I help you?" she asked, through the half-open front door.

"Yes, lady, you have room for rent?" he asked.

"Yes, I do." She didn't know quite what to make of the young man's accent, which was vaguely Continental, possibly Eastern European.

"I am Emil Nagy, and I would like please so much to see it, if is no trouble?" He seemed to state everything as a question, but he seemed nice enough, so Ella stepped back to invite him in.

"It's on the second floor, if you'll just follow me," Ella said pleasantly.

"Thank you, please?" Emil said.

She made her way up the stairs, the young man following behind her, bumping his head on the overhang halfway up the steps. She heard the thump and looked back over her shoulder to see her prospective boarder rubbing his brow.

"I'm sorry," Ella said, solicitously. "I should have warned you about that."

"Is all right, lady, please. No problem for me. I do it many times. All the time in Hungary I am bumping my head. My mother was saying I would be crazy or in hospital many times if I didn't look more where I have been going."

"You're from Hungary?"

"Yes, but I have been here since four years now. After the revolution, I am coming, and my brother, Gyorgy, here to make new living here in the U. S. of A."

They reached the top of the stairs, and Ella led the way back toward the room she had planned to rent. It was of moderate size, neatly organized, and had been freshly painted. The furniture was largely that of Willie and Daniel, but was in good condition, if not particularly stylish. On the whole, the effect was one of comfort and efficiency. The young Hungarian looked around appreciatively, and nodded his approval.

"Will you be asking much to be renting this room?" he asked diffidently.

"Fifty-five dollars a month is what I had in mind," Ella said. "That includes breakfast and dinner, of course, provided you don't keep unusual hours."

"Oh, no, I am keeping regular hours, since I am having a good job," Emil assured her. "I am working for Westinghouse, at laboratory."

"Oh, what do you do there?" Ella asked, more out of politeness than curiosity.

"I am making research in electronics. I am having a degree, from Hungary, and am learning things here, too."

"You must be terribly lonely, so far from your home and your family."

"Oh, no, my brother is coming here with me. From Hungary."

"Oh, when will he get here?"

"Please, lady?"

"Your brother, when will he be here?"

"He is already coming here, with me."

"You mean he is on the way now?"

"Oh, no. He is already coming here. He is working with me at Westinghouse."

"Oh, I'm sorry. I misunderstood."

"Is all right, lady. I am not learning English to speak well yet. I am going to school to learn speaking it better soon."

Ella took this to mean that he was already in school. "How do you like school?" she asked.

"I am not knowing. I am starting soon, but not yet."

Wrong again, Ella decided that it would be better to get down to the purpose of his visit. "Well, do you think you might be interested in the room?"

"Yes, I am thinking I would like to rent it, please, lady."

"Are the terms satisfactory?"

"Please?"

"The rent, is it acceptable?"

"Oh, yes. When can I be moving in?"

"Well, I'll have to check your references, of course, but if there is no problem, then anytime you like. Just let me know, so I can be here to let you in. We'll have a key made for you, and you can come and go as you like."

"That sounds like it would be being nice."

Without further discussion, the arrangements were completed, and Emil took possession of his room on the following Monday evening. He turned out to be a pleasant young man, although conversation proved to be difficult enough so as to be rare. Ella was a bit uneasy in the first few weeks, but after a month or so, things had settled into a routine. Emil, perhaps because it was the closest thing to home available to him, got in the habit of watching the Lawrence Welk show with Ella, who studied the bandleader's syntax in an effort to facilitate her conversation with her boarder. It seemed to help, and they gradually became friends, Ella teaching him the intricacies of canasta, and Emil telling her stories of his life in Hungary, horrifying her with the details of his narrow escape from the Russian troops who had been sent in to put down the abortive uprising of 1956.

Katherine was appalled by the idea of her mother having a stranger in her house at first, but soon got used to the idea, and Emil was soon treated as part of the family by everyone but Willie, who maintained a cool reserve, and Daniel, who was seldom at home in any case. Ella was proud of herself, and of her new-found confidence, which was greatly bolstered by the success of her plan, though still tenuously rooted.

TWENTY-SEVEN:
Willie

Talk about crazy, that foreign guy my mother took in was something else. Not that he was wild or dangerous. I couldn't really say that after seeing some of the things I've seen here, but he was just a little strange. I didn't like him at first, and I guess it was because I was a little jealous. We never got along, Mom and I, after she told me I was being selfish, and I guess it was because she was right that I got a little offended. It was around the time that Louise and I had come to the conclusion that there was no point in continuing our marriage. It was clearly going nowhere, and I was at loose ends. The only thing I could think of to do was to go running back home, I suppose because I could pretend that I had never been grown up at all, and that would make it easier to pretend that things were all right. If I were young enough to be my mother's son, there could be no marriage dissolving around me like so much sand at the beach, Louise would soon be a figment of my imagination, and everything would be fine. I always felt that things were going just a little out of control, and I didn't want to face up to the fact that it was mostly my fault and that if anything was to be done, I would have to do it. It would be a lot easier to go back home and let Mom take care of it, like she took care of everything when I was a kid. When Emil showed up, it wasn't that easy. I don't think it was a case of Mom choosing him over me, so much as it was her understanding that taking me in, like a lost puppy, wouldn't do either of us any good. I resented Emil at first, though, because I started to think of him as a rival for my mother's affections. I just couldn't accept the idea that she had made a decision to live her own life, and Emil was a constant reminder of that. It got to the point where I couldn't even go see her unless I was sure he wouldn't be there. I didn't want to see him. I even started waiting in my car, parked at the corner, until I saw him leave before I would drive on up and park in front of her house. I don't think she realized it, but maybe she did. She always used to say, "You just missed Emil," or something like that. I guess maybe she was trying to let me know that she knew it was deliberate without coming right out and saying it, because she didn't want to hurt my feelings.

I guess he was a nice-enough guy, all right, but he was a little odd. Him and his brother. They were two of a kind, and between them they seemed to know about sixty words in English, and they didn't even seem to know how to put them together. I remember when Emil decided that he would make a hi-fi set for Mom, which was a waste of time, because she had about as much interest in music as she did in sports-car racing, but he wanted to do it, and it was something that he knew how to do, since he was an electronics engineer. Every time I went over to visit, there would be a mess of wires and electronic parts on the dining-room table. It was a big round table, but there wasn't room on it for anything but the stuff Emil was working on. Mom even took the fruit bowl she always used to have in the middle of the table and moved it out to the kitchen. That made me mad, because I would always sit in the living room with her when I would visit and I'd go get a banana or a tangerine from the bowl. Now it was all the way out in the kitchen, and she didn't seem to bother with it much. Half the time I visited, it would be empty. She said Emil didn't like fruit much, so there was no point in keeping it around, since it just spoiled before anyone ate it. I reminded her that I always made sure to eat some, but she told me that she had to pay more attention to the kind of food she brought into the house now, because she had a responsibility to her boarder. It made me feel like I wasn't really welcome there any more, and it was just one more proof that my life was slipping out of control and there didn't seem to be anything I could do about it.

Maybe that's why I started drinking. Not that I didn't drink before, but I really started hitting the sauce around that time, mostly because I liked the way I didn't feel anything when I got really drunk. There was this real hollow feeling inside after Louise left, and I was trying to keep it filled with booze. It didn't really fill it, but I didn't notice it so much when I was loaded. I didn't notice much of anything, when I was loaded. Anyway, Emil kept working on this hi-fi, a stereo set, it was, I think, and the damned thing seemed to keep on growing, just like it was alive. Everytime I saw it, it seemed to be larger, but there were always just as many pieces on the table, still waiting to be soldered in or wired together or added on somehow. I used to ask Mom where the hell she was going to keep the damn thing. I told her that if it got any bigger, she would have to add a wing onto the house, but she just laughed and told me how happy Emil was when he was working on it. I asked her once why it made so much difference whether Emil was happy, and she just said he was a nice young man and she didn't see any reason why he shouldn't be allowed to be happy. I kept thinking to myself that I ought to have the same right, but I never said anything. I guess maybe I was afraid she would just laugh or, worse yet, tell me that it was up to me.

I know now that she would have been right to say that, but I didn't know it then. I was going around looking for somebody to make me happy, instead of trying to be happy. The difference doesn't seem like much, and I don't think I would have appreciated it until I got here. It was Doctor Johanson who made me see that I was here mostly because I had never really learned to be independent, and that as long as I was waiting around for somebody to make me happy, I never would be. When I look around at the other patients here, I can see myself in a lot of them. Most of them are worse off than I am, but that wasn't true a few weeks ago. I guess I'm lucky to have somebody who cares about me enough to make me care about myself. I know my mother cares, but I didn't know that for a while, and I couldn't stand it.

I used to sit around and make fun of the record player that

Emil was building, and I watched, hoping that he would never get it finished. It seemed to be taking him so long that I was sure he would never get it all together. I used to talk to him about it, and he tried to tell me what he was doing, but I didn't really want to know, so I just shook my head, and asked a question every once in a while, mostly because I wanted to distract him. It never seemed to work, though, because he would always go right back to the place he had been soldering before I interrupted him. And he never got mad, either. I guess he just liked doing it so much that he could enjoy being around all those wires and tinkering with them. It probably helped to know that it would sound nice when it was all put together.

Finally, when he had been working on the thing for about three months, I went over one afternoon, and it was all together. Emil wasn't there. Mom said he had gone over to Gyorgy's place because Gyorgy was making a cabinet for the stereo and it was time to put the electronic stuff in the cabinet. I asked if it worked, and Mom said she didn't know but that Emil said it would. He just didn't want to try it out until it was mounted in the cabinet. You'd think it was some kind of work of art. I was annoyed that the bastard was so sure of himself, so certain that that damn thing would work. When Mom said she had to go to the store, I told her I would hang around until she got back, because I wanted to talk to her about something and I also said I wanted to hear the stereo when it was put together.

When she went out, I walked over to the thing, still sitting on the dining-room table, but all by itself now. All the wires and spare parts that had been lying around for so long were gone. I looked at the thing close up, and all the wires were in place, soldered together perfectly, and there was no wasted space anywhere. There wasn't even a piece of wire too long anywhere. Everything had been cut just right and soldered in place very neatly and cleanly. The damn thing looked perfect, and I could tell, just by looking at it, that it *was* perfect, and I knew it would work, and I didn't have any more doubts than Emil seemed to that it would be a wonderful thing to listen to. I figured the cabinet Gyorgy was making would probably be a wonderful thing to look at, too, and I got really angry. At first, I just wanted to push the whole damn thing on the floor and jump on it. I wanted to smash the whole fucking thing into the same shapeless pile of disconnected parts it had been when I first saw it, as if that would render what Emil had done absolutely meaningless. I didn't see that it wouldn't have made a bit of difference, because it was the doing of the thing that counted for him. I don't have a doubt that he would just have started all over again, no matter what kind of damage I did to the thing. He probably wouldn't even have gotten mad.

I got control of myself, and I decided that I could get even with the little twirp without making a mess of his stereo, and maybe even make him look just a little bit foolish into the bargain, if I played my cards right. At first, what I wanted to do was to take some of the wires apart and resolder them in different places, make the whole thing go haywire when he turned it on. If I got lucky, I might even fix it so the whole thing would go up in smoke. If that happened, I knew Mom would get pissed and tell him he couldn't make anything like that in the house any more. I looked around for the soldering iron he had been using, and I found it in the credenza, but when I plugged it in and started to look at the insides of the damn thing, I knew that I could never disguise what I had done. There was just no way I would be able to resolder any of those wires without making it obvious that somebody had been tampering with them. Instead, I decided that if I just pulled a couple of them loose, underneath someplace, it wouldn't work, and I'd have that satisfaction without anyone being the wiser, and that smug little bastard might come down a peg or two when he started to think that his wonderful construction wasn't so perfect after all.

I found a couple of wires that were more or less out of sight and looked like they might be easy to disconnect. I gave one of them a yank. At first, it didn't want to come loose, so I yanked a little harder, and it finally gave. I did the same thing with another wire, and then a third, resisting the impulse to work my way from one end of the damn thing to another, taking the wires apart one by one. I toyed with the idea of crossing the wires, but that would have been too obvious. I decided that the best thing to do was to put them back close to where they had been soldered in the first place, figuring that they would be harder to spot that way. Then all I had to do was sit back and wait for Emil to come and watch the look on his face when he plugged the thing in and found out that it didn't work.

I went out to the kitchen to grab a piece of fruit, but the bowl was empty except for a dried-out tangerine. I opened the refrigerator, looking for a beer. Since neither Mom nor Emil drank, I struck out again, and contented myself with a glass of lemonade, which must have been a big drink in Hungary or something, or else there wouldn't have been any of that, either. While I was pouring the lemonade, I heard the door, and then two voices, Emil's and Gyorgy's. I went into the dining room with my lemonade, and Emil said the same thing he always said when he saw me, "Hello, Meester Weelie, how are we being today?" I just grunted, and he told me he and Gyorgy were going to put the stereo in the cabinet, which they had in a station wagon out front. They wanted to make room for it first, so they pushed a couple of chairs out of the way in the living room, then went out to the street again, soon bouncing back through the door with a long, low wooden cabinet that looked more like a coffin than a piece of furniture. Emil pointed to it when they had set it down and told me that it was handmade by his brother, Gyorgy, and wasn't it a beautiful "theeng"? I nodded, and sat down to watch the fun. I have to admit that they both really knew what they were doing. The cabinet was a perfect fit for the electronic components, and they slipped right into place. Emil screwed them down and plugged it in. He went up to his room and came back with an album by somebody named Bartók, which he proceeded to put on the spindle of the turntable. He pushed a couple of buttons and waited for the music. The arm of the turntable moved over the disc, and it set down without a sound. He stared expectantly, and Gyorgy had his hands all ready to break into applause, but nothing happened. There wasn't any sound. The arm was moving properly, and the needle was tracking through the grooves, just as it should, but there was no music.

Emil mumbled something to Gyorgy in Hungarian, then said "I am not understanding, Meester Weelie, why it must be not working." I just shrugged, and he looked back at the machine, opened the cabinet doors in front, between the speakers, and looked inside with a small pocket flashlight. He got up quickly, unplugged the machine and went to the credenza, coming back with the soldering iron. He knelt down, plugged in the iron, and lay on his back for a couple of minutes, poking around inside the stereo. Then he got to his knees, unplugged the iron, and replugged the machine. This time he was rewarded with perfectly reproduced sound. He looked over his shoulder at me, let his eyes stare into mine for a long moment, then just shook his head without saying a word.

He never did say a word to me, or to Mom. The next week he moved out, and I never saw him again. Mom didn't either, but I think she got a postcard once, from someplace in California. I was glad when he left, but I guess that was about the worst thing I ever did, except for some things I did in Italy during the war. But that was different. There was no excuse for what I did to Emil's stereo. All I could think of was getting even with the little smart aleck, who never did a thing to me. I didn't even stop to realize that I might be hurting my mother a lot more than I might be hurting Emil. I guess that's exactly what I did, because she never took in another boarder, even though she could have used the money. I think she got sort of attached to him, and having him leave so suddenly, without any explanation, may have been just a little like having him die on her, and she wasn't really ready to deal with another loss like that yet. I guess she didn't want to take the chance of getting attached to anyone else at all. I guess I fucked up again. Maybe that's why I'm here.

TWENTY-EIGHT

EMIL is gone. The surrogate son has left her without a word. In bewilderment and desperation, Ella turns her affection on the earth, hoping that in the green lives she shepherds there will be durable communion, her rooted charges unwilling to leave her ministering hands, and unable to leave her if they would.

She has taken to rising with the sun, and often can be seen by busier neighbors on their way to work as she sits in her window watching the birds that have come to rifle the lawn and make off with the cache of worms drawn by Will's attention to the turf. It is almost as though her life has been circumscribed by the fence that marks the limits of her property, life and land coincidentally narrow. And even the land is not free and clear. Daniel has seen fit to borrow money she didn't have, and rather than plead poverty in evasion, or decline in honest annoyance, she has taken a mortgage on the house and yard, placing the garden at risk as it has never been in nature. She is self-conscious of her weakness, but much of her will and most of her pride have gone with Emil, their departure as mysterious and unannounced as his.

The summer had been unexpectedly warm, and the plants are doing better than they should, taking advantage of her lack of interest to grow beyond the borders allotted them, the hydrangeas hanging now over the pavement by the house, their slender branches taxed to rupture by the weight of the flowers. There are weeds among the vegetables, and the wealth of peaches on the tree Will fought so hard to save has sundered other branches from its trunk, the tears and fractures pulling the bark taut against the wire Will had so laboriously wound about its wounds, now nearly hidden. The ground itself is sweet and sticky with the fallen fruit, now fit only to draw the bees who tire of the asters and lilies that loll about unwatered, as often as not, nearly wilting beyond recall in the dry late-summer heat. In all this wealth of color and fragrance, it is only the roses she bothers to tend, coming out, just after sunrise. The slick street is still damp from the late, light rain that slipped in while she was sleeping, or trying to, an uncomfortable prisoner in walls of cotton and chenille.

Here and there, rainbows glow in the early light, spread out on the tar of the street for all the world like exotic birds exhausted by a night flight from somewhere she can't imagine, or disheartened butterflies who no longer have the will to evade the net and choose to lie still and spread-winged, waiting for the pin that will fix them in time and space. The rainbows slip in shade and shiver under the hiss of early tires. An occasional faint splatter of some water loosed by the wind and the quiet remarking of the leaves are the only sounds.

This morning, Ella has resolved to struggle against the enervation that has pinioned her, and to restore the garden to the ordered promise it held last fall. She has resolved to try to salvage what can be saved and uproot what has died. Her hands are not those of angels. They are slightly fat, heavily veined, and, here and there, when they cup a flower, they betray a muscularity ill-suited to the delicacy of their labor. Each flower is cupped as one would heft a fruit, firmly, against the weight, yet gently, to avoid a bruise. Her slippered feet whisper in the damp grass as she makes her way along the bank of roses.

She is acutely aware of the fact that she is alone this morning, alone as she had not been for forty years, as she has perhaps never been, and she cannot erase the months-old memory, fresh as if it happened yesterday, of her life vanishing in a surge of green foam, against blue lips mumbling a language she did not know and had not time enough to learn. She sees again the quiet morning furniture, the shuddering fall; she hears the awful groan and the more terrible silence that followed. Here, in this very house, within a stone's throw of the hospital, the one she hated and he ignored, he died. The quiet avenue of trees, so old their heavy branches intertwined like ancient fingers of lovers, led pointlessly toward the ward he would not live to see, his eyes glazed over, sightless, even as his stretcher was lifted into the ambulance for the half-block sprint too late to be of help.

Last night, as most nights, she replayed on her ceiling a thousand scenes from the long movie that was their life together. She has been rendered a captive audience of one, her career of actress in the film now over. She saw their first meeting, heavy as she was then with another man's child. Then John was cold one day she can't quite remember, knowing it doesn't matter anyway, one day in sixty years; at seventeen she was a widow and a mother twice, though not for long, the first child leading its father underground.

And Will—God, wasn't he wonderful. Or at least he was there, and for that she was grateful, grateful then and grateful still. These were his flowers, too; they were ours, she thinks. And how they planted them, watered them, fed them, cared for them as if they, too, were children, which perhaps they were, in their own way. Such a small thing, to have shared a garden with her husband, and yet how it mattered now, mattered as it never had, with him gone. These green, living things were links to him, their tender shoots buried in the same earth he now lay under, and maybe he would, somehow, someday, find his way back to light, slip up, some small part of him, through a green and tender stem some summer soon, and she knew she'd know, she'd feel his presence waiting silently in the green, watching, still caring as he always had.

And the church, how feeble it all seemed now, all those penitent Sunday mornings, the solemn maundering for the dead she had witnessed countless times, feeling pious, useful, good. What did it matter now, how did it help, could it help at all? She falls to her knees now, not praying, but digging at the roots of a blue hydrangea, its huge globular flowers nodding to the quiet hum of her snatches of song, which were not mournful, nor joyous, either. They were music only, music in its purest form, music as it must have been intended to be, comforting, full of a solitude appropriate to the time she found to be hers, monastic in its solemnity, its quiet acceptance. She knew it was not homage to God so much as an expression of her new knowledge that she was on her own. No Will. And no God. Alone.

She wanted to restore the garden that had been theirs, to carry on the struggle against entropic, cluttered growth that sought only to erase all trace of their influence, to cover over the space that had been theirs alone with random, wild greenery, insolent, arrogant in its self-assertion. She got to her feet and continued her review of the ranks of roses. Caressing a particularly exemplary bloom on nearly every bush, whispering apologies for her recent indifference. At each successive step she saw further evidence of her neglect, and by the time she reached the back of the garden, where the fruit trees sagged under the weight of their scorned generosity, she was appalled at the weeds that grew among the tomatoes and the beans, stooping to pull the worst of them. As if galvanized by imminent disaster, Ella goes indoors and drapes herself in a heavy blue denim apron, its pockets full of gloves and shears, and hurries back with such determined haste that her very urgency seemed to magnify the pace of the wild decay she sought to stem.

Determined to proceed in an orderly manner, she makes her way to the back of the house, preferring to start from the secure and relatively sparse area beneath the kitchen window. She falls to her knees among the weeds and tangled edges of the lawn, clawing at the illicit growth with both hands, anxious to create an ordered space from which her dominance could reassert itself in linear forays into the jungled stretch of flowers along the fence. She assembles a mound of weeds behind her as she goes, baring a regularly expanding rectangle of sandy earth, still dry under the matted weeds despite the rain of the preceding night. She pauses to survey her progress, then, with a cry, she reaches for the shears and uses them more like a knife, and like a club. "Oh my God," she cries. And again, "Oh my God, it's back!" There, a last demonic affront to Will's memory, springs the rambling rose, its arrogant sprigs in tender defiance peeking through the dry soil as if to see if he is still about.

Outraged by the spiteful resilience of the single plant Will despised in the entire garden, Ella can't control herself and bludgeons the tiny sprouts into green-and-yellow pulp, which lies there in the gray sand the way an insult lingers in the mind long after one's failure to respond with withering disdain, an open wound on the broad, defenseless sweep of pride. In her heart, Ella knows that even this savagery is not enough, will not revenge her husband or change the course of time, and she turns with vicious energy on rose after rose, wielding her shears like an angel of death, slashing wickedly from side to side, severing flowers from their stems and crushing them beneath her feet, where they ooze like pools of thickening blood, their soft petals pulped and darkening bruises on the greenish-yellow margin of the lawn. Up one row and down the next she rages, her frenzy gathering violence as she goes, until not a single rose can be seen above the ground, the bushes now ranged in stunted ranks, like columns of dispirited prisoners, defeated in a war they do not understand. Oblivious of thorns and sharpened splints of rosy stems, she casts aside the shears and tears in naked energy at the remaining stumps, bending them with her feet, twisting them off at ground level, leaving battered stumps where her favorite flowers once had grown. Her fury spent, breathing heavily, she falls to her knees in the middle of the lawn and folds her arms across her heaving bosom, glaring into the garden like some brutal parody of Michael at the gates of Eden, and even in her stolid anger, she knows her rage is pointless.

"Damn you," she whispers, then looks up at the sky, where the sun has begun to burn through the haze, and her eyes begin to tear against the light, the drops coursing down her cheeks in merciless parody of life-giving rain and the promise of a renewal she can't imagine.

TWENTY-NINE

WILLIE lay in a stuporous fog, the effect of too little sleep and too much beer, and barely heard the phone when it rang early one Saturday. He groaned to cover the persistent ringing and turned on his stomach to bury his head under a pillow, but the dull buzz seemed no less insistent. Reluctantly, he turned over and groped for the receiver, cocking an eye at the alarm clock as he did so. Still unable to read the dial, he mumbled, "What time is it?" instead of saying "Hello."

The response was entirely too chipper for the hour and the condition of his head. "Hey, big brother, it's nine o'clock. You must have really tied one on last night, buddy."

"Who the fuck is this?" Willie grumbled.

"Who else, you asshole? It's me, Danny!"

"Oh!" Willie managed, shaking his head to clear it. Then, realizing what he had just heard, he sat upright in bed, and yelled, "Hey, how the hell are you? When'd you get in, Danny? Where are you?"

"Hold on, hold on! I got in last night," Danny answered. "You feel up to company on short notice?"

"Sure! Come on over. Just give me a few minutes to wake up, and I'll put some coffee on. I'll need it, even if you won't."

"Okay, buddy, be there in about half an hour. See you then," Danny said.

Willie slowly threw his legs over the side of the rumpled bed, then slowly edged forward, and groaned loudly as his bare feet hit the cold linoleum. Sitting motionless on the edge of the bed, staring dumbly around the disheveled room, he hoped he would recognize his robe, when and if he saw it. He lay back for a moment and snuggled his pillow into a ball, cradling his head on the soft cushion to collect his thoughts before trying to rise again. What seemed to him to be only moments later, he jumped with a start, aggravating the thumping in his skull, when he heard a loud tattoo on the window. Running over to yank the shade, he cringed away from the insane flapping as it spun madly until the tension in its spring was exhausted. He rubbed the grimy glass to make a peephole and, bending his nose to the pane, saw a bearded figure gesturing wildly and shouting so loudly that the words were lost. It was his brother, dressed in watch cap and peacoat, unseasonably warm, though it took him a second or two to recognize the familiar features under the unaccustomed foliage.

Finally, Willie was able to make some sense of the peculiar communication by reading his brother's lips, and he realized Danny was saying, "Let me in, you asshole!" He mouthed an okay and moved toward the back door of the small house he had rented when he and Louise decided that their marriage was taking a toll too high for either of them to pay. He tugged on the doorknob. At first, the door refused to budge, and the greenish glass rattled perilously, threatening to shatter. He saw a bulky shadow outside the door, yelled "Push!" and gave the knob another hard yank. Flying suddenly backward as the knob pulled loose from the shaft, he landed in a heap, and narrowly escaped the shower of glass splinters and shards that erupted inward, pursued by his brother's hands.

"Damn it all to hell, Willie," he heard, dimly. "Why didn't you tell me the thing was so weak. Look at the wreck here now. Jeeesus!" Immediately on the heels of a vicious thud, the door flew back. Danny turned to Willie with a grin and said, "I guess you didn't get around to making that coffee yet, huh?" He laughed loudly. "I'll just go put it on. You can straggle on back when you get yourself together. See you later."

As he thumped on through to the small kitchen, Willie could hear Danny rattling around searching for the coffee. There was a crash and a muffled curse. Danny shouted, "Hey, Will, where the hell do you keep your coffee—and something to make it in?"

Willie realized there would be no solace for his aching head until the coffee was perking, so he carefully picked his way into the kitchen and sat heavily on one of his two wobbly kitchen chairs. He put his head gently on his arms and said into his sleeve, "Under ink!"

"What?"

"Under ink!"

"Ooohh, under the *s*ink," Danny said.

"Don't do that," Willie pleaded.

"Do what, make coffee?" Danny asked.

"No. Don't say ssssink like that."

"Why not?"

"The *s* hurts my ears. I've got a bitch of a headache."

"Sssso I ssssee." Danny laughed, opening the metal cabinet under the sink and falling to one knee to peer in among the jungle of pipes and cans. He rooted around, clattering several of the tins together, then exulted, "Gotcha!" He began to search for the coffeepot. The water swelled nearly to the sink's brim as he reached in for the plug, then drained away with a convulsive gulp and a prolonged gurgle, each of which seemed to go into one of Willie's ears and collide with the other in the very center of his skull. He put his hands to his ears and let out a subdued "Gaaaaaaahhhhhh!" When he was certain the noise had subsided, he resumed his former posture. Danny worked for a while without further conversation, interrupting the mild clatter of his activity with snatches of popular songs from the forties, hummed in a saw-edged baritone.

With a loud "Ta da!" he announced the conclusion of his search for the missing pieces of the coffeepot, quickly scoured them under a steaming stream of hot water with a handful of Bon-Ami cleanser and pierced the sealed lid of the coffee can, deeply inhaling the coffee-laden air that welled up around him.

"God, Willie, I've had some bad hangovers in my time, but I never saw one like this!"

"Like hell! I've seen you sometimes so bad you got a headache if a butterfly went by!"

"Like hell you have," Danny snorted. "You never saw the day I ever needed more than a cup of coffee and a beer to make me right as rain, no matter how much I had to drink the night before."

"Come on, Danny, I remember one time you came home with a flowerpot on your head, and you kept telling Mom you were Napoleon. I thought for sure she was going to skin you alive, and then disown you. But you could always sweet-talk your way out of or into anything with her. She never did get your number."

"Hell, you're just jealous, that's all." Danny laughed.

"Damn right!" Will responded. "And so would you be, if the shoe were on the other foot."

"Oh, hell, you shouldn't talk, buddy. It's not like you didn't have Pop on your side whenever it counted."

"Yeah, sure, but Pop looked out for everybody. With you and Mom, it was a little different. Like you were special, or something. I never could figure that out."

"Sounds to me like you really *are* jealous, Willie," Danny said, turning serious. "Shit, I never meant anything, but if you were like me and got into as many messes as I did, you'd feel grateful for anything like a guardian angel that came along. You know what I mean?"

"Sure I do. That's exactly what I'm telling you. You had a guardian angel and I didn't."

"But you didn't need one like I did!"

"Well, who gives a shit?" Willie said, the beginnings of a smile tugging at the corners of his mouth. "That's all over now, anyhow, and I'm going to bed."

Danny sat down to wait for the coffee, and in a short time Willie was back, seeming more alert than when he had left. He pulled up a chair and joined his brother at the table.

"I thought you were going to bed," Danny said.

"I'll never get any sleep with you making a racket out here."

"Well then, why don't we drink a little anesthetic instead of the coffee?"

"Why not?" Willie agreed. "You always *were* a pain in the ass."

Danny pulled two quart bottles of Miller from the refrigerator, and slammed the door shut with a bang. He looked quizzically at the bottles and turned to Willie, saying, "You getting the churchkey or am I?"

"If you think I'm getting up again before I finish one of those bottles, forget it. It's on the side of the refrigerator."

Danny fetched the bottle opener and pried both caps loose before retaking his seat. "Bottoms up," he said, handing one to Willie and tilting the other back with a luxuriant sigh. "Aaaahhh, that's better," he said, slamming the bottle down on the table. It was now nearly half empty. "Big brother," he continued, "you know what I think? I think we better get our asses in gear."

"What's your rush?" Willie inquired.

"I got a friend I want you to meet."

"Who is she?" Willie asked with some suspicion. "I don't really feel up to any female companionship this morning."

"Not she, he. It's some guy I met last time I was home. His name's Jimmy."

"Well, who is he, and why would I want to meet him?"

"He's just a real interesting guy, that's all. He used to be in the merchant marine, and I met him through a couple of buddies of mine. He lives in a shack down behind the War Memorial Building."

"What?"

"Yeah, it's true. He's sort of a bum, I guess, but not really."

"What do you mean? Either he is or he isn't!"

"Well, I mean he doesn't go on the road or anything like that, you know. He's not a beggar or anything. He just lives down there because it's cheap, and he gets by on some kind of pension or other. Anyway, he's a real pisser. He tells some stories you wouldn't believe. I think you'll get a kick out of him."

"Okay, already. You convinced me, but at least let me wake up a little. My fucking head is killing me. I can't even stand to breathe right now, let alone go traipsing down to the woods to talk to some fucking hobo. Just let me get myself together."

"Okay, great! I'll see if I can straighten out this mess, or at least find out how far it reaches into Pennsylvania." Danny turned immediately to a clamorous reorganization of his brother's kitchen. He made what progress he could, but by the time Willie returned, this time dressed to go out, there was little discernible improvement in the dreary and disorderly kitchen.

"All finished?" Willie laughed.

"Shit, are you kidding? Hercules couldn't do this place in a week!"

It was a warm fall afternoon, the bright sunlight cutting through the seasonal edge, but it threatened to turn cold, and chilled down quickly under every passing cloud. The bus trip through the usual semisnarl of downtown traffic was quick, the pace interrupted only by an occasional traffic light. Once, Danny leaned over to say something to Willie, but the latter was unresponsive, and Danny did not trouble himself to speak again.

They got off the bus at the corner of Broad and Market streets, and made their way quietly down the steep angle of Market, in the general direction of the river. To their left was a long row of boarded-up businesses—hardware stores, bakeries, delis, liquor stores, a paint store—while on their right was a three-block-long stretch of vacant lots, which were a sandy yellow, marked with the broken ends of bricks and cinder blocks, which were the only evidence that the lots had ever contained anything other than the small, desiccated patches of weeds that grew in scattered clumps all over the leveled area.

"I see Ben's is gone," Danny observed, breaking the silence for the first time since they left the bus, as they neared the intersection of Market and Lamberton.

"What?" Willie asked distractedly.

"Ben's Deli. It's gone," Danny said.

"Oh, yeah. They moved most of these places out of here a while back. They're going to tear most of this area down and put up more state buildings."

"That's good. It'll make it look a lot nicer."

"Sure, but it's just going to make the city poorer. They won't get any taxes from the state. But that's the way they do things around here. When I had my real-estate license, I was handling some houses down here, but I couldn't give them away, because everybody knew what was going on," Willie replied angrily.

"You sound pretty bitter about it."

"Hell yes, I'm bitter! I'd still be in the real-estate business if it hadn't been for that bastard Delmonico. He gave me a tip on something that was supposed to happen over by the old coal-port, and I nearly lost my shirt. I was lucky I had had a couple of good years before that or I wouldn't even have been able to unload the business. As it was, I just about broke even. That's the last time I ever listen to that guinea son of a bitch."

"Shit, Willie boy, that's a hell of a lot better than you usually end up doing. You can't blame that on Dom."

"For Christ's sake, Danny," Willie retorted. "What the hell do you know about business? You haven't even been able to hold a steady job for more than six months at a time since you left home. At least I was able to take care of a house, a wife, and a couple of kids."

"For a while."

"Damn right, for a while. I'd be doing it yet if it wasn't for that asshole of a doctor who ran me down."

"That asshole of a doctor saved your life, pal. Don't forget that."

"Yeah, sure! If that jerk hadn't run me over, I wouldn't have needed anybody to save me in the first place! Don't *you* forget *that*. Pal."

They lapsed into silence and began picking up their pace under the influence of anger and adrenaline. Willie looked frequently at the empty lots to the right, as if they formed an unbroken, sweeping metaphor for his entire life, and particularly for the bleakness of his future, which he had begun to believe was a desert of the most arid expectation. Danny, on the other hand, seemed to have shrugged off the conversation and its bitterness rather easily and was soon whistling unconcernedly, swinging his hands about.

Willie began to grow irritated by Danny's demeanor. It seemed to him that Danny was indifferent to his fortunes, as if everyone should be capable of his irresponsible approach to life, able to escape into the anonymous freedom of the sea at will whenever reality intruded too boldly into his life. He speculated on his own feelings and realized that he might be more than a little envious of that carefree approach to things that had seemed to preserve Danny from the injurious knocks he had received, an approach that seemed to give him some hidden resilience that could be discerned in the sprightliness of his walk and the absence of lines on his heavily tanned, almost leathery face.

"Maybe I should be more like that," Willie mumbled half aloud.

"What's that," Danny asked, as if he couldn't care less.

"I don't know. I was just thinking out loud. Forget it."

Danny nodded. Then his face stiffened a little.

"What's the matter with you," Willie asked.

"Jesus, I really miss the old man, you know? I never realized I would, especially when he was chewing me out. I even used to wish he'd croak on the spot, and sometimes he'd get so mad, I thought he would. It makes me feel guilty when I think about it, almost like it was my fault somehow. And it sneaks up on me when I'm not expecting it."

"That's stupid, Danny. He had a stroke, that's all. It wasn't anybody's fault. It would have happened sooner or later, no matter what anybody did."

"I know, but look at me, will you? Look at us! What the hell is wrong with the two of us? I keep telling myself that if I hadn't given him such a hard time, it would have been later, rather than sooner. Then I look at me, what I am, what I do. I don't know. . . ."

"There's no point in thinking like that. Mom was talking the same way, and God knows, she never gave him a hard time.

It's natural to feel that way, I guess. It's just because there's nothing else we can do about it. Somebody dies, and you want him back, so you blame yourself instead of having to deal with the idea that there was absolutely nothing you could do about it."

"Yeah, I suppose so. Still, I wish to Christ I had been better to him when he was alive."

"We all do, but it's too late to do anything about it now."

"Not really!"

"What do you mean? He's dead, that's all there is to it."

"Yeah, but there's still Mom. Maybe we can make things up to him by looking out for her better than we did him. I think he'd like that, if he knew we felt that way. Maybe it would make things easier for everybody concerned."

Danny trailed off. Then he broke the self-imposed silence with a whistle. "What the hell, it's all water under the bridge, I guess. What the hell . . ."

"Why don't we get on down to this friend of yours. We can talk about that later, all right? How much farther is it?"

"Not far, just down through those trees over there. It's right on the water, and it's pretty well hidden, but I think I can find it okay."

"You better not have dragged me all the way down here on a wild-goose chase. I could still be home in bed, you know," Willie warned.

"Yeah, I know. But why should you be home in bed, sleeping one off, when you can be out tying one on?"

"You don't think I'm in shape to do any serious drinking, do you, with this head?"

"I've never known you to be in any shape but."

"Well, you got me there, Daniel," Willie chuckled. He didn't feel much like laughing, thinking about Danny's suggestion that they might, somehow, have been responsible for their father's death. He knew there was no direct connection, but it was a good, sharp hook to hang his collected guilt on, and he couldn't shake the feeling that he did, somehow, have some bills about to come due.

They made their way across the wide expanse of the riverside highway with no difficulty. On the opposite curb, Danny paused uncertainly, looking up and down the river, finally spotting the pathway and, grabbing Willie by the upper arm, moved toward it briskly. Their careless passage filled the air around them with the sudden hum of disturbed insects and the brittle debris of seed husks and dying weeds. The smell that arose from the increasingly dense undergrowth was of dry musk, a pungent attack that Willie unconsciously associated with childhood games played in vacant lots and open fields. The path was obviously well traveled, and Danny plodded on with confidence until he reached the first of the tall trees.

There, he stopped again, and looked about to take his bearings. He spotted his signpost and struck out in a new direction among the trees, which were still well leaved, although golden and red. The trees were largely sumac, with a sprinkling of oaks and maples. The hum of an occasional car could now be heard. In addition, there was the soft gurgle of the river, and birds song and but noise. Danny had not broken the silence he had assumed upon crossing the highway, and his characteristic chatter would have been welcome to Willie. He started a tuneless whistle, but Danny turned to shush him, placed a finger so firmly on his own lips that they flushed white to either side of the fingertip, then turned and continued on his way, swatting at a swarm of gnats which suddenly erupted in front of him. The trees had begun to thin out as they drew still closer to the river, and suddenly there was a clearing, in the middle of which a small, rickety shack stood, seemingly held together by ragged strips of tar paper nailed to the outside walls. The roof appeared to be plywood, covered with tar paper. Danny again halted, turning to his brother with a broad smile, and said, "There she is! I knew I could find it."

"I see it, but I don't believe it," Willie informed him. "What the hell is it doing way out here in the middle of nowhere, and why the hell would anyone want to live here?"

"That's Jimmy for you. I told you he was a little crazy. Let's wake him up."

He strode swiftly across the clearing and began rapping vehemently on the frail plywood door. The whole construction seemed to teeter perilously, but there was no indication that Jimmy, or anyone else, was inside. He gave the makeshift handle of the door a tug, and it swung toward him. Willie could see a feeble glow of artificial illumination within, but no one acknowledged their arrival.

Danny stuck his head in through the doorway and called, but there was no response. He edged into the shack, and Willie gathered that it must be divided into at least two rooms, because he could hear the squeak of hinges, followed shortly by the slam of a door. "Come on in," Danny shouted from inside, the thin walls of the building barely muffling his voice. "There's nobody here, but we might as well wait a while."

Willie stepped in and immediately looked for the source of the light he had seen from outside. There was a battered card table against one wall, with a pair of bridge chairs, and a small kerosene lamp in the middle. It was surprisingly light inside. The other furnishings were rudimentary and makeshift, consisting largely of fruit boxes, which served as bookcases, a pair of small tables, and cabinets. In the latter, he noticed a few canned goods, three or four cardboard food boxes, and a variety of condiments in bottles. Jimmy's bed must have been in the second room. The wall that divided the shack into chambers was made from the end panels of fruit packing crates, still wearing their colorful labels. The only other furniture was a long narrow couch, both arms sprouting tufts of rusty cotton, which lay against the wall opposite the bridge table.

Danny flopped down on the couch with a groan, rubbing the calves of both legs vigorously. "I'm not used to so much hiking, big brother." He sighed. "I guess I must have been away too long this time."

"Oh, I don't know." Willie laughed, in spite of himself and his profound irritation. "I haven't been anywhere at all, and my legs are killing me, too."

"Yeah, but they were never right after that accident, anyway. I don't have that excuse," Danny responded.

"I'd be more than willing to trade excuses with you, if you can manage it," Willie responded sharply.

"Come on, Will. You know I didn't mean anything by that. I just meant that I could understand why you might be tuckered out, but *I* should have been able to make this hike without much of a strain."

"I know, I know," Willie snapped. "I'm just a little bit pissed that I came out here at all, let alone to find nobody here. This guy must be awfully interesting to drag anybody out in the middle of the woods. Where is he, anyway?"

"Search me. He's almost always home, except when he goes into town to get his mail, or to buy supplies."

"How the hell does he manage, even if he *does* have some kind of pension?"

"Well, as you can see, he doesn't exactly live high off the hog. How much could it cost him to live here?"

"I didn't mean the money angle," Willie explained. "It must be really boring. I think I'd go nuts if I had to live like this. This place isn't much better than the shacks I saw in Italy during the war. In fact, I'm not sure it *is* better. One thing's for certain, though—they used the same architect."

Danny laughed, and began searching the room, hoping to find a bottle of water to quench the considerable thirst the dry weeds and dusty air had created. Willie, too, was thirsty. "I don't suppose there's such a thing as a refrigerator in this dump, is there?"

"Are you kidding?"

"I didn't think so."

"That's the main reason Jimmy is so fond of whiskey, I guess. He never has to worry about keeping it cold."

"More likely he uses it as anesthetic whenever this place

gets to him," Willie ventured, "and I'll bet he needs it pretty often, too." He looked around with no effort to disguise his distaste.

Suddenly, Danny jumped up with a loud shout, and Willie wheeled in time to see a tousled gray head entering the doorway, followed immediately by the gnomish body upon which it rode.

"Danny me boy!" the diminutive figure bellowed. "Where the hell have you been? I haven't seen you in months!"

"Hey, Jimmy, you're looking good, old man," Danny shouted, reaching out to help the new arrival with the three large bundles balanced precariously in his arms. He grunted as he lifted the two largest of the parcels, and Willie noted the clank emitted by each as Danny set them on the bridge table. "Holy Christ, what's in these things? They weigh a ton."

"Potables, me lad, potables."

"Hunh?"

"Ambrosia, Daniel. The nectar of the gods. J & B, if you catch my meaning."

"Gotcha!" Danny nodded. "Willie, grab the other bag so Jimmy can dig up some glasses and we can toast something or other." Then he introduced his brother to the comical dwarflike man. "Jimmy, this is my big brother, Willie. You remember my telling you about him last time."

"Yes, of course. The motorcycle patrolman, right?" he said, winking at Willie.

"That's the one," Danny said. "It's good to see all that booze hasn't affected your memory any. Now, how about we get some of that J & B out. I'm thirsty as hell."

"Sure thing! How about you, Willie?"

"Why not? I'm sure as hell not going back through that jungle out there until I have *something* to drink. You got any ice?"

"Now where would I keep a thing like ice around here?" he said, waving his arms in a sweeping arc.

"Can't blame a guy for asking." Willie laughed. "I don't exactly *require* it, anyhow. It has the distressing tendency to melt, and dilute my booze."

"Ah! There's a man after me own heart, Daniel," he said approvingly.

The three sat drinking and exchanging stories for the better part of the afternoon, Jimmy regaling the brothers with stories of odd characters he had encountered in his nearly thirty years in the merchant marine. He had sailed under several flags, largely in the Pacific, and spent most of his time on short hops in the Far East, leading a bizarre life which might have appealed to Joseph Conrad if that distinguished author had been blessed with a sense of humor. As the afternoon wore on, and the stories became more protracted and the laughter they provoked more prolonged and less controlled, Willie began to feel a vague sense of unreality creeping up from behind and insinuating itself into the floor of his consciousness by degrees. It began to seem to him as though Jimmy were himself a creature of fiction and that it was precisely that unreality about him that appealed to Daniel, who attended to every word of the older man as if it were some gem of Oriental wisdom.

Less under the storyteller's sway, Willie could devote a part of his mind to objective analysis, and he came to feel that he, too, was attracted by the carefree fabulousness of the life style described but, he felt sure, not lived by the old man. It was as though Jimmy were some modern Homer, a foot-loose fictioneer, and the stories he told were too perfect in their construction to have been true. Missing from his narration was the sense of futility and the debasement of poverty that formed so integral a part of the lives of the people who populated the tales. They did not convey, in any real sense, the feeling of a life *lived,* but, rather, of a life one would have *preferred* to have lived, if only life were not so unruly as to impose its grimmer realities.

By five o'clock, the men had finished the better booze Jimmy had brought with him, and they began to hit the cheap wine. With the change in booze, a new tenor crept into Jimmy's voice, an edge of barely concealed despair, as if some pain, deeply buried, was lubricated by the liquor and slowly slipping loose from the iron grip of wishful thinking that had held it so long in check. It was there, Willie knew, and intact, waiting to be uncovered, lying in wait like the remains of a woolly mammoth, flash-frozen and perfect in its integrity. The difference in the old man's tone was a subtle one, and seemed to have escaped Daniel's notice, but it was there nonetheless, evident in the posture as well as the voice. He seemed to be shrinking into the shadows as if there was the only place he could hide from the ruined thing he carried inside, a painful reminder he could ignore but not escape.

Willie watched the eyes of the man turn inward, and toward the ceiling, as the alcohol more and more affected his perceptions, and he knew that the Jimmy he was watching, so outwardly rapt, was not the amusing gnome before whom his brother sat enthralled. It seemed to Willie that there were two Willies in the room with the other two men, one who betrayed his kinship with Daniel in posture and outward fascination with the skillfully woven words, and one who reluctantly extended his hand in greeting to the inner Jimmy, joining his phantom hand to the gnarled claw that scratched its way up from the belly of the old man who sat there spinning fables in order not to see the peculiar thing to which he was giving birth.

Daniel's head was drooping forward, and his shoulders slumped, as he fell more and more under the influence of the alcohol, and Jimmy's voice seemed to sag, giving Willie the impression that Daniel was merely an incarnation of the imagined life Jimmy had so longed to lead. He, too, was slowing down noticeably, his voice now seldom above a whisper, the hoarse laughter all but gone, surfacing now and then as a harsh, parodic reminder of itself until finally it vanished completely and the droning voice had given way to the exaggerated silence that lingers in the wake of a speeding train late at night in open country, where its sound can carry for miles over the dark vastness that lies, as real and dangerous as any sea, between the islands of refuge men build for themselves. Willie stared in silence at the now unconscious men before him, his drink in his hand, dangling as though it were the last word the sleeping bard had uttered, the one tangible proof that he had spoken at all, the lone memento of a life hard won by the weaving of words and the denial of pain. Willie turned the glass over and over in his hand, minutely examining its surface from every angle, the way an ambitious scholar explores the surfaces of a poem, searching for the one door that will reveal the splendor of its deepest chambers, nestling among the stones like the burial chamber of a pharaoh. Like most incarnate words, this, too, had long since been rifled, and Willie was reduced to draining the glass through the one apparent opening. He tossed it carelessly into the corner, where it smashed against a heap of dead soldiers.

Willie got shakily to his feet and staggered over to the table, where a single bottle remained unopened. He downed the wine in convulsive gulps, then he staggered backward to the sofa and closed his eyes, screwing the lids tightly down against the light he did not want to see and, with a shuddering sigh, passed into blessed insensibility.

A sudden noise awakened him with a painful start that echoed and re-echoed in the caverns of his skull, which had bloomed to four times its normal size and was far heavier than usual. He refused to open his eyes until the first throb had died away, and spent the time speculating on the source of the noise, thinking at first it was his own voice, slipping out in one of the uncontrollable moans he had taken to uttering in recent months. He opened his eyes, one at a time, on darkness, realized that the lamp had long since burned out, and that it must be very late. There was no ambient light in the shack, since the lamps that lined the highway, though very bright, were screened by the heavy vegetation through which they had passed on their way to the shanty that afternoon. He sat up, ignoring another siege of throbbing, and groped in his pocket for matches, lit one, and made out in dim outline, beyond the full reach of his meager illumination, the shape of the table, upon which sat, if he remembered correctly, a second kerosene lamp. He got gingerly to his feet and shuffled softly toward the table, taking care not to make any noise that might awaken his two sleeping companions. In the darkness, he groped for the chimney of the second lamp, knocked against it with his extended fingertips, and caught it with the same motion, heaving a sigh of relief at the narrow escape as he placed it carefully on the tabletop. He reached into his pocket for a second match, struck it on the rough wood of the table, and brought it to the wick of the lamp, which began to smoke, to glow, and, finally, to catch fire. As the flower of light bloomed in the shabby interior of the shack, he replaced the murky chimney and turned to see where Daniel was, but the spot where he last had been was vacant.

He turned toward Jimmy's chair and saw no one, then turned to allow his eyes to sweep the room, a movement that came to an abrupt halt and dissolved in an exploding moan, which slackened his jaw and glazed his cobwebby eyes. The first thing that registered was the greenish tongue that lolled from the slack mouth like a piece of spoiled pastrami, thick and dusty, dangling toward the chest of the man who himself dangled from the soiled rope he had knotted carelessly about his neck; he dangled just above the battered crate he had used to fix the rope to the two-by-four that helped support the roof, a fragile support, but not so feeble it could not stand the added weight that hung nearly motionless in the silent, bug-filled air.

Willie closed his eyes, as if to deny the validity of his vision, or as if he preferred to see nothing ever again, rather than face the bloated myth that swayed ever so gently before him, the first faint odor of decay reaching delicate tendrils tentatively in Willie's direction. He groaned again, in a tone as despairing as the cry that had first awakened him, and as he slipped back into the insensible state from which he had so recently been ripped, he was still unsure whether that sound had been his own cry or the last desperate fable woven by Jimmy, his final lie squeezed into gibberish by the pressure of the grimy rope from which he now hung suspended in lifeless space, a gnomish comma, fading into thin air like a story for which he had no other ending.

THIRTY

Ella had always dreaded passing through these grimy streets, and now they seemed even worse to her, the gritty pavement litter grayed by the smeared windows of the bus, the general oppression further heightened by the sharp sunlight, which seemed more yellow than usual, perhaps because the leaves had begun to turn. She sat uncomfortably, her hands in her lap, restlessly twitching. As the bus stopped at each traffic light, she turned her head this way and that, as if trying to absorb the whole city on this single passage. It all seemed new to her, because she had seldom traveled through this part of town.

The oldest buildings, dilapidated windows askew in their frames, the paint, usually gray or grayish white, peeling back from the underlying wood in great curling sheets, were as novel an experience as the newest government buildings in the heart of town. As new as the hard gray stone over Will's grave. In a curious way, it was that stone around which her world had begun to revolve, from the moment of its emplacement. Just as Will had been the reason she lived her life, and the reason she sometimes wished to end it, now his tombstone provided her with the only reliable point of reference.

She wondered what Will would have thought of her making this uncommon trip on her own, without so much as a word to a soul about where she was going or why. When Willie had called her late the night before, she had thought it was one of his horrible jokes, the kind he often indulged in when he had had a little too much to drink and had begun feeling restless and put upon by a life that had seldom, if ever, been firmly within his control. When she had finally realized that he was not joking, her instinct had been to hang up, to slam the phone back into its cradle with enough force to shatter it and utterly extinguish, not only the voice and the trouble on the other end of the line, but communication itself.

She wasn't yet sure what Willie had been trying to tell her, the story pouring from him in slurred fragments, tumbling over themselves like stones in a landslide, racing one another to the bottom. She had repeatedly asked him to slow down, to speak more distinctly, but no attempt to impose order on his rambling, even crazy, speech had had the least effect. When he had finally and abruptly hung up, with a last whimpering request that she come see him first thing the next day, she had felt relieved, as though the phone call had been a trial in itself, rather than a warning of one yet to be endured. She knew only that Willie had been picked up by the police and was now confined in the state mental hospital on the northwest edge of town. She didn't know what he had done, or allegedly done, to require confinement, and was hoping that she would discover her trip had indeed been the result of a bad joke. She was even willing to forego the luxury of outrage if only it were nothing more than a joke, but she knew in her gut that it was not going to be so simple. Not that Willie was likely to be in serious trouble; that couldn't be, because she knew him as well as any mother knew a son, and while he had been unpredictable, even wayward, it surely was not attributable to insanity, even temporary in nature. It had to be just his high spirits and the tough time he had been having off and on for years that had caused him to get into an occasional scrape. Ever since the motorcycle accident, Willie had been, more often than not, down on his luck.

Ella knew it was the disappointment at having to leave the police force that had been at the root of his difficulty, and although they might have been able to keep him on after the accident, he would have been confined to a desk job, and that would have killed him slowly but surely. He had seemed to live for the excitement of being a motorcycle patrolman, finding interest and reward in the most commonplace of duties so long as he could go to and from the scene on the big, noisy bike. He liked nothing better than to come roaring down the block, especially if he knew she and Will would be on the front porch, helmet and goggles obscuring his features almost entirely, the small puffs of his trousers billowing in the wind that whipped along both sides of the bike. He would screech to a halt in the nearest available space, gun the engine to a full-throated roar, and dismount. He'd make a great show of kicking the bike up onto its stand, remove his thick leather gloves with an elaborate flourish as he strode toward the porch, and pull the goggles up over the front of his helmet as he reached the bottom step. It was so predictable a routine, and so elaborate, but Ella had never had the heart to tell him how silly it all seemed, because she knew that the display was all for her benefit, and that of the neighbors, who would all run to peek out from behind their shades to discover the source of the racket. No matter how often he went through the ritual, and some weeks, particularly in warmer weather, it might be three or four times a week, the neighbors would look, some of them lingering at the shades long after they knew that nothing unusual had occurred or was about to. Then it was all over, in a matter of minutes, wiped away as cleanly and surely as if it had never been.

It had been fortunate for Willie that his unintentional assailant possessed the skills to become his savior, as well. It was generally conceded, after the crisis had passed, that a delay of just a few minutes might have cost Willie his legs, and possibly his life. Ella had never once doubted that Willie, despite the pain of repeated skin grafts and the agony of physical therapy, was a lucky man, although he could not be said to share her certainty of his good fortune.

His recovery had been slow and laborious, marked by fits of despair and heavy drinking, mostly brought on by the pain that persisted long after his recovery had been pronounced to be complete, or at least as complete as it was ever going to be. One leg had been broken in several places, while the other was less severely damaged, with the result that one leg was nearly two inches shorter than the other, and it gave Willie a rolling gait that was nearly comic, even to those who were privy to its origin. The psychic damage was far more difficult to measure, however, and Ella knew the somewhat checkered career her son had led since the accident was directly attributable to his unwillingness to relinquish his attachment to the profession that had been so suddenly and irretrievably denied to him.

The bus was now slowly working its way through the last stretch of grimy streets, with their clutter of smelly trucks and small factories, which huddled together like refugees awaiting deportation. The overwhelmingly chemical smell of the air was seeping into the bus through its air-conditioning system, and Ella wrinkled her nose unconsciously, then reached into her handbag for a small, scented hankie. She brought it to her nose and looked out through the front windshield toward the more suburban, tree-lined avenue that lay immediately ahead, with its large white frame homes set well back from the street on huge, immaculately tailored lawns. She was trying to ignore the suspicion, which lay at the base of her brain, that Willie *belonged* in a mental hospital, and concentrated on the comforting belief that some administrative solution was all that would be necessary to obtain his release. She would then take him in and nurture him again, as she had twice before since he had first left home.

The bus picked up speed. Its stops were more frequent, but were shorter. Instead of long walks that culminated in long waits, the people who lived out here on the edge of the city seemed to have individual stops a few steps from their homes. Ella had refused to take Will's diatribes against the well-off too seriously, assuming that he was merely exaggerating things out of his own sense of frustration, but she had to admit that it must be nicer to live out here than it was in their neighborhood. Even though the street on which they lived was pleasant enough, it was surrounded on all four sides by decaying, or soon to be decaying, blocks of homes, which had been sold by the very people who now left the bus on which she rode to the people of whom she was afraid—rough-skinned Irish drinkers, dark Italians who

329

smelled of garlic, and blacks who sat around in the evenings drinking wine and sweating in their sleeveless undershirts.

Will had scoffed at her fears, partly because he worked every day with these men, and others like them, and partly because his sense of himself would not allow him to admit that he was afraid of anyone. When they had first taken the house on Commonwealth Avenue, the neighborhood had been inhabited largely by small merchants and white-collar workers, but lately it had begun to change. Will had been unalarmed, preferring to believe the change meant only that things were getting better for some people, rather than that the neighborhood was getting worse, or going downhill. She remembered the countless impassioned arguments between Will and Willie, arguments that threatened to break out into real donnybrooks, the balled fists of both pounding the kitchen table into submission when they could not force a change in one another's thinking. Will asserted that men were only as good as they were allowed to be by a system that offered them a quart of milk in exchange for a gallon of sweat, while Willie countered with the jaded weariness of a man whose occupation consistently brought him into contact with the blood and carnage created by the worst of men, and, Will had been forced to admit on one occasion, the worst in the best of men.

Ella used to sit back and listen to the arguments, smiling when she was able to predict, word for word, the response to a particular point made by either of them. There was such vehemence in their voices and flailing arms, it was difficult for her to see how they could have been father and son having a discussion, yet their movements and passions were so similar she couldn't see how they could have been anything *but* father and son. She was always careful, during these marathons, to avoid taking sides, since both were hard-headed and more stubborn than any man she had ever seen. There was never a concession from either, not until the day Will died, and not really then, except that Willie had seen to it that his father's casket was carried by some of the more radical members of the old man's union. For Ella, and she suspected for Will himself, that was concession enough.

Now she was on the way to God knew what kind of man, waiting inside a prison full of sick minds, and she wanted the trip to be over, wanted the bus to turn around and head back the way it had come, as if the mere act of returning home would achieve the purpose for which she had come. As she tossed this foolish idea around in her mind, the homes on the right side of the street gave way to a huge expanse of grass behind a high iron fence. There were small beds of flowers, some still in bloom, despite the coolness of the late September air, and others long since gone to gold. The flowers had to be mums, she thought, since nothing else bloomed this late in the year, nothing in the way of a common garden flower, anyway. Her eyes fell on a large red-brick building, some of its windows in the process of being washed by a handful of workmen in white coveralls. Well, it doesn't look so bad, after all, she thought. Then she saw the sign that stood beside the mortared pillars that marked the only break in the fence. It said "New Jersey School for the Deaf" in fancy lettering, and she knew that her desire to avoid the waiting unpleasantness had led her to take the deaf school for the state hospital. The realization plunged her into a foreboding depression even deeper than that she had felt before. She closed her eyes wearily, tightening them so she could feel the pressure.

"Hey, lady," the bus driver yelled over his shoulder. She looked around and saw that she was now the only passenger on the bus. "You wanted to get off at the nut house, right?" the driver continued. "Next stop is it."

"Thank you, yes," she said with exaggerated politeness. "I did want the 'nut house,' as you so nicely put it. I am going to pay a visit to my son, who is not an employee, if you understand my meaning." She fixed the man with an icy stare, and the faint red at his collar rose slowly up the back of his neck to his cheeks.

"Sorry, lady. I didn't mean nothin' by that, you know?" he whispered. When he pulled over to the curb at the gate of the hospital, she rose and walked majestically toward the front door.

Ella stared at the driver, and he seemed to cower in his seat, then she turned gracefully, stepped down from the bus and headed straight through the front gate of the hospital. She nodded briefly at the gate attendant, who sensed from the vigorous determination of her stride that he should not challenge her progress. She paused to take stock of the grounds and find the way to the administration building. On the lawn in front of each of the buildings was a staked sign, neat black lettering on faded white background, but these signs were of no help because they merely identified the buildings by name rather than function. Choosing the Roosevelt Building as a likely candidate for the headquarters of the hospital administration, she walked briskly up the cement path that led to a low, broad flight of stairs and a wide portico, marked at each end by imitation Greek columns. Directly inside the tall glass doors was a tiled vestibule, across which was another pair of doors. She grasped the knob and tugged, but the door stayed shut. She gave the knob a turn and tugged again, but it still refused to budge. Then she noticed a small sign, hastily penned on an index card, which read "Ring Bell and Wait for Admittance."

She pressed the grimy black button cupped in tarnished brass, hummed impatiently, tapped the toe of her shoe on the gritty tile, and was about to press the button again when it swung open and a nurse stepped out, looking over her shoulder and gesturing to someone still within.

"That's right, Mabel! That's a good girl. Come on with Toni now," the nurse cooed. Ella was prepared to see a small dog trot through the door behind the nurse. Instead, a shrunken gray-haired woman stepped from behind the partially open door. Her hair hung in long, greasy strands along both cheeks, and the loose gray smock she wore was torn in several places, one of its sleeves hanging loosely by a few shreds of material. The whole garment was spattered by a rather ugly reddish-brown substance the nature of which Ella did not care to guess. The nurse continued to gesture toward the woman and cooed her name again and again. "That's the girl, Mabel; come along now, and I'll take you home."

The woman spied Ella, gave a shriek, and stepped back through the door. The nurse turned and saw Ella for the first time.

"What the hell are you doing here?" she asked fiercely, and glared at her.

"I'm sorry, I . . ." Ella mumbled. "I'm trying to find the administration building, and I thought this might be it."

"Who are you? Are you a patient here?" the nurse asked suspiciously.

"No, I'm not a patient. I . . ."

"Well, who are you then?" the nurse interrupted. "Mabel, you stay inside there for a minute. I'll be right with you. All right, dear? That's a good girl. You wait." She turned to Ella with a fierce countenance and again demanded to know why she happened to be in the vestibule.

"I'm here to visit my son. He called me last night and said he was here, and I want to see him," Ella explained.

"He said he was here? In this building?" asked the nurse.

"Well, no, not in this building, I guess. I mean, he said he was here at the hospital, and I was just trying to find the administration building so I could make arrangements to see him. Could you tell me where it is?" Ella stammered nervously.

"I could, if I thought you ought to know. I'm not going to tell you anything until I know what you're doing here."

She pulled the door closed, and Ella noticed for the first time that the glass panels were heavily laced with wire, and that the glass was far thicker than one would expect. The nurse pushed a second button, which Ella had not noticed before, and a loud buzz could be heard. A moment later, there was a pounding of footsteps, the door swung open again, more violently this time, and a burly black man stepped out.

"Ed, this lady says she's here to see her son. Do you know who she is, or who he is?" the nurse asked.

"Naw. I never saw her before, but that don't mean nothing,

Toni. Shit, there must be hundreds of nuts I haven't seen around here. This place is full of them." He laughed, and Toni joined him.

"That's just what I was telling our friend here." Toni smiled, and Ed laughed again. "I think we better take her over to admitting and see what we can find out. Will you give me a hand?"

Ella began to get indignant. She shook her arm loose from Toni's grasp. "Now you look here, miss," she began, "I don't have to . . ."

"You have to do exactly what I *say* you have to do until I find out otherwise," Toni said, and grabbed Ella's arm again, a little more firmly this time. As Ella was about to reiterate her objection, Ed grabbed her other arm, and the three of them began to move toward the front door, largely propelled by the burly man, Ella firmly held by the arm on either side. The big man bent forward to wrench open the door, and stepped through, pulling Ella, then Toni, through after him. He began to march her across the portico and down the stairs. Ella was too astonished to say anything more, and decided that it might be easier to let them take her to their destination.

They crossed the broad lawn at a brisk pace, heading toward a building that was a larger version of the one from which they had just come. Ed was chuckling, and Toni was grimly silent. When they reached the front of the building that seemed to be their destination, Ed continued on past the front steps and turned left, walking in close to the building. Ella saw a narrow white sign jutting out over a narrow doorway toward the rear of the wall; it said "Admitting."

Ed stepped gallantly aside, gestured to Ella to step through the open door, and bowed chivalrously, saying "After you, Miss." Ella stepped in, followed by Toni, and she heard the big attendant say good-bye to them as the nurse stepped up to the large counterlike desk that cut the room in two. There was no one behind the desk, and Toni briskly rapped on the small bell alongside a rather untidy pile of papers. Ella heard a rush of footsteps, and a man appeared from a room behind the desk.

He was dressed in white shirt and duck pants, the color of which seemed the starker alongside the bright scarlet of his belt and suspenders. He smiled pleasantly at Ella and looked questioningly at Toni. "Hi, Toni," he said pleasantly. "What's up?"

Toni gestured toward Ella with her shoulder. "It's her," she said.

"Who is she?" the man asked.

"You tell *me*," Toni responded. "She claims she is here to see her son, but I found her skulking around over at Roosevelt, in the vestibule."

The man looked inquiringly at Ella. "I see," he said, and Ella was not so sure he *did* see, but resolved on the spot that he *would* see, after the swelling in his eyes went down, because she was determined to blacken them both if he didn't get to the bottom of this misunderstanding at once.

"Who are you?" he asked Ella kindly.

"Who are *you*?" she shot back at him.

"I'm Dr. Steinmetz, a resident here," he explained with a hint of irritation.

"Well, I pay your salary," Ella spat at him with a withering look. "I am a taxpayer in this state, and I came here to visit my son. I don't appreciate being manhandled by a pack of fools, and if I don't get to see my son, and pretty quick, the whole lot of you will be damned sorry. My name, as if it mattered, is Ella Donovan, and you damn well better not forget that too soon, because I'll be back here as often as it takes to get my son out of here."

"And who is your son, Mrs. Donovan?" Dr. Steinmetz asked, leaning away from the fury of Ella's attack. "I'd like to help you, but you'll have to give me some additional information."

"Before I give you a damn thing, I want an apology from this idiot," said Ella, glaring at Toni, "and from the damn fool who nearly wrenched my arm out of its socket dragging me over here."

"I'm sorry for the inconvenience you may have been caused, Mrs. Donovan, but surely you must understand that Toni and

Ed were just doing their jobs. As their employer, you ought to appreciate that fact," said the foolhardy Dr. Steinmetz, smiling at his mild joke.

"Don't you smart-mouth me, you buffoon. I've boxed the ears of bigger rascals than you in my time, and I'm not so old I can't do it again if I have to. Just take me to my son, and you can forget the apology. You probably don't know the meaning of the word, anyhow. Doctors never do. They're so damn high and mighty with their X-ray machines and penicillin, it's a wonder they even come near sick folks. Now, are you going to take me to my son, or am I going to have to twist your nose a little first?" Ella demanded, astonished at her own ferocity. She was not used to dealing with unpleasantness in so forthright a manner, but she had been angry ever since the unfortunate bus driver had made his slip, and was spoiling for a fight. At the moment, she was willing to do battle with anyone who so much as hinted that she might have to wait to see Willie.

Intimidated by her persistence and the thinly veiled threat of unnamed violence that lay behind it, Dr. Steinmetz decided that accommodation would be his wisest course of action, if only this damned woman would tell him enough so that he *could* help her. He shuffled a few papers and then stepped briskly to a small table behind him.

"Where do you think you're going, you ninny?"

"I'm, ah . . . I'll just, you know, look in the admitting ledger to see where your son has been assigned," he stammered. "It'll just take a moment to check the records. Let's see. Donovan, Donovan . . ." he mumbled, making a great show of running his finger up and down the pages of the ledger. "Aha," he said, turning to Ella with a big smile, "here he is. Donovan, Willie. That's him, isn't he? I mean, is that him? Your son? Willie?"

"Yes, that's him. What have you done with him?"

"Nothing, nothing. He was just brought in for observation last night," he explained. "By the police, it says here," he continued, barely suppressing a smirk. "I wonder why?"

"Could be he ran into another one like you somewhere,"

Ella ventured. "He probably ripped his ears off. What do you think?"

"Oh, no, I, uh . . . I don't know," he said, his surge of superiority quickly evaporating.

"Well, where is Willie?" she asked, tapping her fingers on the desk top.

"Mr. Donovan is currently in the reception ward on the second floor of the Randall Building. I'll arrange for someone to take you there right away."

"Thank you, Mr. Steinmetz," Ella said, somewhat dubiously.

"You're welcome, Mrs. Donovan," he said with relief. "And it's Doctor."

"Excuse me?"

"It's *Doctor* Steinmetz." Ella stared blankly at him, and he cleared his throat and said uncertainly, "You called me *Mr.* Steinmetz."

"Yes, I did, didn't I?" She turned to look at Toni. "I called him Mr. Steinmetz, instead of Dr. Steinmetz, and he's upset, you see. What would he do, do you think, if I took him by the arm and accused him of being a patient here?" She laughed so hard she had to bend over to catch her breath. She wiped away the tears that had begun to run down her cheeks and smiled at her perplexed auditors. "Just joking," she said.

"I'll call someone to take you to your son, Mrs. Donovan. If you'll just wait over there on the bench, he'll be right with you," said the doctor, anxious to restore some semblance of control to the situation.

"As long as it's not that Ed fellow. I'll have bruises for a week, I think."

"Certainly. I understand. But I'm sure Ed meant you no harm."

"Well, I don't know about that, and I sure as hell mean him a little harm. Tell him he better watch his step, and find some errand to run if he sees me coming," she warned. "I like to get even."

Dr. Steinmetz turned to the telephone and mumbled a few words into the receiver. Ella couldn't hear what he was saying because he had turned his back and cupped the mouthpiece in both hands, so she resolved to keep a watchful eye on the ensuing events, determined that she would not find herself right back where she had started some twenty minutes before.

In a short time, a shuffling little man came into the Admitting Office. He cocked a thumb at Ella and asked, "This her?" Dr. Steinmetz nodded, and the recent arrival said, "Big mother. Ed better look out, you ask me." He laughed as Steinmetz blanched and sought to hide his embarrassment at this unexpected betrayal of confidence by immersing himself in some papers. The short man laughed even harder at Steinmetz's obvious discomfiture, then winked at Ella. "Follow me, lady." He dashed out the door, and Ella followed to find him lighting a cigarette on the cement slab that functioned as a stoop for the Admitting Office. He shook out his match, tossed it over his shoulder, and stuck out a small hand to Ella. "Name's Vinnie," he said. "What's yours, lady?"

"Ella Donovan," she told him, wondering what manner of ninny she had now been entrusted to.

"I'm a trusty here, but don't worry, I'm okay, you know what I mean?" he asked, bobbing his head in reassurance and winking on alternate bobs.

"A trusty," she asked, growing more uneasy. "What's a trusty?"

"You know, like in them pitchers with Jimmy Cagney, in the jailhouse. They have guys there who are okay. They can't let 'em out, but they're okay, so they let 'em do stuff, help out, sort of. That's a trusty, see?"

"I guess so," she responded, more uncertain than ever. "You mean you're a patient here, don't you? And they let you walk around on the loose, even send you to take unsuspecting people like me from place to place?"

"You got it, lady," he said cheerily.

"I see. Well, watch your step. You lay a finger on me and they'll take a week to find the pieces."

"What pieces?"

"The ones I'll make out of you if you step out of line."

"You're all right, Ella. Yessirree, you're all right! I kinda like a lady wit spunk."

"Don't you spunk me, buster. Just take me where I'm supposed to go."

He turned abruptly and began walking at a brisk pace back in the direction from which Ella had come a short time earlier. She walked warily behind the little man, watching for a false move, or a move that could be so construed, but Vinnie neither did anything out of the ordinary nor said another word until they reached a broad, two-story building directly to the rear of the Roosevelt Building.

"Here it is, lady. Just go in and tell 'em what you, who you want to see and stuff, and they'll take care of you okay," Vinnie said softly.

Ella thanked him and stood back to look at him, half expecting him to disappear rather than walk away, so unreal had her afternoon been thus far. He looked back at her, and she noticed that he was staring blankly somewhere to her left. He waved diffidently, then turned to walk away, saying over his shoulder, "Take care of yourself, Nellie. Be seein' you."

Ella watched him move off, until he turned a corner of the building and disappeared, his odd shuffle reminding her a bit of Chaplin. She turned to mount the steps, prepared for anything but the commonplace as she reached the door to the Randall Building. As she stepped inside, she saw a large open area to the rear of a desk, behind which sat a thin, birdlike woman, wire-rimmed spectacles depended on her frail bosom from a beaded chain. The woman's hair was gray and pulled tautly behind her head in a bun not unlike Ella's own. She looked up expectantly as Ella approached the desk.

"May I help you?" she asked.

"Yes. At least I hope you can," Ella said warily. "I'd like to see my son, William Donovan, Jr."

"Oh, yes. We've been expecting you, Mrs. Donovan. Dr. Steinmetz called to say you'd be coming. Please have a seat. Dr. Johanson will be with you in a moment." She smiled.

"Thank you, Miss . . . ?" Ella said, pausing for the receptionist to fill the blank with her name.

"Casey." She smiled. "Susan Casey. And you're quite welcome. It can be very upsetting to visit a close member of the family under these circumstances, so I always try to offer whatever assistance I can."

"You have no idea how rare, and welcome, that attitude can be, Miss Casey." Ella smiled, beginning to relax for the first time since her arrival. She turned as she saw some motion out of the corner of her eye, and a tall, blond man, clad in a long white smock, crossed the room to stand at Miss Casey's desk.

"Is Mrs. Donovan here, Susan?" he asked.

"Yes, Doctor, right over there," she responded, indicating Ella with a nod of her head. The doctor walked over to Ella, extending his hand as he drew near. His grasp was warm and friendly, and she noticed that he covered her hand with his free hand as they shook in greeting.

"I am very glad you've come, Mrs. Donovan. We were trying to reach you earlier, but could get no answer when we telephoned. How is it you're here?"

"Well, Willie, my son, called me last night and told me where he was. He asked me to come to see him, which of course I would have done even if he hadn't asked. And if I may say so, I've had no end of trouble trying to see him ever since I arrived."

"What do you mean?" the doctor asked, wrinkling his brow.

Ella briefly sketched the events of the past half hour, the doctor occasionally interrupting to ask a question or two, particularly when she described her encounter with Vinnie and the retribution she promised to visit on the hapless Ed should she ever have the ill fortune to encounter him again. When she had concluded, he apologized and promised her that he would have the front-gate security tightened in order to prevent the likelihood of a recurrence, explaining that it was essential that hospital staff challenge any stranger they encountered, on the possibility it might be a wandering patient or an unauthorized visitor.

"Now, I'm afraid, we have more serious matters to discuss," he said.

"When can I see Willie?" Ella demanded, still not completely mollified. "Is he all right?"

"We won't know how well or ill he may be for a few days yet, I'm afraid. I've ordered some tests, and the results will not be available until the day after tomorrow, at the earliest. Physically, he is well, except for a few bruises sustained in a scuffle with the policemen. His clothing was a mess, and his watch was broken. His mental well-being is far less certain, unfortunately."

"What happened? Why is he here in the first place?" Ella pressed.

"I'm not conversant with all of the details, but I believe there was an incident involving a former merchant seaman who had been living in a shack down by the Delaware River. The police were called by someone who refused to give his name, claiming that this hobo had hanged himself. When the police arrived, the hobo was hanging from a roof beam. Your son was also present, although he refused, or more likely was unable, to identify himself and got rather violent. The officers who brought him here said that he had obviously been drinking heavily."

"Well, I suppose he does drink a lot. Once in a while, anyway," Ella replied, speaking slowly in order to avoid worsening the doctor's already dim view of Willie. "He gets it from his father, I guess. Will liked a drink now and again. But Willie was never mean, and neither was his father. They both react the same way when they get to hitting the bottle. They get . . . got, I guess I should say; his father's passed away almost a year ago now. Anyway, Willie would get real playful when he was drinking. Mischievous, you might say, I suppose. And his father was the same. I never knew Willie to get into a fight, at least not without good reason. He would fight once in a while as a child, as most boys do, I think, and I punished him for it, but since he's been grown, I never knew him to hit anyone."

"I'm still puzzled as to how he knew to contact you, and how he managed to do so. When the police brought him in, he refused to tell anyone who he was, whether he had any relatives, that sort of thing. He wouldn't answer a single question. If the police had not found his wallet on the floor of the shack, we still wouldn't know who he was. We'd have had to wait until a fingerprint check was run, or until someone reported him missing. You say he called you on the telephone?"

"Yes, he did," Ella said. "Last night, at about two o'clock, I think. I was scared to death when the phone rang. I was sound asleep, and the phone never rings at that hour. Not unless it's bad news, anyway. I guess you might say this is bad news."

"Not necessarily, Mrs. Donovan. It might actually be a good thing this happened. If there is something seriously wrong with Willie, we can try to determine what it might be, and treat him. If this hadn't happened, he might have gotten hurt, or hurt someone else, if this were to happen again. Or it could be a symptom of some neurological disturbance that we'll be able to treat appropriately. If he hadn't been brought here, it might have gone undetected until it was too late to correct."

"I suppose so, and I hope you're right," Ella said uncertainly. "Still, I'd like to think it wouldn't happen again, whether you find something wrong with him or not. Do you have any idea at all what it might be?"

"I do have a couple of things in mind, but I won't know anything definite until I see the test results. We'll have to keep Willie here, under observation, until we're sure it's safe to release him."

"Can I see him now?"

"Yes, I suppose that would be all right. But I want to caution you not to say anything that might upset him. And it's not particularly pleasant upstairs."

"Why not? This is a public hospital, and everybody should get decent treatment here."

"Oh, I can assure you that he is not being treated poorly. It's just that the circumstances of his admission were such that we felt constrained to take some . . . precautions."

"What sort of 'precautions,' Dr. Johanson?"

"Well, the circumstances that led to the police being called, his refusal to tell us anything at all about who he was, and the way he continued to struggle with the officers forced us to confine him in the reception ward for those of our patients who may be criminally ill."

"Whatever do you mean by that? 'Criminally ill.' Why I never heard of such a thing. Since when is it a crime to be sick?"

"That's not what we mean by criminally ill, I'm afraid, Mrs. Donovan. We mean that he may be inclined to engage in criminal, or otherwise violent, behavior, and we must protect our other patients from that possibility. And we also have to protect the criminally ill from themselves. But you can rest assured we try to be as civilized as possible under the circumstances."

"I think I better see him right now, if you don't mind. I can't say I'm pleased to hear what you've been telling me, Doctor," Ella said. "Do you mind if we go now? I'd like to see him as soon as possible."

"Of course. I'll take you up right now. Please leave your handbag with Miss Casey, and follow me."

"Leave my handbag? Why?"

"Regulations, Mrs. Donovan. And not without cause, as you'll no doubt see. Susan, please take Mrs. Donovan's purse and hold it for her until we return, would you mind?"

"Not at all, Dr. Johanson. Here, Mrs. Donovan, I'll keep it under my desk, where it'll be safe." Ella handed her purse to the receptionist.

The doctor took Ella by the arm and led her through the

door opposite the one through which she had entered. Across a small hallway, Ella noticed a narrow, brightly lit flight of stairs, painted pale institutional green. The doctor led the way, pausing once or twice to allow Ella to keep pace with him. At the head of the stairway was another hall, and a thick, small-windowed door, steel-sheeted and barred. The doctor took a heavy metal key from the pocket of his smock and inserted it into the keyhole of the massive lock.

As the lock gave an ominous snap, the doctor pushed inward, and the door swung away from his thrust on well-oiled hinges. He motioned to Ella to step through, and, she found herself in a small room roughly the size of the hallway from which she had just come, painted the same pale-green color. Another barred and windowed door, as massive as the first, stood across from the open doorway.

Ella was beginning to feel a bit queasy and looked at the massive security devices in stunned disbelief. She began to shake her head from side to side, and could not speak for a moment or two, then said, "I can't believe it, Doctor, I just can't believe that my son has to be locked in a place like this, just like a wild animal. I'm sorry, I just won't believe it, no matter what you say."

The doctor gave her arm a kindly squeeze. "I'm sorry, Mrs. Donovan. I'm not sure he has to be in here, either. But until we know what's wrong with Willie, we have to assume the worst. You can imagine what kind of people there are in this world, perhaps, when I tell you that the doors you see here are not just desirable. For some of our patients, they are essential."

Then he turned to the second door and unlocked it, motioning Ella through as it swung back away from them. She stepped through into a dimly lit corridor and noticed a small counter immediately in front of her, not unlike the check-in desk at a motel. A fat man in grimy, sweat-stained whites looked at her, then smiled over her shoulder at Johanson, who was closing the door.

"Hey, Doc, what's happenin'?" he asked.

"Hello, Curly. Just taking Mrs. Donovan here to the receiving area. Her son is a new patient, brought in last night."

"Curly is one of the best people we have here at the hospital, Mrs. Donovan, not least because he can pick up a desk in each hand, if he has to."

"Come on, Doc." Curly laughed. "You're exaggeratin' again. I gotta empty the drawers first. At least on one of them." He laughed again, and Ella felt a faint stirring of uneasiness at the idea of strength being a desirable quality for a hospital attendant. He turned to Ella and asked, "Your son the one the cops brought in last night?"

"Yes, I believe so," Ella said. "At least that's what Dr. Johanson tells me."

"Don't believe everything you hear from the Doc. He's what we call a bleeding-heart around here, cause he believes he can help everybody that comes through the door. Ain't that right, Doc?"

"Come on, Curly. You know as well as I do that there's nobody here that believes *that*. And if I am the most optimistic, you're a close second," he said. "Curly's only problem is that he wants everyone to think his heart is as hard as that bald head of his."

"All right, Doc, let me go get Donovan before you ruin my hard-earned reputation for being a tough guy." He smiled again in Ella's direction, then went through a doorway behind him. The doctor led her down the gloomy corridor to a large squarish room, sparsely furnished and badly in need of a paint job. The furniture consisted almost exclusively of long, picnic-style tables, painted the same pale institutional green she had seen in the halls, and narrow, low, red vinyl-covered sofas, backless. The former were scattered at random about the middle of the room, and the latter were arranged along three of the walls. High up on the fourth wall, on a steel-bracketed shelf, was a large-screened television set, its wooden cabinet chipped and scarred.

There were a number of people in the room, about half of them dressed in the same kind of nondescript gray smock she had seen on Mabel, and the others, clearly visiting friends and family members, were dressed in dull-gray or brown cloth coats, flower-print dresses, ill-fitting pants and shirts. Most of the visitors seemed themselves to be suffering from severe depression, and as Ella allowed the significance of her present whereabouts to sink in, she, too, began to feel a heavy weight slowly descending on her spirits, which had been none too good to start with.

"Why don't we sit at one of the tables, Mrs. Donovan?" Dr. Johanson said.

Ella nodded dully and moved to the nearest unoccupied table and sat down. She felt, rather than saw, the doctor move to a place across the table from her. She found herself absorbing the smallest physical sensation, smells, sounds from out of doors, distant bells ringing in some other part of the building. It was as if her mind had no presence in the room, were somehow barred from participating in the limited activities going on around her. She concentrated on framing her reaction to Willie's arrival, hoping she would not betray her true feelings to him and upset him further.

The doctor was watching her closely, perhaps trying to gauge what her response to seeing her son might be, perhaps looking for some clue that would explain her son.

She scrutinized his face, which was not unkind, and attempted to hear the murmured conversations going on around her, as if they held some key to what her own conduct should be. The murmurs were almost identical from table to table.

She heard a stirring behind her, and turned to see Curly coming through the door and a hand swinging behind him which she knew to be Willie, even though the rest of him was obscured by the burly attendant. Curly headed straight toward the table where they sat. "Here he is, Doc," he said. The big man smiled at Ella, gave her a wink, and said, "Don't worry, Mrs. Donovan. I'll take good care of him as long as he's here," then turned and went back the way he had come.

Ella struggled to stifle the impulse she felt to leap to her feet and embrace Willie, who stood facing her, at an angle. She squeezed her eyes closed for a moment to suppress the tears beginning to well in her eyes, and said, "Willie, oh, Willie."

He did not look to Ella to be insane in any way, or at least he manifested none of the symptoms she associated with mental derangement. He was not drooling from the corners of his mouth, his eyes were not rolling wildly in their sockets, nor was there a maniacal edge to the set of his jaw. He was just Willie, who and what he had always been to her: a slightly pudgy man, no longer young, but not old, either. Through the blank stiffness of his stare, she could see the slightly impish grin that would flicker across his face from time to time when he was explaining how he had gotten into, or out of, his latest scrape. He was her son, and he did not belong here. Even the dreary institutional clothing seemed out of place on his rounded limbs, stretched almost taut over his burgeoning paunch. Where the other patients seemed to Ella to be lean to the point of emaciation, their faces angular and haggard, Willie looked fit, if slightly overfed.

His face was bruised above his left eye, which was swollen, and there was an angry red welt across the back of his right hand, running up under his cuff. She suspected he probably bore other signs of the struggle of the previous night, but his physical condition seemed otherwise to be normal and healthy.

Ella noticed that the doctor had not responded in any way to Willie's arrival, and the strain of the silence was beginning to tell on her. She looked at Willie as though she would pry from him by the sheer force of her will the explanation the police and hospital staff had been unable to elicit. But there were those eyes. So flat and motionless. He seemed more to be looking through her, than at her. It was as if he could see the wall behind her, and was fascinated, hypnotized by something only he could see, slowly and laboriously climbing up its grimy surface from the baseboard.

"How are you, Willie?" Ella asked, unable totally to suppress the quavering of her voice.

Willie batted not an eye, nor did he respond to her question.

He continued to stare at the wall behind her, or at the invisible barrier that stood between them. Ella looked at Dr. Johanson, hoping for some guidance. He nodded to her, as if to say "Continue," and she turned back to Willie.

"Are you all right, Willie? Did they hurt you?" There was still no response. Ella stared back at him, trying to force some flicker of recognition, her eyes boring straight into the expressionless wastes that were his. So motionless were they that Ella was not even certain that he was blinking his eyelids. Every muscle in his face seemed frozen, or carved from a soft stone the color and consistency of flesh, utterly and perfectly immobile. She reached out to take his hand, half afraid that he would recoil from her, but he did not move. He did not even shuffle his feet or move his head to look down at the strange hand held in his mother's own, for that is how Ella had begun to think of it, lying there in her grasp as motionless as a wax image. True, it felt like a living hand, it was warm, and she could feel the quiet thump of his blood coursing through the veins in his wrist, but there seemed to be no internal motive force.

She pressed his fingers with her own, hoping to feel a response in kind. She tugged on his arm, saying, "Sit down, Willie. Here by me," patting the bench beside her. Willie remained motionless, and she tugged again, repeating, "Sit down, Willie, please."

"Mrs. Donovan," Dr. Johanson said, "please don't upset yourself. It will not make matters any easier for Willie, assuming he even knows who you are at this point."

She turned to the doctor, imploring him to do something, her eyes now full of the tears she had controlled so long. "Can't you do *something* for him? There must be some medicine. I'm his *mother,* Dr. Johanson. There must be something you can do that will make him recognize me. He must know I'm here, he must, please . . ." She broke off in mid-sentence, the rest of her words drowned by the sobs that were now achingly torn from her throat.

"Mrs. Donovan, I'm doing all I can, you must believe me,

but there is only so much I *can* do. It is essential that Willie cooperate if treatment is to be successful, but if I can't reach him, well . . ."

She turned from the doctor's hopelessness back to her own frantic need to force a word or a glimmer of recognition from her son, who had not changed his position. "Willie, Willie, I . . ." But she broke off, turning in desperation again to the doctor. "What's the use, Doctor? He can't hear me, can he." It was a declaration of fact, but the doctor nodded as though it were a question.

She turned to Willie and again stared at the lifeless features, hoping to see a momentary thaw in their glacial aspect, or a shallowing of the motionless depth of the eyes, some betrayal of life behind his inanimate façade. She was disappointed.

Curly came in and took Willie by the arm, and her son turned automatically in the direction of Curly's pull without looking at the man or hesitating to allow his glance to linger on his mother. Not once in the course of his stay in the reception area had he looked at Johanson, or at anyone else in the room. His gaze did not wander for a second from whatever area happened to lie directly in front of him. There had not been a flicker of emotion.

"Willie's condition is very severe at the moment, Mrs. Donovan. We have a patient here with a similar illness, and we have made some considerable progress with him. When he first arrived, he was not eating or speaking; now he does both, though not much of the latter and only enough of the former as is necessary to keep body and soul together. Still, as long as we can keep him alive, there is the possibility that we can effect further improvement in his condition. I have every reason to hope that we may have as much success with Willie, possibly more."

"Why do you say that?"

"Well, in my experience, if you can succeed in reaching a patient who has totally withdrawn, it is usually an indication that you are very close to determining the source of the patient's problems, and it is often a simple step from that discovery to a complete cure. The other patient has been with us a little over two years, and it took us nearly a year before we could get him to eat. We were forced to feed him intravenously before that, and to keep him heavily sedated to prevent his removing the IV or otherwise attempting to do himself harm. Once we got him to eat, it was a matter of only several weeks before he began to speak, though he is still not exactly talkative."

"Two years? Did you say he has been here for two years, and that's all you have to show in the way of progress? Do you mean to say that Willie will have to be here for *years*? I thought we were talking about a few days, or a couple of weeks, at most. You can't mean that my son may be confined here for that long! You can't mean that."

"I'm afraid I do mean just exactly that, Mrs. Donovan," the doctor said.

"Oh my God," Ella groaned. "My God in heaven." She covered her face with her wrinkled hands, and the doctor shook his head sadly, staring dumbly at the stricken woman. He studied the backs of her hands and wondered at the strength of spirit it must have taken to endure the years of hard work mutely witnessed by the muscular fingers and heavily veined forearms. And for what? he asked himself. Why do people struggle so to endure? How can they stand the inevitable failure? What use was it for this woman to have raised a child, against enormous odds, only to see him end up a silent balloon of a man who could not even recognize her, and would not if he could?

The doctor reached out a delicate hand to pat Ella on the shoulder. She neither looked up nor ceased the shaking which he could feel through his fingertips. Down the hall, Ella could hear the dull thud of the door to Willie's ward as Curly swung it firmly shut.

THIRTY-ONE

FALL came, its golden litter a blessing, drifting in whispering clusters to cover the lawn, and the months-old ruin of the roses, now reduced to withered stumps. The leaves collected against the fence, slowly mounted in snowlike drifts over the domed tulip bed, where, for the first time in twenty years, there were no bulbs lying in the warm brown soil like so many promissory notes of spring lying in a vault. It was as if autumn erupted and sought to preserve Ella's garden for all time, to arrest its development, as had the ashes of Vesuvius that of Herculaneum, waiting for future excavation so that someone would know what it had been like for Ella Donovan without her husband. The ruined roses would give mute testimony to the dimensions of her suffering and some perceptive archaeologist would be able to reconstruct the final days of her happiness, and its abrupt end.

Since Willie had been committed to the state hospital, she had been at loose ends, at odds with the world. Her newly discovered independence now seemed worthless to her, and she closed herself off from those few friends who were truer than Will had predicted. Pat Flaherty and his wife still called on occasion, though Ella had little enthusiasm for company. Daniel was predictably incommunicado. Katherine did her best to rekindle the spirit Ella had come so close to mastering, but when Willie was hospitalized, Ella's enthusiasm reached a low ebb. Even her posture reflected the toll taken by recent events, the robustness of her figure, which would have been taken as confirmation of vigorous health in happier times, seemed now to be the collapsed ruins of a more stalwart person pulled down by forces beyond her understanding and as irresistible as gravity.

It was as if the glow, the vitality of her, had collapsed inward and, like a neutron star, she were spinning in place, gathering gloom to her bosom and suppressing all light.

It was only November, and Will had not been gone even a year, and now she had Willie to deal with. He was making progress, but it was slow and agonizing. In the two months he had been hospitalized, he had gradually come out of the shell that had so securely held him the first morning she had visited him. He talked to her, he talked to the doctors, sometimes even to other patients, but it wasn't really *Willie* she saw, only some strange cartoon man who looked like him.

Time moved so slowly now, sometimes it didn't seem to move at all, as if it had come to a grinding halt, rendering every clock as useless as the one-handed watch that dangled on Willie's arm, the watch Will had given him last Christmas, and with which he refused to part, even when Ella had promised to replace it. She sometimes thought that's all it would take to set things right, just to replace that hopeless parody of time on Willie's wrist with something real, something that moved, that marked time's passing instead of mocking the very idea of it.

She was not unaware of the transformation she had undergone, but her will to fight had been exhausted, and the very knowledge of her inability to struggle against events only served to heighten her depression. Now, with the anniversary of Will's death little more than a month away, Ella sat on the front porch idly playing with the arm of the two-seater swing as she rocked slowly back and forth. The sun was bright and hard-edged, with that palpable light peculiar to the season burnishing the leaves and deepening the sky's blue until it seemed like that ocean at the edge of the universe beyond which there was nothing. She watched the shadows of the high clouds glide silently along the street, the sunlight on the remaining leaves on the maples out front waxing and waning like variable stars. She noticed that the paint of the swing was already showing signs of wear, though it had been little used since Will had repainted it, and there was a film of gritty dust, which flattened to black smudges under the slightest pressure of her fingers.

It was a beautiful day, and she felt more disposed than usual to enjoy the crisp air and the last surge of color before the winter bleakness, already imminent in the intermittent breeze. She felt it would be soothing to walk, to enjoy the air and the smell of autumn, the burning leaves smokily wafting, camouflaging the sharp industrial scent of the city.

She went indoors and found one of Will's heavy woolen sweaters, wrapped it about her shoulders, and went back to the porch, descending the steps with such tentativeness she was not sure she would reach the bottom until her feet were firmly planted on the pavement. She looked westward, but the hospital sealed the block, as if to foreclose passage in that direction. With listless gait, she set off in the opposite direction, quickening her pace under the brisk impetus of the air to a leisurely stroll. Much of the green was gone, though here and there were patches of grass, yellowing but clinging tenaciously to the last vestiges of their color. The leaves, gathered in raked clumps, were largely brown, as if the gold of single specimens were illusory, or merely borrowed from the sun.

The bright sunlight flickered and waved from the windows of the row homes on either side of the street, bright blades of fire which harmlessly licked at her, almost as if they were willing to sacrifice themselves to burn in her blood, restore some color to her cheeks. The trees were nearly barren, arid fingers all the more bereft for the few leaves still clinging to them, most hopelessly withered and dark, wrinkled brown, deepened by the shade that sheltered in their curled palms. It was a weekday, and except for an occasional housewife cleaning a porch or squeaking a chamois across a damp window, the street was deserted. After a couple of blocks, she lost interest in the sights and gave herself up to the scent of decay and the relentless rhythm of her walk, which seemed mechanical and beyond her control. She walked on, mindlessly, for several minutes, and soon came to the end of the street, breaking out into an unrelieved glare where the sun, unrestricted by the broad sweep of Wetzel Field, was harsh and unremitting.

She stood on the curb for a moment, undecided whether she should turn and go back or across the street to the deserted diamond. At last she resolved to walk in the open, to feel the heat of the sun on her face and back, the dark wool soaking up the light, letting it through her clothing to her skin. She entered the gate and walked out to the infield, where the grass had been gouged into desolation, the dry earth staring back at her where countless feet had run for the better part of the summer. In the outfield, there were a half-dozen bald patches, barely distinguishable in the yellow grass, the desolation perfectly silent. She stood staring at the summer wasteland, and it was hard to imagine that any life could have existed here. It seemed a place as barren as the moon. That this bleak meadow could ever have been the source of joy seemed inconceivable to her. Try as she might, she could not hear a sound, not in fact or imprisoned cheers from summer crowds lingering in the rafters of the grandstand, which seemed alien, its row upon row of seats so empty it seemed that no one had ever sat upon them.

She remembered coming here years ago, when the boys were young, to watch them play, to cheer them on, Will bellowing and cursing a blue streak at those foolish enough to oppose a team that numbered both of his sons among its starters. She had never cared for baseball, and could not understand how anyone could enjoy watching someone hit a small sphere with a slender stick so that someone else could run and pick it up. Will was rabid about the game, never more so than when his sons were playing, and this place had been the scene of more than one family triumph, and the source of considerable agony. All of that seemed so far away now it might never have been were it not for the persistent echo that seemed to resonate within her.

She shook her head, less in dumb wonder than in an attempt to dislodge those memories, as if she could shake them out of herself and watch them spring to life like the teeth of Cadmus, an army to wage war against the life that weighed so heavily upon her. She thought, for a moment, that she could reconstruct the past, that she could make things as they once had been, and that all that she had lived through in the past year would cease to be, or at least lose its power over her. But even as she wished, she knew that it was not to be. She knew that nothing could be undone, and that the only stone that could change her life had already done so, and begun to gather moss, lying there in the shady silence above the pond. Sadly, she shook her head and turned to go, signifying her acquiescence to the irresistible and her renunciation of her faith in the impossible. As she reached the gate, a cloud passed overhead, momentarily obscuring the sun, and its mitigation of the harsh light that had bathed the field restored, for one brief instant, the green that was no more than a memory of grass.